THE SUNDERLANDS

also by Anastasia King

WORLD OF AUREUM SERIES:

The Sunderlands

Kings of Shadow and Stone

World of Aureum Series, Book One

THE SUNDERLANDS

ANASTASIA KING

The Sunderlands by Anastasia King
World of Aureum Series: book one

ISBN 978-0-578-56009-0

Anastasia King Books, L.L.C.
Anastasiakingbooks.com

Orders by U.S. trade bookstores, wholesalers and all other business inquiries, please contact Anastasia King via anastasiaking@anastasiakingbooks.com

Cover and Interior Art: Micaela Alcaino
Editors: Chloe Szentpeteri
Revisions by: Breanna Diaz and Sophia Behrman
Formatting: Zachary James Novels

This one is for the little girl who wrote in secret, who burned her journals full of stories, and grew up and got a "real job."

It's my pleasure and privilege to finally say…
Welcome to the World of Aureum

PRONUNCIATION KEY

DIFFICULT NAMES:

Keres: *Kehr-z* or *Keer-ees.* | Coroner to the God of Death

Liriene: *Leer-een*

Silas: *Sigh-lass*

Indiro: *In-deer-oh*

Osira: *O-sigh-rah*

Cesarus: *Ceh-zar-us*

Resayla: *Ree-zay-lah*

Herrona: *Heh-row-nuh*

Ivaia: *Ih-vye-uh*

Riordan: *Ree-or-dahn*

Hero: *Heer-oh*

Rydel: *Rye-dell*

Darius: *Dare-ee-us*

Arias: *Ah-rye-uhs*

Emisandre: *Em-ih-sahn-druh*

Iantharys: *Ee-on-tha-riss*

Famon: *Fay-mon*

Diomora: *Dee-oh-more-ah*

PART 1

MIDWIFE OF SOULS

"Under the darkened skies
We lapse into our deepest thoughts.
Midnight's canopy,
A question of truth or lie,
Is strung by stars
Witnessing our faults.
Then, interrupted by the dawn,
Our guilt is absolved
By the sun."

—Keres

1: DEATH

Yesterday, they shook me out of bed with the news that one of the nine dying soldiers was choking. I didn't wash my face, didn't dress. I ran.

If I hadn't left her side to begin with, it might have ended differently. The healers never abandoned the nine. Despite my exhaustion, I refused to walk away until a bent-boned elder told me to take a rest. Obeying earned me the overwhelming despair of cradling the soldier's lax body in my arms until she died.

Tonight, the silence wakes me. The blankets caught me in their net as a current of eerie peace tows my mind from panic. At last, I'm not fighting for air. My mouth is gasping, but my rigid muscles are relaxing. My eyes adjust to the darkness. My mind chokes on the memory as I lay on the shoreline of nightmare and reality:

Water. There was nothing but water filling my head and lungs. I was sinking. Drifting in a relentless current. Kicking against the hand wrapped around my ankle. Was it pulling me deeper or to the surface? Was the chill in the water or in my blood?

My stomach uncoils as I sit up, careful not to wake my sleeping family. The eerie hush of the night moves neither my sister nor father. A wave of bile washes away the dull ache in the back of my throat. I push the sweat-soaked blankets to the foot of the bed and shift to the edge. A headache splits my skull. Not enough sleep, not enough air. Every time

I have that dream, I hold my breath. I dangle my pale feet for a moment above the black soil. The earth looks like an abyss, and I shake away the thought before touching down a toe.

The wind hisses against the tent walls. Did I imagine it spoke my name? *"Keres."*

I wait until silence again fills my ears. The night air attempts to soothe my skin as I pad over to the washbasin. Memories of my dream splash around in my head. I try to drown them out, but the silence that woke me is less mollifying.

"Keres," it says again.

That voice is as familiar as my own. It's not the wind. I grip the sides of the washbasin and my stomach boils from the stress of hearing Him again. "Mrithyn," my spirit responds. His call makes my blood sing in my veins, and a dull chorus fills my ears. His voice echoes in my bones.

I become keenly aware of Him. He's no longer brushing his hand against the tent walls. He's no longer outside, deepening the darkness. In the mirror's reflection, I watch His shadow creep along the floor and walls. Its black limbs unfold and curl in unnatural ways. Its fingers grasp and unfurl, stealing inches of the room. The shadow stands to its full height, taking up the wall and towering above me. My knees buckle as I realize why He's here, but I cannot bow to Him. Tonight, the God of Death comes to take who is dear to me.

A moan breaks the silence. At the sound of breathing, the shadow melts off the wall into the black ground. My older sister stirs in her bed. I count her breaths, settling my own.

"Liriene?" I test the air.

My eyes slide toward the other bed in the far corner. I wait for any sign my father still breathes there. A loud snore cracks the air, and I let out a short breath. The threshold darkens once more. Like a cloud passing over the moon, the phantom darkness crosses back over it to rejoin the shade of night. He's not here for them.

I resist the urge to run into the night and chase His shadow. To throw myself at His feet, clutch the hem of His garment, and follow Him down to the land of the dead with the souls He's harvested tonight. I should be among them. Instead, I turn my back on them and my guilt. Death passed over us. I should be grateful He isn't greedy.

In the looking glass, a blank-faced reflection meets my gaze. I splash my face with water and grab a washcloth to scrub at my once golden skin. This past week has wearied me to the bone. I haven't slept a full night since the day before the last attack. I push my hair behind my long, pointed ears.

The wind catches its breath. My eyes pinch shut as I count. *One. Two. Three.* The wind sighs, sated. It's done then. The last of them have died. My shoulders drop under the weight of my realization. The washcloth splashes into the bottom of the basin harder than I intended.

I wonder, if I hadn't forsaken my duty to the nine, would it have saved them? The thought spurs me to dress up in my usual light undergarments and worn leathers.

Yesterday, I tried to save a life. Tonight I can't fight my thirst for blood. While that soldier died in my arms, I called for water for her. I pressed it to her parched lips. I demanded magic and herbs, everything and anything to save her. Our resources were wearing thin, spent on the nine soldiers who each bore horrific wounds. Barbaric weapons had devastated her armor.

Our efforts did more harm, keeping the nine on the brink of suffering instead of letting them sink into oblivion and peace.

"They will pay for this, Katrielle." Who had I been trying to assure? Her or myself?

She couldn't speak above a hoarse whisper, but her eyes held a desperate plea and a warning which I scorned. *"Coroner."* Every breath hitched in her lungs, blocked by the blood in her throat.

I lost my temper at her calling me that. *"You will not die."*

Someone spoke from behind us. *"Coroner, Hayes is dead, we need you to do his rites."*

I ignored the healer, refusing to leave Katrielle even for a second now.

My fear and regret were the last things I could offer her. I demanded she live, but she wasn't strong enough to resist. The wounds were grave. Blood filled her lungs, and she sputtered as she tried to tell me not to cry. I told her she was my best friend, my right hand, and she nodded her head, her eyes hanging low. I asked her how I could fight those who had done this to her and our fellow soldiers if she died. She smiled, and I knew what she'd meant by it.

"She's losing too much blood. Why is she bleeding so profusely now? She was stable just hours ago," I said as I supported her full weight in my arms. Her head rolled back, jerking upward as another fit of coughing arrested her body. More blood splattered my bare feet.

"The Humans will shed more blood," I told her. *"You must be with me to fight them. If we don't stop them, they will kill again. Stay with me!"*

She smiled. *"Tell, Liri—-"*her last words were interrupted by a sudden loss of air. Her lips turned an ugly shade of blue, her brown eyes bulged as her chest shuddered and deflated. And then her eyes closed, and her murderers' fate sealed with them.

Tonight, the God of Death finally owns all nine souls. They'd fought together, died within days and hours of each other, and now they go on to the next life together. I'm not sure what tomorrow holds for me without my comrades, but I know what tonight will.

After Katrielle died, the healer demanded I perform the rites for her soul. I'd put off performing all their rites of passage to the world of the dead. I felt like if I did... I'd be giving up on them.

THE SUNDERLANDS

"Not until the last one takes his final breath," I told the healer. A painfully futile attempt at dissuading Death from claiming them all. Their wounds had defeated their bodies. In truth, their suffering was over, but for the rest of the Sunderlands' Elves? We were damned and barely surviving.

Footsteps shuffle outside the tent and it sounds like they're hurrying toward me. I throw my bow over my shoulder, tripping on my belt as I push past the curtain into the night.

"Coroner," an ancient voice whispers, catching me before I can slip away. She flings herself toward me, and I glimpse the silvery tears streaming down her weathered face. She grabs my shoulders and leans her face on my chest. Her hand-bones are curdled by age and dig into me as she weeps, "Oh, Coroner." She crumbles against me. I grimace not only because her fingernails dig into me, but because she called me that. *Coroner.* I hate my title more and more with every soul I'm forced to midwife during death.

I don't extend a hand of comfort; I refuse to cry in front of her.

"Vigilant Chamira," I say, straightening my spine so she's forced to let go of my shoulders. We address all the healers as Vigilants.

She leans back and opts to hang from my shawl, pawing at me as she struggles to find words. Her clear blue eyes glow with desperate sorrow—which I recognize but will not mirror.

"Mrithyn, blessed be His name, has claimed the last of the nine souls." She dabs at her eyes with calloused hands before gesturing for me to follow. "Come. It is time to say goodbye. Come do—"

"No." I cut her off, pushing her aside.

Trying to brush off memories with her touch. How many times did the ten of us sit in Chamira's tent getting minor wounds cleaned and bandaged? Now is not the time to count.

She reaches for my shawl again; her lips tremble and hold back a response. I grab her hands and place them on her own chest. I note the ferality of my green eyes reflected in her wide blue ones.

The silence in the air shouts at me, screams at me to go to the deathbeds with Chamira. Her faltering mouth utters everything she wants to say without a sound.

Since the attack, the sounds of suffering polluted the air. The cries of loved ones; groans of agony, healing incantations, and prayers to every God in the Pantheon. It was the worst attack yet. Now, silence buries the camp once more. The same wound gaping open in my heart widens Chamira's eyes, but now is not the time to look back.

There will be more bloodshed.

Hurrying past the nine bodies of my comrades, force myself not to search for Katrielle's face among them. Not to check whether her hand is dangling off the bed. I imagine it folded against her chest. Chamira hobbles after me, sniffling, and an icy breeze reaches for my back. I spin on my heel, startling her to a halt.

"No, Chamira." I point to the ground, ordering her to stay like a dog.

Somebody behind her draws my eye. For a second, I fear our voices have woken my sister or father. But now the presence is gone. I pause, searching the shadows of my tent entryway for the tall, cloaked man. A black hood hid his face, but I felt his eyes.

"Why do you run, Keres?" Chamira grabs at my attention again, "Your responsibility—"

"Don't you lecture me."

"You're in pain—"

I grip her shoulders and shake her. "You're out of line." My voice carries into the shadows.

I see the cloaked figure again behind her. I look up and it disappears. Focusing back on her, I sense eyes on me.

"I will not kneel at her deathbed, fold my hands, and do nothing."

"The rites are no small thing," she argues. "There is nothing else except the rites, Keres."

"Call me by my name once more and I'll send you with the nine." I shake her again. "You will call me Coroner. That's who I am. Do you understand?"

I hate my title, but I am not allowed to be less than what it entails. Chamira and the rest of our kin get to grieve—I don't have the luxury of being *Keres*, not now. Right now, I'm no better than Death.

Chamira whimpers and nods.

"My power, my responsibility, goes beyond useless sentiments and prayers. You have your role and I have mine. Perform the rites yourself," I assert.

She shakes her head, dropping her gaze. Tears follow it. "Coroner, you know the doctrine. As Mrithyn's Instrument, this is your duty. Comforter of souls—their bodies need care. This is your ministry!"

"Enough," I snarl, releasing her but stepping closer so fast she flinches. She recoils, drawing her brown shawl around her chest. "Don't tell me how to do my duty, healer, when you failed at your own. You didn't save them. How effective was praying when she coughed up blood? I'm not here to scrub the blood from their skin—I'm here to clean the stains of war from this land."

Chamira breaks down, turning from me back to her own tent where the corpses decorate her front yard.

"Do your part and I'll do mine," I add.

She returns to the deathbeds and although I will not help, I watch her shoulders quiver as she goes. I shake off the tension making my own muscles tremor with adrenaline from the argument.

I move deeper into the shadows and track her every movement. The flush of heat under my skin succumbs to the night's chill as I watch her pace between the nine cots. She starts by burning sage, setting it in the censor, and waving it over the bodies. She mutters her prayers with strangled sobs. The smoke rises into the sky, soft and swift as souls on the wind.

She was right.

I turn and leave. I should be with the old bat, performing the rites, choking on tears and that fragrant smoke. Its scent follows me, and my stomach hardens as I point my eyes ahead. An owl's voice in the distance echoes the thoughts in my head. *"Who will pay? Who else will die? Who?"*

Home becomes foreign when those you love go into the ground beneath your feet. Every step away from Katrielle's body rings into the earth and my mind, reminding me of a lesson I gleaned from my studies of Mrithyn and his realm of eternal rest: the dead become the earth the living walks upon. Tread in memory.

As the Coroner, I must fulfill my true duty to the nine tonight. Not the way Chamira was begging me to. My way.

It doesn't take many steps for me to reach the outskirts of the camp. It doesn't take much effort to put distance between myself and the task of praying for my dead friends' souls.

The short walls of the clangrounds and our watchmen are all that stand between me and my other duty. I tighten my belt and search for the guard who stands a certain way. Back straight, neck tall, and legs apart—that's him. Predictable. Shoulders set with determination to protect those sleeping behind these walls. Bow at the ready and helmeted head aimed at the forest beyond the camp.

I remember his blind spot and creep into it. Tonight, of all nights, sneaking past him proves difficult, and he coughs low in his throat when he notices me. I draw up my shawl over my stark white hair, realizing my head is a beacon at this blackened hour. If only covering my hair could mask the fact that Death marked me as His own.

My wearing red garners as much attention from my kin as my

whitened hair does. A constant reminder of my status, like a flag signaling just how much I don't fit in. If I think about that, I'll weep for the company of my comrades.

This guard will not question my sneaking off the grounds. He won't follow or try to stop me. Still, I look back over my shoulder and connect with his tracking stare. His honey-colored eyes gobble up the distance between us as I wave a dismissive hand. His sandy blond hair crosses his brow as he nods.

I disappear between the trees. The sun will soon chase away the shadows. Light will absolve what I'll do in this darkness. The moon catches my eye; a pearl in the sea of deep blue above. I stifle my grief and replace it with the familiar rush of adrenaline and angst in my blood.

2: ABSOLUTION

Tonight, I will take matters into my own hands. Pausing at the bank of the River Liri, I frown. The memory of my nightmare jumps into my head. Rubbing my hand over my eyes does little to wipe away the thought, but I must ford this river every time I make this journey.

I wade into the frigid water and recoil. The chill makes me want to turn right around and go home. A shiver quakes under my skin, and I question my decision. Should I have stayed with the fallen soldiers? The thought of their frozen faces chills me more than the water that laps at my knees. *Keep going.*

I choose the shallowest parts and tiptoe across fallen logs, staying out of the icy grip of the river as best I can.

As I approach my destination, pulses of energy reach me like a scent wafting on the wind. A thrumming begins in my stomach and my bowels turn to water as the strange sensation ravages my nerves: the wards.

I do not shy away from the energy or the rising panic it creates in me. Anyone else would flinch at the sight of the decrepit hut, ruined beyond repair. A normal person would retrace their steps. They wouldn't take their eyes off the utter darkness behind the shattered windows. It sucks the starlight in and extinguishes it. Anyone else would heed their burning instinct to run, like a mare from a serpent— from the whirling tendrils of shadow that reach for passersby through the open door. That hungry door swings, creaking on its hinges.

Striding through the doorway, I disregard the claw marks dragged over the threshold. The pitch dark throws its hands over my eyes and the door slams shut behind me. I wait until the mirage spell melts away, falling like scales from my eyes. The atmosphere around me glimmers and morphs into a clearing in the forest. An illusion blown away by the wind, the hut disappears. Beyond the Veil of magic, a loft perches in the branches—content as a sparrow in a ship mast.

I shake the chill from my back and arms. The sight of the house in the trees would usually pull a smile from the corner of my mouth but not tonight. The full moon is settled on the roof, and every star of my favorite constellation winks into the clearing. The appeal of the night sky is useless in cheering me up, paled by the sight of my Aunt.

She stands at the foot of a staircase that winds around the burliest tree trunk. Awaiting me. Her silver eyes beam even brighter than the stars. Not with joy at my return, but with fervent power awaiting release.

🔲🔲🔲🔲🔲

I've stood at the foot of a mountain and looked up. I've knelt before a shrine to a God and begged. I've looked into the eyes of Elven victims as they lay dying. I've also smiled in the faces of their murderers, my prey. No experience compares to standing in front of the woman who raised you and seeing your very origin in her eyes.

My mother's sister wrought everything I am. She sees pain and fury where I hold back tears. My Aunt knows the names of my fears and the depth of my despair. She's raised me in my mother's stead to face those fears and rise when I fall. Her eyes have looked on me with pride more times than with discontent. But the look she gives me now breaks me down to nothing: understanding.

Ivaia understands the pain I bear each time I come to her after an attack on my people. She is not part of the clan, but she pays attention. Not only does Ivaia understand the loss of someone dear, she understands the darkness in my mind quickly filling the void created by yet another death. Midnight thoughts, as innumerable and as constant as the stars. She sees the shadows my emotions are dragging my thoughts into. She steps forward with that mother-knows-all smile and embraces me. It's easy to put on the mask of the Coroner in front of others—not her though.

For the next few minutes, I'm aware of nothing else but the mesh of her gown as it grates my wet cheek. The warmth of her fur cape she's invited me into. Her hair smells of lavender. Fingers lightly caress my scalp. Her skin cools my fevered soul. She bears all my weight in her unfaltering arms. As my shuddering voice quiets, I realize she's singing a song from my childhood.

I look into Ivaia's eyes and remember the first time I saw her. I had just woken up days after my mother's death and was shocked, thinking mom was somehow at my bedside, alive again. The same long golden hair and a wide smile. But the voice was startling, unlike my mother's. Ivaia spoke as if she didn't know how to interact with a seven-year-old:

"Your mother's gone now, but I'm not. Your sister locked herself in the garden. Gods know what for. We can still see her through the gates. But never mind that. I'm here now. We never met, dear Gods, where are my manners?"

She stooped awkwardly at the side of my bed. *"I'm your mother's little sister, not the older one. Your father knows I'm here and has approved me taking you back to my house, not the castle. It's a hut..."*

"I don't want to leave," I said.

She swatted away my rejection like it was an insect.

"Rubbish, darling. Look at you! So ill and grimy even Mrithyn didn't want you. It's only for a few days." She dragged the covers off my shivering body.

"Come now, put on this shawl." She tossed a red bundle of fabric onto

my head. *"You'll end up right back in the earth if you don't bundle up. Weather's turned against us. Seems Nerissa is mourning your mother."*

That was that. She swept me up with a swish of her long black skirts and cloak.

Ivaia isn't rough with me now like she was then. She allows me to regain my footing and scrub my face with the backs of my sleeves. Taking my hand, she leads me up the stairs of her home. Much like the first time I visited her loft, I stare at each step. Each plank of wood is more unsteady than the next; winding up and up around the grand tree she's chosen for her stairwell. When I was small, I thought I'd fall through the spaces between them. She held my hand like this when I lost my mother, and now, thirteen years later, after I lost my closest friend.

The lanterns in the house cast whimsical shadows over the eclectic furniture. Plants brought in from the forest crawl along the walls and hang from the ceiling's wooden beams. Many have grown wilder since the last time I was here. A few more pelts have been added to the furs lining the floor.

My uncle lounges shirtless between two long-leafed plants. One hand holds a book near his nose and the other is tangled in his shoulder-length blond hair. A fire crackles in the pit, toasting his toes. I hang my bow on a peg beside the doorway and fall onto the cushion the same shade of green as my eyes.

"Ah, there you are, Keres." He snaps his book closed and perks up. "We were expecting you a few days ago when we heard about the ambush."

His eyes dart between my tear-stained face and Ivaia's somber one.

"How many?" He asks.

For too long a moment, the only sound is of the fire chewing on the wood.

"Nine," I say.

The door behind me clicks shut and Ivaia catches my eye as she removes her shawl. In the light, her silver eyes seem almost clear, tinged with blue. Her golden hair, twined and braided in sections, falls to her shoulders in an edgy chop. It hides her long, pointed ears.

The heavy fur slips off her frame. Her dress looks like it's made of cobwebs. Long, delicate, and the same silvery blue of her eyes. It clings to her curves and covers only what it must. Her arms remain bare, and her long legs are exposed through slits in her dress. Most of her fine tattoos are on display. Some are simple, colorful stains like Riordan's. Some are black, dense line-work. All are illustrations of the things she loves in life. Stories on her skin.

Despite the hour, she doesn't look like she was prepared to sleep anytime soon. A broad silver band crosses her brow, taming her mane, with coin-shaped pendants dripping off it. A heavy, intricate necklace to match it rests at her throat. Tiny, silver ingots line her ears from lobe to cartilage. She's gorgeous. Almost nothing of her resembles our family in the West. As she intended.

Riordan and Ivaia look at each other.

"Keres lost her childhood friend among the nine." She abandons her fur cape, losing it in the menagerie already warming the wooden floors.

"Katrielle?" Rio's hand goes to his chest. "I'm so sorry, Keres."

He leans forward onto his knees and reaches toward me. I grip his hand and am rewarded with a consoling squeeze. Before we speak, Riordan insists on setting a miniature feast on a mat before us. He passes me a cup of something hot. This tea is my favorite. Lilac and honey.

"Katrielle..." I wipe my eyes and straighten my spine. "Kat and eight others were scouting close to the clan Hishmal. The Dalis seem to be moving south." I glance into my half-empty cup. "We've thought they might be bolstering their numbers, claiming more territory. We still don't know. The nine were ambushed before they could learn much."

"Once the Dalis breached our borders, we shouldn't have assumed they would stop." Rio thinks aloud.

I shrug. "Whichever direction they're going, their presence is growing quickly. We've been running routine perimeter checks once a month. A group would go out and gather as much information as they could about their encampments. Each patrol found more discouraging information as time passed."

Ivaia takes up a spot on the floor and leans against Riordan's knee.

"All nine who went out are dead. All we can ascertain is the strength of the Dalis warriors and weapons, judging by the wounds they inflicted," I say, taming my voice.

I hate this. The Dalis presence is a blight. I can't stop emotion from breaking through my words, the same way we can't stop them from staining the land with innocent blood.

"You said nine?" Riordan asks. "I thought Indiro never sent out troops of an odd number. His superstitions and all."

"He doesn't," I say. "I was to be the tenth soldier that night. It was a full moon."

"Oh." Riordan nods, closing his eyes.

"Indiro accompanied me to mother's grave, as he always does. I keep thinking I should have been there with them instead."

Riordan makes a tsking sound in disagreement. "You cannot change the outcome."

I swallow hard, my mouth getting drier. "We couldn't push them for more information as they died. They were maimed. How they made it back to camp is beyond me." I ball my fists. "The Dalis see us as animals or less, here to be butchered. But they cannot see how much less civilized they are for thinking so?" I ask.

Ivaia's eyes wander to the floor where her fingers wind in strands of the fur rug. Riordan presses his fingertips together in front of his nose and leans back in his chair.

My face feels hot and my skin stings where my salty tears ran their course. "I don't think they were far from home when the attack happened. Kat... they impaled her through her side. Their injuries were beyond anything we know how to heal. Our efforts were ineffective."

I think back on my harsh words to Chamira. She tried everything she could, I know she did. I watched her try for two days. My eyes blur against my will.

"Kat hung on, stuck with that thing jutting out of her until we dared remove it. We repaired what we could, but the internal damage was greater than we realized. She seemed stable for a little, but started coughing up blood and—"

Two sets of hands reach for me as I fight back a sob. My chest hurts. She was my dearest friend. Closer to me than my sister.

"I know," Ivaia says.

I hold my breath and blow it out through pursed lips. Needing to focus, I look at them and tell myself not to cry. It's remarkable how alike their eyes are, how they give off the same energy.

They're both fair-headed, but his coloring leans more toward a warm rich color, and hers is cool platinum. Their eye colors are inverted but the same: Hers are silver, streaked with blue. His are blue, sparkling in places like crystal. Two sets of diamonds. They exchange glances.

"I don't understand this," Riordan says, standing up.

Ivaia shifts backward to lean on her hands. "This is Human brutality at its finest. What reasoning is there to be done beyond this understanding?"

"Oh, come on, Iv. What's changed in the last few months? They went from bartering with us to butchering us. The clans have always been right where they've kept us. Underfoot. We're at the ends of their swords and at the mercy of their King. His hostile mood swings are tearing our land asunder. Every day we fight for our way of life against the North. That's the point. These attacks are happening more frequently and unprovoked!"

Rio is right. The darkness of men spreads throughout the forest uninhibited, and there's no ray of hope for the Elven clans as we toddle on the brink of extinction. Merciless hands usher us closer to the edge every day.

"Man is perching in our forest, armed to the teeth, setting up military camps among the four remaining clans," Riordan continues. "This is war. One we didn't ask for."

Ivaia glares at him. "If you don't count our spying on them as a provocation."

"There is no justifying their actions," I retort. "The Dalis have a more secure foothold now. They don't have to worry about us fighting them off, because we can't," I say, wiping my nose. "They used their dealings with us as leverage. They sowed seeds here. Now, we're outnumbered and overpowered— they don't require a reason to fight. They're just picking us off like pests. And the Queen allows it."

The Dalis are not the only ones to blame for the state of the Sunderlands. The Elven Kingdoms responsible for protecting the clans have withdrawn. Their absence has allowed these Human territories to scar the landscape. I've been wondering, more and more angrily, why no one comes to our aid. Granted, the Dalis don't attack clan campgrounds outright, but anyone out walking in the woods is fair game.

The Elven Armies could match the Dalis in weaponry and force— an advantage the clans don't have and desperately need. Clan-dwelling Elves are docile, bound by traditions of pacifism. Our warriors will defend the clans, but they are not trained or equipped to grapple with an army. Only I possess power to rival them, gifted by the God of Death. The sole predator that can match them, but a lone wolf, nonetheless.

I've read of the Elves that came before us; their blood ripe with magic beyond what we know now. Ancient texts claim they were more connected to the Gods, too. However, our ancestors protected their secrets so well, they've been lost even to their descendants. The Children of the Sunderlands' Forest today are simple folk. I suspect great power lies dormant in our blood. But there are centuries of nonviolent tradition barring us from awakening it. Everything is fucking working against us at this point.

"Who knows if this loft will even be safe anymore, come a few more months?" Riordan says, rubbing the back of his neck with one hand, the other planted on his hip. His linen pants hang low off his hips making him seem even taller. "Keres is right. An entire sodding army has squatted on the kingdom doorstep and there's no word from anyone." His words always come faster the angrier he becomes, along with a flurry of gestures.

"The Cenlands have sent word—" Ivaia says.

"Okay, let me rephrase. *Help* hasn't come from anywhere. No one is coming. Your niece sits on the throne with half her mind gone out the widest window. When the clans need their kingdoms most, she's revoked the crown's protection. If her mother could see—"

"Enough," Ivaia says.

"No, Iv. It isn't enough. Gods know what Hero is doing or what she's planning, but our people are perishing every day. It is not enough."

I agree with Riordan. Something isn't right with my cousin. But considering her current situation, little *could* be right.

"Ivaia," I try to ease the tension building between them. "You know the Ro'Hale Kingdom better than any of us. You may not know Queen Hero, but you know everyone else there." I look at Rio next. "You know your brethren in the Knight Order. Can either of you think of what might be going on *around* Hero since her mother died? Hero's not the

only one suffering the loss of Herrona, the entire kingdom must have felt
it."

Ivaia shrugs. "I don't know why Queen Hero hasn't helped the clans.
It is not my job to guess what could go wrong with an entire kingdom.
Especially not one I haven't been a part of for more than a decade. We
all have our roles, Keres. You know yours," She says, avoiding my
question and my eyes.

Riordan throws his hands up, leaning his weight back onto one leg;
a bony hip brandished in her direction. She folds her arms across her
chest. The glance between them reminds me that only a diamond can cut
another diamond.

"The crown has come to Hero prematurely." Ivaia relents, "The
armies will not follow a little girl in the wake of a Queen who ruled them
for nigh twenty years."

"She's hardly a little girl, so that can't be it," I scoff. "She's a couple
years older than me, around Liriene's age. I'm sure she has enough
experience—or at least studied well enough under her mother."

"We do not have time for this now." She swats my interjection away.
"You must go out tonight, Keres, and hunt. Alone."

Riordan flinches. "What?" He opens his arms towards her, and I
know he thinks she's gone mad. "Ivaia, darling."

"It's been three days," she says and holds up a quieting hand. "And I
know why she was late in coming here but the task is still at hand."

"Alone?" I ask. She usually goes hunting with me.

Riordan crosses the room and sits face to face with his wife, shutting
me out of their conversation.

"Ivaia, you know this is wrong. She's grieving and doing an exercise
alone will be too much for her. The amount of discipline she needs under
these circumstances... She's bound to lose control and you'll be the one
who set her up to fail."

The rational part of me agrees with him, but the hungry part is growling objection. It's not the dark out there that scares him or even the beasts—Human and animal alike, I know it. It's the darkness within me that does.

"Riordan, my love." She smiles like she's thinking he's just as crazy. "This is the best time for Keres to prove what she's learned. It's during difficult times we must exercise our faith in the Gods."

She turns back to me, inviting me to join her side of the argument. I clasp my hands behind my back and look between her and Rio.

"I respectfully disagree, Ivaia. I came here to hunt, but not to do it alone."

Although I'm dying to do something, she wants me to do this as an example of piety. That's not what I came for. I came to take control in the way I know how—not to cause more chaos.

"Let us drink their blood," The Death Spirit howls in my head.

"If I go out there alone and I lose control, there will be consequences," I say.

Ivaia's smile flies off her face as if I'd smacked it across the room. "Exactly. So, don't lose control."

"An army marches into our land." Riordan takes her limp hands in his, taking her attention off me. "For many moons, you and Keres have gone on these hunts. Seeking justice, seeking balance. But while our numbers dwindle, more of them come from the North. Maybe these hunts need to stop altogether."

My brows shoot up at that.

She yanks her hands back and rises to her feet. "For many moons, she and I have gone hunting together, yes. It's time she does this alone."

He follows her, keeping steps behind her as she busies herself with packing up my belongings. She loads my bow onto my shoulder. She ignores my desperate expression and Riordan's protestation.

"You or Keres or both of you. It doesn't matter. See the bigger issue. Keres and her self-control aside. The few we are and what power we have, we are not affecting our cause. Your actions are like throwing grains of sand at a wave," he says.

She growls her annoyance at him.

"Who are you even doing this for anymore, Ivaia? You say it's the Gods, but I fear it's yourself. This isn't for the people anymore. What are you trying to prove?" He adds.

I freeze at his words. The temperature in the hut drops several degrees when Ivaia looks at him.

She takes one heavy step toward him.

"You cannot understand what it means to uphold a responsibility given by the Gods," she says.

Another meditated step, and he watches her feet move closer.

The bells on her anklets tinkle.

"You cannot understand the burden of power or the weakness one must overcome to wield such a divine gift. To battle selfish desire and carry out the will of the Gods—that is the true fight Keres must endure time and time again. This is not a skirmish with Dalis warriors in the dark, this is what Keres must do to defeat the darkness in herself if there's to be any hope for the Sunderlands. Keres must prove herself worthy and in control of her power. This is not futile."

Riordan rakes a hand through his hair, and drops her gaze, shaking his head.

She turns to me, jabbing a finger toward my chest. "Mrithyn came to you tonight, didn't He?"

I close my eyes and nod my head, remembering the hooded figure in my tent doorway.

"He wanted you to perform your duty to the dead. He wanted your worship. Did He not?" She asks.

My eyes spring open as she inches closer to me, those little bells sounding more ominous than they should.

"Your Spirit does not want to linger at the side of deathbeds. You run here every time this happens. I'm giving you free rein and the chance to prove you deserve it. If you want to be the Coroner that kneels in prayer, go back home. I know that's not you, and tonight is different than any other hunt. Don't pretend you're not roaring inside."

"I am. Rio does have a point, though. These hunts don't make the Dalis any more afraid of us, if anything it makes them angrier."

"This is war, Keres, but you are an Instrument of the Divine—your wrath is mightier." She flashes a wicked smile at each of us. "Just because Riordan doesn't understand what we do for our Gods and our people, doesn't mean you should forget what it feels like to be out there doing something *right*. For the glory of our people and the Pantheon. If you can focus on that truth, I believe you can maintain control."

She turns to Rio. "You think we do this to exercise our pride or to cope with our grief? No."

Riordan and I exchange nervous glances. I can hear our heartbeats racing.

"Keres is not here to grieve. Tell him, Keres. She hunts because she hungers, and this appetite was given to her by the God of Death." A bitter laugh drops off her tongue as she turns back to me. "You crave vengeance. Katrielle was a victim. All nine of them and countless others."

Her eyes search mine for the same understanding she has always shown me. Something inside me wants to echo her words with a wide, hungry grin, but I swallow the growl in my throat and straighten my spine. My inner monster paces with quick, heavy steps behind my rib cage.

"You and I, and every Elven Child of Aureum, we are all victims of

Human terrorism. But you are a victim who has the power to claim vengeance for us all. You must learn to trust your God-given abilities. You ran from one task tonight; you ran to this one. This one engenders change and you know it. Order and balance. We must balance all things. Blood for blood." She shoots a disdainful look at her husband.

"If you go with me, we have a better chance at making a real difference. I haven't had enough time to prepare for this kind of situation." I try to hold the lamp of logic against her emotional speech.

"Life will never give you enough time," she snarls. "Death will not wait for you to be ready. And neither will our enemy. You've made mistakes before, you've lost control before. Show me what you have learned. Now. When it really hurts, show me you can turn that pain into power."

"Keres, the choice is yours. You *can* go home. You don't have to hunt." Riordan stretches his disapproval over Ivaia like a net.

He's wrong. There is no going home. Not while my Spirit thirsts for the blood of my enemies. Ivaia knows my darkness well. My inhibition is not stronger than my cursed thirst. I resist her words because if I don't, it will be all too easy to go out there. To give in to the desire for the freedom she's tempting me with. Without her there to rein me in, my hunger might just consume me and the most dangerous parts of me want it to. That's the point.

"You will never make peace with the monster inside unless you let it out and face it," Ivaia speaks in my direction but throws her attitude in his. "And right now that monster is raging."

I pause at the top of the steps and stare out over the banister. From this height, I am equal with the mighty trees. The wind blows, bowing the trees at my feet. Despite the hour, the darkness deepens. Promising fealty to me before the dawn comes for me.

My blood races, my palms sweat. That familiar, unearthly thing crawls along my bones, gnawing at my muscles to move. Ivaia's hand alights on my shoulder, and I tear my eyes from the tree line.

"Meet me at the Shrine when it's finished," she says, and I follow her down the stairwell.

I don't say goodbye or even mutter an agreement as she bids Riordan a goodnight and goes her own way. I thunder down the steps. My bow knocks against my leg and the crescendo of a drum of war beats somewhere deep within me.

3: DARKNESS

"According to our history, the world began with love.
    The God of Death, Mrithyn, encountered the Goddess of Life, Enithura.
    He loved her for her vibrancy and creativity.
    She loved him for his serenity and honesty."

Katrielle and I were children when we met. We sat next to each other one day in school. It was a tedious lecture, and we both struggled to stay awake in the back of the class. So, the teacher forced us to sit at her feet. To test her, the tutor told Kat to recite a verse about the Pantheon of Gods:

"They created our world, Aureum, to be their kingdom.
Thus, in a world born of Life and Death, everything that lives must die.
From the Principalities come Creation's Powers and Laws.

The Children of Life and Death are those Who comprise Aureum:
Adreana, Goddess of Night. She is the Dark and Secrets.
Oran, God of Day. He is the Light and Revelation.

There are the twin Gods, born between the day and night:
Taran, God of Earth. He is Phenomenon, he is Disaster.

Nerissa, Goddess of the Sea and Air. She is Discovery, she is Mystery.
The Dominions of the World are Elf, Man, Monster, and Spirit, as well as
all between them.

To the Deities and their Dominion, came friends and rivals:
Imogen, Goddess of Peace and Order.
Ahriman, God of Chaos and War.
Elymas, God of Magic and Wonder."

My muscles tense at the memory, as my bare feet glide over the familiar ground. The mist parts ahead of my every step and curls around the roots of the towering trees. I push aside draped vines of crawling plants, scattering the moonlight beaming through the leaves and gilding the fog with silver. Insects buzz and chirp; an orchestra set in the balconies of branches. Memories consume me as the smells and sounds of the ancient forest permeate my senses.

Katrielle had worshipped the Goddess of Night above all others. She found comfort in a higher power who could see you at your darkest and not judge you. The memory of the first time I saw Katrielle is now polluted by the memory of the last time she looked at me.

"Very good child!" The teacher had said as she passed Katrielle something sweet to eat. A reward for pulling off the impossible—making the teacher believe we cared about her boring lessons. I watched as she crumbled the cookie between her teeth, and she smiled until some fell out of her mouth. I laughed at her. Her brown curls were wild around her ecstatic face, her mouth so full she could not retort.

The image of her losing crumbs through her smile is stained by the memory of blood dribbling from her mouth. I wipe away escaped tears and spit the image into the dirt. My tears are futile. Prayers proved useless too. Still, I can't help but look at the sky and question the Gods.

My eyes search the space between two clouds, a doubting devotee staring out my temple window.

Mrithyn. He stalks my every step. Anticipation gnaws harder at my stomach the further I wade into shadow. My eyes flit to the moon. Adreana. The God of Death and the Goddess of Darkness plague my existence. One God to incite the inner riot that is grief, the other to watch silently as it consumes.

Katrielle used to look to Adreana as a guardian of secrets; she swore she felt safer knowing nobody could see her fears and desires in the dark. I see Adreana now as the only God who shows us the truth. Who reveals our fears and desires. During Her hours, the universe reflects what we all are: darkness scarred by starlight. I see myself in the face of the night sky, through the branches, and am glad I'm alone to face that.

I'll miss Katrielle every day, and every night I will remember what she taught me about the Dark Goddess. A beautiful being, although useless to me now. Is this what the Gods are good for? When you need them, they are here and far away at the same time. Are the Gods untouchable as your other self in the mirror, only present when they want to show you something silently? Our teacher always insisted they loved their creation, desiring an interactive relationship with us. I don't believe it.

"Teacher, which of us is like Adreana?" Katrielle had asked.

Our teacher folded her hands behind her and chewed on the question. Her long nose pointed toward me, blue eyes glinting with mischief.

"Oran is a juvenile God. He toddles across the heavens; his mirth is the rays of the sun. Daily, he beams upon creation and is content with what he has." Our teacher raised her arm and fluttered her fingers.

"Adreana is a fierce and wise being, eldest of the Hallow-children. She sweeps Oran up in her arms and hides him under her veil like a babe when the monsters

come out to play. She dims the world to keep its secrets hidden for sake of his innocence and our shame. She turns his face beneath her long black hair and grants us our repose."

"Keres, with her long black hair, then. She is like Adreana." Katrielle pointed me out in class.

"And you are like Oran, Katrielle." She enjoyed our reactions: me scowling and Kat giggling.

"So, I have to protect her from monsters?" I jerked a finger at Katrielle. "She can't even chew her food properly."

The teacher's hands landed on her hips and her eyebrow cocked. Katrielle's lips puckered and then trembled. She wiped her hand across her face, scattering the crumbs. I looked at her and frowned right back.

"I can't protect a blubbering fool like her."

"Now, Keres," the teacher said, "Imagine what Liriene will say...."

My sister's name rings through my head like a bell. I realize where I am. I'm not too far now, the trees are sparser here.

I wade deeper and deeper into the dark blue of the night. Only those who know their way should walk this far into a night in the forest. I am not the sole danger walking between these trees. Mrithyn walks freely in the land of the living, and Adreana oversees our dreams, but it is War that took my comrades from me.

My skin prickles at the cool caress of the night. The knot in my stomach unwinds, and my nipples perk up at the chill licking my neck. A pair of golden eyes tracks my steps. When my emerald eyes meet their stare, they disappear.

Once, I overheard a Dalis soldier telling his comrade to beware the wolves in these woods. He should have warned his friend to fear those who walk among the wolves instead. Still, I'm thankful for the rumors, the stories tossed into campfires. The lies that burn into impressionable minds. They stay there, glowing like embers in the back of their heads.

Those are the thoughts that will keep them away and us alive.

When I'm not around, it's true, the wolves are the most dangerous predators lurking behind these trees. So, let the humans stay in their beds, jumping out of their skin every time we howl. They may be here, but they are not home like we are.

I'll have to reach my destination before sunrise if I want to avoid the same mistake the nine made. They fucked up and collided with a Dalis patrol. However, my chances of survival are much higher than theirs was. I wonder, if I had been with them, could I have saved them? That's a painful thought.

"Turn your pain into power," the Death Spirit echoes Ivaia's words in my head.

I determine the hour by the position of the stars and moon, referencing the slant of shadows cast by the trees. Sunrise is in a handful of hours. The thought of orange and red streaks painting the sky hastens my steps.

Not only does Mrithyn charge me with the responsibility of guiding souls, He grants me the power to take them. The only problem is I'm cursed with an unslakable bloodlust.

Each attack makes me more restless, hungrier for justice. Sometimes, I worry that it's not peace I want at all. Sometimes, when I was alone with Katrielle and we told Adreana our secrets, I prayed for war. A war so brutal and earth-shattering— a war to end all wars. I prayed for bloodshed, propitiation for those lost to us. And Katrielle did not bat an eye. She bowed her head and uttered an agreement. Adreana knows what horrible darkness my soul craves, but no matter how I pray she proves useless every time.

4: THE HUNT

Green looks otherworldly in the dark. Life blossoming from shadow. A chill runs up the spine of a tree ahead of me, making its leaves shiver. Trembling in and out of the moonlight, the undersides of the leaves take on a sickly color. The grass and moss garnishing the ground roll out like a verdant carpet toward my prey's hiding place. Even the fog takes on a bluish-green haze, interrupted by the black stalks of the trees. Silver starlight bounces off the caps of enormous white mushrooms. The air smells of fire and pine.

Hesitation haunts my every step. I resent Ivaia. She always has to be right. She looked at me and saw a monster waiting to come out to play. She played on the sinister thoughts running through my head to persuade me. Rio looked at me and saw a girl mourning her childhood friend. As a knight, he understands the impact of losing a comrade. They both know how pain can be a motivator. Riordan understands how it's dangerous. Ivaia sees only how it's useful. He sees pain as blinding; a weakness. She sees it as cleansing oneself of weakness.

To prevent the arrow from grazing my skin as it launches off my bow, I wrap my hands in leather strips. Riordan prays with a strand of glass beads wrapped around his fists: one bead for each God of the pantheon. Ivaia wears hers as a circlet taming her wild blonde hair. I lost the string of beads they gave me, and it would have been useful right about now. I hope Riordan, at least, is somewhere praying for me. One strong hand wrapped in beads, the other gripping a dainty teacup.

The forest adopts a burnt-hued glow as I approach an unnatural clearing. Walls of gnawed down trees stretch toward the sky as if in one last attempt to grow, curving into a full circle around the human encampment. Their wood is slammed together and bound by arms of iron. My home camp aims to live in peace with its neighbors, trees included. Here, these damned creatures destroyed everything to make room in a place they do not belong. Burnt earth, their destitute clearing. Mountains are the backbone of their encampment, which faces the shadowed forest. Scarred territory, stricken with a disease that goes by the name, Men.

Sounds of revelry gobble up the air with the pillars of smoke from their bonfires. Roguish voices chirp curse words like demented birds perched on chopped-down branches. They spend their nights crossing swords out of boredom. Drinking to fill their emptiness.

I take a position in the shadows. *Remember what you've learned, Ker.*

On the hunt, Ivaia goes into a place in her mind that houses years of experience and discipline. Fearlessness. In Ivaia's world, she's on one side of a scale, these men on the other, and the weight must always be even. They killed nine, so nine will pay. Blood for Blood. We've hunted together countless times. She's equipped me with lessons in fighting and magic. Ivaia and Mrithyn have both vested their unique powers in me.

The God of Death is here in all things around me. He is in the rotting wood of the walls, the decaying leaves, the ashes. His power is in my hands as they nock an arrow to the bow; heightening my senses as I survey the camp. What isolates me from Ivaia is what both sanctifies and corrupts me: The Death Spirit.

She has never understood the blight on my soul. My curse. Controlling my thirst for bloodshed is antithetical to my Divine nature.

As safely as her lessons live in my head, an untamed Spirit of desolation inhabits my bones. The Death Spirit does not discriminate, and it does not cower. It hungers.

"You crave vengeance," Ivaia said. *"Keres is not here to grieve."*

"Yes," the Death Spirit says.

The Dalis will see me, they'll look into my eyes before I take their lives. And they will not see a young woman, they will see Death.

I take a deep breath and close my eyes, trying to steady my hands.

Nine. Only nine.

Footfalls crunch into the leaves ahead, bringing me out of the stillness in my mind. A soldier stumbles into my line of fire. I withdraw the bowstring as he tugs his belt loose with one hand, lifting a bottle to his mouth with the other. His trousers drop to his ankles and he pisses in the dirt. I loosen my grip on the arrow. His head jerks back as the arrow enters his eye socket. As if in slow motion, his legs go out from under him. His arms flail, his back thuds against the ground, and I recoil at the sound of the glass bottle hitting a rock.

This one will be for Meir, one of the nine.

Back into my hiding place, I stifle the need to drink in the scent of blood on the breeze. It burns my nostrils and narrows my vision. Peering out from behind the tree I'd chosen for cover, I ignore the gorgeous shade of crimson oozing out of his skull. I need a better position, away from the first body.

I creep around the walls like a vulture circling a carcass. Burying my thoughts in the back of my mind like an arrowhead deep into bone. A guard is leaning against a tree up ahead. I check to see if he's alone; vision burrowing into the shadows and uprooting every detail.

He's alone.

I sneak up behind him, crouching as low as his own shadow. The smell of fire wafts on the breeze, his comrades on the other side of the wall begin singing off-pitch:

> "Wallow, wallow, or walk on with pride.
> Follow, follow, in Ahriman's Stride.
> The Gods are listening to the voices of men.
> When we call upon Chaos or Imogen.
> War, war, we conquer and toil.
> More, more, 'til there's blood in the soil.
> Wallow, wallow, or fight on with pride.
> Follow, follow, in Ahriman's stride.
> He gives us the weapon, he gives us the war.
> He leads us and brings us the spoils of war..."

Their screeching masks his scream as I grab him, digging my claws into his shoulder. My knife traces a bloody smile across his throat. Holding his limp body up by his shaggy brown hair, I adjust my stance to his dead weight and drop him into the dirt.

Jaren.

I wipe my blade on my leathers before sheathing it. Jaren used to start the singing around the campfires. His voice was stunning, bright as a crackling fire. Now he's dead on a cot; voice forever silenced.

I hear footsteps and a conversation looming above me on the wall. Two guards walk at a lazy pace, rounding the curve of the embankment. *They're just coming to me tonight.*

"I swear, it's like they wait for the trees to move on their behalf."

"Well, there's not much he could have done, anyway. Not with my knife at her throat and my cock in her cunny." They share a laugh.

"Must have not liked the poor bitch if he didn't lift a finger."

"They're spineless. It's too easy to—"

I shoot an arrow into his open mouth.

My next arrow nestles into his friend's eye before he can scream. They fall off the wall and land at my feet. Whipping the knife back out, I drop to my knees at one's side. The arrowhead perks up out of his throat. Refusing to give in to death, he gasps and writhes. With a flick of my blade, the rapist's pants tear open. Unable to suppress the growl in my chest, I sever his prized appendage. I rip the arrow from his mouth and replace it with his cock. I seethe as he sputters, and I watch until his body stops moving.

Katrielle.

This one was for her and for the female he raped. I look toward the other body, limbs bent at ghastly angles.

Hayes.

Kat and Hayes would have been wed tomorrow.

I hear a gasp behind me and whirl toward it. I jump to my feet as a soldier's light blue eyes flare at me. I stare back for a moment. My mouth runs dry and a thirst for blood erupts like a geyser inside me.

Oryn.

No more feeling, no more memories. Only vengeance, only bloodshed. I lunge for him, the bloody arrow still in hand. Dodging his sword, I stab the arrow into his sword upper arm, forcing him to drop his weapon, before grappling with him to the ground. Our struggle isn't quiet. My bare feet paw the earth as I fight to get on top of him. We roll over, trying to keep each other at a distance but still in a lethal hold. He bucks between my legs, hands reaching for my face and hair. Grunting, I throw all my weight behind the arrow and plunge it into his neck. He screams. I yank it out and stab it back in until I've broken a sweat. The sound of his gasps beneath the arrow subside into the sounds of blood bubbling up in his throat.

His men are coming for him, for me. I sense them before I see them. Above the groaning of the desecrated forest, I hear their staggered breathing. Mine are the unrivaled senses of a predator. I hear the blood whooshing in their veins, pumping with adrenaline as they run toward that silenced scream. I taste blood and note that he had scratched my lip. I smell fear in the air. My hands should be cold where the wind licks at the blood on them, but all I feel is fire.

Nilo, Lucius, Cassriel, Leander.

I don't look, I shoot. The next Man falls. *Six.*

My arrow will not miss so long as Mrithyn's power courses through me. That familiar, otherworldly beast gnaws at my rib cage, begging to be unleashed. Its roar fills my lungs, blasting Ivaia's lessons out of my head. Another arrow nocked and ready. Dawn has walked into the clearing and stopped short at what it's found.

Turning from the sunlight that threatens to expose me, I prowl into the last of the fleeting shadows. I repeat the last three names over and over in my head.

Nilo, Lucius, Cassriel.

My heart beats their names, louder and louder until it's all I can hear. That creature within me breaks free of its cage.

I see him. My arrow rips through the air and sinks into a wide eye. Again, Nilo's empty eyes stare back at me from his deathbed in the camp. My grip on the bow tightens.

I hear him. I spin on my heels, arrow biting at the bowstring, ready to soar. It strikes him through the temple of his skull.

"Remember, they don't see you as a person," I hear Lucius's voice. *"Remember, all they see is someone in their way."*

There is now a palpable panic in the air. I've raised an alarm that's sparked outrage in the camp. I stop searching for another shadow to drift into. I stop counting my own steps. I stride into that orange glow of time between day and night, a beast in the stillness of dawn.

A smile breaks across my face as another man crosses my path. His scream tells me he's glimpsed the terror living inside me. Another arrow meets flesh and bone. The silence after his scream sucks the air out of my lungs like a vacuum where his soul once was.

The phantom breeze caresses my face, soothing the part of me that is so like it. So bitter, so brutal, and unforgiving. My mind swims with the smell of blood thickening the air. Mrithyn's entropic power is taking hold of the nine bodies that paint the soil red.

Mrithyn despises the war, the perversion of His power. Mortals were never meant to kill. All the blood staining this land calls to me. Keres. He's in me too, His might reaching for souls through my very hands.

Fix it, fix it. Make it right.

I hear the echoes of long-lost heartbeats. The earth itself seems to pulsate beneath my feet. A bleeding heart, one threatening to stop.

Balanced. For every beat, a moment of silence. All must be balanced.

My mind is drifting in the waves of bloodlust now. I twirl on my toes, head tilted as I listen for more footfalls. The moan of a man grieving the loss of his comrade breaks the silence and I move toward him, greedy for more souls. I hear him breathing, and I smile at the thought of silence.

"Nine." Heavy hands fall on my shoulders, pulling me to a hard stop. "Only nine."

My eyes darken at the sight of those bright, clean diamonds in Riordan's head. A gasp catches in my throat as he ushers me back in the direction of the loft.

"What?" The question escapes me but we both know it's already answered.

Only nine. Only nine. Only nine.

His hand stays on my back, reassuring my direction.

"I should have never come here alone—"

"You're not alone, Keres."

We're running now. His long sword is drawn, and my bloodied hands cling to my bow.

"Hey! Elves!"

Dirt flies up from our feet as we skid to a halt. I snarl, flinging myself toward that voice— but I falter. We're surrounded. A human steps out of the shadow and his arrow trains on Riordan.

5: DAWN

Everyone wonders what dying is like. It's a natural thing to ask. At a curious age, we ask our elders, as if they had died before. When a sparrow falls from the sky, we question the bittersweet nature of everything. We ask our Gods when we cannot answer each other. But when the Gods do not reveal their secrets, we make up our own answers.

We spin our own web of understanding, entangling ourselves in beliefs like a child would cocoon themselves in a blanket.

Folly. Faith is not benign. Sometimes, our faith tricks us.

Pulling a blanket over our heads can be comforting but it is also blinding.

I don't blame anyone for trying to assuage the pain of reality with faith-based balms. Nobody can resist asking the question or dreaming up its answers.

"What is dying like? Like going to sleep and never waking up."

But there's a preeminent question we should all be asking, with a much more harrowing answer… "How merciful is Mrithyn?"

I have faith in one thing: The men at my feet saw my God before they died. As I brought the dead justice, the living begged me for mercy and I gave them the final answer. From the looks my prey gave me, I believe dying doesn't feel like going to sleep.

Blood is pulsing from a Human's severed leg and he's gripping the new end of it in disbelief. I don't hear his voice, but I know he's praying as I put him to an end. The blood stops squirting and pools beneath my bare feet.

Riordan is face down in the dirt and he's covered in blood. The birds aren't chirping or welcoming a new day. A Man is sobbing, realizing it's his last morning. The Death Spirit is snickering with sadistic glee, back in its cage within me. Riordan isn't moving.

After that, everything comes in waves of sounds, smells, and sensations. My slippery wet hands roll Riordan onto his back. My legs almost give out with the strain. I check his throat with shaking fingertips before laying my ear to his chest. He groans as his eyes flutter open.

"Rio! Wake up." I shake him by the shoulders. A large cut decorates his wide forehead. His blond hair is muddy and blood streaks his face. I push resurfacing images from my mind. "We have to go."

He staggers, rising from the ground, regaining his sword and sheathing it. Eyes locked on the trees between us and safety the whole time. He doesn't once look at the massacre of bodies. Never looks down on me or what I've done. He places his hand on my shoulder for support and we run. The forest hurtles past us as we flee to the safety of the loft.

Once we're close enough to feel them, the wards overwhelm me. The magic draws out every bit of panic left in me. I stop him, commanding him to face me as I scan him for injury.

"What happened back there, are you all right?" I ask although I know very well what happened back there.

"I'm fine, Keres," he says and catches his breath.

He unbuckles his sword belt and leans on the hilt of his sword like it's a walking stick. I see he's bleeding from his leg and a little from his brow. He rolls up his trousers and reveals a gash. The blood on his armor is someone else's.

"Bastard knocked me unconscious, but then you...."

I can't breathe. I can't—

Doubled over, hands braced on my knees, I empty my stomach onto the ground. I cough and gasp for air. A tremor takes hold of every muscle, stealing control of my legs, and I buckle. He catches me.

Riordan's eyes meet mine, concern filling them to the brim. He's saying something but I can't focus on his words. My chest heaves against panic's tightening grip on my lungs. A stabbing pain gnaws at my chest and a dull ache balls up in my throat.

We fled like shadows that run from the sun, and no one had followed. A glorious morning broke open the sky, filling the clearing with shades of pink, red, and orange. It reminds me of the blood I hunted for tonight. The thoughts in my head sound like a conversation between two people.

"You should have wiped them all out. Why didn't you kill them all so none may follow?" My inner Death Spirit growls.

"I should have stopped at nine. You're no better than them, beast." The second voice belongs to me, or at least who I was before the Monster moved into my body.

Two spirits, one mortal and one belonging to Death Himself. Or myself. I don't know anymore. I rake my hands through my hair trying to push away the intrusive thoughts.

"Keres," the Death Spirit roils in my head, taunting me.*"Nine, nine, nine."*

Riordan's soothing words find space in my mind at last. "It's over."

The crisp morning air settles my shivering muscles. The chill relieves the sweat on my brow, my palms, and finally fills my desperate lungs. I look up into his eyes again and nod. A weak smile trembles on my mouth.

"Ivaia is waiting for you at the shrine."

"I'll bring her back to help you," I say.

"I'm fine. If I hadn't come, you'd be the injured one right now. Maybe." He straightens my shoulders. "Go. It's been a while since I wielded my sword but recovering from battle is muscle memory. Don't tell her I stopped you. I don't want to upset her."

"Okay, I won't tell her," I nod. "Thank you, Rio."

I turn to go but he stops me, remembering something. "We told her this hunt was futile, that we were throwing grains of sand at waves. Tell her how you felt, what happened to you. Not the Men, not me. She must hear reason. These hunts are getting more dangerous for *us* instead of those it should hurt—the humans. She needs to see that and come up with a new plan. I know you can help her see the truth."

⌯⌯⌯⌯⌯⌯

"He interfered." Her voice cuts through the cavern, echoing off the walls. Our meeting spot is a makeshift temple in a cave beneath the mountain. Ivaia is kneeling in prayer before the shrine.

Well, there goes the big secret.

"Ivaia, I needed… He came right before—" I sink down to my knees beside her and bury my head in my hands. The acrid smell of the blood staining my hands assaults my nose. Tears stream into my mouth with salt, dirt, and dried blood. They taste like poison and I wish they were.

"Keres," She says.

The only sound to follow is that of water dripping somewhere in the cave. I rise from the cold ground. My eyes burn from sweat and the stench of my stained skin and clothes. I stare up at the statue of the God of Magic, Elymas. Her gaze flickers from His gilded face to my twiddling hands.

Behind the shrine, a deep pool of water stretches out to the far end of the cave. I strip out of my armor, dropping the heavy leathers into the

41

dust. I let go of all other senses as I walk into the cold water until it reaches my neck. Sunlight slips through a hole in the cave's ceiling. The intrusion of light unsettles me, and I force myself to wade deeper into the pool where it's darker.

"Keres." I hear her gentle voice behind me. "You can't swim. Don't torture yourself."

I don't listen. Right now, I feel no specific desire to float or sink. Stained and in need of cleansing, I am breathing and drowning all at once. I deserve punishment, for the water to scourge me. The weight of the water shifts over my collarbones and its silvery chill kisses my jawline. A gasp escapes me, the desperate need for air overwhelms me. I kick my feet, hoping to push off the bottom of the pool but am met by bottomless, swirling terror. I propel myself upward with aimless hands and spit a surprising amount of water out of my mouth.

A swell of water grows beneath me at the command of Ivaia's magic, and I rise with it. It's difficult but I manage to maneuver in the water as it ebbs and flows into a taller wave with me at the crest. I glimpse Ivaia's rings on her dancing hands before the wave collapses toward the brink of the pool. Delivering me back onto the dusty cave floor, naked and coughing. The water recedes at her command and she rolls her eyes from me to my filthy clothes.

"Stay put." She returns moments later with one of her own gowns. The frail material does little to fight the chill that's soaked into my bones. My pale, long, wet hair drapes over my shoulders. My skin is colder where there should be material on my back but there isn't, because this is Ivaia's dress.

"I always keep extras in that chest over there. We're quite a walk away from the loft." I huff in response.

Again, she positions herself before the shrine, taking ample time to pin the circlet of glass beads into her hair. She closes her eyes and bows deeply at the feet of Elymas. For several breaths, I watch her twist and stretch into various positions. At her leisure, she brings her head to her ankles in a way that baffles me.

She pops an eye open and demands, "Tell me about the hunt."

As if my retelling of a night filled with bloodshed is perfect for her meditation, she awaits my response.

"I failed. It should have only been nine."

"And how many did you kill before Riordan interfered?" Her voice strains as she bends backward.

I mull over the details in my head and remember, "Nine, actually, but he stopped me from the tenth. We almost got away; we were running. And then..."

"And then you protected him." She's standing upright again, still as Elymas behind her.

"I slaughtered them," I say.

"How many?"

"All those who stood in our way. I lost count."

"So, you did it. He put himself in danger." Ivaia says. "You killed the nine you went for. *His* interference made you—"

"Iv, did you hear me? I couldn't stop. No part of me wanted to. He stopped me."

Her hands make their way up to her hips as she processes.

"Riordan is okay, in case you were wondering," I add.

A thought flashes across her eyes like lightning and she turns back toward the statue. She places a hand on the chest of Elymas before resting her head on it.

"And you only used the bow." The statement is filled with disappointment.

"I used the knife too, I mean—"

"You did not use magic."

I swallow my response and look at the figure of Elymas. I've seen this statue countless times and never noticed its eyes. They seem honed on me, tracking my movement as I approach Ivaia.

My power manifested in my first few years of life. I was younger than anyone else in my family was when their magic awoke. However, in thirteen years, never once have I used my powers to kill.

"A poisonous snake who bites and gives no venom," Ivaia says.

She's right, but, "If my bite is deadly, venom is overkill."

She looks up at Elymas, a silent prayer on her lips, a silent response on His. Birds chirp outside, and their shrill voices travel along the cave walls. She lights three candles on the shrine. A breeze enters the cave, marking its territory on my wet skin. Finally, her diamond eyes meet my emerald stare.

"Keres, you have a fear in your heart, and it cripples you. If you were to use the gift of magic Elymas has bestowed upon you, you would gain confidence."

I shift from one foot to the other.

"The Gods chose you." She turns and continues lighting candles all around the shrine. "A God may choose *any* mortal as their servant to bear their power. Mrithyn has chosen *you* as His. Elymas has no servant." She glances at the statue. "Though many have tried to gain His favor."

She looks at me over her shoulder, eyes reflecting the firelight.

"He's gifted us with power, you and I, as He has gifted our bloodline for generations. As *He* has gifted many Mages throughout Aureum. Of what must be thousands, none are like you."

I busy myself with scraping dried blood and dirt from under my fingernails.

"Two Gods, two gifts. The power of Death, and the power of Elemental Magic. Control over life and nature." She allows her words to sink into me.

"A soldier." A flame dances into life upon the candle wick. "An instrument of the divine," She waves the long lighting stick drawing with its smoke. "A Mage." She blows out the flame. "A three-headed hound."

I drop my hands to my side and meet her stare.

"What's in that head of yours? Ignorance or blatant disregard for the Gods' will?" She snaps.

I press my lips together and roll my shoulders back, trying to dismiss the tension building between them.

Ivaia narrows her eyes. "All these years of training you. For what?" A laugh lilts off her tongue, and pangs in my ears.

She doesn't understand. Then I remember Riordan's words.

"All these hunts! For *what?*" I ask.

She pauses.

"Ivaia, understand what this is doing to me, to our people. This balances nothing. I lost control— I raised the alarm of an entire army camp— you think there will be no consequences for this? You think they will go back behind their walls when a little girl killed a bunch of their soldiers? You think this will inspire fear in them, make them stop terrorizing our people and leave, but it won't. They answer to King Berlium. His power. Not mine. And we need Queen Hero. Not me."

"We don't need that child," she says.

"Ivaia, this power is not good enough. We need an army. Not an Elf standing in the shadows with a bow and bloodlust." I decapitate my confidence for the sake of the truth. "These hunts make us feel better. They're not actually making anything else better."

"Do you know what men see before you take their life?" Her question startles me.

I lower my eyes and see my bloodied armor on the ground.

In the past, I've stared into a looking glass for hours, trying to summon the beast inside me. Searching for a glimmer of the darkness brought out of me by violence. I remember the ninth kill, his eyes wide at the sight of me. They all look at me that way before I kill them. As if I'm their worst nightmare. Half of me has always wanted to know what I look like at that moment. The other half dreads the truth.

"An executioner with the abysmal darkness of Death in her eyes. A cloud of white hair floating around a jagged face. You speak to them." Her voice lightens. "I don't know if you hear yourself, but you speak in a divine tongue. A voice comes out of somewhere deep inside you, out of the realm of the Gods. Your voice sucks the air out of lungs, your throat swallows up life like a chasm into the pit of the earth." She approaches me.

"Stop." My voice cracks.

I've tried to maintain my emotional armor for all my second life. Ever since my mother's death, I've fought and grown stronger, colder. Worse than anything life's done to me. Now, this. Nine more weak links in my armor.

I've always resisted the dark, intrusive thoughts the Death Spirit summons. Trained hard and fortified my resolve. Now, it's all crashing down. Everything I've buried deep inside has been unearthed. The cage I've kept my overzealous monster in is unhinging. And Ivaia is pushing me in ways she never has before. It's like I'm trying to run upstream, and the current is constantly pulling me down. I know I'm strong enough to keep moving forward—I have the power of a God within me. But now the question is whether I want to. Do I deserve to?

"When you move in on your prey, time slows. You tear these Humans from the world with a smile on your face." She brushes a strand of hair behind my ear. "A reaper whose bones call for blood. Death Incarnate."

I pull out of her grasp, shaking my head in disbelief.

"Imagine the smile on the face of the Gods at the sight of you." She laughs under her breath and turns toward Elymas's statue. "Imagine His power coupled with the power of Mrithyn. Lightning at your fingertips. Water beneath your feet." Her voice deepens, the weight of it slamming against the cave walls as she looks back at me. "You are fire and you must learn to burn."

She holds up her hand. In her palm, a blue fire bursts into existence. She raises her other hand, encased in a frost. "Ice."

I take a breath as the surrounding air raises every hair on my body. "Water."

I feel the water in my body respond to her. My body goes rigid as she takes control of my blood.

"Air."

The beads of water on my skin evaporate into a gentle whisper against me, ravenously stealing all the breath from my lungs. My eyes roll back after catching sight of her widening smile. After a few breathless moments, my vision returns, and my lungs expand. I fall to the floor gasping as she lowers her hands.

"Earth."

A guttural rumbling sounds from deep within the cave. The water ripples and dust falls from above. A fissure opens in the ceiling. Cracks of golden light and shadow break over her face. I jump out of the way of falling rocks.

"Ivaia!" I move as more dust and rocks splinter out of the cave ceiling and attempt to bury me. The cave crumbles in on us, dust shrouds us.

I react.

Large chunks of stone and gravel float around us, frozen in the air by my outstretched hands. The weight of the mountain is falling on top of me, and I strain with a cry to push it back up into place. I struggle to stand, forcing all my magical energy against the tumbling mountain. The cave ceiling floats up and begins piecing itself together. With a final gesture, I heave the fissure closed and collapse to the ground exhausted.

As the dust settles, echoes of her applause clap against the cave walls.

"Strength that moves mountains, Keres."

"You're wrong."

I scramble to my feet, toes tangled in the too-long dress. "You think you understand what this means. I've been chosen by a God, my own life spared on one condition—I kill for Him. You pretend to know what this kind of existence feels like or should be like."

She lifts her chin and her mouth forms a thin line. I straighten up and point a finger at the statue of Elymas.

"You believe the day might still come when your beloved God will notice you." Laughter drops from my mouth like a stone into water.

"The Gods do not see you, Ivaia. They do not see any of us. They see this world and what we have done to it. The Gods bestow their power, and with it, responsibility to fix their world."

I pound my hand on my chest. The beast behind my ribcage recoils.

"This is not strength. This life comes with a curse. You marvel at the monster the Gods have made me into and what the curse does to me. *A three-headed hound.* Still, only a dog bid to do Their will. And you envy this?" I ask.

The clear voice of my conscience quiets the voice of my cursed soul and the sound of it echoing off the walls is like cool water to a parched throat.

She laughs, "Ignorant fool. You squander your gifts on self-pity and loathing. Yes," she says and throws her hands up. "I envy your gifts. I'm blessed with power but was never chosen as the servant to the God I love most. And you, Keres, the blood of my own. You disgrace Their will. I will never understand why they chose a child like you when I have been a faithful servant."

I stop, astounded at the confession.

Knowing the truth now, I curse her.

Ivaia will never respect the differences between us. She doesn't understand how these hunts unravel me. I keep losing people and I keep taking lives, but it's never enough to set the world back in order.

My life has been off-kilter from the moment I died. No matter how many suffer or how many Men pay, I can't avenge anyone. Not even myself.

Why did Mrithyn choose me? How was cursing me with His "gift" a change in the balance? If I don't learn how to control this monster inside me, it won't be anyone's saving grace. The Sunderlands needs a warden. To stem the tide of bloodshed, not drown it in a crimson tide.

Ivaia wants to play God through me. She wants to use me as if she understands how to. I gather my belongings, my ill wish hanging in the air between us, and desert her. She follows me from the cave, calling my name with a softened voice, but I ignore her and quicken my steps.

6: The Birth of Terror

The Past

King Adon couldn't look; his head stayed buried in his hands. The leader of Ro'Hales armies knelt by his wife's bedside, powerless. Vomit tinged his throat. His palms were sweaty. Cold darkness loomed at the edges of his vision. Was he spinning, or was the room?

Her heavy breathing made him dizzy. It had been hours of this toil, this pain. Her screams dissipated into sobs. His fear brought him to his knees. Everything threatened to go black, and then there was nothing but red. She was losing blood.

The sweat beaded on his brow and ran in rivulets down his neck. His mouth was dry; he needed water. Too many candles were lit, too much light and heat.

Footsteps shuffled around him. He stood frozen in place. Felt more like a ghost watching her body lose all color and energy. Her lifeblood pooled between her legs. A baby cried somewhere in the corner of the dimly lit room. He tore his eyes from his wife, searching for that sound. A nurse turned, bearing the child in her arms. She settled the squealing bundle of blankets into his arms before he realized she had even moved.

The baby's eyes opened, and her cries ceased. *My Princess.*

"Darling," the Queen whispered. He turned back to his wife as the nurses made themselves busy with the blood beneath her, the smell of it sharpened the air.

"Let me see her," she said with a pale-lipped smile.

He laid the baby onto her mother's chest before pressing a kiss to his wife's head. Her small frame shook with what seemed like both a laugh and a cry. She was perfect; he stared at her in wonder. Then he looked to the babe and ascertained she was perfect too.

The nurse's flitting movements caught his attention. All the blood.

The power between his wife's trembling legs amazed him. The baby demanded their attention again and he couldn't stop the tears as they flowed from his eyes. His hand lingered on his Queen's forehead. So much power in her body, to bring forth and sustain life. His knees buckled. Again, he knelt by her side.

This was their third child, but he never grew accustomed to the phenomenon of birth. He never forgot to worship her life-giving power. Queen among all women, the mother of his children. A piece of the Goddess of Life dwells in every woman; he was sure of it.

"Praise Enithura," he said.

"King Adon." The nurse startled him.

His eyes flew to his wife. Her face was gray, her green eyes lacking their usual luster. He removed the baby from her and passed her back to the nurse. The Queen's head drooped to the side, her body going limp once the baby left it.

Fear erupted in his throat; a cry and a scream, "Atyra!"

He gripped her frail shoulders in his hands, but did not have enough power to hold her back from the brink of death. The blood was leaving her without a sign of stopping. He'd fought and stopped wars. He could not stop the bleeding.

There were things his Queen Atyra would have done as the babe's mother, and he tried to remind himself of them. In the middle of the night, when the infant wailed, and he sobbed beside her cradle, he prayed. Sometimes he prayed aloud, to the Gods or to the spirit of his dead wife.

"There were things you would do, I can't remember. I can't."

As time passed, the nurses stayed by his side. They taught him how to be both father and mother to his children, and he tended to his children as carefully as he did his kingdom. Deep down he knew the ability didn't come only from the nurses' guidance. It came from his wife, from the place in his soul where he bore the memory of her. In time, his love for his wife overflowed into his love for their daughters.

"Bring the child to the Oracle," Attica, one of the nurses, whispered to him as they watched the growing baby sleep. "It's what she would have wanted."

Atyra and Adon had presented their elder daughters to an Oracle in the palace temple around the same age. Each Oracle made claims different from the rest. Of the first daughter, the Oracle had said, "Stillness in her blood. Chaos in her wake."

King Adon and Queen Atyra never understood the riddle until it became apparent their firstborn had no magic. Her only power was her remarkable beauty. Like her mother—black swirling hair, sapphire blue eyes, porcelain skin, and a tender frame. Herrona, a name meaning, "her mother's likeness."

Atyra's love never failed him, it morphed into something bigger than their marriage. It split between him and their firstborn daughter. Both received a fair amount. But with a woman like that, having to share her never felt fair. With a daughter like Herrona, he didn't mind so much.

The second-born child lured amazement out of the Oracle who'd blessed her after birth.

"Mother of nations, bringer of light. Power will drop from both her palms into two pools. One pool like blood, the other like starlight."

These words baffled the King and Queen, too, until Resayla exhibited outstanding beauty coupled with alarming power. Magic-touched. Blond of hair. Her eyes the same forest green as her father's but flecked with gold. Her features were not as soft as Herrona's. Sharp facial bones and a pouting mouth. Her eyes were large, and she was long-legged and spindly.

This third daughter was a princess unlike her sisters: Ivaia. With hair and eyes like the sun and the sky. Blue like that in her mother and eldest sister's eyes, seams of blue sewn around the edges of her clear silver eyes.

"She will grow to have great power, like her sister." The Oracle whispered. A laugh rippled her youthful face. "Power that begins and ends inside her but continues on through her."

The King's sunken eyes searched the Oracle's as he tried to understand. "How great will her power be?"

The Oracle's eyes were vacant, the trait of one without physical sight. The trait that sets Oracles aside from other children. The Blindness struck at a certain age, and forever demarcated their lives from their peers. His wife's absence made room for new fears throughout the years. Now, alone before an Oracle with their last-born daughter, he prayed his child would never lose her sight.

"Greater but not the greatest." The child Oracle lifted her small, plump hands. "Your Queen is no longer at your side. She is beneath your feet."

Tears welled in his eyes and he clutched the infant to his chest.

"She lives on in them: Her beauty, her spirit, her power." Her scaled eyes widened as if the revelation thrilled her. "The three daughters born of you, born of her, they are birth, death, and rebirth. Go again into the earth at the end of your days and the beginning of theirs, a happy father, a solemn king."

Years later, Ivaia was a blossoming little girl.

"You brought down a mountain in your birth," the King whispered to her one night. He found her asleep in the grass after training in magic with her sister all day. He scooped her up in his arms. "You've been powerful enough to shake a nation since the beginning of your days."

Of the three, Herrona was the most like their mother. Her true power was seizing a room's attention. Everyone listened to her, everyone respected her, and everyone loved her. King Adon couldn't deny it. And as she grew in age, stature, beauty, and grace, he was sure she would bring kingdoms to their knees as Queen of her time.

He emptied coffers of gold employing the finest tutors to educate the three of them. Herrona and Resayla were studious and bright. Resayla trained her magical abilities, starting at eight. The youngest was in her eleventh year of life when her magical ability first manifested. Ivaia's power was greater than her sister's. Magical studies swallowed up Ivaia's interest.

By seventeen years of age, Ivaia had learned all she could from the tutors and the mages her father paid for. She grew restless, careless, and rebellious. Herrona was preparing for her coronation. Resayla was studying politics. Meanwhile, Ivaia began sneaking off the castle grounds and into the woods. One night, Herrona had stayed up late awaiting the return of the youngest princess.

"I have found a God," Ivaia declared upon return.

"The Gods are never out of reach. You can visit the temple any time and you know that." Herrona raised an eyebrow.

"No, Herrona. The Gods do not live in temples of stone and earth. They are out there, in the world, in nature, in all."

"And which God has so captured your heart? Have they made you a mortal servant?" Herrona's eyes appraised Ivaia's body for a change.

"Not a servant, yet. I have devoted my life to the God Elymas, Lord of Magic. I have found a purpose."

Resayla stirred in her bed, groaning in protest at their volume. Herrona bowed her head in thought, closing her brilliant blue eyes. Ivaia did not dare interrupt her contemplation.

A few moments later, Resayla sat up, hair tangled and eyes creaking open. She stretched and pushed the covers back.

"What are you two on about?"

Herrona smirked at Resayla and then turned back to Ivaia. "I believe you."

Ivaia wept with joy.

"But——" Herrona lifted a long-fingered hand, "You will go to worship, accompanied by a knight. Never after dark."

Both Resayla and Ivaia exchanged looks.

"The both of you. My first act as Queen will be to find you each a knight protector."

Resayla rolled her eyes and shuffled back to bed. "You mean a husband."

Herrona pursed her lips and waved her hand at Resayla's response. "Long has it been a tradition in this family, that the princesses should receive a guardian from the order. I will put it off no longer."

Ivaia's eyes were far away, but her mouth quirked up at the corners.

The next day, Herrona ordered the finest knights in the kingdom to present themselves to her. For Resayla, she chose a handsome, hardy knight.

"Resayla, my first act as Queen is to choose Indiro Aval as your knight protector." This stunned Resayla. The most battle-worn knight became her closest companion. Where she went, he followed, and he cared for her. They left the kingdom shortly after.

"Ivaia, my second act as Queen is to choose Riordan Gale as your knight protector." Herrona smiled. Ivaia's jaw dropped when she first laid eyes on her knight. A tall, muscled man with eyes like diamonds and hair like gold. She imagined them alone in the woods together and blushed.

After Herrona's coronation, King Adon died from what appeared to be a broken heart, and Herrona met her first challenge as Queen. Rumors flew like arrows about a newly blind child in the castle village. The Gods chose a new Oracle. Herrona knew there were traditions and there was a ritual she had to perform. Her first task as Queen was to lead the kingdom in pious celebration of a holy phenomenon. The Veil Ritual was as old as the Ro'Hale kingdom itself.

Her father had taught her everything. She knew it all by heart but now she must act. They presented the child to her in the temple. All her hair had fallen out, as happens with all new Oracles. Her eyes were wild, although glazed. As if she were scouring the darkness for a glimmer of hope. Herrona, being merciful, knew what she must do.

"For ages, our traditions have exploited these children chosen by the Gods. While we worship the Gods' decision to use the child, we forget about the toll paid—their loss. No longer can we ignore their pain."

Ivaia marveled at her elder sister. Herrona gained fame that spread beyond the kingdom, for her acts of kindness to the Oracle children. They were no longer left to wallow in blindness and visions on the temple floors. They were elevated, treated with dignity and honor. She desired for them to be clothed richly and always accompanied.

Herrona ordered for mages to enchant any kind of animal the child desired to be their companion. They received rooms in the castle. The temple priests stocked the library with books for the blind. Tutors traveled to court to help the children learn to read with their hands and adjust to the loss of sight. These changes affected all Oracle children who outgrew their connection with the Gods.

Herrona inspired Ivaia. The beauty of the religious culture awed her.

"How gracious the Gods are to use us and be a part of our lives," Ivaia pondered.

Herrona, signing her name on each scroll, put her quill down and looked at her sister.

"Blessings and Curses, they both exist in our world. You must give up something, sacrifice something of yourself to become an instrument. The Oracle has suffered a great loss so we may gain. Do not diminish that."

Ivaia nodded in solemn agreement, realizing her error.

"Magic," Herrona continued, "Is a great force that runs in our bloodline. The gift of such power requires we lose something too: Our pride, our comfort. Not everyone looks upon Mages with high regard in this world. Our people do, but most others do not."

Ivaia nodded again.

"As women with power, we must lead and take blame, act, and lose. Myself as the Queen, and you, my little Mage. Never forget, our power does not come from victory or strength, skill or reputation. Power comes from the ability to see what is right and do it, even if it costs us. It is a weakness to chase accomplishments only for self-glorification. It is a failure to be selfish, not to see what our words and actions do to others."

She rose from her desk and walked to a shelf beside the window. Scanning for the book she wanted, she added, "I see it in you, Iv. The drive." Ivaia waited. "I see your passion to serve the Gods, your heart for religion and tradition. Your enthusiasm and willpower to make a difference."

Herrona was smiling, Ivaia could tell by her voice, as she bent to pluck a book from the bottom shelf.

"It is in our blood, to feel as you do. It's who we are." She presented the book to Ivaia with a broken smile. "Mother's diary."

Ivaia's eyes widened in disbelief. "How—"

"Father gave it to me when you were born. In it are her prayers and wishes. She, too, loved the Gods. She prayed that at least one of us would do great things with our gifts and ambitions."

Ivaia caressed the worn leather journal.

"I'm sure it would please her to know that not one, but all three of her daughters are powerful and righteous." Herrona turned her skirts back toward the desk, seated herself, and dipped her quill in the ink. "Keep to it, Ivaia."

On their daily walk, Ivaia confided in her knight, Riordan. "The God of Magic, Elymas, has gifted me with great power. My father used to tell me about my prophecy from the Oracle. Over and over he told me because I asked him to, over and over." She chuckled.

Riordan smirked.

"Power begins and ends inside her but continues on through her."

Riordan pondered her words but did not interrupt her.

She stretched out her arms. "What else could that mean? I believe the Gods will choose me one day, as a vessel through which their might and power will be demonstrated. My sister says power comes from helping others, and that's what I want to do. I don't want to have power and do nothing. I want to use it. For good, for the will of the Gods, for our people."

She looked up at the skies.

Riordan loved her passion. "If you feel so moved, who is to deny it will be that way," was his only response.

"I must try my best to prove myself. Will you help me, Rio?"

He walked towards her, one foot in front of the other, hands in his trouser pockets. A long sword slung over his shoulder. He dropped it to the floor and stepped closer again. She felt a flutter in her belly as his eyes locked on hers. One step closer and they were toe-to-toe. He brushed a wild curl behind her ears and smiled.

"You want my help?" He scrunched up his face, and she giggled. "You want to change the world, Iv. Do you know you already have?" He touched his nose to hers and closed his eyes. "My world was forever changed the day the Queen gave me you."

Ivaia lifted her eyebrow. "I believe she gave *you* to *me*."

He smiled and bit his lip. She tilted her head to kiss him, but he stopped her, their mouths nearly touching.

"I will follow you to the end of the earth and beyond," he promised. Their smiles faded, eyes searching each other's faces.

She grabbed him by the shirt and stepped on his toes. She wrapped her arms around his neck, kissing his mouth hungrily. He held her against him with one arm on her bottom and knotted his other hand in her hair. He pressed his tongue into her mouth and explored the taste of her.

"I've been dying to do that," he whispered when he pulled back.

"You have?"

"I want to do so much more," he said and smiled. "Do you want me?"

"More than anything," she said. The truth of her words surprised them both.

A gasp escaped her as he guided her to the ground. Kneeling over her, he removed his tunic. He opened her long legs, which trembled at his touch, and bent down to kiss her belly through her mesh gown. His blue eyes flashed up at her and he watched her as he lifted her dress and pressed kisses onto her inner thighs. She twirled her fingers in his long blond hair and writhed to sate the urge burning between her legs.

His fingers held her legs, controlled her movements as he lowered his mouth onto her. She whimpered as his tongue swirled over the sensitive peak between her legs. Every attentive kiss sent shivers through her body. He stroked her until she screamed, and his name echoed off the trees.

Climbing back up her body to face her, he thrust himself inside of her and gripped her throat. Her body arched in response, curls flattening in the grass. He filled her body with his promise until she was overflowing with pleasure.

That night, he brought her under his cloak to the ink artist in the kingdom village. An old woman with weathered hands that were still steady. She illustrated their devotion to each other on their skin. Pressing ink into their bones with a sharp tool: One on each of their left palms.

"You are my Queen, and I am your King. We are allegiant to no one else but each other."

They pressed their palms together and swore an oath to each other. Blood seals. He bandaged her freshly inked hand and kissed her fingertips.

When she returned to her living quarters, and he returned to his, she vowed to herself to learn as much magic as she could to protect her love. She prayed.

"What magic is this? And which God might I thank for this new gift? Elymas, is this a spell? Mrithyn, know that if you take him, you are to take me as well. Adreana, do you see my secret love and weep? He is beautiful. And who might I pray to for protection of my mate? Imogen, make a pact with me, to let only peace and safety follow him."

She waited in silence for a feeling of comfort, but none came because she was in love and it made her feel a vulnerability for which there is no comfort.

7: Clan Ro'Hale

Keres

The gates creak as they open; an argument between metal and wood. As I reenter the campgrounds, I glance up at the walls and the guards looming twenty feet above my head. Their attention stays on the forest. The white stallion insignia decorating their breastplates stands as proudly as they do.

Afternoon sunlight floods the campgrounds, running its golden fingers along the treetops. The sounds of a hammer falling on an anvil and children's laughter greet me.

Silence quenches the conversation between the two guards behind the gates. One with brown hair, one with black. Their dark eyes follow me, tracing my body. Either they're noticing my weapons and gauzy dress, an odd combination, or the generous curves of my body. I pass them and push farther into the center of the camp.

The fragrance of bread and smoked fish fills my head. I don't eat any animal of the earth. Do not take a life if it is not necessary. Still, my mouth waters with hunger. Near the armory, female shovels stew into her husband's and children's bowls. The youngest groans as his mother's cooking slops into the wooden bowl in his tiny hands. The father quickly defends his wife, scolding the child who sniffles and agrees to eat all the carrots.

Another female is coming in from harvesting, her basket laden with ears of corn and potatoes. It's so heavy she bears it between her arms, leaning it on her belly like she's with child. She trips over her skirt and a potato rolls over the brim of the basket. A nearby hunter in brown leather armor stoops quickly and picks it up for her, dusting it off on his breastplate before placing it back in her basket. He smiles and she blushes. She nods and sidesteps him, but he holds out a hand to stop her, offers to take her basket and walk her home. Nervously, she passes it into his brawny arms and busies herself with twirling a lock of her long black hair around her finger. They pass, nearly hitting me with the basket as they stare at each other with moon-sized eyes. I overhear him complimenting the fragrance of her hair.

Long black hair. Smells like jasmine.

I force myself to ignore the empty beds that decorate Chamira's yard. *Buried.*

"Delicious blood stains the forest ground now," the Death Spirit preens.

No one knows *exactly* what I did last night. No one except my sister knows of my hunts with Ivaia.

I watch my kin bustling about camp as I near my tent. I try to remind myself that this hunt was for them, but it feels like a lie. If I pray there will be no repercussions, will the Gods prove useless again?

"We should tip the scales. Balance makes no sense. If we just let loose and slaughter the Dalis, we'd nip our problems in the ass," the Death Spirit insists.

"No," I say aloud and drop my weapons on the ground.

Ivaia's dress tears as I rip it off my skin. Silk and linen undergarments don't make me feel more comfortable. My eyes are blurring, and my face feels hot. I want to swallow the air; it's so hard to breathe. There's that nagging pain in the back of my throat again from choking back the tears. I pass a shawl around my shoulders to fight off the chill in my blood.

I will not cry. I refuse to break down. Instead, I force happy memories of the nine into my mind. I force myself to smile. I will not grieve for them; they would not want me to cry. We were soldiers. They were not weak, so I won't be either. I sit on my bed, zoned out, for longer than I care to notice.

My fists eventually uncurl. My chest loosens and my stomach growls. I turn my feet toward the gardens in search of something to eat. I stretch my shawl overhead and drape it over my hair.

The winding path to the gardens has been overrun by mushrooms and crawling plants. I take my time; the lowering Sun a salve for my nerves. I eventually shove through the gates to the garden and scan the territory.

Of course, my sister is here: knees pressed into the soil; hands busy with weeds. Dirt streaks her sweaty face. Despite years in the Sun, her skin has maintained its opalescent sheen. Her blue shift is crumpled and stained. She loves that dress. It makes her already vivid features more profound. I try to sneak past her to the large harvest storage tent. She knows I'm here without looking in my direction.

"There you are." She grunts, tugging a large weed out of the soil. She holds it up like a trophy and turns her attention to me. Looking between the weed and me as if we're the same to her: A problem.

"You left again last night." Not a question.

"I had to." I swallow hard, watching her rise to her feet. She's a great deal taller than I am and lanky too.

In a couple of steps, she's at the small fire burning amid some logs in a pit. She throws the weeds into the fire, a small smirk covering her lips. Her mouth naturally turns up at the corners, so I never know if she means to look so snide. Again, those gray eyes shine in my direction.

"You're not fooling anyone, Keres."

I absorb the sight of her standing beside that fire. Her straight, silky red hair matches the thirsty flames in hue. If she were magic touched or a God's servant… she'd be terrifying. I'd never wish it on her, no matter how poorly we get along.

"Fooling anyone how?" I ask.

"Oh, come on, Keres. You're so arrogant. Walking around in your *red* shawl, back after a long night."

"You don't know what you're talking about." I wave her off.

"Chamira came to see me this morning," she says.

I don't flinch at her words like she might have expected me to.

"She says you refused to perform the rights for Kat and the other eight last night. You agreed to do it when the last of them died, but you went back on your promise. She also said you were in a foul mood."

"Foul mood?" I inch closer to her, uncurling my fists. "My best friend just died, and no one understands why I'm in a *foul mood*?"

Liriene lowers her gaze. "You speak as if you care but then you disappear on these reckless hunts. You say you're helping but nothing is changing."

I try to interject but she stops me by raising her voice, "You act so important because you're Mrithyn's child, but when your people need you to be who you are supposed to be, to fulfill your duty, you run away."

A hundred responses jump in my head but all of them sound like Ivaia so I stay quiet.

"You haven't got me fooled, Keres. I can see what's happening to you."

I cross my arms over my chest.

"Your soul…." her voice trails off.

I notice her hands are warped into fists also.

"Your soul is being corrupted by the power of Death, the power to kill. This power is doing more harm than good, as all power does. It's rotting your judgment."

"Stop," I say, "Don't you think I know I'm cursed?"

"But you're not fighting it." The color of her cheeks competes with the shade of her hair, and her eyes seem more silver. I think she's about to cry.

I choose my words carefully, "I am, Liri… I'm not trying to fool anyone."

I look between her and the fire. The smell of the burning weeds makes me cough.

"Which is why I'm being honest. I had to go. Ivaia was waiting. I was late. Chamira knows how to do the rites and honestly it hurt too much. Did *you* go to the burial ceremony?"

She smooths her locks behind her pointed ears, revealing the elegance of her neck and oval jawline. "No."

Her slim face looks gaunter as she purses her lips, distorting their natural rosebud shape. Her sharp cheekbones are more profound with the expression. She lifts her pointed nose and rounded chin. Eyebrows raised like rainbows above her glossy eyes.

"That's not the point. You say you *had* to go? Untrue. You wanted to. Painful or not, you did not want to do right by Kat."

"Of course, I did! She was my best friend!" I say. "Which is the exact reason I left, Liri. I killed a human in her name."

"Two wrongs do not make any of this right!" She says.

"He was a rapist. I heard him talking about—" I feel my skin flushing.

"Keres, stop. Your eyes are getting stormy. You know how much you frighten me when you get like this," she protests.

I force my words back down my throat. She picks at her fingernails, weighing her next words. I see them bubbling up but she's biting them back behind her lips. Her short temper wins and she throws her hands up.

"He was a rapist, the other was a thief. They were Human. All these reasons are excuses to live just like they do," she says.

"*Live* like they do? This is not living. We are barely surviving."

"And suddenly that's *your* problem?" She scoffs, redirecting her attention to her filthy hands. "You know what your duty is."

She treads on silent feet toward the running brook that cuts through the garden plot. She stoops to rinse her hands in the sparkling, running water. Her eyes lock on mine once more, the shimmer in them like that of sunlight on the water. I always thought that her eyes held the same gray swirling depth of river water. Fitting, since mother said her name means 'daughter of the River Liri.'

"Keres," she hisses, snapping me from my thoughts.

"What?" I spit back.

She closes her eyes as if the perfect words are on the underside of her eyelids. Her lips press into a thin line as her eyes spring open, darkness boiling within them. "No more."

I glare at her and plant my hands on my hips. She stands and mimics my pose. Fire and Ice, the two of us. I roll my eyes away from her stare and proceed toward the harvest tent. I don't hear her footsteps, but as I reach the entryway, she pulls me backward. Her hand tightens around my wrist. I grimace at her wet hands on my skin.

"No more." Something like a plea touches her wispy voice. It startles me.

I tear out of her grip and push into the tent. She follows. Of course.

Using my shawl to form a makeshift basket, I start picking various root vegetables and legumes out of harvest baskets. Mushrooms are my favorite. Liriene occupies herself with organizing some of the stock. No doubt contemplating her next words. Wanting to escape the tent before she can harass me further, I clutch my little bundle of veggies and quicken my steps. I cast one final glance in my sister's direction.

She doesn't reciprocate it, but she asks, "Did Katrielle say anything when she died? Anything…"

I suddenly remember. "Yes."

Liriene spins toward me, eyes glistening.

"She wanted me to tell you something, actually." I narrow my eyes. "But she died before she could say it."

Her eyes fall to the ground, her shoulders crumple. I await an explanation for her question.

"She was a good friend to you," is all she says.

I hug the bundle of food in my arms. "She was."

Liri turns back to her vegetables and I turn to leave. I collide with something hard.

Honey brown eyes, shaded by sandy blonde hair, meet mine. My meal probably squished after walking right into his muscled chest. His arms float at my sides as if he meant to catch me. I step back, mouth open to speak but no words forming.

"You," he says as if to apologize.

"It was my fault, I wasn't paying attention," I say.

A sudden smile. My eyes go to his mouth, my cheeks flushing. He presses a hand to the bundle of food between us.

"Allow me." He takes it without breaking eye contact.

I look back toward the tent to see Liriene standing there, observing us.

"Silas," she says. He moves only his eyes toward her.

"You're late." She quirks her eyebrow at him.

She is his Ivaia. Bossy and expectant.

I take my food back before he can protest. Tilting my head toward her, I order, "Go on."

His smile fades. "I'll see you."

He shoves his hands into his trouser pockets. His biceps tighten with the movement. We move in an awkward dance around each other and leave a conversation on the ground between us.

Their footsteps retreat into the tent as mine hurry back toward my own. Her laugh in the distance bounces off the trees. Birds squawk in reply.

They've been close since childhood. Liriene is twenty-two and he's only a little older. She could go from wanting to burn me at the stake, to forgetting I existed if he was around.

Breezing through the heavy beaded curtain, I hurry toward the small table in the near corner of the tent. Vegetables roll across the surface as I shake out my shawl.

Fire sparks with a snap of my fingers and leaps onto the small pyre laid out in a shallow ditch at the center of the room. Smoke billows up through the round hole in the roof of the tent. I drag a cauldron, still filled with the broth from last night's soup, toward the fire; and slam it onto the cooking rack. Brandishing a knife, I begin ripping the skin away from the potatoes.

Silas and Liriene have always been inseparable. It wasn't any different when we were children. There was a time before I was born when they were all each other had. When I was born, more children came to Ro'Hale. Thaniel came from Hishmal. Darius and Hayes came from Massara. They became fast friends with Liri and Silas.

Someone told them to, "Go pick berries," and they would scurry off, swinging their baskets at each other's heads. At seven years old, I still followed my mother's skirts down to the River Liri. The other children wandered haplessly into adventures and trouble I'd never know. I was meant for a different kind of trouble.

Some things changed when I became a soldier, but Silas and Liriene still ran in different circles than me. Katrielle was the common denominator in our friend groups.

Nowadays, Liriene has Silas working with her in the gardens by day.

He guards our walls at night. It's an unfortunate lapse in availability since we're getting married in two days. With the attack and loss of the nine, I haven't spared a thought for wedding gowns and ceremonies. How could I?

After I finish supper, I scrape all leftovers out of the pot with my fingers into a large wooden bowl. Father will be home soon, and it's best that supper be waiting for him.

For the first time in what seems like ages, I look at my bed across the room. Warm and inviting, seducing me. I realize how tired I am. I wash my hands in the basin and pad off toward the welcoming heap of pillows. Falling onto the furs and blankets with a heavy thump, I can't help but let out a groan of relief.

"Long day?"

I jump up, startled by my father's voice. He chuckles as he walks into the tent and right over to the bowl of leftovers. He points at it, eyebrows raised in my direction. I nod and watch him as he leans over the bowl on his elbows. Lazily, he drags the utensil I left beside it through the stew, looking for a mushroom. He takes a bite and closes his eyes, mumbling something in approval. He scoops the bowl up and sways a bit as he takes another bite. My father loves my cooking.

"You know, Keres," he says with a full mouth, pointing his utensil at me. "Your mother was very fond of long days. Days of work spent problem-solving and debating. She loved it." He laughs, almost choking. "But not because she loved to work. She thought a hard day of work made a bed feel better at the end of it." He laughs again, turning toward the chair lined with furs by the little fire.

"Did she love food as much as you do?" I smile.

"Mmhmm. Wild Salmon. That was her favorite. With tomatoes. I never understood it. She ate tomatoes… What was the other thing?" He waves his utensil in thought. "Ah, lemons. She ate tomatoes and lemons like they were apples. Boggled me."

I snort at him. I love lemons too.

A few moments go by, filled only by the sounds of him chewing and humming with satisfaction. I get up to fetch him a drink. As I pour what's left of our water from the pitcher, his humming gets louder. I steal a sip before passing him the glass.

"Keres." His pleasant demeanor cracks. "I'm aware the last of the nine passed away this morning just before dawn."

I wring my hands and nod.

He frowns and puts the empty bowl down between his feet. He swallows all the water and then continues analyzing me with pursed lips. "*Keres?*"

"Katrielle," I say, plopping down on the floor beside the fire pit. I poke at the burning wood with a metal rod and watch the sparks float up toward the darkening sky through the smoke hole. Moonlight is leaking into the room in silvery droplets. "She's gone."

"I'm sorry. We are all feeling this loss. As we do with them all."

I look at him, but his eyes are far away, fingers pressed together in front of his nose.

"Have you visited Lysandra or any of the other families?" He asks.

"No," I say. "I haven't been able to bring myself to. It's just—as the Coroner it's just so much responsibility."

He nods, closing his eyes as if to hear me better. "Must be especially taxing since we're talking about your friends, Ker Bear."

I thrust the rod into the fire, awakening more sparks. I look at him from the corner of my eyes.

"When I became clan leader, I confided in your mother." He stares up at the moon. A smile breaks over his face, but he pretends to cry, "Resa, I can't do this. They want me to perform the rituals, train the armies, feed the people, teach the youth, rally the old, and lead with a smile."

I snort at his theatrics.

"And you know what your mother said to me?"

I shake my head.

"She said, 'Kaius, it's your duty, honor, and privilege.' And that really struck me."

He smiles again, "And then she said, 'you aren't weak. You're so strong. And wise. And handsome.'"

I squint my eyes at him. "Did she really say that?"

He laughs again. "Well, maybe not all those nice things at once. Your mother was a woman of few words. She's where you get your broodiness from." He nudges me with his foot. I open my mouth to protest but he's got a point. Being a servant to the God of Death makes one broody.

"Daughter, I think... for someone of the lesser sex, with your education and skill level, you're doing fine. Maybe now you're just truly realizing the weight of a man's work like your mother did at that moment."

"What are you talking about?" I flinch.

"Duty, honor, privilege. A man knows these words in his bones."

"That a *female* reminded you of," I interrupt.

"Well, there's never really been female servants to the Gods. Mostly males all throughout history, especially never a female servant to Mrithyn. *His* is a particularly difficult responsibility to cope with. I'm just saying, I think you're doing fine. You're realizing your limits and that's okay—good, even. There's nothing else you can do anyway."

Ha! He doesn't know about my hunts with Ivaia.

"So, because I'm a female, there's not much more I can do? I'm supposed to just excuse myself from the *particularly difficult responsibilities?*" My own words hit me in the face.

"Why are you getting so upset?" He rubs a hand over his black hair, smoothing the wispy curls down.

I shake my head, let out a deep sigh, and lie, "I don't know what to think anymore."

My dad is an ass sometimes, but his diseased thoughts just helped me clarify my own.

Am I just going to excuse myself from the struggles of being what I am? To be mediocre, to be genteel and safe, to be static? Fuck no. But is there really much more I can do? If I delve deeper into this dark power, will it consume my soul like Liriene thinks it will?

He stands and walks over to his corner of the tent. He searches under his pillows and blankets until he finds his smoking pipe. A cloth pouch of herbs rests on the small table beside his bed. He stuffs his pipe with the heady-smelling herb and lights it in the firepit. He begins blowing O's over my head.

"There's a new Oracle in the kingdom," he says.

I raise my eyebrows. "Another child went blind for the Gods?" I scoff.

He opens his hands like *'what do you want me to say,'* and shrugs. "I do not question the Gods or Their methods."

I sigh. "How old is she?"

He inhales and puffs out two rings that cross over each other. I shift my position on the floor, awaiting his next words.

"Not sure. Young as they usually are, I'd assume." He fiddles with the mouthpiece of his pipe. "When Resa was born, your grandfather presented her and her sisters to the Oracle in the kingdom. I always wanted to make the trip to take you girls, but you know how busy I am."

I smile and recreate his moping expression, "So busy!"

He laughs, choking on a smoke cloud.

"Anyway, go see the Oracle sometime. On your own. She might be able to help you define your beliefs."

"You mean like a pilgrimage?" I ask.

He throws his hands up. "I guess, if you wish it. Your wedding is in two days. The Veil Ritual started in the kingdom today, so you have some time," He wiggles his eyebrows, earning a scowl from me.

"I will go after the wedding." I blow a smoke ring out of the air. I jump up to my feet, plant a kiss on his cheek, and grab a book from under my bed.

"Going to the war tent?" He asks sleepily.

"As usual," I say over my shoulder, as I replace my scarlet shawl around my shoulders. I kick a pebble across our threshold and follow it out into the twilight.

8: The Coroner

Reclining in a chair in my corner of the War Tent, I open a dusty book titled, "The Hands of Gods." A brief account of those who have served the Gods. It's shabby and incomplete, and I've read it a hundred times. It never tells me anything new, but it's oddly comforting. It should help ease my mind. I need to sleep.

It's easier to cope with anxiety when you've identified it, tucked it under the covers of a book, and can look at it when you want. This book has become a journal of sorts. I've annotated the margins with my thoughts about the Gods and their servants. I'm sure the author would be pissed, but that's how I learn from the books I read. By writing all over them.

My mother brought the book—among many others—from the Ro'Hale palace in the lockable trunk. She'd acquired the small, portable library before she married into the clans. I inherited its entirety since Liriene doesn't know how to read. I've offered to teach her, but she thinks it's inappropriate. Well, father has convinced her it is. Most females in the clan are illiterate, except me because I'm special or whatever.

Right Hand of Death.

My people call me the Coroner, servant to Mrithyn. A mortal who oversees the passage of souls. Mrithyn exists in all living things, His power of entropy is a force of nature. It was mortals who perverted this power, who began killing. Death can only claim a soul from a body that has failed it. He cannot kill. He is peaceful.

Mrithyn is called by the anguish of dying souls. When mortals are at war and blood flows in rivers, it awakens Him. According to the book I'm reading, the Coroner before me existed over a century ago. The Gods only call out servants when they deem it necessary. Mrithyn uses Coroners to stop the aberration of His power.

Ahriman, the God of Chaos and War, is the natural enemy to Mrithyn. He incites riots in the hearts of men, lures out their wrath, and is the origin of all dissatisfaction. Those who lust, who idle, will seek Him out and do His work. I can't understand how there could ever be a time for a servant of War to rise. If the purpose of divine servants is to better our world, what could an instrument of war do to benefit the world of Aureum? There is no servant named in the book, but a guess at such an Instrument's power is scrawled in a shaky hand. As if the author feared to even imagine it.

This book says there is only one Coroner at a time. As the mortal Instrument of Mrithyn, I have earned an appropriate level of reverence from my kin. I'm one of a kind. Still, fear stains their beliefs. They misunderstand me, my power.

As a mage, I'm already sanctified. As a servant, I'm akin to the divine. Some see me as a Goddess. An Oracle. Some believe I bring death. The last Coroner, whose name was Geraltain, was also feared by his people. I don't blame anyone who's terrified of a Coroner. We possess the Death Spirit... or it possesses us. Either way, we're far from righteous.

What the hell am I doing here? I stare at my hands, the pages of the book beneath them. Blood pulses through me. I'm alive. And I shouldn't be. I've been living on borrowed time since I was seven, and now I'm twenty. Nobody gets that it still freaks me out I'm even here. How could they? They don't know what truly happened to me. It's still boggling *me* to this day.

Either way, here I am. To fix the world. How am I supposed to do that with the power to kill? It's been my lifelong question. My conversation with my father got me thinking, and my well-loved yet insufficient book tempted me again. Maybe there's something in here I'm not seeing. But the more I read it, the more I see the abrupt ending, and the more I question.

"You are asking the wrong questions," the Death Spirit hisses in my head.

Cue the delightful little curse on my soul. A bloody pleasure. I bristle at the intrusive thought and shake my head.

I'll ask whatever the hell I want. Like, whose idea was it to force a God's nature on a mortal? Did they really expect this to work? The book says nothing of whether Geraltain was cursed as I am, but lists his many horrific deeds.

I wonder if my curse is bloodthirstiness because I'm the mortal hand of Death. Does the servant to the Goddess of Life get blessed or cursed? Blessed with boundless lust for life, ambition, eternal life satisfaction? Or maybe they're ridiculously fertile. I almost laugh at my own thoughts. Imagine, the servant to the Goddess of Life is cursed with an overpowering need to procreate. What would their power even be? The half-blank book can't tell me.

An hour into the book, a hand slams down a piece of paper on the desk I'm using as a footrest.

I cast a lazy, "Hello, Indiro," over my pages. I know that temper anywhere.

"Coroner, you're aware the last of the nine died last night?" He asks through gritted teeth. I drop the heavy book on the desk and glance at his scrawl on the paper.

Katrielle

Hayes

Cassriel—

"Well aware." I lean onto my elbows and press my fingertips together in front of my nose. With an expectant wave of my hand, I meet his dark brown eyes. "And? Do you want to proceed with their burial ceremony, or will we postpone it until the end of the week? Surely, there will be another attack and more casualties. Easier to pile the bodies at this point than dig individual graves." I've run dry of emotional energy, but I know I didn't mean that. He knows it too.

Indiro places his hands on the desk, bringing his long nose toward me. His gray hair, loose on his shoulders, shadows his face.

"There was already another attack."

I jump to my feet, matching his intense stare. He growls as he pushes himself off the table. He stalks over to the map that dresses the largest table in the room.

Tiny, hand-painted figurines representing the clans and the Dalis soldiers dot the map. White horses are for us, the Ro'Hale Clan, red birds for the Massara Clan, green fish for the Hishmal Clan. Brown bears mark the Humans because they gather under the banner of the Grizzly King.

Black bears surround the white horses, but we're standing proud as ever. The red birds are dwindling. They're still holding the border with the Baore. The clan, Allanalon, the oldest clan out of the four remaining, is represented by two blue snakes. I've always wanted to go see the other clans, but I've never left my own. Except to hunt.

He swipes a trembling hand across the map, scattering all the little figurines of green fish. He turns back to me, shoulders rising and falling raggedly.

"Hishmal has fallen."

Indiro bends down and picks one up out of the dirt. He stares at it before squeezing it into his fist. His shoulders jerk. My brows shoot up in surprise. He rubs his hand over his eyes, but he can't stop the tears. He thuds into the nearest seat. I rub my hand in circles over his back until he stops, staring and lost in thought.

Did I predict this consequence of the Hunt? I told Ivaia there would be consequences if I'd gone alone. Did I cause this?

"There's a human encampment close to here. Elves must have attacked them, and they lost many soldiers in the dead of night. Shortly after sunrise, they marched their remaining forces on the clan. Hishmal never stood a chance. They burned it to the ground," he says.

My blood stands still in my veins. "Burned it to the ground?"

"Everything is dead, there's not a worm in the earth. My friends, my family. Ashes."

"And the Dalis? Have they retreated? Did they take the grounds?"

"Let's go after them!" The Death Spirit rumbles within me.

"No," I silence her and clench my fists. *"More will die."*

"Take it? There's nothing left but the gates. Elistria Kingdom soldiers put out the fires and drove the Dalis out, but they wouldn't have stayed. The earth is burned, there's nothing there." Indiro says. His red-streaked eyes searched mine.

"Queen Hero isn't going on the offensive," I say.

"She won't," he says.

"She might."

"When your mother left the kingdom to come dwell in the clans, she asked me if I wanted to stay behind. Live out my days at court. I never looked back. But maybe if I'd stayed... if I'd rejoined my brothers in arms, I'd have been close to the captain of the army. I would not have sat idly by while these dogs swarmed our land and killed innocents."

"You also would have missed out on the family you've found here."

He shakes his head and presses his fingers to his brow. "I feel like I failed a test."

I turn back toward my desk. Folding the list into my pocket, I pass him and head out of the tent. I desperately need air.

I was supposed to be the tenth. If I'd been there with the nine... if I'd been able to control myself last night, I wouldn't have woken the wrath of an entire military camp.

"It's fine," the Death Spirit muses in a bored tone. *"Now, what are we going to do about it? Crying doesn't help."*

Last night was as much about my desire for revenge as it was about the nine, I'll acknowledge it. I'm clutching a piece of crumpled paper with the names of my dead friends written on it. Still here while everyone in Hishmal is dead.

My Death Spirit, the tainted side of my soul, knows no boundaries and feels no regret. The side of me fighting for control hates myself. It's like I'm running in circles all the time, and Death is always right behind me. Nowhere to turn without seeing Mrithyn's fingerprints all over my life.

This is who He's made me into. I'm supposed to be the lone guardian raising a lamp to light the passage from our world to his. To walk the shoreline between the world of life and the waters of death, to ford the river time and time again. To lay the fallen to rest, to comfort those left behind. This is who I became when Death knocked, and I opened the door.

His fingers brushed my long black hair behind my ear, turning each strand white as the full moon. His hands wandered along my arms, strengthening my muscles, lengthening my bones. He set fires in my veins. His hands covered my mouth, my eyes, my ears, changing all my senses to those of a predator.

He placed a seed of darkness on my tongue; a mite of his power, and I swallowed it. I wiped a streak of blood from my mouth with the back of my hand. It took root in my soul, turning it blue and dark as the midnight sky, sparking stars into existence within me. Blue like fire, deep like eternal slumber. And when I awoke, I was something from a nightmare. He filled my mind with solemnity; I could not grieve my loss.

"*Mrithyn made no errors,*" the Death Spirit purrs.

A cold breeze chases after me as I turn a corner and come to face Katrielle's tent. Her mother must be inside. Lanterns are lit. I spin on my heel, trying my best not to notice the darkened horizon, where black smoke still stains the sky.

I cannot sit and cry with Indiro, and I can't keep running. I will fulfill my obligation to the nine by performing the rites and comforting those they left behind. Lucius is the name that screams at me from the paper first, so his family's dwelling is the first place I'll go.

Perhaps Ivaia was wrong. Maybe I've been running away from what's right this entire time and straight into the arms of my worst influencer.

Nobody is glad to see me and no one truly accepts my condolences. As expected, I don't feel any better. After visiting the eighth house, I lift my red shawl over my hair and head back toward Katrielle's house. The steps up into her old home stretch before me, the darkness of the night threatens to swallow me whole. I glance up at the moon.

"Adreana," I whisper.

I wait for a silent moment, for a wave of comfort to overwhelm me, but none does. Because I am Death's right hand and there is no comfort for that.

Her mother is crying. I hear her meek sobs through the window.

"Lysandra," I call out.

The crying stops and footsteps shuffle. I straighten my back, preparing myself to see the pain in her eyes, the anger. I half expect her to turn me away, to curse me.

The gray-haired woman, much smaller and stouter than me, folds back the entryway curtain. She knows my red shawl.

"Oh!" She bursts into tears and launches toward me.

Her thick arms wrap around my neck and her wet cheek presses into my own. I struggle to keep my balance or my composure as she weeps on my shoulder, trying to manage words.

I shush her gently and stroke her matted grey hair. We sway in the doorway, and my throat tightens as I try to offer some words of consolation.

She holds me back from her face to stare into my eyes. A faint, sad smile trembles on the corners of her mouth. "Keres, come inside."

Lysandra pours me a steaming cup of tea with shaking hands. I offer to take the pot from her and pour her a cupful.

"I spoke to Hayes's brother this morning. He isn't doing well. Left early, traveled to Massara to be with his mother," she says.

I wrap both my hands around the cup's warmth and think about Darius. I didn't know Hayes well, but I know the fear of losing a sibling to this war. That alone is hard to live with. I can't imagine actually going through it.

"I can't imagine any of us are doing well. I myself..."

She wipes her eyes and pats my shoulder before taking a seat across the table from me.

"I don't know if I should go forward with my wedding," I say.

She makes a clicking sound with her tongue and shakes her head.

"It feels wrong. It's inappropriate to be marrying and celebrating when we lost them."

It feels wrong to be breathing while they're not.

She waves her free hand while she lifts her cup to test the temperature of the tea. She braves a small sip and then another.

"We need something to look forward to in times like this," she says.

I shrug, leaning back in my chair. My eyes wander over to Katrielle's side of the hut. Lysandra has stripped the bed and folded the blankets into a neat pile at the head of it. Her collection of books is still strewn beneath the bed.

"You can take what you like," Lysandra whispers.

I look at her, incredulous, but she goes on.

"Kat would have wanted you to have those books. Gods know how many hours you spent wound up in blankets like caterpillars in cocoons. Always reading into the wee hours. Adreana must have a special love for you dears after all the time you spent awake at the wrong hour. Snoring through the day." She laughs, catching her face in her hands and the laugh turns into a sob. Water lines my eyes.

I push my chair out, and it scrapes along the wooden floorboards of the hut. I sit on the floor before her bed and reach into the collection of storybooks. Taking one out, I leaf to the page I know is stained with berry juice. We would eat and read. Eat and read. Dirty fingers pawing through the delicate pages before stuffing our faces once more.

I snicker at Katrielle's hand-written note on the cover of a book, "The Pantheon of Aureum." She wrote the note when we were children. *"Oran and Adreana are jealous of me and Keres."*

I sift through the books we spent the most time with, making a short stack of the ones I would like to keep. Lysandra brings me a string to keep them neatly together.

"Oh!" Her hands flurry as she remembers something. I load my parcel of books onto the table and swallow the last bit of tea in my glass. Lysandra's movements in the darkened back room of the hut intrigue me. She emerges holding something. She pulls open the drawstring pouch and slides a string of beads into her plump hands.

"See, Kat told me this was to be your wedding gift." She holds it up by the end of the string.

"The white bead is Mrithyn." Her voice shakes. "Orange for Elymas. Oran, yellow, and Adreanna, dark blue. Gold is Katrielle and Red is you," Tears stream down her face. "The clear glass one is, let me think." She pinches her eyes shut.

I know she's remembering Katrielle's voice the night she detailed each bead to her mother. I can picture her excitement over her beautiful present for me.

"The glass one is the future, the stone is the past. She got that from the river." She smiles at me, tears slipping down her cheeks with the effort. "And this amber-colored one, look at it, darling."

I take the beads in my hand to examine the amber bead. "It's an ant."

I gape at the fossilized bug in the amber and turn it over between my fingers. "The ant is the present time," I say.

She wipes her nose on her sleeve and nods. She holds up a finger, "That's it. Those were her words."

I dangle the beads in front of my nose, staring at the little ant frozen in time.

"Be strong, she always told me," I say and slip the beads back into the pouch. "Wherever you are, whatever you do, be like an ant. Be strong, no matter whether anyone notices. Mountains move, one pebble at a time," I recall.

"That sounds like her," Lysandra smiles. "Thank you for coming, Keres."

"Before I go," I look at her toes. "Katrielle's last words...."

I need to make eye contact for this.

"Go on, dear, I'm okay," Lysandra lies.

"Her last words were for my sister, Liriene. She died before she could finish telling me what she needed to say. Did she leave anything for my sister?"

Lysandra sniffles and dabs at her eyes again. "No. I don't believe so. They'd gotten into a fight the day before Katrielle left with the patrol group. I saw them arguing but I don't know what it was about."

"Oh," I say, not knowing what to make of it.

"Katrielle was out of sorts that night. She wouldn't eat her dinner; she was very upset. She even said was reconsidering the wedding."

"What?" I ask. *She didn't come to find me to confide in me.*

"She didn't tell me why. I figured it was premarital nerves. She must have been so stressed. After the argument, preparing for the patrol, and with the wedding a couple of days away. I told her to take the next day to think while she was out walking in the woods. But then...."

"I see," I nod. "Well, she's safe now." I try a reassuring smile like I've seen Riordan do.

"Yes, that she is. At peace." Lysandra fakes a smile too.

Katrielle's belongings in tow, I kiss Lysandra's cheek and head home. As I turn the corner of the hut to take a shortcut behind the tents, I'm met by three brilliant sets of eyes in the dark.

"Shit!" I jump, swinging my load of books at the nearest body.

"Sorry, Keres, we didn't mean to scare you," Thaniel says.

I look him over, noting he isn't wearing his guard leathers like Silas and Indiro are. A casual tunic and linen pants. Brown hair in disarray and a sleepy look in his eyes. Did they wake him up for this? Whatever this is.

Silas steps up, golden-brown eyes smiling in the dark. Indiro is beside him, eyes still red from crying earlier.

"This can't be good." I huff at them, passing the heavy books into Silas' strong arms. He offers to take the pouch too, but I shake my head and fasten it to my belt.

"Keres," Indiro says in hushed tones.

I lean closer, looking around for anyone else who might overhear us.

"Last night..." He stares at me.

"You knew," I breathe.

"It wasn't your fault." Indiro shakes his head. "You were getting justice for our own, and you handed their asses to them. They blamed Hishmal and attacked because they were looking for you. We know it, you know it, but we all know it's their nature that burned Hishmal into the earth. You didn't tell them to do it." His voice is shaky, I've never heard it this way before.

"That's bullshit, Indiro. My actions got an entire clan killed. And now—"

"Now, we want to go with you. We want to hunt," Silas says. "We can't go out against them without you. This is war, Keres. Nilo was my cousin. No matter how much it hurts, we have to expect and accept that any of our actions may cost lives."

"It's a war nobody else seems to be fighting. The four of us, it's not enough," I say.

"Technically, there's five of us," Thaniel pipes up.

"Who is the fifth?" I ask.

"Come to hear what we have to say, Ker." Silas' voice turns silk-soft.

I puff stray hair out of my eyes and nod my head toward the war tent.

"Too risky. Someone will hear us." Silas protests.

"Then where will we go?" I ask, wondering if we're quickly becoming rebels against our own leader, my father.

"Let's take a walk." He gives me a crooked smile.

He slings my books over his shoulder, pushing his free hand into his pocket, and saunters off into the forest. Indiro pushes Thaniel forward by the neck. I follow the three scoundrels into the dark.

9: The Fifth & The Tenth

Silas stokes a campfire to life. The flames devour everything in the pit, puffing up and boasting a brilliant red. Its fragrance fills my head, heavy in my lungs, and its warmth is an enticing relief from the cold air of this dark autumn night.

"Someone will see that," I warn.

Silas gives me a smirk and shrugs. "We're doing nothing wrong. Simple Elves huddled around a simple campfire. Scared of the wolves or of Man?"

"I fear no Man and I *am* a wolf." I rub my hands on my shift. "Gods be damned, it's freezing though."

"Well, I hope your blood's hot," Indiro says as he plops down and unfurls a map on the ground. Silas and Thaniel peer at it as I lean closer to examine his markings.

"We're here." He drags his index finger across the illustrated trees, scraping his too-long nails against the paper. "And the attack on the nine happened here. The attack before that happened here. And now... Hishmal." His finger lingers on the marker.

Thaniel says, "They're moving south."

"Yes," Indiro sighs. "Hishmal." He jabs his finger into the center of a large angry 'X' on the map. "Has fallen. We know the Elistrian army responded to their horns, but it was too late."

Silas and I exchange glances. He offers me a comforting smile, but I look away into the swirling fire, bringing my shawl around my chest.

"I spoke to your father." Indiro looks up at me. "And he has no intention of sending out more scouts."

Silas stands up, crossing his arms. Indiro watches him. I continue staring into the fire.

Thaniel asks, "So, are we supposed to be blind out there?"

Indiro rubs his scruffy chin. "It would seem our chief would prefer we don't go 'out there' at all."

"*Fuck the orders,*" the Death Spirit growls in my head.

"Not sending out scouts is foolish. If we can't see when and where they're coming from, how can we defend ourselves?" Silas spits on the ground.

"Kaius wants to wait for the kingdom's reinforcements," Indiro says half-heartedly.

The Death Spirit yawns. "*Fuck that, too.*"

"They haven't outright attacked any clans before this morning," Thaniel says.

"And now that Hishmal has fallen, who's to say they won't attack us or any others?" Silas replies

I try to memorize the patterns of the flames in the seconds they exist, whipping like flags in the wind. Then I glance from the fire to Indiro, to Silas. The map unfurled in the dirt, only visible because of these desperate flames.

"Oh, so we're just supposed to sit on our hands?" Silas asks.

"No," I say, eyes refocusing on the fire. My cheeks feel warm, my palms are sweating. In one breath, a seething pillar of brilliant red and blinding smoke, in the next, ash. We are like these flames, and the wind is like our Gods. Breathing life into us in one moment, snuffing us out in the next.

Three sets of eyes are on me. I look at the fire reflecting in their eyes. Leaning forward, I warm my cold hands and the beads of sweat evaporate.

"No, we will not."

"That's my girl," Indiro claps his hands. I smirk at him.

"What will we do?" Thaniel plants his hands on his hips.

I look at Thaniel. "There isn't much we *can* do though. You all know the consequences of hunting Men. But I refuse to sit on my hands. There has to be something we can do." I look to Silas. "You said there were five of us. Who else?"

I'm thinking… if we could get more support, perhaps, the clans could form their own coalition. Without the aid of the kingdoms.

Silas bends to poke the fire with a twig. "Darius. He's pissed about Hayes."

"Pissed is probably an understatement." I shake my head. "They murdered his brother. But Lysandra said he went to Massara to be with family."

"Aye, left this morning. But not to be with family, to get his armor." Indiro says. A shiver chatters my jaw.

"Darius is not enough. We need to rally the clans." I scoff.

"We don't have time for that," Silas says. "Darius just got back an hour ago. He's eating supper and will come to meet us here." He scans the trees. "Our numbers aside, I don't think it matters a great deal with the Coroner amongst us." Silas flashes a smile at me. "A dragon amid mortal men." He hisses through his teeth as he drums his fingers down my back.

My stomach flutters at his touch. "I may be the Coroner, but I am one person. Like I said, it's smarter to reach out to Massara and Allanalon while we can."

Indiro contemplates my suggestion, his jaw ticking as he stares into the fire. "Massara won't help us, they have ties to the Baore, but Allanalon might not either simply because how close they lay to the border. Prime targets."

"A coalition would solve that problem though. A militant force—" I say.

"Militant? We're not an army. No amount of preparation will enable us to battle with the Dalis. Ro'Hale and Allanalon would still not be enough." Thaniel adds, "We have more hunters of animals than slayers of Men among us. Women and children—"

"Alright, ye of little faith." Indiro holds up his hands. "It's an idea. This is the reason for this meeting. To discuss ideas. We might not *need* an army if we can come up with a good idea. Battles are often won by wits."

Silas nods. "Well, we can't make plans without Darius. He's one of our advantages. And wits aside, I still want to run a Man through with my sword."

"What's so special about Darius, is he a fierce warrior?" I ask.

"He's been by my side since childhood. I know his true strengths and weaknesses. Plus, he's a brute in battle. Besides you and Indiro, he's the only one out of us who's killed Dalis Men. Trust me, we need him."

My legs stretch out, toes toasting. Too many times, my eyes wander to Silas. I find him watching me, I catch him smiling. Struggling not to think of the horrific reasons we meet in the dark, I allow myself to smile back. I doubt it's an attractive smile without an ounce of heart in it.

I think of Ivaia's words, *"You tear souls from this world with a smile on your face."*

Self-image forever distorted, I turn away from Silas. He doesn't know what he's getting himself into with me and the homicidal guest my being houses. He'll never understand.

"If we hate him so much, we could just kill him." The Death Spirit's laugh echoes in my skull. *"We don't— I don't hate him."* I blink. *"I don't hate him. I hate the Dalis. The Dalis we can kill."*

"More than nine?" The beast asks.

I try another thought. *"Mrithyn chose me for a reason. Mrithyn has a plan."*

"He surely does," she simmers.

Indiro lights his smoking pipe. He and my father have a matching pair. I remember the pipes Katrielle and I had stashed in a sack, stuffed in the hole of a tree by the river. We'd smoke herbs until our heads spun and the only safe place for us was the ground. Clouds rolled over us, turning hours over in the sky. I look up at the clouds above, glimpsing them in patches as they pass over the thick branches. I wish I could go back to lingering beneath purple skies and story-telling clouds with my best friend. Or even further back than that to the day I—

A rustling in the shrubbery behind us lifts us all to our feet. I glance to my left, feeling Silas' arm brush against mine. He's armed. I'm not. I take a step behind him, and the bushes rattle as something large pushes through them.

He curses and we all lower our weapons.

"By the Gods, Darius, if that's your idea of meeting us for a secret meeting, you'll get us all killed." Silas sheaths his knife, his jaw tightening as he stares at the gigantic soldier who's emerged from the shadows.

"Darius," I nod and give a wave, curious to meet the one Silas has spoken so highly of.

His face drains of color. "What's *she* doing here?"

I furrow my brows. "I beg your pardon."

His footsteps crunch leaves and snap twigs as he stalks towards me. "I cannot pardon you for what you did."

THESUNDERLANDS

Silas is between us faster than I have time to react, his knife at Darius' throat. "Speak that way to her again and I'll rip your tongue out from beneath your chin."

"Guys," I put a hand on either of them. "Closest companion one moment, an enemy the next?" I ask Silas.

Indiro interrupts, "Sit down, Darius. You're misinformed."

Darius pushes Silas out of his way, glaring at me as he settles in a spot next to Indiro.

"Misinformed? Or is she lying?" His massive muscles coil like pythons under his too-tight tunic. His chest heaves in a deep breath as he calms himself. His brown curly hair is tied atop his giant head. Eyes like coal burn into me.

Darius isn't just a mountain of solid muscle and raw physical power, he's a volcano. His temper rivals mine. But I understand why he's angry.

"Darius," I speak up.

His eyes flare. Silas flips his blade and catches it by the hilt. He goes on twirling it as he sits down, eyes like daggers aimed at his friend.

"I wasn't there," I say.

Darius jumps to his feet. "Like hell you weren't!"

Indiro's hand flies to Darius' forearm, the size difference unsettling. "The lot of you boys have learned better under my wing than to speak without thinking. Listen to the girl."

"Where were you? You were to lead that group of scouts. I saw the orders. I saw your name on that list," Darius says.

Silas spits into the fire again. The flames protest, finding new paths into the smoke-filled air. Indiro mumbles something about boys and men under his breath. Darius cracks his knuckles and awaits my explanation. I watch his massive hands kneading out the tension between his bones.

"I wasn't there," I repeat.

Our eyes search each other for a glimmer of weakness. Neither of us finds it.

"We could take him," preens my Death Spirit.

"I was at my mother's grave," I say.

His brows raise in realization, his muscles uncoil, and he sits again. "The full moon."

Everyone knows I visit my mother's grave under the full moon. Not because they care but because they watch me. Fearfully.

Readjusting my shawl, I stab the burning logs with the stick Silas dropped. Darius' eyes lower but I keep mine fixed on him. Deepening lines slither across his face, cracking his tan skin. He snaps his attention back to me, eyes smoldering like the campfire.

His heart is pounding against his ribs and the monster within me knocks on mine in response. The blacks of his eyes dilate. I can hear the hairs rising on his skin. Muscles tensing, his knuckles popping. Teeth grinding. I sense it all and I understand it better than a spoken word. If there's one thing Death has taught me, it's that bodies don't lie, and his truth is atavistic: Fire. His body is relaying one promise. *"If you touch me, I'll burn you."*

"My brother. Hayes didn't deserve to die," Darius growls.

"None of them did, lad. It's good you're angry because now we will do something." Indiro frowns.

Darius glares at me once more. "Kaius isn't allowing the scouts out. He said—"

I thrust the stick into the fire, "Fuck what my father says. That's why I'm here, you ass. Don't you get it? We're going after them."

Indiro and Silas smirk at each other. "Aye, Lass."

Darius clears his throat, "Alright, Princess. Well, you must know…" He looks at each of us, "We heard you deserted. That you led the group out and when they came back you were nowhere to be found."

My jaw drops. "Who said that?"

"Lucius's father said he was in the war tent when they wrote the orders. He also saw your name on that list. You were the tenth, Keres."

"I heard it too," Thaniel chimes in.

"Doesn't matter, my sweet." Silas pulls my attention off the others by taking hold of my cold hand. *My sweet.* I feel my face heating and not from the campfire.

"Mackeron? A lie." Indiro spits on the ground. "Mackeron is an honest, Hishmal-bred Elf. He's been my friend and second in command for twenty years, ever since I came to the clans. He knows of Resayla's full moon tradition. He should have expected where Keres would be. At her mother's grave." He stands. "Besides. I had her name removed. I went with her to honor her mother. We refuse to let the barbarians steal that right from us. And so, the nine went out instead of ten." Indiro clears the air.

Darius pockets his hands. "Fine, whatever you say, Indiro. Just tell me how I can help?"

"You can start by never calling me princess again," I say.

Silas chokes on his swig from a calf-skin canteen. Silas passes the canteen to Indiro who takes it and snorts, "Aye, Darius. Last poor sod who called her that ended up cold in the earth." Followed by a healthy gulp of whatever is in it.

Darius rolls his eyes, locking his full lips around the canteen when it's his turn.

Thaniel looks warily into the canteen when Darius passes it to him, and sniffs it. "What's in this?" With no one's answer, he tests a sip and coughs.

I grab the canteen from his hand and finish it.

"Damn, Ker!"

I quirk an eyebrow at Silas as I pass it back to him. "I know you've got more where that came from. Liriene is no secret keeper."

He reaches down into his rucksack, producing three more canteens.

We pass all three around, sampling the varying liquors. Conversation about the nine can't be ignored and Darius is the first to tell a story about his brother Hayes. I remember the story, it's a funny one. Katrielle told me about it. Silas and Darius reconnect, mourning the loss of their third companion, Darius' twin brother. Thaniel speaks fondly of Leander, and Indiro curses Cassriel for dying. We say each name aloud, all nine. In my mind's eye, the faces of the nine humans I killed appear and disappear with each name. Indiro redirects the conversation to the map and goes over the plan.

"And that's where you come in, Keres."

I cast a wary eye at the spot he's marked on the map, before taking another swig.

Head starting to spin, I lean forward on my knees and point to another spot on the map, "Who's that again?"

Indiro laughs at my slur, "Me, ass."

I nod and a shiver sneaks down my spine. Silas' warm hand runs from the point between my shoulders to my lower back and stops. I look into his honey eyes, and Gods know if it's the liquor, but I smile again, only worse this time. More like an idiot.

"Alright, it's time to move out," Indiro says.

"I second that," Thaniel stands and stretches.

Silas lifts me under my arm, "I'll escort the fearsome Coroner home. I know she doesn't want to wait for you saps to finish pissing in the dirt every other mile."

"Miles!" I burst out laughing.

His eyes widen and he loops his arm under mine as I stand on unsteady legs. "That's right, did you not notice how far out we came?"

I cover my mouth as if I can stop my giggles from falling out of it. "No."

I pinch my eyes shut, swinging my head, "No. I was thinking about Kat!" I drop my weight against his shoulder, as tears and laughter pour out of me in tandem.

Indiro casts him a look.

Silas nods. "Alright, Keres. Let's go home."

"I'll walk with you." Thaniel chases after us.

"Darius will stay with me," Indiro says to nobody but Darius.

The two of them walk on either side of me and I lilt between them. As if they're each holding either end of a necklace string and I am the bead, sliding from end to end. They speak to each other of armor and weapons. My smile stretches across my face from Silas to Thaniel.

"You're lucky we are men of honor, my dove." Silas chuckles as I stumble. "You're in quite a compromised state."

Even through the stupor, my predatory senses are picking up his body's signals.

"*You're* lucky. I might have kissed you." I laugh.

Thaniel's brows shoot up. Silas licks his lips.

"Both," I add. "I might have kissed you both."

"I don't share, Keres." Silas' eyes flicker with amusement.

"And I do not fancy you," Thaniel stutters.

Silas' amber eyes are brighter in the dark. His lips look delicious. I realize we've stopped walking, and the two of them poise to catch me.

I try to turn away from them, but their footsteps match mine. Silas is not letting me get away. His eyes rake over my body. My nipples are hard from the cold and I notice his gaze catching on my top.

The thrill of being watched like prey by these two soldiers forces me to stop swaying and bite my lip. My cheeks warm again and my mouth runs dry. This is a different kind of hunger. Silas is hungry too, I feel it in the energy he's throwing off. His vibe is running rampant all over my skin, tantalizing me. Since when do I blush like a little girl? Thaniel looks more concerned, but Silas looks…

"Fuck." I breathe.

"Mhmm," Silas steps closer to me.

The hours are getting heavier; the stars are falling—or I am.

The next thing I know I'm in someone's arms and my mind goes darker than the sky.

10: Hark! The Heralds of War

Standing in a field of flowers, staring at the ground. My eyes pierced through the earth, boring a hole down to the core of the world. From it came water and shadows. The shadows swam in the pool at my feet. I waded deeper into the liquid nightmares and the depths took hold of my ankles. I sank into the earth, swallowed up by this world into the belly of the next. In my stead, a river flooded the field, and the flowers died.

"Wake up, dammit!" A bucket of water empties on me.

I fall out of my bed, gasping for air.

"Oh, right. Sorry. Didn't think that one through."

"What the shit, Indiro!" I wipe water from my eyes and with it goes the memory of the drowning nightmare. There is no field of flowers. No underworld. Just Indiro towering above me.

A low laugh rumbles in his throat. "I tried; I really did. Ask your sister. Even stripped the blankets off you first. You seem dead when you sleep, and hellish when you wake, lass."

"That's because you nearly drowned me," I say.

"Someone drank too much last night," he says.

"What?" My sister's voice comes from somewhere to the left.

"Too much herbal tea, Liriene. That stuff will kill you," Indiro says.

I shake my head like a water-logged wolf. Indiro reaches his hand under my arm and swings me up. My nipples stand up against what's now a thin excuse for a sleeping gown. He looks to Liriene instead, approaching her where she sits at our small table. She watches him with wary eyes, her red hair glowing like a fiery halo around her sleep-swollen face. I turn as he places one hand on the table and one on the back of her chair, caging her in. I pick clean lacies and leathers out of my dressing basket.

Out of the corner of my eye, I monitor his hands. He twirls a loose strand of silky red hair around his finger and she looks up into his eyes. They carry a conversation not meant for me to hear. I press my lips together and focus on preparing for battle while he distracts her.

Armored, I opt for my short bow, tossing it over my shoulder. I sheath a dagger and a knife on either side of my hips and consider switching my bow out for something that doesn't require range.

A soft giggle flits through the air from behind me and it tempts me to look at them. I haven't heard Liriene laugh in a long time. I shake my head, deciding not to care and not to bring my other weapon even if it may be a close-ranged battle. My arrows won't fail as long as Mrithyn's power courses through me—which is always.

"Alright, you old war hound. Are you ready?" I call over my shoulder.

"Where are you two going?" Liriene asks.

"Officers meeting. Then an exercise. Be back for supper."

I hear footsteps turn toward me. Indiro's hand lands on the back of my neck and he pushes me out of the tent with a goodbye to my sister.

"Old, am I?" He growls at me and chuckles

"Twice her age," I sneer back.

He sighs. "Aye, well I'll be damned if I can't smile at a pretty lass with long red hair. But I've got a kindred love for you and your sister." He pats my back. "And I've a right to, you can't change it. Now, off with you. The boys are waiting by the river."

"What about you? Off to terrorize more maidens?"

He kicks the dirt at me. "I'll follow."

I bounce on my toes instead of walking away.

"Out with it then." He folds his arms across his chest.

"You knew." I look across the path at a female with three brats hanging from her skirts as she washes linens.

"I didn't want to ask last night with them there, but who told you?"

"Aye, I knew about your little escapades with the forest witch, if I glean your meaning."

Forest witch.

He reads my face. "Silas. He said he sees you on his watch."

I roll my eyes as if I'm not surprised.

"Mind yourself, I pressed him for the information."

I shoot him an incredulous glance and then continue watching everyone in earshot.

"I've got a duty to your mother, you know, to watch after Liri and you." His frown-lines deepen. I avoid his eyes.

He grabs me by my shoulder, pointing one finger at my nose. His long gray hair falls forward, shadowing his sharp jawline and dark eyes. "Mind yourself, lass."

I shrug him off and lift my hands. "Alright." I turn, "I'll see you out there."

He grunts and his footsteps kick up dirt in the opposite direction. I pick up the pace as I near the camp borders. I break into a run toward the river. The river's voice reaches me before I see it, and then the other voices. Deep, charismatic timbres. Cursing and arguing, and a voice like thunder. Darius.

I slow once they come into view. Thaniel is wearing armor this time, they all are, and heavily equipped. I tighten my grip on my bow, settling the lump in my stomach. I remember Indiro ruined my chances of getting my first meal.

"Did you eat?" Silas asks at my approach. Gods bless him. He passes me a piece of bread with smoked fish on it. I frown at the meat but decide it's better than nothing. I gobble it down as fast as I can. Darius watches my every bite. I ignore his hard-pressing gray eyes.

"We were just discussing your brilliant idea of an Elven coalition," Darius says.

I meet his gaze.

"And we decided we would not talk about it out in the woods where the wind can carry our voices and plans to the wrong ears," Thaniel says.

"We can talk more about it later," I say.

"We will have another meeting," Silas says.

"Yes." I nod at him. "Can we go over the plan again?" My head is fuzzy from all the drinking last night. I want a clear goal, a reign on my thoughts to control myself when the killing begins. I can't let my Death Spirit take over again.

"Indiro will meet us here," Silas rehashes the plan, making it sound like we're going for a stroll. "The patrol will come through here and we will have them surrounded."

"And then we'll do to them exactly what they did to my brother," Darius snarls.

"We need at least one alive, Darius," Silas says. "We need information on their strongholds. A coalition, if we can even muster one, will mean nothing if we don't know what we're up against."

"Keres." A brittle voice breaks my concentration on the map Silas holds.

"Yes, Thaniel?" I glance at him.

His gaze is steady, his shoulders relaxed. "You brought a dagger, right? We will need to be stealthy, but if they catch us it will be a close fight." His voice softens.

"Yes." I flash a smile as I whip it from the sheath on my belt, slicing through white beams of sunlight. The glint off the blade shows the contrasts of color in his hazel eyes.

"Good." He turns to Darius. "You going to behave yourself, or will we all have to mind you?"

The corners of my mouth flinch in surprise. He just reminded me of Indiro.

Darius' stare goes over Thaniel's head, landing on me. He looks me over, appraising my bow and blade. "I will if she does. You'll only use the weapons?"

You used only the bow. . . . A poisonous snake who bites and gives no venom.

"What?" The word stumbles off my tongue.

Silas' eyes dart from my mouth to my fists. I wring the tension out through the tips of my fingers.

"We all hear stories of the Coroner's power, but none of us have ever seen it." Darius shrugs and looks to his brothers-in-arms for confirmation. He lifts his hand toward me. "Mage, soldier, and Goddess of Death? Sounds like today will be very interesting." He awaits my retort.

"I am not equal to the God of Death."

"But you share His power. To kill." Something sinister surfaces in his smoke-filled eyes. "Is it true you're cursed?"

I study Darius for a couple of breaths, looking for something trustworthy. He radiates danger. Every hair on the back of my neck stands up when he licks his lips. Sunlight complements his glowing eyes but does little to calm my nerves as I look into them. His dark curls are a beautiful contrast to his searing stare. He looks like fire in the dark.

I stare a little too long and step closer.

"I am. Cursed to thirst. Blood is no small tribute to the God of Death and to me it is everything. Vengeance is my life's purpose. Blood sings to me, and the screams of my enemies light me up inside. That fire is all I feel in battle and the chill of Death Himself is the only thing that soothes me. So, don't take it lightly when I warn you not to test me, Darius of Massara. I am cursed, and you'd be wise to stay out of my way."

Looking at Darius brings a feeling I've never felt before. He doesn't take me seriously; he doesn't fear me. No one has ever looked at me like I'm harmless before—like I'm a joke. Not even my comrades looked at me like that. They knew I was a weapon. He looks at me like I'm an ordinary woman. A plaything. *Fool.*

Darius' mouth twitches. Dark humor fills his eyes. He opens his mouth to speak but bites his plump lower lip, stopping himself. The muscles in his square jaw feather, and he rolls his shoulders back to stand taller. He towers over me by a few feet, but I'll climb his body like a tree to wrangle that neck if I must. He does not understand who he's messing with.

"Enough."

The authority in that voice forces me to look at Silas, but his mouth is still. The command came from Thaniel. I turn to face Silas and Thaniel and see them again as I saw them last night in the dark, with moonlight scratching at their beautiful faces. Drunkenly, I said I wanted to kiss them both. Thaniel turned me down, but Silas turned me on. Thaniel looks at me now with the same sternness Indiro always has.

"Ker, you remember what you said last night?" Silas interrupts, reading my thoughts aloud.

I suddenly feel naked standing among these three soldiers. Their eyes follow my every move, assuming and appraising. They don't know me, but they yearn to understand this enigma of a girl with whom they will battle beside. Death's Right Hand or a flower with untouchable thorns?

Most people can't stand to look me in the eye, but since last night they've been watching my every move like they are watching a God. Darius paces behind me like a hungry wolf and Thaniel's cracking his knuckles as he tilts his head toward me. Silas lets his eyes wander over my armored body. They're as curious about me as I am about them. What will they do with me when they finally see the taint of my soul? Loathe me, fear me, or pity me?

"I remember." I force my best sly smile, refusing to feel embarrassed. "And nothing has changed."

In what feels like two steps, Silas has his arms around me. Instinctively, I place my hands against his armored chest, and the cold of the metal sends shivers up my arms. He pulls my head back by my hair and kisses me. My senses are cheated the warmth of his mouth and the wetness of his tongue as he pulls away as quickly as he touched me.

"I still don't share." He smirks "You will walk with me."

He takes my hand, pulling me to his side. Dazed and confused, I allow it. Thaniel and Darius clean up from our quick meal and then we begin our march south. Nobody's ever kissed me before. Did it even happen? It was so fast—anticlimactic too.

These males walk very fast. I fall behind a few steps, watching their long legs stride farther and faster than my own. I imagine each footstep taking root in the earth, and growing tall as the surrounding trees. Their bodies ripple with masculine power. The surrounding forest brushes across my peripheral vision like green and brown watercolors as I rush to keep up with them. I focus on the songbirds as every step we take toward this battle distorts their tune into a hymn of war. Their shrill incantations seem to follow us, carried on that cold familiar breeze. A shiver runs down my spine and I jog to catch up.

Darius turns a wary eye on me, and I on him. Footsteps that aren't our own distract me.

A signal from Silas breaks our rhythm and we all stop short.

A bird cawing in the branches above draws my eye. It's huge and black, and its feathers ruffle as it throws its head back and screeches. The sound catches in its throat as an arrow nestles into its chest, and we all watch the heap of dark feathers plummet to the ground.

Someone pushes me. A hard wall of muscle and armor goes up between me and all else as my body catapults toward the base of a tree. Darius wraps himself around me and we slide through dirt and leaves between the tree's roots. His knee bruises me but my elbow knocks his chest.

I catch a glimmer of the inferno in his eyes as I push my disheveled hair back. Dry, broken leaves tangle in my hair.

One by one the voices shout and echo. Our plan is obliterated. This isn't the patrol we planned to ambush. Not here. Is this what happened to the nine?

"Behind the trees!"

"Earth-fucking scum."

"Come out, Savages!" the Humans shout.

Darius and I lean around the corner of the tree. I ready my bow and arrow as his massive body covers the back of me protectively. His right leg comes against my right leg and he leans out further to see the Dalis men past the end of my arrow.

Dark thoughts blossom in the forefront of my mind like black roses. Surrounded by the sound of hearts beating, men drawing their swords, beads of sweat rolling down the skin of someone's neck. Breaking my trance, I look at Silas and Thaniel. They're ready to attack but look to me first.

As I focus back on the Humans, my inner Death Spirit whispers, *"Kill them."*

"Kill them all!" A Dalis Soldier echoes.

104

I knock my knee against Darius, signaling him to move out. As if my touch sent an electric shock into his body, he jolts up. Battle axe and shield raise as he roars at the three men. Thaniel and Silas scream and follow behind him. I stay at range, rethinking and redirecting my aim. The angst in the boys' voices reverberates off every stone and tree. Their furious words catch on every branch and leaf like a forest fire.

"For Hayes!" Darius roars again. His axe clangs against a Dalis Soldier's shield.

Thaniel flurries his twin short swords between two men armed with chains and maces.

I pick a target and shoot. My arrow rips through a soldier's shoulder, forcing him to drop his mace as Thaniel's blades lurch into his abdomen. Thaniel moves with roguish brevity toward the other soldier, slicing his inner thigh and then his abdomen.

Silas kneels, blocking the heavy swing of a great sword with his shield. In the seconds it takes the swordsman to regain control of the massive sword used with two hands, he regains his footing. His footwork is quick; he moves with conviction, twirling around the lumbering soldier and cuts him down from behind.

I quarrel with myself: *Move. No, watch.*

Before I can decide, the boys have already turned the tide of the fight. The blood is on their hands. I don't move, I watch.

"This is for Nilo!" Silas' voice cracks. My throat is tightening up again. I understand now the power in Riordan's words to Ivaia that night. I've been attempting to take justice into my own hands alone for too long. I wasn't the only one suffering. This is why Indiro has become so bitter towards my father for his passivity. We all deserve the chance to fight for what we love, to take back what we have lost in any way we can. What little chance we have at making a difference—we deserve it.

"One victim given the power..."

Ivaia's lessons turn from gold to gall.

"We are all victims of the Human terrorism."

Riordan stands up in my head and puts his hands on his hips.

"Who are you even doing this for anymore? Throwing grains of sand at a wave."

My heartbeat pounds in my ears, the blood rushes to my face.

"We need an army! Not an Elf standing in the shadows with a bow and bloodlust!"

Liriene looks at me like I'm a weed, a problem.

"Your soul is being corrupted...."

"This is what I was created for," the Death Spirit silences them all.

A different scream breaks through the air. I launch myself out of hiding toward Thaniel's voice. I drop my bow and draw my blades, charging toward his cry. I skid around the bend of a tree and find Thaniel on the floor with only one of the twin blades in his grip. His free hand clutches his side and he's covered in blood.

A soldier hovers over Thaniel, dragging his longsword through the dirt in a circle around him. The beast rattles my ribs, begging me to let it out and stop the Man.

"And who would have thought, I'd be the one to finally end you?" The Human sneers.

Thaniel stares down at his attacker.

"Hey!" I draw the Dalis soldier's attention.

His dark eyes shoot to me, confusion and surprise widening them. I bare my blades and charge toward him. His eyes bulge with shock, but I realize it's not the revelation of my inner monster that's taken him aback. I skid to a halt.

He stumbles and falls backward, as another Dalis soldier side-steps from behind him. His bloody dagger, loosely tethering his hand to the falling body of his comrade.

"Mathis." Thaniel gasps, attempting to crawl toward the Man who killed his attacker.

This so-called Mathis drops his blade and runs to Thaniel. He helps him to a sitting position in his lap, and Thaniel clings to him. Their bloodied hands check each other for injury and Mathis gasps at Thaniel's wound.

Confusion stifles my urge to kill him. Turning my aim toward Mathis, I yell, "Explain this!"

Thaniel holds up a hand to me, stretching his other arm between me and the Human. "Keres, don't."

Mathis stands to his feet, regaining his dagger. He pushes past Thaniel's grip and matches my fighting stance. Thaniel struggles to his feet, plunging a fist into what I now realize is a massive stab wound.

"Thaniel, stay out of the way," I command.

Instead, he stands beside Mathis. "Keres, he's not the enemy."

I spare a glance at Thaniel's desperate expression. *He's protecting this Human?*

"He's Dalis! Explain yourself," I hiss.

"Can you not see he's injured?" Mathis asks.

"Keres, Mat is...." He looks to Mathis, who nods. "I love him. Please, lower your weapon."

"He is Human! This is not right. Elves and Humans do not belong together. He's a threat—"

"No!" Thaniel flurries his dagger. "You need to trust me."

"Why should I? How do I know you're not conspiring with the enemy?" I ask. "How do you two even know each other?"

"We met on patrol," Mathis says. The Death Spirit and I growl at him, our voices intertwining.

"Mathis, go." Thaniel holds my gaze and shifts into a ready stance, to fight me and protect his lover.

"I can't let that happen, Thaniel. He was with them. How do we know he wasn't one of the Men who ambushed our nine? How do I know he didn't kill Katrielle?"

Mathis takes a step backward. "Thaniel, she's right. She has no reason to trust me."

"She should trust *me*," Thaniel answers.

My stomach turns and winds into knots, and my throat is running dry with every breath. I shift on my feet, "I trust no one." Unhinging the cage door and setting my beast free is easier than I expected.

Death takes the reigns. As quickly as I shift into the Other state, I lose complete control.

It happened so fast: The screams, the prayers, the bloodshed. Then a collision of talons, blood, and fangs. My inner monster came out to play, but there was another kind of beast nearby. Frenzied, my senses missed its presence. The creature came out of nowhere.

I'm on the ground when I finally regain my bearings. The blood is coming from me. I wrap my hand around the gaping wound on my shoulder. I try to shield myself from the massive beast that injured me. The wind from its wings blasts into me. It lands before me and its impact shakes both the trees and my bones. Its talons, decorated with my blood, sink into the earth.

I lurch backward, crawling as fast as I can from the creature before me. Wings like fire, eyes like gold. The beak of a bird and the body of a lion. The Gryphon's eyes don't move from mine.

I hear Mathis muttering prayers to Ahriman somewhere to the left.

"Don't hurt her," I hear Thaniel's voice. The weakness in his voice drags my eyes from the Gryphon's hypnotic gaze. His wound is killing him. Grief overwhelms me as I realize what I'd done.

"She's the Coroner," Thaniel speaks for me, despite how I've hurt him. Mathis's jaw drops, eyes dilating with fear.

The Gryphon paws the earth and says, "Mrithyn's hound."

He speaks and his voice shatters all thoughts. I'm lost in it.

"White Reaper." He snaps his jaws at me. "She's lost all respect for Life while serving Death. Even the life of your own kin?"

Heat blossoms in my face. My senses are overwhelmed by the sound of his auburn wings feathering out to their full breadth. His heart sounds like a drum in a cage of brass. His talons rip the earth apart beneath his paws. His mane is a halo around his face, bright like righteous fire.

"You would kill your very own for standing between Death and the Man he loves?" The Gryphon turns away from me as if he cannot bear to look at me. "Geraltain would have never been so corrupted by his power."

I jump to my feet, startled by the mention of the Coroner before me. I search the ground for my lost weapons.

"Don't bother," another lustrous voice crashes into my mind. I spin on my heels and am toe to talon with another Gryphon. Turning, I realize there are more. Five in total. The one before me sizes me up.

"So, it's true. Mrithyn's given another mite of his power to yet another Elf of the Sunderlands."

"Geraltain was from the Sunderlands?" I ask.

"From Massara." The Gryphon hisses.

Darius comes jogging into the clearing, running toward Thaniel. A Gryphon pounces from a tree branch and Darius skids in the dirt. "Shit! Fuck!"

One of my blades is by the Gryphon who attacked me; who stopped me from killing Thaniel.

"Altair," he calls his kin.

"Yes, King Arias?"

"Fly the injured one back to the Ro'Hale clan. I need to speak with the clan leader." He turns toward the one snarling at Darius.

"Kaltain."

"Yes, my Lord?"

"Let the Man go and escort the Elves and the Coroner back to their clan. Allow the Coroner to regain her weapons."

Well, there goes our one potential hostage for questioning.

"Where is Silas?" I ask Darius.

"Here," the familiar voice bounces off a tree. Silas steps out of cover, hands raised, as another Gryphon nudges him from behind.

"And what was the plan? To wait 'til the last minute to rescue your friends? As if you could take on all of us. Or to flee?" The Gryphon taunts him. It stalks around him, shaking his head. I furrow my brow at Silas who lowers his eyes to the ground.

"He was waiting for my signal, actually." Indiro's voice perks up somewhere behind the Gryphon, catching the beast by surprise. My eyes dart back to Silas, who dares another glance toward me, and the corner of his mouth picks up for only a second.

"Arias?" I question my attacker, watching Mathis exchange a glance with Thaniel before running off into the forest. I hope the wolves get him.

"Yes, Coroner." He doesn't deign to look at me.

"King Arias, of the Moldorn Gryphons. The Heralds?" I scan the territory and the beasts' faces before counting the heads of my comrades. Indiro nods at me. I turn back to Arias, King of the Gryphons, "If you're here in the Sunderlands that means—"

"Yes." He turns a cold, yellow eye on me. "War is at hand."

PART 2

QUEEN OF BONES

"When a shark smells blood…"
She takes a step toward me,
head rolling over her shoulders
and eyes closed as she takes in
a deep breath through her nose.
"They go absolutely mad."

—The Huntress

II: DUTY

As we enter the gates, we are welcomed by gasps and wide eyes. The sight of Thaniel's mangled body draped over the back of a Gryphon earns someone's scream for Vigilant Chamira. The five Heralds of War march in unity through the gathering crowds. Like prisoners to the gallows, Darius, Silas, Indiro and I follow them to the war tent. My father steps out, brows shooting up and mouth open but empty of words.

"Kaius," King Arias says. A baby's cry interrupts the silence of the audience, followed by his mother's desperate hushing.

"Welcome!" My father opens his arms, remembering to bow at the end of his smile. "Heralds of the Moldorn."

He catches sight of me and the others and confusion crosses his brow.

"A not so pleasant encounter," the one called Kaltain sneers. Altair echoes him.

"We saved your soldiers in the forest. They ambushed a Dalis patrol."

I spot Liriene's frown in the rows of faces; her red hair like a torch in the crowd.

"Were it not for your Coroner." Arias steps out of the way for my father to connect with me. "Your warriors might not have needed our help at all."

My father raises his hands once more, his brow lines creasing deeper. "I don't understand."

"Neither do I understand why Mrithyn's servant crossed blades with her own brother."

Chamira points Altair toward her tent, glaring at me as Thaniel whimpers from his place on the Gryphon's back. I hang my head as murmurs break the silence of my kin.

"We stopped her from killing that soldier."

"I wasn't trying to kill him, but to kill the Human he was protecting. He got in my way." I speak up.

"Such ill-discretion and lack of self-control is evidence of the chaos consuming these lands." Arias disregards me, but someone in the crowd accuses me of lying.

My father folds his hands behind his back, straightening his posture. "If you have come, King Arias, chaos has begotten war."

"As it always does. The Heralds of War have journeyed from the Moldorn to the Sunderlands." King Arias addresses the entire clan now. "News of attacks by the Baore's Dalis on your people has not fallen on deaf ears. We came to investigate the rumors of a Human militant presence growing here and have found it to be true."

The expressions vary throughout the crowd of faces. Some look to my father with hesitance, some to each other with relief. Bright eyes appraise the Gryphons with wariness and bore into me with disdain.

"We came to question your leaders." He turns back to my father. My father's expression solidifies. "Kaius, Shepherd of the Clan Ro'Hale. Queen Hero of the Ro'Hale Kingdom. King Gemlin of the Elistria Kingdom. Leto, Shepherd of Massara," Arias lists. "You can imagine our surprise when we found the Dalis had utterly destroyed Hishmal. This urged us to come hold all those accountable for the deaths of the

Sunderland's Children."

"Hold us accountable?" My father scoffs. "King Arias, I mean no disrespect, but King Gemlin and Queen Hero have made their stances very clear. We receive no military support from the kingdoms sworn to protect us. They do not equip us to defend ourselves from the Dalis."

"So, you do nothing?" Kaltain hisses. His voice reminds me of a snake's. "While the Children of the Forest burn to ashes. Their screams carried on the southern winds to our throne room in the skies. We answer a call and question, why? Was your very clan not the erection of an accord between the kingdom and the clans? You expect us to believe the kingdom has abandoned its own subjects that dwell here? Your daughters are royalty, your right hand and his ward are knights of the Queen's legion. What is the reason for the disconnect between the Queen and her own blood?"

"Whoever called you here might have informed you that Queen Herrona is dead and her daughter, Hero, sits on the throne." My father. "You'd do better to ask the new Queen why she estranges herself from those she swore to protect." My father says. "Who called you here?"

"That is not important."

My people find their voice, some cursing my father and some thanking the Gryphons.

"Enough," Indiro's voice rings out. "Our clan leader is not the only one to question for our fate, neither is our late Queen nor the child ruling in her stead. King Arias," Indiro steps forward to my father's side. "You come to question the victims. You should travel north and pay a visit to King Berlium, the father of this war."

At that, my people shout agreements.

"King Berlium will be dealt with, as will his armies," Arias silences them. "The Heralds do not take sides. We challenge the negligence and abuse of all leaders. As shepherds of the clans, it is your responsibility to advocate for your clan. The High Council and its Magisters are responsible for the Kings and Queens you are subject to. We are here only to investigate and warn." King Arias pauses before adding, "Hishmal is a blood blot on the map. Your soldiers are being killed every day. You live in terror and you cannot walk the lands you were born to rule. You are oppressed and succumbing to their power. None but your Coroner has taken any action."

I perk up at the mention of me. *How does he know about my hunts? Who called them here?*

"For years, this girl ventured into the dark and diseased forest hunting those who hunt you. While you slept, she claimed the lives of your oppressors. She claimed vengeance, and in silence, she carried out her duty to your dead." I feel all eyes trained on me, Liriene's well with tears. "Only one has stood against an army of darkness. Until today. These brave soldiers joined her in hunting the Dalis."

"You said she nearly got them killed! What of Thaniel?" A male shouts.

"You yourself, King Arias, bested our Coroner. You stayed Death's right hand?" Another asks.

"Tell us, does a God bleed?" A woman mocks.

"One against an army has not brought about change."

"Months of secrets."

"The attacks may very well be retaliation for her actions!"

"She is to blame for Hishmal's destruction!"

"If we hand her over to the Dalis, whose blood is on her hands, they will stop hunting the innocent!"

The voices mingle, I stop listening. Blood roars in my ears.

Arias' voice soothes them, "The spirit of one may be greater than an army. Although alone she would not win, every fire starts with a single spark."

My face heats, my palms sweat. I try to ignore the clashing remarks of condemnation and praise for me and Mrithyn. This King of the Gryphons, this Herald of War, drew blood from me. No one has ever done that before. He shamed me in battle, denounced me, and judged me. Now, he speaks for me. How does the same mouth mock me and call me blessed?

"If your child can do right by her people, even if it costs her everything, how can you do nothing?" Arias turns away from my father. I know his words have wounded his pride. Indiro's hand rests on my father's shoulder but his eyes settle on me.

An arm comes around my shoulders. I blink at the face of Darius. His coal eyes are on fire with pride. Redeeming me from the cruel accusations my people still toss at my feet. I should have never expected to look down and see roses, anyway. Silas, behind him, peeks his head around to flash a smile in my direction. King Arias heads back towards the gates, followed by his soldiers.

"Coroner, a word," he beckons. I push past the crowds, turning my back to my sister and father. Willing to go anywhere to escape the disapproval my kin are aiming at me like flaming arrows. I am no hero, and I know it well. I follow the band of Gryphons back into the darkening forest. Realization rushes into me as I rub my arms, smearing the warm blood from my shoulder. My body must have been in shock. I've never been injured like this in a battle. I've caused so much death up. And now Thaniel...

"Keres, is it?" Arias asks

"Yes." I keep my eyes low.

Kaltain and Altair circle around me but the other Gryphons keep their distance.

"I see a fire in you; a light burns where others see only darkness."

Much to my dismay, my eyes blur again.

"We cannot honor your actions, as we are neutral in this war. But we can honor your intention."

"You've been led astray in this hunting ritual," Kaltain adds.

I raise my brows, "How did you know about the hunting?"

"I told them." A familiar voice says.

I whip my head around. "Rio!" I run into my uncle's arms. He catches and steadies me. I quickly check for Ivaia.

"She isn't here. She doesn't know what I've done."

I look up at his warm face, those diamond eyes. "Why? She will, Rio, she seems to figure everything out."

"I told you. The world doesn't rest on one set of shoulders. The hunts have cost us more than they have gained. You've known nothing but her teaching since childhood. Suffering through it. I couldn't stand it anymore. My wife is changing, she isn't herself. I fear for her. For the first time in over twenty years, I do not trust her." Riordan turns to King Arias.

"Your people tire of war. Hope is dwindling. The force of the Heralds isn't what this delicate situation needs. The new Queen has abandoned the clans, we know it, and she needs accountability. But there's no predicting what our confrontation will stir her or her subjects to do. And so, we have need of you."

"Me?"

Riordan rests his hand on my shoulder, "Yes."

"You are the Coroner."

"What can I do? I have no formal training, no political knowledge. I'm not prepared to take the throne at all. Ivaia would be more—"

"Ivaia has earned the position she's in. She serves no one and no God, only herself. Never again will she be welcomed in Ro'Hale," King Arias says.

"I am a warrior. A hound as you called me," I say. "What could I do?"

"We need you to go because you have every right to, and the power no one else has. A God goes with you," Riordan says.

"We need Queen Hero to stay on the throne but others oppose her. If they deposed her, King Berlium of the Baore will try to plant a usurper there, ready to replace her with his own puppet King," Arias adds. "King Berlium killed his own father, uncle, and brothers to take both the Baore's two thrones. He seeks to rule this Province too. Her reign is in question, and she is weak. He will strike."

"So, you want me to go to the kingdom? To do what, exactly?" I scan all the gold and silver eyes staring back at me.

"Spy."

I laugh. I curse. The weight of the word, the sting of it in my ears. The Death Spirit within me bristles with excitement.

"Spy on my cousin, my Queen? And report to who?" I ask.

"Our people lack the power they need to fight back in this war. We need information we can report to the High Council— evidence of the Queen's negligence or of the Baore's reaching influence." Riordan chimes in.

"So, why isn't the High Council already involved in the Baore?"

"They've tried to intervene but Berlium has grown too powerful. They want Queen Hero and King Gemlin to ally and act. Ro'Hale and Elistria have a duty and they aren't upholding it."

My body suddenly feels too small, my rib cage too tight. "Surely, we have allies who can—"

"Usually, the kingdoms gather information on the problems of the province and report it to the council or its agents," Arias explains.

"But the kingdoms are the problem," Rio clarifies.

"The Sunderlands clans are on their own," Kaltain adds.

"So, you want me to go spy on my cousin to make sure no one tries to dethrone her and get information." I take it all in.

"Observe. Gathering information is your sole mission. Your people need proper advocation, not more derision, not a rebellion. If you stand up beside Hero and make yourself known as her weapon or personal guard, you will attract the exact attention we're trying to avoid. We need to know what is wrong at court before we can fix its relationship with the clans." Arias's voice is a haunting, melodic shiver across the air.

"We also suspect the kingdom is under the influence of a higher power."

"There's a new Oracle," another voice interjects. We all startle at Indiro's ghost-like presence. I've always wondered how he moves, silent as a shadow. He holds his hands out at his sides.

"The child, Osira." He joins the circle, and the Gryphons make way for him.

"So we heard," Arias notes.

Indiro and Riordan exchange a curt acknowledgment of each other. They must know each other, both former Knights of the Ro'Hale Legion. It seems the blood between them isn't warm.

"If another Servant is at court, the Oracle would know," Indrio says.

"If there is, could this servant be the hand of Ahriman, The God of Chaos?" Riordan asks.

"It's very possible. Why else would Mrithyn also raise up his servant in the Sunderlands?" Altair adds.

"Our sources also speak of another servant to a God rising in the East," Arias says.

"A servant to which God?" I ask.

"No one knows." He seems to frown, in his weird Gryphon way.

"Well your sources sound unreliable," I say, earning a glare.

"Gods aside, we need to know what's changed in the hearts of the Queen's men," Indiro adds. "The armies can't be satisfied with sitting on their hands. Not while she executes innocent subjects in the search of her mother's murderer. I know those soldiers. They would rather fall on their swords than desert their duty to the kingdom and clans." He shoots a glare at Riordan.

My jaw drops. "Wait. Queen Herrona was murdered? Hero is executing innocent people!?"

"That's what Hero believes, and she's killing those who deny it. Trying to torture an answer out of her court. Nobody is stopping her. She may be as bad as King Berlium," Indiro says.

"Well, it sounds like the answer to our question is Hero. She's the problem, and it sounds like you know full well what's going on there." I look Indiro up and down. "No wonder the soldiers won't march for her. She's a bloody tyrant."

"Perhaps she has ordered a stand-down and they believe obeying their Queen is their most important duty. Most men would fear committing treason." Riordan lifts a brow.

"No. Not the men I knew. They would have never chosen the Crown over what was right for the Province. Not many of them, anyway. Something has changed in the ranks, I suspect. We need to know what's going on with her Captain."

"Anyway, no one can force you, Keres." Riordan regains my attention. "But now you know why it must be you. If we will send anyone into the mess that may very well be the handiwork of Ahriman, we need to send an Instrument of the Divine. You know I would go with you if I could, but I must stay with Ivaia." He looks to our war chief. "And I'm assuming Indiro has duties to attend to here with all the attacks."

"I must prepare for any retaliation for our actions today."

I take a moment to mull over their words. I can't determine a reason not to go. Except for my impending wedding. I can tell my father I wish to go on my pilgrimage to court to see the oracle. He suggested I go. It's a chance to escape the hatred my kin are feeling toward me for what I did to Thaniel. A chance to do something other than what they have trained me to do: Kill, serve the Gods, and please my family.

"I will go." The words run out of my mouth, smooth as water.

Indiro claps his hand on my back. "That's my girl."

"Can the Heralds offer any protection to my clan?" I ask King Arias. Humor flickers in his eyes. "Clan Ro'Hale has more than the Coroner. There are others who will rise in your absence."

"Who?" I look at Indiro.

"Trust your people, Keres," King Arias says before turning to Riordan. I look at Indiro again and he just smiles at me, crossing his arms over his chest.

My uncle and the Gryphon King exchange brief words before Heralds wish me luck and set off. Off to rebuke another Clan leader, I guess.

When Riordan is available again, I ask, "Has Ivaia told you what happened?"

"That you stood up for yourself? Yes." Riordan smiles. "You should come visit before you go. Make peace with each other."

I nod and kiss his cheek before I join arms with Indiro and head back to camp. Before we reach the gates, Indiro stops, taking hold of my chin.

"When I left you this morning, I went to the war tent to retrieve my shield. A letter arrived for me, from your uncle. He told me he had summoned the Gryphons, and that they were coming. To prepare your father. I made my way as fast as I could to reach you poor sods in the woods, but the Heralds were already there."

I nod. Thank the Gods, King Arias caught me off guard and saved Thaniel from me.

"When Arias called you after he made your father blush, I had to slip

123

away to pen this." He presses a letter into my hands.

"The moment you turned to walk with them, I knew what they would ask you."

"Am I allowed to read it?" I cock an eyebrow at him.

His drawn mouth explodes into a fit of laughter. "Agh, Keres. My little white-haired witch. Still asking for permission. Read it when you get to court."

I agree and we part at the gates.

Mentally preparing myself for the onslaught of Liriene's special type of disapproval, I shove the entryway curtain aside. She's sitting on my bed, looking through the books and trinkets Lysandra gave me.

"Those are my things," I say.

"War has come." Liriene turns her cold gray eyes on me.

I watch her play with the string of beads Katrielle made for my wedding gift.

"It would seem so," I say. "Picking which of my things you will inherit when I'm dead?"

"These were Katrielle's things and now she is dead."

I meet her cold, watery stare.

"Katrielle is dead," she repeats.

"Yes, Liri. Wishing it were me instead of her?"

She doesn't answer.

"She made that string of prayer beads for me." I don't know what else to say and begin stripping off my armor.

"Did she ever kiss you, Keres?"

I pause before pulling my jerkin off, not sure how to answer. "Liri—"

"I heard Thaniel's lover stood up to you in the forest. And you would have killed them both. Tell me, was Katrielle your lover?"

I don't know what possesses me, but I charge toward my sister and catch her by the hair. Her utter shock escapes her throat. I fling her lanky frame to the floor. "How dare you?"

She laughs, her hair matted across her face. She tucks a knot behind her ear and faces me. "Dear, Keres." Laughter interrupts her and my hands ball into fists. "I heard Thaniel's lover crossed you and feared—" She wipes a tear from her eye. "I feared you tried to kill them out of anger about their sex."

"I despise the Human for what he is, not for what he isn't. I'd have felt the same if Thaniel had taken a female Human lover."

"I figured as much, little one." She dusts her skirts off as she stands again. "I could not believe you would harm them both for being male. Knowing your love of Katrielle then led me to wonder if you'd been jealous. How Thaniel's lover, a Human, might live. And yours would be dead..."

"Kat was not my lover."

"I know." She smiles.

"Then why on earth would you ask me that? What's your problem, Liriene?"

"She was *my* lover." Liriene whispers, all signs of laughter fading from her face. The air hits my lungs like an arrow. She approaches me, one hand knotted in her skirt.

"I needed to know whether you hated Thaniel for his lover's sex or for his race. Because I loved Katrielle." She searches my eyes, "I could not bear to grieve her loss untruthfully. To hide my tears."

I remember Katrielle's last words. Lysandra said they had fought. That Kat wanted to postpone her wedding to Hayes.

"Asking me if she was my lover was your way of confessing she was yours?" I shake my head. "Makes no sense, Liri."

"How does one confess such a thing to another person... without first confessing it to oneself? Our love is what others consider unnatural. But what's unnatural about love?" She laughs again through her tears.

"Katrielle was marrying Hayes. If she had loved a female, if she had loved you, I would have known." I try to deny what's so obvious now. Katrielle had always been the common thread between me and my sister. She was my closest friend, fought alongside me. Died in my arms. But Hayes, Silas, Darius, Thaniel, Katrielle, and Liriene... they'd grown up together. They shared a different bond.

Liriene stares at me. The silence between us billows like smoke from a clash of fire and ice.

"What of Silas, then?" I flail my hands.

She looks confused, "What of him?"

"Oh, come on, Liri. Everyone knows how close you two are. You've spent more time with my future husband than I have."

"Silas and I are friends—"

"Katrielle and I were friends," I hiss. I jab my finger into her chest, "You cannot believe you loved her more than I did. Or that you have some sick claim on her, her stuff, because of... whatever you did with each other. She was my closest friend since childhood. She might have turned to you out of fear of her impending marriage. You might have seduced her—"

Liriene slaps my face. Hard.

My hand flies to my cheek instantly, noting the stinging flesh. But deep inside my head burns hotter. My veins fill with fire, my lungs fill with smoke. My skin turns a lurid blue as my wrath and magic collide within me. Liriene's triumphant smile shatters into a look of horror as I smolder in front of her.

"Your— Keres! Your eyes!"

My voice splits into multiple tones as I speak, "Come sister, try that again." I grab her and my touch sizzles her skin. My magic boils as my temper burns. She breaks out of my grip and gasps at the red handprints I've left on her pale skin. The smell of burnt flesh taints the air. She goes running from the tent. I follow her out, steam rising out of my pores, smoke lolling off my tongue. My hair whips around my face as the heat inside of me rises into the afternoon air. I spark screams of terror in my neighbors as I move fast as wildfire.

"Liriene!"

I whip around a corner and catch sight of her red hair. I spit sparks into the dirt as she turns to face me.

"Your eyes! They're black as jet." She stammers, tripping as she walks backward away from me. I reach for her again—

"Keres!" A familiar baritone runs up my spine. I whirl around and am stopped by the heavy hands of Darius.

12: TEMPTATION

My touch scorches his skin as he grabs my arms.

"Darius!" My voices collide, crashing back into one scream of frustration.

"Keres, stop this."

I can hear his flesh sizzling, but he locks his hand around my arm and pulls me away from the crowd still gathered from the audience with King Arias. I quickly check the crowd for my sister, Silas, or anyone else that would be as shocked as I am to see Darius put his hands on me. Most people still watching only look relieved I didn't fry Liriene.

Darius silently veers me off the campgrounds. Steam pours off my skin where we touch. Once we're among the trees and out of earshot, I jerk free of his hold and slug a fist at his face. He catches my fist with one hand and his other hand flies to my throat.

I claw at him, but my fiery touch seems to lose its effect on him. Pushing me back against a tree, he steps between my legs and brushes against the apex of my thighs with his knee. His smoke-filled eyes burst into flames, matching the fire within me.

"Listen, Killer." He licks his lips and tightens his grip on my throat, making me scratch at his hands. "You want to take it out on me, try. You want to play with fire?"

I gasp for air, tapping his arms as a sign of surrender. He loosens his hold on my neck but doesn't back away, keeping me pinned against the tree with his knee.

I catch my breath and use it to say, "Don't forget who I am!"

He leans his head back and laughs.

I shove him off me and stand up on my toes to get closer to his face. "Who do you think you are?"

He grabs me by my hair and pulls me in closer, fiery eyes darting between mine and my mouth. Struggling to keep my feet on the ground, I grab onto his armor.

"The beast has fangs." A snicker breaks through his lips. "Settle down, Killer, or I will burn you right back." My instincts tell me to believe him.

His use of the word 'killer' as a pet name angers me even more. Luckily, emotions incinerate his resolve first. He draws in a sharp breath. I can feel and hear his heart pumping as adrenaline courses through his veins with the same urgency and disparity as the magic rushing through mine. Beads of sweat crown his brow as he nears closer and closer to the fire within me. I feel the heat of his body against mine. There's fire in him as well, but it's primal, not magic. Unadulterated angst and masculine energy.

He pulls my head back by my hair and bites my neck, sending shivers of his own dominant power into me. One hand firmly grips my breast through my thin shift and the other writhes around my center. His touch dares me to submit, drawing my body to his own. I buck against the full weight of him, the fire beneath my skin still boiling and turning his hands red as my cheeks must be now.

"Easy, Killer."

"Stop calling me that," I say.

"Would you prefer princess?"

We glare at each other, his fist still knotted in my hair.

"Didn't you hate me yesterday?" I ask.

"Would you prefer I hate you?"

"You've never even looked twice at me before," I say.

"And now you're all I see."

"Why?" I ask.

He bites his lip and something wicked lights up his ember eyes. He shakes his head and leans into my neck again, nipping at my fluttering pulse, caressing my skin with his tongue where he bit me. I hope there's no mark. Silas...

"You don't hate me. You like me, but want to fight with me. Overpower me?" I stutter nervously. I've never been touched by a man before. His hand falls to my breast again, squeezing a small sound of protest out of me.

"Fight you. Fuck you. A little of both." His breath fans against my neck.

I feel heat blossoming on my face and pooling between my legs, and attempt to push him away again. I've never explored my sexuality with another person, only on my own. That doesn't mean I don't think like he does, that I don't want all the things I've fantasized about. All bodies know how to respond to touch and temptation.

Darius moves faster. Locking his massive hands around my tiny wrists and holding them at my sides.

"I haven't been able to stop thinking about how you challenged me last night. Then, I saw you going after Liriene. All that fury and glorious fucking power.... Makes my dick hard to think there's a girl who might be as savage as I am. I bet you know how to use those fangs. I like it when a woman bites. I bet you could handle everything I'd give you."

"What would you give me?" I lick my dry lips, trying to stare back at him with the same unwavering intensity he's giving me.

"Unbridled passion." He nips at one of my trapped wrists. "Pleasure that would show you what true fire feels like." His eyes glow hungrily when they lock with mine again.

"I don't think you can handle me, soldier." I laugh him off, trying not to reveal that my stomach is tumbling into my toes.

"Oh?" He scoops me up in his arms. His muscles snaking around me as he evens my weight out in his arms.

"Put me down."

"I could break you." He maneuvers my body in such a way that makes every inch of me still.

"Could break your back over my knee." He searches my face. "I don't know if I believe the things people whisper in the dark about you."

I steady my breathing, holding onto his arm.

"She's dangerous." He whispers against my ear and I recoil.

"Wicked."

The pounding of his heart matches mine.

"Fucked."

I flinch at the word. "Put me down," I say with less conviction.

He obliges, allowing me to my feet again.

"You don't scare me, Killer." He cracks his neck, looking my body up and down. His stare is hungrier than Silas' was. More feral.

"Walk with me." He starts off, leaving without a glance back at me to see if I follow.

I weigh my options: go back and face Liriene. Or....

At the bank of the River Liri, we stop. I try to keep my distance, but he pulls me back by my shift, tearing it a little.

"Where do you think you're going, killer? I'm not done playing with you yet."

"And what's your game?" I growl, snatching my shift out of his hands. "To take what belongs to another man?"

"Do you?" He clasps his hands behind his back and straightens up to his full height. "Do you belong to any man?"

"No."

Silas is a promise, not yet binding. I've always wanted him. I thought Liriene wanted him too. Now, I think I might want something else.

"And have I actually taken anything from you?"

"You... you bit me and ripped my shift!"

He drops his head back and laughs. The sound is riveting. The sexiest laugh I've ever heard.

I draw closer to Darius until our faces are inches apart. I lay a hand on his chest. I can feel and hear his pulse, his lungs moving. His muscles tighten at my touch. My hot breath comes out in small puffs of smoke still.

He kisses me. His hungry mouth sears me to my molten core. I push against him, but he kisses me harder. He forces his tongue against mine, the cool wetness of his mouth extinguishing the flames in mine. He pulls away, leaving a gasp and sparks on my tongue. His eyes are burning wilder than before. My first kiss with Silas turns to ash.

The rumbling voice of the river echoes the blood in his veins. The tension in his body is building. The flames inside me are nowhere near dying down.

Without warning, he steps back and begins taking off his armor.

"What are you doing?" I ask.

"Going for a swim. Care to join me, Killer?"

He removes his breastplate and undershirt. Then, has me back in his arms before I can blink. I shout in protest, but he flings me into the crystalline water. He comes right in after me and lifts me from under my arms to hold my head above the water as the smooth current dances under us.

I splash him. "I can't swim! Get out of my way!"

I attempt to get out of the water. Bristling with the acute realization that I am out of my element. The water's movement, gurgling against my skin, makes me feel sick.

With powerful strides, he drags me deeper into the water though I try to resist. Forcing me to focus on paddling to stay above the surface. My lungs are struggling to take in air. He grips my face in his still-warm hands and brings my mouth to his. Once again, his tongue brandishes through my mouth.

His method of calming the heat inside me sparks a new flame in my core. I will drown again today, either in the same waters or in him. He holds me. My skin is still hot. I kick until his hands catch my legs and bring them around his waist.

"You don't want to go under, do you?" he asks.

Thankful for the chance to get a good height above the water's surface, I allow him to hold me up. The water's movement threatens to knock us over, and I wrap my arms around his neck as we falter in the current. He shuts his mouth and I stare at it. I moisten my lips, tasting the river water.

He kisses me again. In this kiss, I taste a morsel of his own internal, burning pain. He dominates my senses, leading me by the tongue.

His brother is dead. A girl I once thought of as a sister is dead.

We're both soldiers, at war with the world and ourselves. But we were never enemies—we. That's not something I'm supposed to be thinking about, but he's putting all thought out of my head.

As he kisses me, he wraps his arms tighter around me, and I lock my legs behind his back. We search each other, searing one another, unraveling our restraint. One fight we do not have to lose is this one: our desires. We do not have to fight each other. And as waves of pain and loss wash over both our lives, we've somehow crashed into each other amid the worsening storm. Setting each other ablaze in a raging river.

I pull back for a breath. "Neither of us wants to go under."

His kiss sends chills running rampant all over my wet skin and fans the flame he's set burning between my legs. He bites my lips, feeding off the energy within me. When he pulls back, I feel every inch of where our bodies are still connected. The water keeps me clinging to his neck, his broad shoulders, allowing him to soothe me.

His lips brush against mine, asking permission for the first time, and I grant it with a returning kiss. The taste of his mouth lights up senses I'd never used before. A chill spreads across my shoulder blades and drapes down the back of my legs as his breath warms my neck. Holding my head back by my hair, he licks my throat and runs his other hand down my backside. His cock presses against my stomach through his trousers and my useless shift. I stop him and look between us. Reaching down a tentative hand, I lock eyes with him. I watch his face as I touch him. I've never touched a man this way before. His mouth parts and a ravenous sound comes out of him.

"Are we to fight fire with fire, Darius?"

He smirks against my neck and continues kissing me. Even in the water, I feel the warm pool between my thighs growing hotter. A new world of sensations, wants, and needs with a broadening horizon. I want to explore; I want to adventure.

I tug on his trousers and demand we wade into more shallow water, nudging my nose against his. He looks to the riverbank and pulls back, pushing me off him and into the water. I gasp as the water kisses my neck, stealing the warmth he gave me.

"Keres, get under water."

"What?"

Struggling to keep my head above the surface, I glimpse a figure standing on the bank.

"Fuck!" I grab onto his shoulders and cling to his back. He bobs lower in the water, working his long legs and arms to keep us both afloat. The current of the river is carrying us but he's keeping us close to where we jumped in. Silas follows as we drift a little.

"Silas," Darius calls out, his voice echoing off trees.

"Water fine?" Silas asks, loading his crossbow.

Darius' body bristles, hairs rising on the back of his neck. Two sounds fill my head: The sound of his blood pumping fast as the river's pace, and the clicking of the crossbow. He aims at Darius' chest, but his eyes are past him, landing on me as I cling to Darius.

"Silas, lower your weapon." Darius' voice is calm.

"No can do, Nance."

Darius flinches.

"Silas," He warns.

"Silas, stop it." I maneuver out of hiding, braving the water. It's been a long time since I've swum in this merciless river.

"Keres, get—"

"You forget who I am, Silas," I growl at him, slapping the surface of the water. "Lower your weapon."

A smile trembles on his mouth, but it doesn't reach his eyes.

"My *wife*." He seethes. "You're the one who has forgotten."

I paddle desperately as he clicks something on the crossbow, preparing to kill Darius or us both.

"Silas, put the bow down before someone gets hurt." Darius tries again, grabbing onto me and making himself my raft again.

I look behind Silas to see if he has come alone. He has.

"No can do, 'Nance." He turns his arrow toward me. "I could have you burned for adultery."

"*As if,*" the Death Spirit snorts.

"We are not married, Silas." *Also, is why he calling Darius, 'Nance?*

His threat sparks a new fever in me. As if Darius senses the temperature shift within me, he squeezes my arm. A warning of ice and water splashes across my skin at the protective gesture. Silas winces.

"And that makes you as good as mine!" Spit flies from his mouth, and he takes aim.

"Elymas, help me."

Darius pushes me under the water. I gasp for air, taking in water as my head is forced below the surface. It muffles the sound of the shot as water intrudes into my body, assaulting my senses.

Water. There is nothing but water filling my ears and mouth.

No.

Rather than sinking, rather than drifting in a relentless current, I submit to the hold of the cold hand wrapped around my ankle. Its chill crawls up my legs, tugging on my waist, enveloping me in power. The icy skin of the water is no match for the fire in my blood.

The next thing I know, we are safe, floating as if we are lifeless, and suspended in an orb of water. Arrows hail against the shield of the river water as Silas shoots and reloads his crossbow. Darius' eyes burn golden with awe.

The sound of the water swirling around us matches the blood whooshing in my head. We do not breathe because we do not have to as my magic encloses us in a protective shield of power and water.

The River Liri... which once killed me, now obeys me. It picks us up like a pebble in its current and delivers us further down the riverbank— farther from Silas. We wash up on the gravel, bodies still mingling together.

"Magic," Darius says, still in shock that I moved the river for him.

Silas screams a curse at us from down the bank, but we are out of range of his bow. We take off running.

"We need to split up. No one else can know we were here together," I gasp out as we run at top speed.

"I'm not leaving you alone out here. He could be right behind us. What if he kills you! Or what if there are Humans?"

"I'm the most dangerous thing out here."

He slows down, so he isn't running too far ahead of me. His legs are much longer, much more powerful.

"Keres, you heard him. He threatened to have you burned. I've never seen this side of Silas. I don't know how many of his words to mark. What if he tells Kaius or Liriene?"

"I doubt he's eager to tell my father he shot at me."

"That aside, he will tarnish your name."

"Am I not tarnished already?" We stop. "Should he be jealous enough to commit murder over a cursed girl?"

"Come on, Killer."

"No, Darius. I don't know what I was thinking."

"What?" His face scrunches. Pain flickers in his coal eyes again.

"I am marrying Silas."

"Is that what you truly want?"

We both feel my unspoken answer.

"Come home with me." He reaches for me and his callused hand grazes my fingers.

I flinch away. "I have to go home. Apologize to my sister."

Silas has a claim on me. And what he saw today will reap consequences my mind fights against the thought of. I want to go home with him. I know exactly why.

Darius inches closer to me and the hairs on my neck stand up. "I never apologize to anyone for doing what I want."

I pull away. "And should I do the same? Forsake my family, our traditions? My own standards?"

"Is that what bothers you? You feel you're betraying your betrothed by being with me. Lowering yourself—"

"Being with you?" I ask.

We stare at each other.

"You know that can't happen," I say softly.

His jaw tightens, and he pulls his hand back.

"Because you believe no one should want your cursed heart or because you've already given it to him?"

"You don't know me, Darius."

"I could get to," he counters.

"You want to know my body, not me." I place my hand over my heart.

"You're assuming that, but denying I might understand how you feel." He leans in closer and lowers his voice. "I find you bewitching. Not many things catch my interest." He smirks. "I'm not your Silas. I'm not charming or gallant. I see what I want, and I go after it. I see something in you that I want. That's all either of us needs to understand."

"And you think I want you too?" I raise my hands.

"Do you know what you want?" He asks.

I cross my arms and stare him down. I can't speak because I don't know the answer to that question, so I just continue staring like an idiot, my face on fire.

"Whatever, Keres." He turns to go.

"Wait."

He grunts.

"I didn't thank you for stopping me. From pursuing Liriene. If you hadn't interfered, I would have regretted the outcome."

He nods, keeping his eyes off me.

"You stopped the arrows." His ember eyes flash at me. "We're even."

"Where will you go now?" I ask, inching away from him.

"Where will *you?*" He counters.

I weigh my options. I could go home to apologize to Liriene. Risk running into Silas again. He might shame me in front of everyone if he is angry enough. Or...

"Have you ever met a witch?" I ask.

Darius raises his brow at me.

13: THE RIVER LIRI

Liriene

Keres' eyes were black as a midnight sky without the moon.

I look up through tree branches at the placid orb glowing resiliently above me, wrapping my gray shawl tighter around my shoulders. I push thoughts of Keres out of my head and remember how Katrielle used to talk to the moon.

Adreana, Goddess of Darkness: Will She hear me if I talk to the moon too? If I cry?

My sorrow feels endless. A bottomless well of tears within me. What's the point of everything without her? She belongs with me. Always has and always will. Not with Hayes. Not in the ground. With me.

I slam my fists into the dirt. I wish I could unearth her. With fists of fury, rip the earth open as wide as the chasm in my heart. Find her smiling beneath it all and reaching for me to pull her up from the grave. I pound the ground with my fists until my knuckles ache.

My life feels like one big joke. I've been good; never asked for more than was given me. Never warred against anyone or anything. Simply loved. My life has been tender. Until, fate twisted me into its brutal scheme. Upended my serene life.

My mother died. My sister died. She revived but as something else. Not the raven-haired girl who liked to play in the River Liri but the

White Reaper that rose from the depths of it. Spat out of the very mouth of Death.

Still, I never questioned the Gods, just Keres. Just her power. I never cursed my mother's killer, never tempted fate; no matter how it crooked its smile at me. I behaved. I was good.

Maybe it's the good people who lose everything. But why? Will I ever find a good enough reason to justify Katrielle's death— my greatest loss? She was the love of my life.

"Adreana," I break down into tears. "If You can hear me..."

A bird calls through the dark and silence.

"She said you always listen." I lift my blurred eyes to the moon. "She trusted You. With our secret. With everything. She swore You granted safety. Only You could see her fears and desires in the dark, she said. Only You could see us."

I clench my fists and hammer the ground again.

"Damn you, Kat. For keeping our love buried. For dying and never listening to me. I told you not to go. You should have stayed with me instead of fighting me. Instead of warring with the Humans." My sobs overwhelm me. "I told you not to be like Keres. Her curse... influenced you. War changed you."

I hug my knees and rock. My accusations might be unfair. I instantly regret my angry words. As if she can hear me. I scoff, fighting against the only truth I know right now. Mother is dead. The Keres I once knew is dead. Katrielle is dead.

Not wanting to see the resurfacing images of her broken body, I replay lively memories of her. The sight of her in armor, one hand on her hip and the other on the hilt of her sword. That was how she looked the last time I saw her whole. I silence the memory of our argument that day.

The memories that left me speechless come instead. The gentle ones.

Her sultry brown eyes staring up at me, her dark brown curls looping around my fingers. The generosity of her breast. The warmth between her legs. Her laughter. She always laughed at my pathetic jokes, but she was funnier. She had freckles that ran from neck to navel. Like the seam of a silky garment.

The humans split her open along that dotted line. Her blood was the most horrendous shade of red I've ever seen. Dark and muddy, nearly brown around the wound. Then a bright and angry color as she coughed it up.

Keres wouldn't leave her side. I wanted to comfort her, but she was there. I asked Chamira to get Keres to take a rest so I could have my chance. When I finally reached her side, her breath was failing. I didn't know what to say or do. I just cried. Not caring who saw it, not caring who wondered why I wept so.

I promised to love her endlessly for the first time aloud in broad daylight. She tried to tell me something, but then she started coughing up blood worse than before. Chamira was the first to come, pushing me aside. Calling for someone to wake the Coroner.

I cursed myself for my uselessness. For not having any real right to be there, besides a love that no one would recognize as valid. If I threw myself across her body the way I wanted to, our secret would be brought to light. She would die alone and the elders would have voted for me to be cast out of the clan. My father being the clan leader didn't mean I was safe.

I lingered when Keres came. She was furious. She commanded the team of healers like a general on the battlefield. Shaking Katrielle awake, she nearly slipped in the blood pooling at her feet. Keres demanded herbs; I was quicker than the others and gave it. She demanded everything. If I could have given everything for Katrielle, I would have.

She demanded water, and I gave it. I would have given myself in her stead.

The night air tucks my body under its blanket of cold, comforting me in my fevered grief. For an hour of wishing I was lifeless, I lay on the ground in the dirt. Wishing I was with her under it.

"Liri." A familiar voice startles me to my feet.

"Silas." I wipe my eyes.

"What are you doing out here alone and on the ground? It's dangerous."

My lip trembles and my voice cracks as I try to explain. He hushes me and pulls me into his arms, dropping his crossbow to the ground to hold me. He pets my long red hair until I finally stop crying.

"She loved you as much."

"Kat refused to break it off with Hayes. She chose him. She chose death."

"No, she chose to protect you. To carry the secret to her grave. A secret that would have destroyed you both in the eyes of all who care about you."

"It shouldn't be that way." I sniffle. "I love her. Thaniel loves Mathis!"

"No one knows about them," he says. "Love is love, Liri. We know that. I wish the entire world agreed. I wish everyone felt that protecting love was more important than protecting pride, hatred, and fear."

I cry again, leaning into him.

"Love is precious. You lost her, but you did not lose her love. It lives on in you." He sighs. "And there are others who have it and give it up rashly."

I lean back to look at him. His brown eyes swirl with pain and I finally register the smell of liquor on his breath.

"What's happened?"

"Keres." He laughs under his breath. "Whoring herself to Darius."

"What?" I push out of his arms. "You have proof of this? This is no light accusation—"

"I saw them in the River Liri together." He rubs the back of his neck. I await further explanation, but I know it's not coming. His rage and jealousy are boiling. He kicks his crossbow away and I flinch, taking a step back. He screams curses and starts punching the nearest tree.

"Silas!" I grab his shoulders. "You'll break your hands."

"Better than breaking his neck," he growls, shrugging me off and puffing out his chest. He paces back and forth.

"How can I marry her now? She defiled herself."

I wipe my eyes, letting thoughts of Kat bury themselves in the back of my mind for now. I've grown accustomed to Silas' mood swings. Now is not the time to mirror his emotion, but to be rational. "This is an arrangement older than either of us. You cannot break it off."

"She's the one who has broken it!"

"What did you see?" I ask, having a hard time picturing Keres in the water or even near the River Liriene. He describes the alleged thrall of passion, but still, I doubt Keres would ever go into that water. Even if she were on fire, she'd sooner roll in the mud.

"Are you sure he wasn't forcing her into the water? To torment her, to—"

"I'm sure! She wrapped her body around him like the snake she is. Kissing him, caressing him. And he, her. I should kill him. *Comrade*." He spits onto the dirt, pulling a canteen of what I assume is more liquor from his belt. He takes a swig. "*Brother in arms*." He laughs. "Do brothers steal from one another?"

"No." I lower my eyes and pace beside him.

He mumbles under his breath as I ponder Keres' behavior.

As a child, she drowned in the River Liri. Everyone remembers that day... How could she go into it? With Darius of Massara? What was she thinking!? "Her power—her curse. It's corrupting her."

He whirls on me. "You're defending her? You seriously think she loves him or that she would choose him over—"

"No." I lift a hand to silence him. "For thirteen years, I've warned Keres of what this power might do to her. Who it will force her to become. What body could withstand the height of a God's power without the very soul being compromised? The God of Death instilled his essence into her. What more should we expect from a God's touch than for it to break a mortal?"

"So, she's broken. Sullied. Soul and standards, apparently." He rubs the budding scruff on his chin. "All the more reason to marry her?" He rolls his eyes.

"Forces beyond our power or Mrithyn's brought you two together. You are bound to each other. Do not abandon her over this foolish dalliance. You cannot walk away."

"Why can't I?" He gets in my face. "Because I'm a knight? Because it is my duty to love her?"

"Do you love her?"

"Since she came into this very world." His voice rumbles in his throat. He screams another curse of frustration, barking like a mad dog at my skirts.

"Love is precious," I suggest his own words back to him. He's still seething, but he stills.

"Love is worth protecting more than pride. As you said. Is it your heart she injured or your pride? Do you now hate Darius, who has been your right hand since childhood? Do you fear losing her? What about your love for her?"

He lowers his eyes and nods, raking his hands through his ragged blond hair.

"Where is she now?" I ask.

"I don't know." He looks to the moon. I follow his gaze. "Still not at camp even at this hour. Neither is he. Yet, here I am, and you're right. I can't walk away even though she's run away. Wherever she is. Whatever she's doing."

I sigh. "Only the moon knows her secrets now."

He nods and I look at him. "She will leave soon."

"What do you mean? Go where?" He flinches.

"King Arias charged her with a task. She will go to court."

Silas runs his hands through his hair. "No."

"If you don't want her to discover your secrets there..."

"I must marry her. As soon as possible. Tomorrow—"

"Silas—"

"No. I can't lose her, Liri. If she goes there... courtiers gossip."

"You want to trap her. So she can't run once she knows the truth." I arch my brows at him.

"Don't put it that way. You know what she will do."

"Buck like a wild mare. Choose Darius or whoever else instead." I chew my lip in thought.

"She has no choice. You said it yourself. I can't walk away, and neither can she."

"What if you were to accompany her to court?" I suggest.

"That would be catastrophic. You know it. My mother—"

"Would burn you at the stake herself."

He laughs, but it's mirthless. "I guess Kat was right about Adreana, then." He smiles at me and looks back to the moon.

"A secret-keeping Goddess," I ruminate. "Trouble is deciding whether that makes Her a dangerous or safe entity."

"Secrets are weapons." His smile fades. "It makes Her the most dangerous."

14: A God Bleeds

Darius and I crossed the River Liri as the Sun fell under the horizon.

We plummet into the shadows of the Sunderlands Forest, keeping our guard up against Dalis soldiers and other wild things. Neither of us speaks, but I fear our hearts are conversing. Telling each other things they shouldn't be. *I feel your pain; I want to ease it.*

Our shoulders and hands brush against each other as we pick our way between trees and sideways glances. His eyes are a torch in the darkness. I know the forest well enough to walk blindfolded, but he is uncharted territory.

Instead of wishing he would say something, I try to figure out what I should say to Ivaia when we reach the loft. Riordan told me to make up with her before I go to court. Can we really resolve this break in trust with our differences?

My stomach balls up at the thought of facing her again. I'd rather sulk a little while longer. I rub the chill from my arms and stop short.

"Should we go back?"

Darius stops too and turns to me. He rubs his callused hands over my bare arms, and I welcome the warmth.

"You haven't even told me where we're going."

"We're almost there…"

I remember the wards and attribute my suddenly shaken resolve to their influence. Never have they dissuaded me from continuing to my family's house. But I feel like I don't belong. Am I shying away from the energy of the wards or from the responsibility of repairing my relationship with Ivaia? Why did I involve Darius in this?

"What am I doing?" I rub my hands over my face.

"Hey, calm down." He grabs me by the shoulders. "Talk to me."

I pause, biting my lip as he looks down at me. Fire in the dark.

I kiss him and take courage from him. He doesn't hold back, pulling my body against his as I open my mouth for his tongue to taste me. He releases me and my resolve is even weaker now. I've half a mind to let him fuck me on the ground right here, right now. But I wouldn't want my first time to be that way. Although I do want it to be with him. I know that now.

Silas' honey eyes flash into my head. I blink them away, staring at Darius. This is not a war I've prepared for.

"Let's keep going." He tugs on my hand and continues walking with me in tow.

"You don't feel it?" I ask as we get even closer to Ivaia's loft.

"Feel what?"

"The wards. Magic barricades my aunt's home from the rest of the world."

"Oh?" He scratches his head and looks around.

"That's her house?" He points toward the decrepit hut.

"That's an illusion."

He looks at me like I'm crazy, brows pinched together. "I like to believe what I see," he smirks at me.

"Perhaps you better start believing in what you feel instead." I put my hand against his hard abs. I feel his muscles tighten. "Don't you feel queasy with panic?"

Confusion crosses his brow. He tightens his jaw and focuses. He closes his eyes, searching his body for the sensation I've described. The ward's energy is hitting me full force. A barrage of discomfort. I step closer to him to soothe myself.

His eyes spring open as I near.

"I feel only this." He takes me in his arms. Our bodies react to one another, like sparks to kindling. Engulfed by the sensations of his touch and the magical vibrations of the wards, my body hums with pleasure. My breath catches in my throat and my vision dims from the heady concoction of the thrill of his touch and panic. Adrenaline spikes my blood and my heart kicks into overdrive. My knees go weak and my core clenches when he says my name, "Keres." But it isn't his voice I hear coming from his succulent mouth. It's the telltale hiss of Mrithyn's.

I collapse in Darius' arms.

🝖🝖🝖🝖🝖

Am I dreaming? A stranger approaches me. A figure emerges from the shadows that surround me. His presence interrupts my thoughts, misplaced as stars would be in a day-lit sky. He is the most beautiful person I've ever seen, even though half his face hides beneath the hood of his long black cloak. A single strand of brown hair crosses his brow, giving me an inkling of what's beneath the hood. Serious, blue-green eyes burn with what seems like hatred toward me.

We're walking together now. A path appears, one gray stepping-stone at a time. No world around us but black emptiness. Oblivion.

I realize I must be dreaming. One moment he's beside me, watching me from the corner of his eye and striding in sync with me. In the next, he is ahead of me, watching as I walk towards him.

He doesn't speak, but I try to. No words come out of my mouth, no voice. With what seems to be my mind, I ask, *who are you?*

He doesn't answer but the corners of his mouth kick up. As if he takes pleasure in me being confused.

Where are we?

Nothing.

How do I get out?

He laughs. The sound rumbles all over my skin. A deep and rich baritone. I feel my face heating with frustration. Why won't he answer me?

He moves to retrieve something from within the folds of his cloak, but before I see what it is someone calls out, startling us both. I recognize neither the voice nor the language. He turns to answer the call but not before locking eyes with me one last time. As if promising to continue this at another time.

Okay, dream man.

I take another step down the stone pathway but lose my footing and fall into the abyss. I awaken from that dream, yet deep in another, feverish, feeling as if I've fallen from a great height and landed on a bed of bones. I feel beads of sweat rolling down my face and neck but see nothing.

"Where are you?" A child's voice screams in the darkness. "I need help. Someone, please!"

I drift towards that voice. Not truly myself, not in my body. My mind is carried like a wisp on the wind as it hisses my name.

"Keres, get up and go. Go."

Why can't I see? I panic.

"Help!" That child's voice cracks through the air like lightning. Flames lick at the edges of my mind. I open my eyes but still see nothing. I only feel seared by the rising heat and my lungs are full of smoke.

"Fire! Fire!" The little girl's voice trembles and she shrieks again, this time in a language I haven't heard since childhood. My native tongue.

"Where are you?" She pleads again. The smallest, coldest hands grip me by my ankles. "I need help."

My awareness tumbles downward in an unending spiral. Farther and farther down a rabbit hole, towards her desperate cries for help. The fire rages around me and I choke on the billowing smoke. I try to answer her calls. *I'm right here, I'm right here.* Her needy hands scratch up my ankles and legs.

"I cannot see!" She weeps and I can't see either. A choir of voices, none of which belong to her or me, begin chanting in my mind. Her screams attempt to drown out their ancient tongue, but they overpower her. Hands that aren't mine claw at my eyes, and I feel warmth and wetness on my skin. Is it sweat? I lift a finger to my eyes and taste the drop. It's blood.

"Let me out, let me see! Let me out!" Her voice prays. Her hands scratch my eyes. I realize the voice is coming from me, from my throat. My mind bucks against the realization that this is not my body. I am the child; it is my voice that is screaming. It is somewhere in my mind that fire is roaring, and the voices of the Gods chant their divine words. Blinded.

"Help me!" I claw at the veil covering my face. I rip it from where it's pinned into my hair. Something growls at my feet. I fall to the cold hard floor. A massive animal rubs against my back, growling.

I stop crying at the touch of the creature I cannot see and feel its guttural growl rumbling in my chest. It soothes me in the way thunder soothes a desert. I lean against the thick fur and knot my fingers into it. My breathing slows as drops of blood and tears tumble down my cheeks. The open wounds on my eyelids sting, but the creature licks away the tears. A Hound.

The servants of the Gods are called Blind Ones. We communicate with our divine Masters, through dreams. I see Mrithyn when I close my eyes. He comes to me in dreams, whispering quietly as a lover in my ear. He turns dreams round in my mind and weaves stories through my thoughts. He laughs and smiles as He watches me sleep. He knots ideas into my fists and tangles starlit fantasies in my hair. His voice mingles with my breath as my chest rises and falls.

The chill of his touch wipes beads of sweat from my brow. He loves me. He chose me; He uses me. He worships me, and what His power has done to me. He tells me I am beautiful. *White Reaper.* When I wake, nightmares plague my reality. Interludes of the peace he gives me wash across my memory and I am comforted by Him.

But this was not a dream.

I wake up for real this time, in my own head and in my own skin. Bleeding from scratches I made on my face.

"Give me the cloth." I hear a voice say. "She's waking up."

My eyes flutter open, but it hurts, and my face stings. I groan.

"Close your eyes, Keres." Liriene's voice sounds close. Am I back home? Last thing I remember...

"So, it was a sleeping spell. See how she's waking up. As if from a deep slumber," My father's voice carries.

"Do mere nightmares make one hurt oneself?" Indiro's voice is unmistakable. I stay still and listen for who's here.

"No." I know that voice too. It stings me more than the scratches to my eyes. "No mere dream has the power to captivate a mind for as long as it held her captive within her subconscious." Ivaia's voice cuts through the room like a silver blade. A cool damp cloth pats against my face. Hearing Ivaia's voice jolts me to realization.

The last thing I remember, I was with Darius, going to see Ivaia. Where am I? What happened? Dare I ask, where is Darius? How long have I been a "captive" as she said? Who held me prisoner in the dream realm, that stranger in shadow or the Elven child?

"Salt would stop the bleeding."

Silas?

"It would also hurt like hell, lad," Indiro says.

"No, he's right. Fetch me the salt. She all but gouged her own eyes out. Let's stop the bleeding."

"Why are the scratches still bleeding? This started yesterday."

Yesterday?

I struggle to open my eyes, groaning as I move my limbs. They feel as if they've not been used for months. My stomach growls angrily with hunger.

"Oh, Gods above. She isn't bleeding from the scratches. She's crying blood."

"Let me see."

"No." I sit up, swatting someone's hands away. I pinch my eyes shut as I touch my face where it hurts. "The looking glass," I demand.

Two strong arms lift me to my feet and lead me toward the looking glass.

"Open," Indiro's voice touches my ears. I struggle to open my eyes and slam them shut once more at the sight of my face. Wild green eyes, shrouded by angry red claw marks and swollen, bloody tears line my face.

"Iv." I turn, unable to see her. I lean back on the washbasin. "Can you heal this?"

"No." She's curt.

Still angry with me, I see.

"There is no blood beneath your fingernails, Keres, no signs you're the one who scratched your face." She adds.

"Then who are we to believe did this to her? A spirit?" I hear the testiness in Liriene's voice.

"I couldn't see." I begin. "I couldn't see a thing. I heard a girl screaming for help. I was not myself. I was her. It was her hands that did this. But through a dream?"

"What you describe is more than a dream, but no less than I expected," Ivaia answers again. "A channeling."

"That's preposterous." I hear my father.

"Is it?" Ivaia retorts.

"I heard the voices of the Gods, not just Mrithyn. All at once. Speaking the ancient tongue." I shudder. "I couldn't hear myself think or scream above their voices in my head."

"Is this possible? There's only ever been rumors of these things happening," Riordan's voice joins.

"It seems real to me," Ivaia sounds like she's shrugging.

"Then who was channeling me? A blind child with the voices of the Gods in her head. And a pet wolf." I don't know why I do but I leave out the part about the stranger.

"The child Oracle, newly blind, perhaps?" Indiro reasons. It makes total sense now, but what doesn't make sense is...

"Why? Why would she connect with me? She doesn't know me."

"I understand it as much as you do, dear." Ivaia's voice softens. "She didn't connect only your minds, she was inside of you. The Gods may be trying to reach you through her. Or you in her. Or both."

"Mrithyn has direct access to my mind at all times I am asleep," I add.

"Then it was not Mrithyn," Silas says.

"What God communicates through pain and fire?"

"Perhaps it wasn't a God at all, but the child herself seeking a familiar," Indiro says.

I fold my arms across my chest as the room falls silent. "How did you all get here, and how long was I unconscious?"

Silence persists.

"Hello?" I shout.

"Two days." My father says.

"Keres, do you remember coming to my house?" Ivaia asks.

I think back to the last thing I remember. Darius. "I remember coming but not arriving," I say.

Ivaia speaks like she's weighing her words. "A… passerby found you. Brought you to my loft."

"How fortunate." Silas laughs under his breath.

"For the better part of a day, I tried to rouse you. When I determined I couldn't help you alone, we brought you here. Your father tried to use his herbs to entice you from your stupor. You were breathing, your heart was beating. But you were gone."

"I came to inquire after you, lass. You can only guess my shock to hear you were in a deep sleep you would not wake from," Indiro says.

"When I arrived, you were screaming. You were kicking your feet at nothing and crying about them burning. You looked like you were dancing in flames. Then scratches started appearing on your ankles. Then your face and your eyes," Silas says.

"It was unlike anything I've ever seen. As if the next world was ripping through your skin to come into this one," Ivaia says. "I tried my best to wake you with magic, but something was holding you. Only when it released did you wake up."

"When Osira decided," I whisper. I blink my eyes open, fighting back the tears from the pain of doing so.

"You should rest," Ivaia says.

"If my eyes were closed for two days, I want them open," I say.

The first face I see is Silas; a snarl on his lips. "And how should we fix her face for the wedding?" He shoves a hand at my appearance.

"We will manage it," Liriene replies.

"The wedding?" I spit back at him. "That's your only concern."

He crosses the room in long vengeful strides and takes me by the shoulders. "You know full well it is not all I am worried about."

He spins to address the entire room. "I caught her in an act of passion with my fellow soldier."

Indiro mutters a curse under his breath. My father's face crumbles in shock, and Liriene casts him a horrified look. Ivaia and Riordan both look to me, more out of concern.

"She thinks she could escape our betrothal by lying with another man."

"I did not lie with another man," I growl.

"I saw you! Down by the river."

"We both know what happened by the river." I bite back.

"Tomorrow." He spins back to my father. "I will make her my wife tomorrow."

"Don't you think this spiritual battle is more important? I'm going to the Ro'Hale kingdom to visit Osira. If she's looking for a familiar, channeling me, or whatever is going on, she obviously needs to speak with me." I gesture toward my eyes.

He wants me to stay and marry all my problems away? I want to run away from all of them. Silas aimed a crossbow at me. Just shamed me in front of my entire family. Now, he demands I wed him tomorrow.

I growl with frustration. "Fuck!"

"Keres! Watch your language," My father says.

I throw my hands up. I feel ashamed of my behavior with Darius now. Ashamed of my growing desire for him. At least I chose him. But I don't know what I'm doing.

There's so much more going on in the world than Darius, Silas and me. Things I don't even understand. Although I feel frightened to think I have a purpose beyond this clan, I'm exhilarated and relieved by the thought of walking away from it all. Marrying someone I do not love terrifies me more than the thought of being attacked or channeled by the Gods. I crave a purpose beyond being the midwife of the dying.

"I don't want to marry you, Silas."

"You have no choice," he says turning his honey eyes on me with a hunger and hurt I've never seen before.

Does he have feelings for me, or is this mere possessive jealousy like I once felt for him? Where is Darius? I can't even ask. All their eyes aim at me. I can't stand it. I'm itching to run out of the tent.

"Come, Silas" Indiro interrupts. "I will help you prepare for the wedding." Indiro plants a firm hand on Silas' shoulder and leads him from my home. Liriene tosses the bloodied cloth into a pile of clothing to be washed. Riordan and Ivaia exchange glances; a silent conversation.

"I'll be outside. Kaius, I desire to speak with you," Riordan says. My father and uncle exit, leaving me with Liriene and Ivaia. The two most bitter women in my life.

None of us speak. Liriene is the first to sit at the table, followed by Iv and then myself. The silence grows thicker. The likeness in our blood heats and cools as our words boil in our heads. Liriene is furious with me for fighting the Humans a few days ago, and for our contention over Katrielle. Ivaia is still hurt by me renouncing her God. Well, she thinks I renounced Him.

"The Coroner hunted again," Ivaia breaks the silence, leaning back in her chair. Her blond hair is frizzy from the humid air, and her sheer blue gown shifts off her shoulders. Liriene watches the movement, eyes widening as she notices she can see through our aunt's dress. Her dark pink nipples stand hard against the thin tulle fabric. I watch Liriene swallow her words.

"Aye." I nod, remembering my regrettable attack on Thaniel and Mathis. I glance at Liriene.

"They also say the Goddess bleeds," Ivaia's mouth quirks up.

"They say many things." I nod.

"Bested by the King of the Gryphons, Arias."

I flinch at the mention of his name. It's true, my pride still stings.

"The Sunderlands is in tatters. Its Coroner renounces her duty. Heralds come down from the heavens, talking of war. I open my door and find a boy holding what appears to be your lifeless body."

"Who?" Liriene chimes in.

"Darius, I think he said his name was." Ivaia smirks at me.

Liriene snorts. "So it's true."

I slap my palm to my forehead. Of course, Silas told her what happened by the river—or at least his version of it.

"Who is this Darius character, the one Silas accuses you of ruining yourself for? He offered me no explanation of himself, just that you were together when you collapsed." Ivaia opens her arms.

Liriene shares a look of disdain with Ivaia. "Penance of Massara, son of Darius of the Ro'Hale Kingdom. Born to two drunks, him and his twin brother, Hayes. His brother was killed in the last attack on our people."

"Penance?" I ask.

She shakes her head at me. "Wise choice," her voice drips with sarcasm.

"Doesn't matter." Ivaia swats away Darius' other name. "You're still marrying Silas. You still need a knight."

"For once in my life, I agree with you, Aunt." Liriene lifts her chin.

Ivaia glances over Liriene's slight frame. Her red hair and bulging gray eyes do little to impress the sorceress.

"You think you have a say, girl." Ivaia snaps at Liriene. My sister shivers at my Aunt's tone. This will be entertaining.

"You may have trained her in your indelible ways and that of magic, Ivaia. But I was the one who bathed and nourished her. You gave her a doctrine, and she lived by it. I gave her life."

"Watch your tongue, bitch." Ivaia leans across the table. "My sister gave her the very air in her lungs. You've only done a shit job at maintaining it."

Liriene bites her tongue. I cannot suppress the smile that quakes in the corners of my mouth. I've been waiting for this argument for years. They've always hated each other but never faced each other. Wish I had a snack.

"And you!" Ivaia jabs her long slender fingers towards me. "Your lack of control without me that night earned the retaliation of the Humans against Hishmal. An entire settlement of Elves— wiped out. Because you cannot control the power the Gods gave you. I've been trying my best to help you, to teach you. And how do you repay me? You renounce Elymas. You make a poor example of yourself in the forest with those soldiers. Your soldiers. You tried to kill one of your own." She stands from the table, hands pounding on the wood. "Damn me if I raised you to act this way! I have given you every tool you needed to manage your abilities, to practice, to take a stand against our enemies. I never treated you like a child, Keres. But you continue to act like one."

My lip trembles at her words, and to my dismay, tears burn my eyes.

"And now your husband to be, before your father, slanders you and denies your maidenhood!"

I stand up, matching her stance, but no words come out of me. I feel powerless before her.

"You are entirely out of control!"

My hands ball into fists as I bite my tongue.

"Do you think you love Darius? Do you think you know what you want? What about what you need?" She comes around the table, getting in my face. "I will prove you wrong and end this dalliance!" Her power glows like the hottest fire in her blue eyes.

"He doesn't matter," I choke on the lie.

"You think he is worth going against your family's wishes? You want to end up like me?" Her words shock me. Liriene is standing now but doesn't dare move.

"I turned against my family and everything I had to be with Riordan. I got myself banished by my own sister. To chase wild fantasies. I ruined my reputation, my honor. And by the Gods, I will love him until I die, but I ruined myself for him. No woman should ever, under any circumstance, ruin herself for a man."

I hate when she yells.

"And you throw your body at the feet of a man who owes you nothing. Have you no shame? No honor? No respect for who you are and how I raised you?"

"Stop." The tears spill out of my eyes.

"Keres, you will go to the kingdom and you will meet with the Oracle. In two days. Tomorrow, I am giving you to Silas myself. Clean up your face as best you can and get your shit together."

"I was coming to you to reconcile," I finally get something out.

"To come apologize for your foolish choices with me, you bring another one of your foolish decisions?" She scoffs.

"I didn't say to apologize—"

She growls, but I cut her off. "I don't apologize for being who I want to be or doing what I want to do."

Darius is the one who taught me those words, and the thought of him gives me the courage to say them with conviction. With that, I stomp over to my side of the tent to pack my things.

"What do you think you're doing?" Liriene tries to stop me.

"I'm done. I'm not listening to either of you. I'm tired of being told what to do. I'm going to court, as I've been saying."

"You can't disobey your husband."

"He's *not* my husband. But even if he was, I would rather answer to my calling than to a man."

"Your calling?" Liriene asks.

"King Arias gave me a task. A purpose. I'm going."

Ivaia's at her side, reinforcing her efforts to stop me. That feeling of being too small creeps up on me again as they unpack everything I throw into my rucksack.

"Keres, stop. Liriene, get the papers."

Liriene is gone in a rustle of skirts and red hair. Her fingers flutter through a chest beside her cot.

"What?" I stop packing.

Ivaia stops unpacking. "Your duty is to no king in the sky, girl. But to your own blood."

"The rights to you." Liriene produces a thick piece of paper, sealed by the sign of our kingdom. She breaks the seal and reveals my mother's handwriting.

"The rights to me?" I spit back at them, flinching as Liriene attempts to hand me the letter. "What does it say?"

"I don't know, I cannot read, remember?" Liriene pushes the paper into my hands.

"It says she gave us the rights to give you to a husband," Ivaia says.

I read the delicately written words and find the cruelest truth: I, Princess Resayla Kalendyrra Aurelian, daughter of Adon Aurelian, King of Ro'Hale, offer my youngest heiress, Keres Nyxara Aurelian of Ro'Hale, to Ser Solas and Lady Seraphina Prycel of Ro'hale, as a gift to their son, Silas.

A bride to be his by promise, an heir to the Mirrored Throne, by blood right.

A royal descendent of the Aurelian bloodline, Keres requires a trained knight and a descendent of the order, the Legion of Ro'Hale, which Silas will be groomed to be for her as her husband.

To come into her power and claim her right to the throne of her ancestors, Keres must accept the hand of the Knight appointed her in marriage.

If I cannot deliver my daughter to her betrothed when she comes of age, I charge her fate to the hand of my sister, Ivaia Jada Aurelian of Ro'Hale; with allowances also to my husband, Shepherd Kaius Lorien of Clan Massara, Ser Indiro Avalon, my dear and faithful knight, and to Lady Seraphina, my closest companion and the mother of Silas.

If none of these should be her Guardian, I charge Master Emeric Dracon of Falmaron to ensure her safety and care.

If Keres should refuse these terms, she is to be cut off from her inheritance and birthright forthwith, and never to return to the kingdom of her mother's birth.

Any child born of Keres and a mate not appointed by her guardians, shall also lose their birthright to the throne.

If all Aurelian heirs are illegitimate, the next heir in line will be of another bloodline, not my firstborn, Liriene Hadrianna Lorien of Clan Ro'Hale, nor her descendants.

I stop reading the letter damning me to marry Silas, damning me if I don't.

"Indiro, your father, and I have sworn to fulfill this final duty to your mother," Ivaia adds. "To give you to Silas, the knight of her choosing."

"So, what am I, property to sell? Cattle?" Anger stifles all the tears that had threatened to well up.

"You're his. By law."

"By your law!" Without a second thought, I run to the firepit and toss the letter into the flames. Ivaia's magic brings it back out before it's burned to ashes and she puts it onto my bed. I begin to smolder with anger.

"You will not understand these things now, but in time you will. I will tell you the truth and explain it all. For now, you need to trust us.

What we're doing is for the best. We have always done what's best for you. Your head is so far up your melancholy ass you can't see it!"

"I have a hard time believing that," I say, crossing my arms over my chest.

Liriene makes a tsking noise, "Yes, we expect you do." A pretty frown takes over her mouth. "It is better this way, trust me."

"You're not going anywhere but to the wedding altar." Ivaia dumps out the rest of my packed belongings onto the bed and that's final.

15: THE WEDDING

I sit on the bank of the River Liri, clutching my knees to my chest. Has it really been two days since I was here with Darius? I shove bread into my mouth.

The water talks to me in its slippery drawl. Starlight drowns in the dark, churning water and resurfaces. The pace of the river steals all my energy; its babble replaces my thoughts. Blood whooshes over my bones the way the water rushes over the rocks, foaming white in places. I think of the letter written by my mother and feel that foam in my mouth.

"How could you?"

A silent stillness in the depth of my heart ripples. A memory stirs, swimming to the front of my mind. I close my eyes and see a woman. Blond hair splayed around her face underwater. Her eyes pinched shut, her lips pursed, holding her breath. That exquisitely sad face pressed up against the surface of the river as if it were glass. Hands banging against the invisible force keeping her beneath the water. Her eyes shoot open, wildly pleading for the river to release her. Her mouth opens in a silent scream, pining for air, and the water fills her lungs. Her eyes are closed; her face is placid. Her hands drift above her head. She sinks into the dark of the river water.

I pick up a nearby rock and throw it in the water with all my strength. Pushing up to my feet, I find another and chuck it. I stone the water until I sink to my knees. How could she die and leave me to them? The river drains me dry and I fall asleep.

Someone nudges me awake at dawn. My eyes still hurt and feel swollen as I blink them open.

"Ivaia and Liriene are waiting." Not the most pleasant words to wake to. "And Silas."

I take Riordan's hand and allow him to pull me up.

"You slept out here all night? Isn't that dangerous?" He asks.

"The combination of Liriene and Ivaia is more dangerous. I didn't want to be home."

We stay for a moment, watching the water. I think of the little girl lost, blinded, and aflame with agony on the other side of my dreams.

"I haven't seen this river in a while. I usually avoid it," Riordan says.

"I wish I could but it's her grave."

"Not only hers," he says.

"I'm assuming everyone's getting ready for the ceremonies?" I ask.

"Preparations are almost complete. Silas is wasting no breath. He had people up all night organizing this."

"They're giving me to him, Rio. Like a prized cow."

He laughs under his breath. "They did the same to your mother and Ivaia."

I shoot him an incredulous look. "More accurately, they gave me to her. To be her knight protector. Silas has been training with Indiro for this his entire life. To be made ready to serve you. That's not someone to take as a husband lightly."

I shrug my shoulders, never having heard someone speak of Silas like that. I didn't expect Riordan to compliment Indiro either.

"That makes him right for me?" I ask.

He doesn't seem to know how to respond.

"Do I search for a certain look in his eye? Will time slow or some force like magic lead me to the realization? When will I know? How will I know if he is the right choice? Do I even have a choice?" I know the answers to these questions, but it feels good to voice them. I pull my hair back, braiding it so it's not in my face anymore. Every fly-away strand seems to find my eyes and I forget about the scratches and keep rubbing at the torn skin. Riordan watches me for a few breaths before speaking.

"Love is a peculiar beast. One that can often change its scales and hide in the most unseemly places. You'll know it only when you step back. When you stop trying to predict its patterns and moods and shades. One day you will look into its eyes and feel its heart. You'll know."

"I know then."

"What?" He asks.

"That I do not love Silas."

Rio sighs and offers me a sad smile.

"What's the story with you two? You and Indiro, I mean." I leap over the gap in the conversation.

Riordan skirts around my question with a brazen smile. "You in a wedding dress will be a sight for sore eyes." He nudges me.

I roll my sore eyes and chuckle. "Fine, don't tell me."

"Don't want to give you grief on your big day," He chides.

"My 'big day' is the thing giving me grief."

He takes me by the shoulders. "There are worse lots in life than marrying someone who's sworn to protect you. No one could have predicted what would happen to you and your mother. She wrote that letter before your birth and ensured that no matter what happened to her, you would have someone by your side. Besides, these are more perilous times, and the costs much higher. The civil war in the Sunderlands has escalated to a degree she and nobody else saw coming.

"Or maybe she did, and that's why she wrote the letter."

We both think about that.

"Either way, think of Silas as a comrade or a partner."

"Is that how you and Ivaia have made it this far?" I ask.

"That, and a lot of jasmine tea." He smiles roguishly. An aphrodisiac. Got it.

"We should get going."

He delivers me to the threshold of the Weaver's tent. He says Liriene and Ivaia are inside and wishes me luck before hurrying off to my home tent. I wish I could crawl back to the river—drown in it for good. Instead, I step through the door and am nearly blinded by candlelight.

"Are all these lights really necessary?" I squint through my swollen, now-fried eyes.

"Better to see your imperfections so I might remedy them," The haggard woman croaks. I glaze over her all-too-eager tone.

"Good morning, Attica." I nod to the Weaver who's dressed me my entire life.

Liriene and Ivaia are at the table drinking their morning herbal brew.

"You look like shit." Ivaia blows on her hot tea, steam spilling over the brim. Liriene raises a perfectly arched brow at our aunt, lips puckered at the edge of her teacup.

"Nothing I cannot fix." The Weaver welcomes me deeper into the tent.

I follow her through a forest of fabrics. Strands of ribbon drip from shelves lined with spools of dyed thread. A rainbow of colors is wound up into neat, workable skeins. Scissors and fabric knives of all sizes, and strips of leather marked for measuring, are all strewn over a massive, u-shaped table. She has me step up onto a small wooden stool between either side of the table and begins plucking my clothes from me. She strips me down and lays my clothes out on the table. I work to keep myself covered with my hands.

"Coroner, this'll be needing mending." She pokes a finger through the shoulder of my top, where King Arias injured me.

Ivaia and Liriene couldn't care less that I'm standing in the center of the room on a pedestal, in nothing but gooseflesh.

"Alright, Attica."

The Weaver circles around me, making my attempts to cover my body useless. "Are you a maiden?" She snaps. I hear Ivaia and Liriene pause their conversation.

"Yes," I breathe.

"Good." She snaps her fingers and disappears into the menagerie of lace and silk. She flings tufts of mesh and garters over the room divider. I stand there, attempting to keep my "maidenhood" intact and focus on my shadow cast by the candlelight. Limbs bent at ghastly angles and my figure elongated. My shadow looks broken.

Finally, she emerges with a parcel in her hands. She slices a sinister scissor through the red thread binding it, unfolds the paper, and holds up a sparse, red, lacy thing. A second piece follows it in her other hand; the whole width of it pinched between her spindly fingers. She places the scarce undergarments in my hands, forcing me to let my breasts go.

I tug the wisps of fabric onto my body, adjusting my full bosom into the feather-strong hold of the lace. There are no straps to support the weight of my breasts, and I fail to see the point of the garment. My nipples point like arrowheads against the sheer fabric, and I bet if I get any colder, they'll cut through the flimsy thing. I step into the matching bottoms, pulling them up over my flared hips.

She tweaks the edges of the flirtatious ruffles at my tail and sighs. "Dainty little thing. The best part of wearing clothes is getting undressed. Your husband will appreciate this tonight." She claps her hands.

Liriene almost snorts her tea out of her nose and starts coughing as Ivaia's glittering laugh heats my skin.

"Now, now! Maybe I should loan her the book, after all. You look like you might need it, Ker," Ivaia says.

"You'll do no such thing," Liriene hisses.

"What book?" I turn, still attempting to cover up what the garments fail to. The Weaver dives once more into a sea of parcels and garments.

"A *holy* book," Ivaia wiggles her eyebrows.

"That book is the damnedest thing on the earth," Liriene argues. "Written by a man, no doubt."

"Oh, no, fool." Ivaia places her steaming teacup in her lap. "Books like that are most definitely written by women."

Turning, I make eye contact with Attica as she brings out a heavy, wrapped garment I can only assume is the gown. Liriene shrieks and dashes over to the old woman's side, spilling tea as she goes. "Oh! It'll be such a relief to see something beautiful again."

I see lace and tulle and am instantly terrified this gown will resemble Ivaia's usual garb. Attica pulls the full length of the dress out and holds it up before me. I gasp. "Mother's dress."

"Yes! Its beauty reminds me of her. And the best parts of you. The more delicate side I know is still somewhere beneath the dirt under your nails—"

"And the blood on my hands?"

She frowns. "Yes, deep under that, too." She puts her hands on her hips and her smile gets a second wind. "I knew it had to be your wedding gown." She bows, flourishing her long blue skirts before returning to her seat by Ivaia. The Weaver helps me step under it and pulls it down over my head. I don't know how my mother dressed at court but among her kin in the forest, her clothes were plain. Neutral colors and soft fabrics. She never even put flowers in her hair like the other females. This dress looks like it belonged to someone else. Someone with a shocking flair for fashion. Someone royal.

The neckline sits off my shoulders. It clings to my ribs and upper arms by a band of elastic gray lace that covers me from collarbone to mid breastbone. The scarlet lace bralette beneath the gray, gasps out in frayed accents over my cleavage. Attica tucks every loose hint of what's beneath the gown back under the dress.

"Some things must be flaunted, some hinted, and some things must be a pleasant surprise."

From the bottom edge of the gray lace down to my feet, a gauzy flowing sheath pours over my curves, whispering around the edges. Delicate as spiderwebs and as silvery gray. The Weaver leads me to a tall-looking glass. Liriene helps her with my hair, tying it back into a loose, simple braid. Ivaia deposits heavy silver dangle earrings into my lobes, and a golden flower-shaped pin into my hair.

Liriene paints rouge to my lips, patting a lighter pink balm into my cheeks. I watch her lips curve as she focuses. Ivaia takes a turn at beautifying me, pressing a tinted powder into the discolored areas around my eyes. Then makes the same efforts with the wound on my shoulder from the Gryphon talon. She arms herself with a thin brush and paints thin black lines above my lashes.

"It'll distract from the scratches."

Last, she spritzes a heady perfume onto my throat and wrists. I am clean and put together, to say the least. My eyes are not as swollen as they were when I woke. I do not feel even a bit more special because I'm wearing my mother's dress. She's the one who forced me into it—along with her sister and mine. Is it ominous to wear a dead bride's wedding gown?

Dawn has blossomed into an effeminate morning with pink and gold skies and whipped, frothy clouds. An audience has gathered in the grass beyond the tent. Liriene disappears from my side, brushing a kiss to my cheek as she goes. Ivaia's somewhere in the crowd. My father is at the head of it all, and beside him are Indiro and Silas.

THE SUNDERLANDS

One look at the path before me and my feet go stiff as a corpse. I ignore the hushed crowd as they swivel their heads. Everyone's craning to see me from their places on the ground, sprawled out on blankets and woven mats. Focusing on my breathing, I try to take a step. Someone coughs their impatience and my temper flares. But I can't look for the offender in the mass of people. I can't look up. I can't move.

A hand grips me beneath my elbow and warmth returns to my body. My knees unlock and I lean into that saving grace of a touch. My eyes meet with Lysandra's. A moment of unexpected weakness threatens to wash away my painted face. Katrielle and Hayes were to wed, but instead of her walking down this path, she's buried near the end.

"I will never have the chance to give my daughter to her love, but I will walk with you," Lysandra says.

I take her hand, tucking her arm beneath mine, and we lean on each other for the full walk down the aisle of flowers and fake smiles. I kiss both her cheeks before she leaves me at the foot of the altar.

For the first time, I give Silas my attention. His sandy hair has been swept into a careful style. Triumph swirls in his honey-brown eyes. His back is straight, and he clasps his hands behind his back. The same way he stands on the wall. He's dressed in a dark gray patterned tunic with long, belled sleeves and sateen trousers. A jeweled blade is holstered to his hip on a thin, silver chain belt.

He holds out a silver ring. A marvelous ruby is perched atop the wedding band. My eyes do not shy away from the size, hue, and sparkle of the gem. I'm always in the mood for that color. I stop gawking and look at Silas. His lips part with a smile as he drinks in the vision of me.

A couple of days ago, this moment would have made me glow. Now, his smile makes me wonder if he's glad to finally own me. If I close my eyes, I can still see his face twisted with hurt and anger. The spit flying from his mouth as he threatened to have me burned. My stomach drops to my toes as he takes my hand. The thought of his right to claim me grates me when each of his fingers touch my skin.

"Children," My father holds his hands up between us. I look to him and catch his eyes on me. Indiro quirks a brow at me, eyes pouring over the length of my dress. He smirks and turns toward Liriene, who I realize is now behind my left arm. She turns rosy with pride at her careful, thoughtful work.

"We come before each other and the Gods to witness the union of these two souls."

I scan the front row of faces and find Ivaia wiping a tear from her crystalline eyes. Riordan flashes me one of his unconvincing smiles. Lysandra is beside them, patting her eyes with a handkerchief. My father drawls on about responsibility, patience, love, and joy.

A gentle breeze tousles the gown, proving the thin long sleeves useless. That silly fear about my nipples stabbing through the lace drags my eyes down to my chest for a quick check.

Kaius talks of knights, princesses, and other obsolete novelties as my attention slips back into the crowd. An array of faces stare at me as if they truly know me or are happy for me. Lucius' father is here, a perfectly odd example of why I'm shocked at the size of the audience since he tried to blame me for the death of the nine. The Vigilants that failed the nine are here to celebrate as if they have the right to, including Chamira. Even the Weaver came to see her fine work on display. All the faces moon at me. I remember their contorted expressions of anger a few days ago when they cursed me. Now, all of them sigh at our feigned romance. All except one.

A head or two taller than most in the crowd, his dark brown curls are bound in a knot atop his head. Wide-set shoulders and his sumptuous lips are dressed in a mocking smile that frays at the edges when we make eye contact. Fire jumps into those coal eyes and my face heats.

I look back to Silas as he decorates my finger with the silver ring. He's muttering something but there's a roaring of blood in my ears. My heart pounds against the frail lace and gauze. I close my eyes and focus on my breathing as my head fills with thoughts of the river. I feel as if my lungs are full of water.

I hate that I'm being forced to marry Silas. Even dead people have more control over my life than I do. I wish I could run out of my own skin. Be someone else, love someone else. And I hate Darius because I do not have the freedom to be with him if I really wanted to.

"Because you believe no one should want your cursed heart or because you've already given it to him?"

I turn back to my father and watch the words form in his mouth until I can hear them again.

"And so, daughter, I give you to Silas." He turns toward my husband.

"Silas, I give you my treasure, my youngest daughter. Do well to honor the gifts you receive this day. Swear to love and serve each other until Mrithyn takes one or the other."

Silas swears it, and I mutter an agreement, thinking of Riordan's advice. An ache boils in my stomach and my palms turn slick. I hate the sensation of sweaty palms—it reminds me of all the blood on my hands.

The ruby stares at me, a single drop of all I've shed. Too soon, Silas takes me in his arms and brings his mouth toward mine. He stops a breath away and waits. I close my eyes and meet his kiss with a tentative touch.

At first, the kiss is nothing like the possessive one he claimed from me by the river before our hunt together. But then reality hits. He is like a stranger to me and my chains have been handed to him. I grab him by the back of his neck and kiss him harder, searching for that promised safety on his tongue. Trying to take control of something. The right choice? No choice.

He wraps an arm around my waist and dips me low to the ground, finishing the kiss with a passionate flourish.

The crowd cheers, music flits into the air, and entirely new fears overrun my mind. The Sun creeps higher into the sky. Soon it will be high noon. Which means it's almost evening. Which means I'll soon face the horror of my wedding night. My mind races through the day, predicting every outcome. Whether I stay or run away now, it's too late and I know it. Here or anywhere, I'm fucking sold and owned.

He sets me back on my feet, keeping an arm around me as the festivities begin. I look at him and that victorious expression of his crumbles into worry. Slipping through the crowd with me in tow, he leads me to a tent on the outskirts of the camp. Music is the only thing that follows us, but I swear I feel a set of burning eyes tracking my every step as my... husband leads me away.

He stops at the entryway, holding back the curtain and giving me the freedom to cross the threshold. I run into the darkness of the tent, my lungs about to burst through my chest as I struggle for air. He follows me in and watches me pace the room. Hands pressed into my ribs; I reeducate myself on the art of breathing.

I realize this dwelling was set up for us. Most of my belongings are here. A newlywed couple's new home. A firepit, unlit, in the center of the room. A long dining table and in the back of the room—*don't look*. Again, my breathing becomes labored. Fuck, I've just expedited the thing I was trying to avoid.

His hands are on my shoulders and my body goes rigid. He turns me to face him, placing a finger underneath my chin. One look into his eyes and I decide we better get this over with.

I kiss him. Hard.

The scent and taste of him ravage my senses. I lose all hopes of my first time being with Darius. This kiss doesn't leave sparks on my tongue but is a clash of hot breath. It keeps my thoughts at bay, my fear—my anger.

"Keres." He pulls away.

"No." I grab him by his tunic, my hands looking for the ends of it and I lift it up over his head to reveal creamy skin and abs sleek as alabaster. He pushes me back, spinning me around to find the laces on the back of my dress.

"Eager, are you?" he snickers.

With quick fingers he undoes each strand, loosening the gown until it's one tug away from falling off me. But then he stops.

Why does he stop?

I turn back to him and separate the fabric from my skin, allowing my body to escape its hold. My breasts are suddenly heavy desire, the stupid red lace chafing them. He brushes his thumb over my nipple, staring for a moment. Ideas threaten to spring up in my mind, so I press my chest against his. He gently lifts the lace over my head, being careful not to rip it. But I don't care if he does.

My bared chest grazes against his and the warmth of him seeps into me. He pushes the bottoms down to my feet with his fingers and drags his hands back up my legs. I allow his touch to wander over every inch of me, closing my eyes and focusing on the feel of his soft fingertips.

"I need to know," he says.

"I have been with no man, Silas."

His jaw sets. He undoes his belt, dropping the dagger and silver chain into the heap of sateen. I open my eyes and look straight at his erection. The girth of it causes me to swallow hard.

I walk backward toward the bed. He follows, and I feel his eyes remain fixed on mine, but I just keep my stare on his body. The edge of the bed hits the back of my knees and his legs hit the front of them as I sit down. His cock is level with my breast, and I wrap a hand around it, examining the velvet softness and pulsing strength.

He lifts my chin. "You don't ever need to be afraid of me, Keres."

"You aimed your crossbow at me, and now this." I stroke his shaft and he bites his lip. He places his hands on his hips and arches his back, his body asking for me to touch him like that again.

"It wasn't the weapon that scared me, Silas. It was your malice. Your threats, the words, didn't scare me. The darkness in your heart did. The place they came from."

"You know darkness well enough."

I bite my tongue. Am I a hypocrite? I think of Thaniel and Liriene. All the things I've fucked up recently. The relationships I've damaged, the people I've killed. Again, I'm wishing I could shed my skin and be someone else. Someone that will love Silas for all he's worth and look upon this ruby ring as if it's a piece of his red heart instead of a drop of blood.

He rolls his head back to me and he takes my face in his hands, so I grip him harder.

"I was wrong." He growls. "I was jealous. I needed to make you mine the minute I saw him touching you." He kneels before me. "I felt the desire between you two. I wanted you to look at me that way. It should have been *me* you wrapped your long beautiful legs around." His hands run up my thighs, gripping onto my hips as he pours himself into Darius' place in my memory of that afternoon. His golden amber eyes shine with hunger, still swirling with jealousy. Yet, here he is. Kneeling.

A Silas I never expected to see.

He folds his hands before his bowed head, as if in prayer. "Keres, I swear never to do you harm, by my hand or my words—again." His eyes search mine in supplication. "Can you forgive me for shaming you in front of your family? For all of it?"

I pull his hands apart and take them in mine. I don't know what to say because I don't know what to feel. I'm naked and he's bowing to me.

His apology is cloyingly sincere. I'm trying *not* to think or feel or speak.

I place his hands around my neck and his eyes instantly come back to mine, only brighter this time. He kisses me and I feel him searching for that same safety I sought in his kiss at the altar. I lace my grip around his forearms and lean back onto the bed. He leans forward, raking his eyes over my body as he positions himself over me.

"Make me yours," I breathe, allowing his legs to come between mine as we move farther onto the bed. I glance down between our bodies and see the truth: I do not fear him. I don't fear his touch. I look down at the part of him that will anchor me in the storm of conflicting emotions and feel relief.

Death is sure. Mrithyn's power is constant—it's *life* that's earned my utter fear. Life is wild and unpredictable. It's not his hands opening my legs as he sits up on his knees between them. It's not that I'm splayed before him like a feast that daunts me either, and maybe those things should. Right now, my mind is reeling with anxiety, my stomach tightening, because of what life may do to me—is doing to me. How can I take back control over my life when I've just become someone's "until death" against my will? Is this a mercy in an unpredictable universe to be tethered to another soul? Is it a punishment to be forever bound by vows?

All too suddenly, his hand grazes across my most sensitive flesh. He massages me, using his fingers—then lowers his mouth onto me and uses his tongue. My mind goes numb as my body's overwhelmed with warmth.

He brings my body to its peak and sends me jolting over the edge. My body relaxes from the thrill and he takes the opportunity to enter me. At first, pain steals all the physical bliss. Slowly, he inches his way into my body, using his hands to continue bringing my body pleasure to mask the pain. He fully sheaths himself inside of me and my body threatens to break. I'm sure he's made me bleed, but he kisses away the pain and begins moving in the depths of me.

I could cry. I could laugh. I could blush. I could bite my lips. Milk and honey, salt and liquor. He takes from me while he gives, and it's a bittersweet exchange.

My body soon forgets the hurt, adjusting to his size. He feels the tension inside of me eventually ease and loosens his control, like a mare bucking at its reigns. Not knowing what else to do with my hands, I hold on to him. Digging my nails into his back as he thrusts harder and faster. My voice shatters, gasping and moaning for him not to stop, and he doesn't. He switches up his pace, angles my hips, and moves my legs to his shoulders with an understanding of what my body wants. I lose track of time; I lose track of where I end, and he begins. Only when he knows I'm satisfied does he ditch restraint and finish with me.

Our connection dissolves into a tangle of limbs. I rest beside him as he winds his fingers in my long white hair. We don't speak a word for a while, as I thought I'd prefer the quiet, but then the silence gets too heavy. My skin begins to crawl with the realization of what's changed. I lay staring at his impressive body as his hands wander still over the curves and edges of mine. I wonder what makes two people belong to each other. A piece of paper? A few governed words? Sex? The bed is as messy as my thoughts.

I must have frowned, staring at his beautiful face because he asks, "Are you still afraid?"

I look into his honey eyes. "Very."

Not afraid of you. Afraid of who I'm allowing everyone else to make me.

16: PILGRIM

"Keres," the wind slithers through the tent, gliding along my naked skin. My eyes open to darkness. Am I being channeled again?

I wriggle out from under Silas' heavy arm and cover him with the fur blankets. I scan the dark room. I slip into my new crimson satin robe.

"Keres," that voice says again. I go still as stone. My skin crawls. I decide quickly: Before the Oracle is on fire. Before she's screaming. Before my eyes shut before she claws them open again. I have to go.

Thunder explodes out of one cloud and slams into another. Lightning fills the sky outside, turning the room near white. The voice of the rain hushes my startled nerves. I fumble for a quill and parchment, sitting down at the table to write a note. I fold it, decorate it with his name and drop it on the pillow next to his. On the small table next to the bed, I notice a thick, old book. I allow myself a second to thumb it open and am more startled by the images within than anything else.

Tangled limbs; illustrations of passion. Sex, sex, and more sex. On every page. My eyes widen as I leaf through the depictions of positions and what I can only imagine are instructions on how to fold one's body into them. My mother's book collection included a few novels with erotic romance, and I relished in secretly reading them as I grew up. But this? *How to pleasure your lover with*—Oh. Too instructional for my tastes.

I flip the book shut and flinch at the sharp shift in Silas' breathing. I glare back at the book and remember Ivaia and Liriene's argument at the Weaver's tent. This must have been the book that horrified Liri and excited Iv.

I find new lace panties and traveling leathers to wear in the chest and wrap myself up for travel in the rain, tugging at the new clothes and pushing them into a large rucksack. My old rucksack is also here, and I realize so are my inherited belongings from Katrielle. I transfer my stuff from the old bag into the new one, tossing some things into the fire pit.

My weapons aren't here. I look at Silas' bare back rising and falling as he sleeps. I wonder if he arranged for my weapons to be taken from me. I wonder if he desires me to retire from my role of a soldier—to take up a more docile occupation. At that thought, I convince myself the bed is cold with him in it, and my feet carry me without hesitation outside to the dark and rain.

Cold assaults my senses, and heavy raindrops slick my leathers. I draw my crimson shawl over my head and closer to my chin, and pull the traveling cloak over it. Red frames my face, but the heavy dark halo of the hood shields me. I secure my rucksack straps under my arms and pick my way through tents to find my old home.

This dwelling with Silas isn't my home, I don't care how many of my belongings are moved into his possession—with me, his possession. Images of us from hours ago haunt my vision. Us.

What a strange new meaning the word holds. Two people wrapped up in each other, escaping the reality of their exchange. He doesn't love me, even if he thinks he does. He doesn't know me. And now that the exchange is over with, I allow the rain to wash the memories away. I stop outside my tent's entry. Everyone inside is asleep from the sounds or lack thereof. No candles are lit within. Still, I wait.

"Child," A voice forgetting to whisper draws my attention from behind me. I turn and face Attica, the Weaver.

180

"I knew you'd be here," she says. *Seriously, what is up with these old women hunting me down in the dark?*

How could she have known that I would be here? Does she know where I am going? I don't speak. I don't move.

"I brought this. You'll need it." She presses a parcel tied with a scarlet string into my hands.

"Your weapons are behind the tent in a crate."

Why is she helping me?

"Thank you, Attica."

"Don't listen to all the rumors there. Secrets." Shadows dance over her face, moonlight distorted by tree branches. I shudder.

"Keep your eyes open, always. The blood in your veins runs with secrets deep as rivers. Do not drown in them again."

The storm ravages the sky and I turn toward the screech of a falling bird. When I look back to her, she's gone.

I'm creeped out. I don't even want to take the time to consider her words, and thankfully I don't have time to because other thoughts surface: different guards will be on the wall tonight. Silas is asleep and if someone sees me leave, I have no reason to trust they won't send someone after me.

Indiro knew I would leave; he gave me the letter—The letter! I look down at the parcel Attica gave me before mysteriously dissolving into the night. The woman is odd.

I tear back the paper and rustle through the familiar fabrics. My clothes are here, all mended. I reach a finger into the folds of a pocket and find the letter is still tucked within. I'll read it later. Taking a moment to shove the parcel into my rucksack, I consider which part of the wall will be easiest to slip through. I skirt around the corners of my tent and find a crate with my weapons leaning against a tree, just like Attica said.

"Oh, Slip, Mama is here." I caress the bow I've named so fondly. I pocket my knives and daggers, sling the bow over my shoulder, and pause. My other weapon gleams in the moonlight, its curved blade bowing to me. Wrapping a fist around its short, iron hilt, I hold up the scythe in the rain and moonlight. It glitters, black and silver. I whoosh it through the air a couple of times and smile.

When Mrithyn claimed me, Ivaia gave me two things: The crimson shawl and this scythe.

"Fitting weapon for the White Reaper," she'd said. *"It's no legendary weapon, like the fabled Scythe of Mrithyn, but it'll do."*

I frown at the memory of her passing this deadly weapon into my clean, child-hands. She taught me to use it. I anchor the hilt to my belt and cover the blade with my cloak. I never wielded it once I fell in love with the bow. Slip belonged to my mother. My father gifted it to me when I turned eleven. It was the same day he informed me I'd marry Silas when I came of age.

Images of Silas' body, naked and panting as he claimed me as his own, drip into my head like raindrops. I push onward. Aiming my steps in a similar direction I walked to meet the boys by the river, I leave home.

Fording the river is never easy, especially not in a rainstorm. Lightning blazes through the sky and I pray it won't strike the water. Stepping across rain-slicked logs and slipping a few times makes me bitter. My feet are soaked and prickled, ice-cold by the time I get to the other side.

"Curse my kind for never wearing shoes." It's such a ridiculous nuance of our earth-worshipping culture. To don shoes is to imply you'd rather be off the earth than be one with it. It's a crime against our traditions. Arranged marriages and bare-footed escapades on merciless terrains, two things on my growing list of reasons to wish I'd never been born an Elf. Let's not forget the blight of our race to be forever subjected to Human terrorism. Wonder what we did to earn that one.

Thunder rebukes the night; lightning punishes its darkness. Eventually, the hour is cleansed by the storm and dressed in new robes the colors of dawn. My mind wanders as my feet follow the map beneath my cloak, which I've been shielding from the rain. I stop when the rain does. Pushing my hood back, I breathe in and absorb the fresh smell of the forest. I stretch the map out on a log and bring a little pouch out from under the cloak. I empty it of its quill and a jar of ink and scratch these words onto the back of the map:

> Under the darkened skies
> We lapse into our deepest thoughts.
> Midnight's canopy,
> Question of truth or lie,
> Is strung by stars
> Witnessing our faults.
> Then, interrupted by the dawn,
> Our guilt is absolved
> By the Sun.

With a satisfied sigh, I fold up the map and deposit it into the pouch with the quill and ink. Rising to my feet, I take a long look in every direction before turning straight ahead.

This way, a path has been cleared and is marked with looming flags and lanterns that don't seem to have been affected by the rain. Magic lights? The path stretches on for what seems like forever, winding through the trees. Magic pulses through the air and I figure it makes the path seem longer than it is. A mirage like the one that protects Ivaia's loft. I take a step and stop. The trees whisper.

I close my eyes and listen to them. They ask, "Why are you here, Our Child?"

My eyes flutter as I seek my answer. It eludes me, running into the

183

depths of my mind. The reply that follows comes out of a darkened, unexplored corner of my head. Do I answer aloud? Do I think it?

"I have come to think." On each bough, I find space to hang my thoughts. If the wind comes to carry them away, let them be lines of poetry whispered through the leaves.

"I have come to grow." Nestled amid the roots of these trees, I find depth in which to bury my troubles. With fear beneath my feet, I turn my face toward the light of the Sun.

"I have come to feel." My bones are as mighty as these trees. I am small but I am not slight, for I am from them. They are the ribcage of my home, the Sunderlands, and I am their beating heart.

"Reach," They say to me in their hushed tongue, "To brighter heights."

My eyes open, wild with the desire to see the earth; this pathway through the trees that tell me I am theirs. The earth vibrates beneath my feet, its energy tingling against my skin. Magic reverberates, echoing off every stone, every tree, each leaf. Filling my body with the hum of life.

Suddenly, I understand why we do not wear shoes. I understand and appreciate everything about what it means to be Elven. A Child of the Forest.

"The blood in your veins runs with secrets deep as rivers." Attica's warning whispers in my head again, but it's silenced by the music of my existence, a call of duty and purpose. An allure of belonging.

Wonder overrides my senses. Green is no longer a color. It's a feeling. The voice of the trees is no longer on the wind, but in my head, singing in my blood. My ancestors call to me through them. I fall to my knees, bowing toward the path that blurs and extends, and the illusion of it falls away into piles of leaves. A magnificent pearl gate stands before me.

It swings open. "Welcome home."

THE SUNDERLANDS

The trees are not trees at all. They're armored guards, tall and clad in silver and jade. Flag poles stretch into mighty pillars and banners unfurl with the insignia of the Ro'Hale Kingdom, a White Stallion. I rise to my feet. The sounds and sights grow more vibrant and melodic with every step I take. Scanning the guards, I count their heads and lose track. Time becomes obsolete. All that matters is I am passing over the threshold, from earth stained with blood on to this... holy ground.

The eyes of a guard peer at me as I pass him, his expression shielded by his helmet.

"Princess."

It's not a question. It's not a greeting.

Maybe I imagined it.

I do not answer; I dare not blink.

I walk into my Kingdom.

"You look just like her. Save the hair." Her mouth stays open too long on that last word. She laughs. The sound of it fills the room, a stark contrast to the fearful silence of her courtiers. She is ill-placed and mismatched in this heavenly throne room. A cacophony for the eyes. Beauty and horror, a vision and a nightmare: Queen Hero sits on a throne of mirrored glass, clothed head to toe in black and bones.

Beneath a ribcage vest, raven feathers tremble with her laughter. A collarbone twice the size of hers perches atop it like a statement necklace that juts off her jittering shoulders. Her gown plummets down to her feet, shifting from black feathers to black satin; shiny as oil. And her crown... *are those finger bones?*

"You lack her manners as well." She snaps her fingers. "My mother had impeccable courtesy."

A person wearing a mask that looks like the beak of a monstrous bird appears at her side. He holds out a silver tray which earns a wide, toothy smile from the skeletal queen.

I remember to bow, but her interest shifts to the ornate golden hand mirror on her servant's tray. Watching her reflection, she tucks rogue strands of platinum blond hair behind her long, pointed ears. She purses her blood-red lips, then smiles at herself, crystal clear eyes widening with pleasure at her wicked appearance. She angles the mirror and shifts from one dramatic expression to another. I straighten my back and take inventory of the room. I have a bad feeling already.

Everyone else is dressed as a beast of some kind. Furs, feathers, spotted hides, and scales. Snakeskin, cottontails, whiskers, and wings. The entire court. Except for one male whose expression is unphased and whose appearance remains unadulterated. His indigo hair and golden skin make an eye-catching combo, but his violet eyes and enticing, opalescent smile catch me gawking. I snap my attention back to Queen Hero, the lone huntress in this court of beasts. This lunatic apparently wears the trophies of her kills, if what Indiro said is true.

"I am sorry for your loss, Queen Hero."

"You must be my cousin." She says. "I could have called you sister for you look so much like the late Queen Herrona." She punctuates each word. "The white." She waves a hand around the crown of fingers and toes on her head to show she means my hair.

"Used to be black," I say.

"My mother's hair was also black. But that's not what I meant. It's white as snow, darling."

"I was marked by the God of Death, Mrithyn. As a child, I—"

"Mrithyn touched you." She gasps as if a God's touch were a scandalous thing. Her eyes pinch shut, and her hands fly to her forehead.

"I cannot imagine. Serving a God—mind, body, and soul." She wraps her hands around the rib bones she's wearing. "The magnanimity of Mrithyn."

She leaps to her feet, clapping her hands in the beaked face of her servant. "A service of worship for Mrithyn, for—"

She holds out a hand to me.

"Keres." I wring out the tension in my hands. "And I must protest." I bow again, not knowing what else to do.

Every eye in the room trains on me. I feel the weight of my cloak, the red of my shawl burning into me, the scythe on my belt biting into my hip.

"Keres." My name sounds perverse coming from her mouth. Like a curse. "Princess Keres Nyxara Aurelian, yes, I've heard about you. Once hidden in the shadows of the Sunderlands Forest, lured out by..."

"My Queen," a hoarse voice croaks from behind the beak mask. "The temple is occupied by the Oracle for the Veiling, you'll remember. We cannot hold a service for the Coroner."

She harrumphs and lifts her skirts, revealing ankle shackles strung with more bones that rattle like dastardly wind-chimes; and pivots away from the servant.

She paces in front of her throne, "Useless rituals. Girl goes blind and the whole kingdom goes mad." She mutters and I wonder if she realizes she's speaking aloud.

Courtiers exchange nervous glances. Hero stops. She scans the menagerie of faces.

"Ah, yes," she hisses. "How could I forget the Child? I've been planning to deal with her."

She stomps one tiny, ill-decorated foot in front of the other, closing the distance between her and me. I notice the mirror still in her clutches. The glass is pitch black.

Coming up to my nose, she says, "Forgive me. My temple is overwhelmed with religious pride and we cannot spare a wink of observance of the Child now. The Ritual is holy, you understand... shall I call you Princess or Coroner?"

I incline my head, breaking contact with her crystalline eyes. "Coroner will suffice. I am more predator than princess."

She raises her hands and laughs, and the court joins her in a choir of forced mirth.

"Someone, run and prepare a room for the Coroner! Squire, parcel and ink!"

The servant passes the requested writing materials to her as I look at a nobleman dressed like a bear and watch his beady eyes recognize the danger in mine. She scrawls out a note and hands it to a maid dressed as a bunny. They exchange glances before the bunny-girl leaves.

"I am here on my Pilgrimage," I say.

Queen Hero's smile falls off her face and the room turns dead quiet. "Were you not sent?"

"Only by tradition."

"Many come falsely claiming that they seek refuge or to offer me comfort. I know why you all come. To seek answers about me." She frames her face with her hands and shouts, "The Queen's gone mad." She's stomping in circles, "The Queen's mother is dead, and her sanity died with her."

Courtiers shrink back from her, looking to me as if they're embarrassed by her outburst.

"The Queen is wearing our skin as her rain cloak and our eyes as her jewels!" She feigns a sob, dragging her fingers down her cheeks and stretching her lower eyelids, "What's wrong with our beloved, Hero?"

She stops. Turning to look at me over her shoulder, uncanny serenity suddenly glazes those crystal eyes.

"Do you know what a shark is?"

I shift on my feet, browsing my memory for the picture I once saw drawn in a book. I've never seen the sea, but I've read about it and its creatures.

"A great predator of the ocean." I remember the rows of teeth, the black endless pits for eyes.

A moan of pleasure erupts in her throat. "Ah, yes. And when a shark smells blood…" She takes a step toward me, head rolling over her shoulders and eyes closed as she takes in a deep breath through her nose. "They go absolutely mad."

"Murder," I say.

"Yes," her eyes flash open, the color of lightning. "My mother screams to me from her grave. Murder! Murder!"

All I can do is stare as she floats toward me like one of Nerissa's monsters in the watery depths.

"I smell blood," she says.

And so, she's gone into a frenzy.

"Have you come to see if it is true—what they say about me?" She frowns.

"No."

"Are you here to contend for my throne?" She bows toward me, an arm sweeping back toward the throne, a mischievous smile daring me to say 'yes.'

"No. I'd rather ensure you don't lose it."

She seems pleased with her little interrogation, but something else bubbles in her eyes. She rubs her fingers along the collarbone at her neck and adjusts the crown atop her sleek hair.

"A Reaper of Souls knocks on my door and promises me safety? Understand if I laugh, my dear." She bounces on her toes and folds her hands behind her back. "Welcome to the land of your mother and mine."

Notably, Queen Hero and I are of similar build. We look so alike we could be sisters. More alike than Liriene and I. This kingdom belongs to our blood. I feel the likeness of her and our mothers swimming through my veins. Along with the secrets, as Attica warned me.

It's so strange, this immense and terrifying presence bottled up in a beautiful, dangerous girl. Beneath the bones and the plume of black. In those eyes, I see a girl as natural as any. She circles around me like a vulture, taking me in. I steal a glance at the throne. If the Gods had desired it, I could have been in that seat. Raised here at court and dumped on to it when I came of age. We share the same blood—we are not so different.

I'm the servant of Death and she's wearing bones. I hunt Human terrorists she hunts her mother's murderer. She rules with fear and intimidation. I am some men's worst nightmare. I see through the facade, straight through the maniac to the girl beneath the exoskeleton, the one who's trying to do right by the loved one that she lost. I see myself in Hero, and I cannot look away from our reflections in the mirrored glass throne. Bloodlust and all, we are the same.

Here I am, wading into the watery grave she's been living in. I know what's beneath her surface. I've drowned in these waters before. Her eyes exude what I've seen only in a mirror. Something I used to call "me," but now in her presence, loses its name.

What would the Gryphons have thought if they came and found her courtiers adorned in the skins and wings of beasts? Something besides the Gryphon King and Osira called me here. I can feel it when I look at Hero.

Hero makes me smile. With her talk of monsters and her crown of bones. Unrivaled power looks good on our family's Mirrored Throne; fearsome and tantalizing. Murdered or not, Herrona's death turned this princess into a Queen I can respect—relate to. Power has never been frightening to me. Raised in it and by it, it's natural to me. I've only ever feared the curse on my soul.

, Looking into Hero's eyes I remember Liriene's fear of the corruption power engenders. All my second life, I've been fighting the Death Spirit for control. Its hunger and ilk feel like weakness—an affront to my morality. Fear is warranted.

Queen Hero turns heads, and some she sends rolling across the floor. Her power is different: it's what holds her spine so straight and tall. It's what clears her throat before she speaks and brightens her eyes. Hero possesses a power too—one I desire.

"I am home," I think and I don't know if it came from the Death Spirit

or from myself.

She's back again, leaning forward over her toes, looking deep into my eyes. Hers are silver and clear as water. I imagine her pupils are the holes of geysers to let out that energy within her. Such an odd color staring into mine.

"So alike," she breathes.

I gather she means alike to her late mother, Queen Herrona. My mother's eldest sister.

"She had eyes like yours. Green as envy."

I tilt my head, not knowing whether that was a compliment.

"Rydel," her voice cracks. She turns away from me, tilting as if she might faint suddenly. Her free hand trembles at her brow, her other wrapped around the mirror hilt with white knuckles. She pales, as if with fear. She lifts the looking glass again, scouring its icy black depths for comfort I cannot see.

A breath later she turns back to me. The blue-haired male is at her side now, and she calms the instant his fingertips touch her elbow.

"Will you come to dinner?" She sighs.

I nod, acknowledging the male's violet eyes briefly and trying to disregard the weird episode of panic.

With that she twirls on her toes, snapping her fingers. The servant returns to her side, allowing her to lay the mirror back on its bed of velvet like a sleeping babe.

I turn and accidentally make eye contact with a courtier dressed as a wolf. His eyes are mismatched colors, and a snarl lingers on his lips.

Someone taps me on the shoulder: A servant with a headdress like rabbit ears, a necklace of whiskers, and a fluffy white and gray dress.

"Your Highness, please follow me to your chambers." She beckons with a finger.

Watching Queen Hero lean into Rydel's undivided attention, I follow the maid past them and into a corridor off the side of the throne room.

Without the distraction of Queen Hero and her court of beasts, I'm awed by the immeasurable splendor of the Ro'Hale Palace. When I stepped through the Kingdom gates this morning, a chariot decked with pearls delivered me to court. From my window, I'd glimpsed rolling fields and orchards, a sapphire lake, miles of village houses, and the spire of a mountain-hewn temple. The views increased in beauty from the tree line to the palace walls. A resplendent jewel of a kingdom nestled in a groove of the mountain range back-boning the Sunderlands. A hidden wonder. Somehow, all those sights, the revelation of the land of Ro'Hale, pale in comparison to the palace.

The walls are white marble, encrusted with opals and diamonds. The fixtures are pure gold and the accents are a rich jade stone. Dazzling white and sleek green, everywhere I look. White like my hair, green like my eyes. I shake my head at the notion I am made of this kingdom.

Golden doors line the corridor which curves off into a sheen staircase that climbs the walls and into a tower. Nadia, the voluptuous bunny servant trails ahead of me. Her dress puffs off her wide hips as she sways her steps. Her luxurious auburn locks put Liriene's to shame— bouncing, frisky curls. Nadia must be more than a servant if she's walking around the kingdom like this.

She flashes her sapphire blue eyes over her shoulder and her sultry voice tells me, "All yours." She splays her hand on a golden door.

I swallow back my words, blushing at the raw sensuality of her persona. I stalk toward the chambers but before even my eyes can cross the threshold, Nadia's got her cashmere soft hand around my wrist. My eyes go first to the place where we're connected, then to the differences between us. Looking down past our joined hands I notice the dirt coating my bare feet, and my overgrown toenails. Her feet are primped from heel to glossy toenail. Her heels touch and all her toes fan out elegantly. She curtsies, lowering so I'm forced to look into her impossibly blue eyes once more. Her smile leans sideways as she brushes my filthy hair back behind my ear.

"Hope I'll see more of you," she says in a husky whisper.

I try to think of something to say but what does one even say to that—to this kind of girl?

Fuck.

"In the pleasure gardens." Her nose crinkles when she smiles. Her eyes do too. She's older than me.

"Perhaps," I say. My voice is rougher than hers.

She giggles and strokes the underside of my hand with one of her dainty fingers. I withdraw my hand and scratch my palm instinctively.

"I hope you'll come." Her eyelashes are so long and thick. I've never even noticed my own.

With that, I turn into my room and slam the door behind me.

Snapping out of my daze proves impossible when I see the room. I only have one word for it: luscious. Never thought I'd say that about a room, or anything other than a sexy mouth. Darius. I shiver at the memory of his kisses in the river and try to replace it with the rightful memory of my husband.

Husband. I shake my head and look around.

The bed. Gods above. I strip out of my soaked traveling clothes, kicking them into a pile near the door. I want them burned. I double-check the lock on my door. Like a child, I run to the bed and sink into it. It feels the way I imagine a cloud would. No. Like—unlike anything I can dream up. My standard for beds rises to the stars. My memories of the wedding bed's satin and fur chafe my mind like gravel on knees compared to this bed. I want to luxuriate in this bed forever and forget—

I sit up straight, hands fisted in the sheets.

Katrielle, Hayes, Cassriel, Lucius, Meir, Nilo, Jeren, Leander, and Oryn.
How can I lay here? Am I not here because of their deaths?

I am, but will I never rest because of their memory? I launch from the bed, shedding my undergarments, and run naked into the adjoining washroom. A separate bathing chamber? I stop short and my curves jiggle. It smells divine in here. I cross my arms and cover my breasts with my hands. If I were a Goddess, I'd want a temple just like this room.

Your niece sits on that throne—half her mind gone out the widest window.

"Stop it!" I shut my eyes and take in the fragrance and warmth. Someone has already drawn a hot bath, and steam is spilling over the edges of the bathtub. I half remember Hero ordering someone to ready my room. I feel filthy, as if I'm coated in blood. I step into the water and slowly sit, melting into a puddle of conflicting emotions.

I pluck a poofy sponge off the gold and marble table beside the tub, and the princess scrubs away the scales of the predator. Blood, sweat, and tears. I shed them into the tub.

For the first time in my life, I sit in a bath of water and refuse to think about drowning. I focus on stemming the memories of my entire life thus far. The thought of Liriene silly with excitement over my wedding dress makes me smile, and then I banish it. Wash it away. Don't think about it or you won't enjoy this glorious fucking bath.

An hour or so later, my stomach reminds me of Hero's invitation to dine with her. Unhappily, I also remember Nadia's invite to the... what'd she call them? Pleasure gardens? I wonder what grows there. I want to go to dinner but I'm lying naked on the bed, polished and soothed. I deign to look at my pile of filthy clothes. Never again do I want to wear them. I walk toward another set of doors, dizzy with perfume and the scent of the candles.

I swing both doors back and squeal. Rows of gowns on my-sized figurines. Aisles of dresses and skirts, blouses and shawls. Coats, hats, and gloves. Shelves—a library of jewelry. I wander into the closet that rivals the throne room in size. Fixed to one wall is a drawing that looks as if a child made it. A little girl wearing a crown beside a woman holding gold scissors. The woman's eyes are red. I wonder why such a disturbing sketch made it onto the gold-leafed wall.

At the center of the room, a velvet couch sprawls out between two round stone tables. On one table is a tray; a single note folded upright with Keres written on it, a bouquet, and a hand mirror that almost matches Hero's. On the other table—a lonely pair of shoes.

I squint my eyes at the odd find. Shoes? In the dressing chamber of an Elven Princess? I pick up the note addressed to me and read it. I assume Hero wrote it, remembering her hand off a letter to the bunny maid.

Keres, these were your mother's chambers. Without previous notice of your arrival, I had my servants speedily prepare the chambers for you, so please understand the dust. My servants will ready the bathing room at the ring of a bell, and the closet has remained untouched since your mother last had use of it. I expect you'll be wanting to explore your inheritance, but we must talk as soon as possible. In private.

Memories of my mother fill up my head as I look around the room. Things I haven't thought of in years come dancing back into my brain, twirling around my skull as I spin around in her closet. Dizzy, I stop and look again at the tray. I'm assuming the servant Hero sent ahead of me is who left a map tucked beneath the note. It's marked.

My mother's riches and those damned shoes will have to wait. They are beautiful, bizarre as they are: made of mirrored glass like the throne.

Queen Hero seems to be on the menu tonight since she's strewn across the dining table. Her skirts are a mess above her knees, and all former bones have been removed, save the one she picks her teeth with. Her platinum tresses are tangled with eating utensils, and her limbs are draped over plates. One leg is bent over the other, toes nearly dipping into some sort of stew. Rydel sits near her feet, staring up her skirts.

She leans up on her elbows at my approach. "Ah, Keres. Hope you're starving."

"For food, yes." I smile, gesturing to her.

She cackles, pushing down her skirts and giving Rydel a mischievous glare. "Thank the Gods you don't have an appetite for me." She kicks a buttered roll across the table at him, which lands in his lap. He dips it in honey and licks it, never breaking eye contact with her.

"If anyone ate you, they'd get bone-splinters in their gut," I say.

She snickers and sits up on her knees on the table, pointing a spindly finger at the chair she wants me to sit in. I take my place and check the table for food she hasn't dipped her toes in.

"Try the lemon cake."

"Cake before meat?" I ask.

"Cake, always, always, always."

I laugh and begin spooning food onto my plate, being sure to cut myself a large slice of lemon cake. I love lemons.

"Just like her!" She points a knife at me, smiling. I know she means her mom and I wonder how long the list of comparisons will be by the time I leave court.

"My mother too," I say around a mouthful of cake.

I catch Rydel staring and try not to stare back, but I don't know whose eyes are safer.

Hero crawls across the table toward me. "Keres, cousin. We must speak openly with each other. I must tell you something."

"I read your note. The one in the dressing closet."

"Good." She keeps crawling.

I look down the table at Rydel who's shamelessly watching her backside.

"Did you get the map?" She stops. I stop. He looks from her to me.

"Yes." I chew slowly. "The Temple. That's where you want me to go?"

"Not me. *Her*."

I lose my appetite and put my forkful of cake back on the plate. My eyes itch where the skin has been healing.

"Who?" I ask although I think I already know the answer.

"Osira. The Oracle Child. Her priest, Dorian, sent me a letter and told me to direct you to the temple. You hadn't yet arrived, but he says they saw you coming. I didn't know what they meant by 'the White Reaper' as they called you in the letter. I realized when I saw your hair."

"She knows I'm here?" My voice drops and I lose focus on Hero as I process.

"She knows *all*." Her eyes glaze over and fury boils beneath the hazy surface. I know that look anywhere: Pain.

"Well, not all. She doesn't know—or she won't tell me. The little witch," She mumbles.

"Who killed your mother," I finish for her, and the shield drops from her eyes.

Unbridled tears spill onto her cheeks and she crawls towards me faster, knife still in hand. When she's nearly on my plate, she stops and sits up with her knees folded to her chest. Her arms wrap around them and she keeps a white-knuckled grip on the knife.

"That's what I've needed to tell you. No one believes me. But I know it." She points the knife at me with a killer's resolve and I remember Ivaia calling her a child. She's no child. She's lethal as a viper.

"No one can help me find the answer. You're the Coroner. You rule the Realm of the Dead. You must help me—"

"Queen Hero, I—"

"My mother was murdered. I know it. And her murderer is alive. I hope he's praying to every God in the Pantheon, because I will find him. Even if I must uproot the Sunderlands Forest. You believe me, don't you?"

We stare into the depths of each other for what seems like a lifetime and I finally understand what we have in common. It's so obvious now. It's written all over her face. I've seen it in my looking glass. That raw pain and fury—the guilt. I can feel it tugging on my heart, the common thread tethering my spirit to hers: We've both watched our mothers die at the hand of a man.

"Yes." The Death Spirit answers in my head.

"I believe you, Hero," I say.

18: THE ORACLE

Whatsoever is in His hand, is still in ours.
For He is in all and all are His.
All must pass from Life to Death,
from our dear Enithura to her beloved Mrithyn.
So we let go at the time He calls,
To rejoin those lost when He's claimed us all.

Instead of jumping headlong into that paradisaical bed, I sit on the carpeted floor of the closet, tortured with infernal memories, staring at the damning evidence that I never knew my mother: Her shoes.

I've got torn parcel paper in a fist, its red string tied around my wrist. Three handwritten letters stare up at me from the floor. One written in my mother's hand, giving me away to Silas. The note from Hero. And the third given to me by Indiro.

Candlelight dances in the reflection of the shoes. The bouquet anoints the room with a strong but sweet fragrance that is beginning to irritate my nose. I look haggard; exhausted to a new level. But the memories won't subside. I allow them to pass before my vision and play out on the mirrored surface of the shoes. They throw themselves at me, glinting with candlelight and hurting my tired eyes. I remember and remember and remember. And then the memories stop, a startlingly finite list of things I can recall. I can count them all on two hands:

Her beauty: eyes, green like mine, and her hair, golden as the sun.

Her voice, soft as rain, telling me not to worry my little raven-haired head about what Liriene was doing running off into the forest with Silas and their friends. Assuring me I didn't need to go along.

Taking me for walks through the gardens to pick lemons and tomatoes.

Sheltering me.

Singing to me.

Dying for me...

Swimming with her in the river.

Drowning in that river and trying to get to her—to save her from that evil man she wept for forgiveness from.

Her bowing before Mithyn, begging Him to take her instead, to allow me to walk back into Life. Giving me to Him, telling Him to make me His servant so that I might have another chance at life. A life dedicated to Him.

The memories end there. My chance of ever truly knowing the woman who gave her life for me is dead—stone-cold and irrevocable. I was so young when my life ended, and when it began again. Her sacrifice made me into a lone guardian, fated to walk the shoreline between the world of life and the waters of death. To ford the river time and time again. To leave her behind every fucking time.

I've never grieved her until Hero looked into my eyes and dipped her question into my mind. *"You believe me, don't you?"*

I recognized the pain, the immensity of her loss, the depth of her grief, the unslakable thirst for revenge. And memory by insufficient memory, I began to feel all those things too.

As if I've just woken up after years of dreams, I realize everything I should have been feeling all this time. And I, too, smell blood.

Mrithyn is here. I feel Him all around me, his whispers dancing along my spine. His promises twirling in my head and making me dizzy with guilt, regret, and grief. These hollow memories clash with His plans for my future, my destiny.

"We are His chosen servant," the Death Spirit says, but my memories tell me I was an accident. I shouldn't have revived that day. My mother shouldn't have died.

Two glass shoes, left behind on a marble table, are walking all over my mind, imprinting me with truth: I never knew her, I never will. A question I've never dared ask before awakens in my thoughts. Was it my fault?

For the first time in my second life, I think of the figure who killed her and remember to hate him. Every drop of blood running through my veins poured into me by my mother rushes to my head—filling it with thoughts more insane than Hero. I wish I could go back in time. I curse the rock on which I slipped, the other on which I split open my skull in the fucking, wild river. I yearn to drive my knife into the heart of the one who did the same to my mother before my innocent eyes. I wish—

"Curse your God and die."

I bolt upright, hand clutching the paper against my chest. My heart is pounding. My throat tightens when I ask, "Who's there?"

I wait, the answering silence roars in my ears.

Throwing the paper on the floor, I stomp around the room, checking every aisle, every window. I look under dresses; I open cabinet doors. I glare back at the shoes.

I'm alone. I look at the drawing of the woman with red eyes and golden scissors.

A tree branch taps on the glass window, but I feel it on my back.

Fuck fuck fuck fuck fuck.

I snatch up the letters, huff out the candle, steal a random garment for tomorrow, and bolt. No more closet, no more shoes, no more memories. No more mother.

Ensuring the closet doors are closed, I catch my breath and then fling myself into bed. It doesn't comfort me. My palms and upper lip are sweating, and my stomach is quivering somewhere by my toes. Goddess of Death they call me. I can handle gore, violence, and dirt. I draw the line at creepy.

"*So, I'm not creepy?*" The Death Spirit asks, mockingly.

"You're just annoying," I answer aloud like a complete psycho.

For hours I try to get comfortable to no avail. I reread the letter from Indiro to distract myself. I unfold it and mull over his elegant cursive script as I pace the room. Shocked every damn time I hit the last word.

Keres, I need you to find someone at court. Her name is Seraphina... She is the mother of Silas and was your mother's dearest friend. When your mother discovered she was carrying you inside her, she journeyed back to court to see Seraphina and arrange your marriage to Silas .

Not for the reasons you've believed. Silas was originally meant to be Liriene's knight. Your mother wanted them to wed. But when you sparked inside her belly, she changed her mind. Seraphina agreed to Silas being raised and groomed to be your husband. And I was to swear an oath to Liriene instead. To become her knight.

Be a lamb and ask the bitch what Resa told her. It's eating me alive and I haven't had the bollocks or time to confront her. I doubt her husband, Ser Solas, would know of their womanly dealings. I want the truth. Why did Resa dismiss me when I served her well all her life? Why did she pass me off like a pelt for barter? Please, little witch. Help.

Another cruel reminder I knew nothing of the woman who bore me. I get up and pace the room. Did mother switch us? She gave away her beloved knight to Liriene? Attica was on to something with her "secrets deep as rivers" warning. Dawn sneaks through the bedroom windows, tapping me on my shoulders. I turn and draw the curtains but open them again when I think of that voice. *Curse my God and die?*

I stare out at the sky where Oran, God of Light, chases his elder sister, Adreana, into a corner of the heavens. I need answers, I need truth. I need... a sliver of light in my dark world. Oran toddles into the sky, dressed in an elysian shade of pink. The giddy Sun peeks over the horizon, topping the spire of the mountain-hewn temple like a flame on a wick.

I need answers. I must deliver this letter to Seraphina. Maybe when she meets me, my mother-in-law can point me in the direction of Paragon Kade. I also need to know what's going on with the armies. Arias was right. Something is wrong at court but not with Hero.

Unfortunately, I understand the blight of her mind, but I don't see why she's abandoned the clans. If I cannot yet avenge my mother, I can certainly try to help her avenge hers, and then maybe she can help my people. Maybe she will revoke Ivaia's banishment. I must keep Hero safe and on the throne.

How can I be the only one bothered by the late Queen's demise? It makes no sense that they all dress up like animals and cower. No one tries to help her, and none believe her. Have they denied her beliefs enough to drive her to start hunting those who oppose her? I sense a higher power at work here. I need to get to Osira first and find out what I'm up against. This kingdom is so tainted with bloodshed and corruption, I can taste it. It's metallic on my tongue. The delicious tinge of darkness and power.

Without a wink of sleep in that blissful bed, I dress up in the blue, ankle-length dress I snatched from my mother's trove. A lighter shade of blue lace wraps around my wrists at the end of its long sleeves. The same detail breathes against my skin at the scalloped neckline and against my ankles. I tie my long hair up with a satin ribbon and push glittering jewels into my earlobes.

The ruby is standing up on my silver wedding band at full attention. Silas hasn't come after me. It's my second day away. A hard, short laugh hits the back of my teeth and I swallow it with the thought of Darius. Now is not the time to think about either of them.

I fold up Indiro's letter as many times as it will bend and nestle it between my breasts— which look amazing in this dress. One new thing I've learned about my mother is she knew style, and she had exquisite taste.

The corridor is empty, and no voices carry along the gilded walls from either direction. I step out and close the chamber doors behind me, trying not to add too much noise to the strange silence.

"I think you'd be a Nymph. Hmm, or one of the Fae."

My back hits my chamber door when I feel her breath near my ear, and I wheel around.

"Fuck! Why did you sneak up on me?" I hold my hand to her throat.

Seriously? Nadia the bunny bitch got the better of my senses?

"Or better yet, *how* the fuck did you sneak up on me?"

"I know a better use for the word fuck." A smirk smears her mouth. "Do you always say it this often or am I bringing it out of you?"

"You certainly brought this out of me," I tighten my grip on her throat, allowing her to feel my fingernails mark her pristine skin.

She may have surprised me, but she didn't beat my reflexes. I don't even want to know why she's calm and comfortable with a hand around her neck. She didn't even flinch.

"I could bring a lot out of you. Things you didn't know you had in you." She breathlessly leans into me and I'm the one who flinches, pulling back. Is she crazier than Hero?

"Nymph or Fae?" I divert, remembering her words.

"For the Pleasure Gardens." Her eyes follow my hands as I plant them on my hips. "I invited you last night, don't you remember? They're open again for our delight."

"How could I forget, Nadia?"

"Hmm... *and* she knows my name." She looks me up and down.

I watch her, raising a brow as she holds up two items. "Nymph or Fae?" She asks.

I look down at the elaborate face masks. One is a blue painted face that resembles a woman, except there're scales along the temple and gills cut into the wood in front of where my ears would go. Yellow mesh covers the eyeholes that would completely hide my own eyes but allow me to see.

"Water nymph?" I ask, pointing to the blue one.

"Yes." She bares her teeth at me, holding it out.

I lean in and reach for the one she's holding close at her side, closing the distance between us.

"Don't you ever fucking startle me again or I'll rip your throat out by accident next time."

She closes her mouth but purses her full red lips as she flashes me those damn blue eyes.

I tie the knot behind my head and fasten the Faery mask on.

"What's a Fae?" I ask.

"Never heard of them?" She ties the water nymph mask behind her red curls and then seizes my hand.

"Nope." I become acutely aware of my sweating palms.

Her hand snakes up my arm and she hangs onto my elbow as she steers me down the corridor.

"Powerful and mischievous Faeries."

I laugh. "Oh, like from the bedtime stories?"

"From the nightmares."

I furrow my brows, but she wouldn't know it because of my mask. I didn't even look at the damned thing. I noticed the blue one first.

I pull myself out of her grip. "So, how do I look? Like something from a nightmare?"

Of course, I'd pick that mask, that persona, and not even mean to.

She laughs and saunters past me, flaring her hips with her strides. "Positively demonic."

I laugh again. For real this time. "Might be. You don't know."

"I like her." The Death Spirit chuckles too.

"Hmmm, I think I do know." She widens her eyes. "You must be a devil if you look so divine."

"That was lame," I chide.

"It was the truth." She tilts her head to the side.

"Gods and devils, they're real." She lowers her voice. "Fae and nymphs and spooky voices… they're just fun."

I jolt at the mention of spooky voices. There's no way she knew about what I heard last night. She glides down another hallway that takes us deeper into the center of the palace. I follow her, not quite sure where this conversation or her directions are taking us. Another set of doors and another long hall.

"Monsters aren't real, Keres." She opens one last white latticed door and sunshine floods into the dimly lit hall. I follow her across the threshold and into a garden. "They're just people wearing masks."

"Princess Keres," A sultry male voice stops me from replying or even getting a good look around. It's noisy, and the sun is beating down on us. Sweat beads on my brow. Rydel steps out of a conversation with two masked people. He's not wearing a mask.

"Welcome to the Pleasure Gardens!" He draws my attention before I can analyze their putrid green, bug-like masks.

I follow his outstretched hands and finally drink in the truly baffling party. Nobody is an animal of prey anymore. They're all creatures of myth. Things I've never seen before in any book. Things I've only ever heard about in Attica's stories.

"Some tea? You're just in time," Rydel offers.

"Oh, shit!" Nadia stomps a tiny foot into the lush grass as she checks her pocket watch. "I'm late. Must go meet my sisters! Bye, Keres." She grabs me and pulls my mask to hers, feigning a kiss. She runs off into the swaying crowd of monster masks.

"Bye." A little off-balance, I turn back to Rydel. He folds his hands behind his back, awaiting my reply.

"Greetings, Rydel. How are you this morning? Yes, tea would be delightful." I try my best to sound like a noble and not think of Riordan and Ivaia.

He plucks a bone-white teacup off a banquet table full of them and pushes it into my hands. I take a sip from it.

"I'm sorry, this *isn't* tea." I cough at the sharp sweetness of the liquor.

He cracks up laughing. "We're calling it Faery wine." He gestures to the other partygoers but no one notices.

"Have you heard of the Fae before?"

"Recently, yes." I sip from the teacup again, already feeling dizzy. "Why do you call it that? Is it magic?" I scowl at the innards of my cup, again forcing thoughts of Ivaia and Riordan to the bottom.

"According to lore, if you drink or eat anything in the Faeries' realm, you belong to them."

"And so, I drank from your cup. Do you think to own me now?" My mouth loosens and I smile at my own brashness.

He opens his arms. "Only to get you really drunk. That's exactly what Faery Wine will do."

I smack my lips together after swallowing the last drop and clumsily placing my empty teacup back on the table. "Where's Queen Hero?"

"Do you wish to see her?" he asks.

I don't know why I asked. I'm supposed to be doing something right now...

"She's installed a chaise for me behind her seat at the head of the table." He gestures to the banquet laden with teacups. It stretches on throughout the Pleasure Gardens, most likely to the other end of it. Hero's chair is not even in sight. An array of ghoulish and impish masks blocks the view. People laugh. Someone juggles. Two girls are kissing, their masks on the ground by their feet. I look back to Rydel.

"Did you mean to say 'beside'?"

"No, *behind* her chair. So that I might always be near to her ear, but out of sight when it matters."

"And why would you need to be in either place?" I fold my arms across my chest, and his eyes follow the movement to my breasts. Maybe they look too good in this dress. Or maybe he's already feeling the liquor. I am.

"You're a vision." He smiles, still staring below my eyes.

"You're her adviser then?" I attempt to regain his attention.

He flashes me a tempting smile. "No. I am an ambassador. From Elistria."

My brows shoot up. "Oh. I thought you were from my kingdom."

Fire spews out of the mouth of someone's dragon mask, followed by the audience's applause. The smoke draws my eye to the orchestra of stringed instruments buzzing like insects in a balcony above.

He shrugs and walks closer. "You'll find that one's allies are often closer than you think, and too often one's enemies are closer."

I look into his violet eyes. No one can deny he is stunning. His golden skin is so rosy in the sun and his smile beams brighter. He's dreamy. He takes on the light of day like a silken robe... and *oh, fuck, I am drunk.*

"Are you implying you're an enemy of our kingdom?" I ask, trying to rub my eyes but forgetting about the Faery mask.

"As much as you are. As well as you, I am religious. My loyalties lie with the Gods above any mortals, queen or consort." His voice is too calm and too loud all at the same time. The glare of the sunlight off the clouds and sparkling off the amber liquor in the teacups nearly blind me. I must get out of here, but he just mentioned the Gods. My thoughts hiccup.

"Where is..." I feel faint. "What." It doesn't come out the full question I intended it to be.

"Coroner, are you feeling ill?" I feel Rydel's radiating presence warming my backside. His arms are around me. Dizzy and disoriented, I force myself to refocus but find no comfort in the jeering, malicious faces spiraling around the garden. My head swings back and I catch my breath as my full weight drops into Rydel's arms. Everything goes dark.

A moment later, I'm awake. Still in the Pleasure Gardens, still surrounded by organized chaos. What the fuck am I supposed to be doing right now? My head hurts.

"Good morning," Rydel seems overly happy. I focus on his violet eyes.

"Keres," I hear his voice, but his mouth isn't moving. *"You're in danger here."*

I blink at him. His smile fades as his eyes bore into mine and his voice slips into my thoughts. *"Unless you tell me the truth."*

"I'm no liar," I think back.

"Are you here to harm Hero, or to help her?" I feel his fist tighten around my wrist.

"You answer that first."

His jaw drops but jumps back up into a wide smile. *"I am here to serve our kind."*

That's a thought the Death Spirit and I can both agree on. *"I am as well."* I start to feel the urge to break eye contact and use my voice.

"Where is Hero's knight?"

"She killed him."

"Where is Paragon Kade?"

"So inquisitive, you are."

"If you want to help Hero, help me," I goad.

He stands and pulls me to my feet.

"If you want to help Hero, help Osira." He releases me from his embrace and all memory of what I should have been doing comes back. My senses too. Reeling from the jolt into instant sobriety, I lose all my Faery wine on the sweet-smelling grass. He hands me his handkerchief. I wipe my mouth and he lifts a hand to insist I keep it. As I turn to go, I overhear someone suggesting the hibiscus tea instead of the chamomile to someone else.

"It's delicious."

The man lifts his mask to take a sip.

"Did you hear anything else about the beast? It has overrun Trethermor," The other man says, daintily gesturing with his own half-full teacup. Fully sober.

I try to catch any slur in their words, leaning closer just as the other spits out his tea. "The apostates, have they fled?"

I take a step back and look to the other for a hint of a smile at tricking his friend into drinking the Faery wine.

"No one knows. How's the chamomile?"

"Truly delicious. Spot on, chap." He smacks his lips together before kissing his cup for another sip.

"Glad I take my tonics from Mormont here in the castle. Poor sods. Wow, but this chamomile is beautiful. What an aroma!"

"Blessed for the Veil ritual, I heard from Arlessa."

I look back to Rydel but he's gone. No one else in the Pleasure Gardens appears to be drunk or sick. What the fuck? I snatch the teacup from the blubbering idiot and finish it off—

"Oy! Miss, there's plenty to go around."

A girl beside me cracks up laughing.

I push the empty teacup back into his still-poised hands and stomp off.

Did Rydel fucking poison me? Was it magic? I don't know who he truly is or what his powers are but after that drunken mind-fuck, I do know one thing: that was the best chamomile tea I ever had.

I run from the Pleasure Gardens and when I'm far enough away from the freak show, I remove my mask and look at it. My anger melts. It's not what I expected. It's gorgeous. The color is pale as the moon and the eyes are almond-shaped. Covered in sheer violet fabric, like Rydel's eyes. The cheekbones were hewn to perfection, sharp and striking. And the whole thing glistens, glowing even in the dimly lit hallway. I don't want to carry it around all day, so I put it on the floor and lean it against the wall. My long dress swishes past it as I turn the corner of the hall. I'll get answers from Rydel later.

I retrace the way Nadia came to bring me here and find my way out of the palace. The village roads are laden with Elves. Orb-like eyes bobbing in a sea of faces. A male Elf catches my attention. His hair looks like liquid, it's so shiny. The length of it washes over his shoulders, pouring down his back. He wears no top, only loose-fitting trousers, and of course, nothing on his feet. His eyes train on three swords toppling blade over hilt in the air. He catches one and then another in an odd pattern, tossing them back up again, eyes never wavering. I wonder why he wasn't performing in the Pleasure Gardens.

A crowd is watching him. Suddenly, the blades are snakes, balled up in his hands, then uncoiled in the air. Then, they're rings of gold, silver, and bronze—ablaze with blue fire. He catches them and isn't burned. He releases them and they spin above his head in flames, flourishing like halos. I'm startled by a hefty female shoving past me and realize I'm watching from the middle of the road. I look back to him and he catches all three rings before tossing them all at once. They burst into feathers, taking flight as large birds. One white, one black, one red.

I applaud him, catching his eyes which I realize now are mismatched colors. One is brown, the other grayish-blue. He bows to me and I don't know what else to do besides smile.

"Splendid tricks." I applaud. "Was that magic?"

"Of a kind." He beams.

"Where did you learn to perform?" I ask.

"In the North." His smile fades. "The village, Falten. There's an institution there where I developed my talents."

In the North? "Correct me if I'm wrong, but Falten lies in the Ressid Province."

"Yes, along the coast." He recalls his birds and they land on his hand, one at a time, transforming back into rings. He pushes them onto his wrist like bangles. "Perhaps, you'll visit there one day."

"The world of Aureum is a large place." I turn to leave. "Perhaps, I will when I'm ready to explore it." We bow and curtsy respectively, and I depart.

Back on the path toward the temple, I devote my attention to the map Hero marked for me. Not far now. I flow with the bustling crowd and count the veiled faces. More than half the market-square denizens are clothed in black, donning veils that cover only half their faces— right down to beneath their eyes. The Veil Ritual, I assume. It means something to me that the entire realm of Ro'Hale's kingdom is observing the Holy Holiday, while those in political leadership are having a masked tea party behind the castle walls. As I near the temple, a bout of nerves halts me.

My eyes wander up the towering spire, squinting in the sunlight. The sounds of villagers chattering and the smell of freshly baked bread fade from my awareness. Feeling small is becoming commonplace. Feeling awed? A crisp, refreshing sentiment.

The temple walls are black glistening stone. Glistening is not a good enough word… I imagine diamonds were somehow crushed and painted into the walls. Or maybe stars hurtled from the heavens to earth and crashed into the temple—shattering into billions of still-lit fragments against the walls. The sunlight reflects so dazzlingly I wish I had a veil too.

The doors are heavy, and they moan as I push both my hands against the sleek black wood. They grind against the stone floor, so I only push them open far enough to squeeze myself through. I push them closed again and face the altar.

It's dark in here, but I like it. I'm sure if I made a sound it would echo. The temple is cavernous. Large candles decorate every available surface; wax melting and pooling on the floor. Pews have been toppled over and shoved in disarray like someone's been flipping them in anger. Heat flushes my skin from the warmth of a thousand candles. And I smell sage. A vague mist engulfs the entire sanctum, blurring the edges and corners. The ceiling vaults up, and up, and up. I have no doubt the spire tip is its end, but I cannot pierce the veil of darkness beyond the candlelight. A lone white tree springs up behind the altar from a patch of black soil. No leaves, just bare branches the color and girth of bones.

A guttural growl rents the peace like a torn curtain. I've entered the holiest of holies and pissed off the monster living within. Heavy paws canter toward me from the shadows. Panting breath and a snarl sound to my right.

I do not flinch. I have never feared a wolf. This one is dreadful, but I know him. He growls at me again, demanding I fear him. But it soothes me in the way thunder soothes a desert.

"Cesarus." A child's voice silences the wolf.

It yawns, baring its jagged teeth, and turns away from me. I watch its hindquarters, letting out a sigh as its giant haunches skulk toward the altar. What a glorious beast.

I take a step forward and swear the flames on every candle burn brighter. I stop and they dim. Another step, another flash. I walk and the light expands, shooing the darkness from the room.

"Keres." The child speaks again. She tries my name a few times. "Keres. Kehr-us. Care us. Will you care for us, Keres?" She asks timidly.

"Osira?" I scan the fallen pews and altar. A girl half my height and fragile in build emerges from the shadows. She's naked beneath a sheer black veil that covers her entire body from balding scalp to toe. Her eyes are callused with grayish blue scales. This is not natural blindness. This is theft of sight.

"Am I still Osira? I hear so many voices in my head. So many names. Yours too, Keres who will care for us," she says.

Cesarus growls at me, but takes his place beside her, making her seem even smaller.

"The Gods cannot change who you are. They simply use you," I say.

"Don't act like you don't enjoy using your God's gift." The Death Spirit chimes in with my thoughts. I ignore it.

"Who am I? So frail a youth, the sublime age of three and ten. Ruined, scarred. Reformed into nothing but a tool. What is Osira besides Theirs now?" Her voice grows in urgency while getting weaker.

"The Gods usually choose a child aged seven or eight to be an Oracle. A pure age. At the latest, ten. Three and ten seems an age at which the Gods would set aside an Oracle and let her rest. Am I mistaken?"

She smiles beneath the veil. Her opened eyes take in nothing of the brilliant candlelight which hasn't dimmed since I approached her.

"No, you are not. I made it through my purest years unscathed. Thought I was free of the paranoia of being chosen." Her lips tremble, "When I thought I'd made it beyond the ridge of my youth, the Gods ambushed me. I lost everything." She's still smiling even as her voice crumbles. "And then I gained other things like divine purpose. Or so Dorian says." Her voice is as small as she is, even monotonous at times.

"Dorian?"

"I," A male voice vibrates off the walls. His creamy robes swish the mist away from his feet. A hood is drawn above his head, and a veil ends just below the eyes. I see nothing of his tall figure, and only half of his long face, but his voice is beguiling.

"Princess Keres," he bows. "We've been expecting you."

Osira whimpers nervously, clutching her arms to her chest and bending to the ground.

"Oh, no."

"What's wrong?" I rush to her side. Cesarus allows me near

216

without a growl and begins pawing at her veil, nearly removing it.

"No, Cesarus. You know she must." Dorian reprimands and the wolf paces back and forth beside her. I lift her chin, seeking her eyes. They're wild, flitting open and closed, rolling back in her head.

"Dorian," I call.

"It's a vision." He stoops and takes her by the shoulders, looking, I presume, into her eyes. His mouth tightens as he reads her blank expression. Osira collapses in his arms and convulses. He scoops her up and lays her on the large stone altar. She writhes as if in ecstasy and we step away from her. For what feels like hours, she whispers raggedly in the divine tongue. Cesarus kneels at the side of the altar, eying his tortured owner.

"What's she saying?" I look to Dorian.

He folds his arms into the belled sleeves of the robe and bows his head. "She speaks with the Gods. When she awakens—"

Osira juts upward, back arched and limbs splayed. A maniacal laugh rumbles in her throat.

"Keres." The voice does not belong to her. It's coarse and too enormous for her body, reaching into every corner of the temple. Chilling but crackling like fire. She sits up slowly, body drifting over the edges of the altar. Her hand rises, pointing as her empty eyes scan the room and fall on me. "There you are."

Again, she collapses. Dorian flings himself to the foot of the altar, catching her as she topples off. Her own voice returns to her body, creaky and exhausted. "Cesarus." Dorian lays her down near the wolf's paws and allows the hound to comfort her as she regains control of her body and mind.

"Osira," I try. She simply lies there silently, until she begins to cry. Dorian presses a silver goblet to her hand, but she swats it away. It clangs against the stone floor, spilling liquid that looks like wine.

"What did you see?" Dorian pushes her.

"I don't understand it!" She growls.

"I will help you," He purrs. "Tell me what you saw."

She considers and then says, "A white hart. A black wolf. In the forest, the black wolf hunted the white hart. Then the river. Then nothing."

"Which river?" I interrupt.

"The River Liri," She says.

"You saw nothing else?" Dorian goads. "You didn't see Keres again?"

"You said my name," I add.

She shakes her head and more hair falls out, sticking to the veil. She's crying harder, curling up into a ball like she's terrified.

"I didn't see you." Her shoulders jostle and her voice shatters.

"You pointed right at me and said, 'There you are,' Osi." Dorian turns abruptly to me and shakes his head as if I shouldn't give her a nickname.

"No. I felt... Death. I don't know," She bleats. "Someone will die. I can't understand the vision. I feel it. Someone is going to die. I don't need eyes to see. A God is coming."

"She must rest." Dorian shields her from me, picking her up and carrying her into an adjoining room with a small bed. Once she's tucked in with Cesarus beside her, he comes back to me.

"When she rises send—" I start.

He stops me.

"Visions and dreams assault the child; she is overwhelmed with revelations. She must learn to interpret on her own. She sees things she does not understand; speaks names she does not know and draws faces she's never seen with her own eyes and wrestles with divinations of the future. She is being used by the entire Pantheon of

Gods." He pauses, pressing his lips together again. "As I told your cousin, the Queen, we cannot hasten her Unveiling. She must struggle for a few more days until she can identify each God by their unique voice, interpret what they reveal to her, and translate their divine tongue."

"Hasten it? Queen Hero has sought to speed up this... process? What is the Unveiling exactly?"

"The Queen has recommended I shave the child's head. She believes it will bring about answers. As opposed to waiting for her hair to fall."

"Is that when she will understand what the Gods show her? When she loses all her hair?"

"Perhaps." He licks his dry lips. "She is being purged of mortal knowledge. Reborn."

"If not then, when? I need answers. A God is coming? Someone is going to die? When?"

"When the Gods will it." He frowns.

I take a seat in one of the few pews still standing and shake off my nerves. Dorian sits beside me. I stare at the tree.

"In three days' time, the ritual will end. And if Osira does not lose all her hair, if she does not realize all of what's being given to her... Queen Hero has ordered for her to be sheared in the marketplace. Or killed."

19: THE WIFE

"I won't allow Queen Hero to harm her," I assure Dorian.

He sighs. "It's kind of you to care. Unless you only care for the answers Osira holds."

"No, not only for that. She's lost one life to live another in service to the Gods. I can understand that. All my life, I've been asking questions Osira will start to voice as she gets older."

He faces me. This close, I can see the outline of his features through the veil.

"Osira told me a God claimed you, but she could not tell me which."

"I have been meaning to ask about that. What is the channeling exactly?"

"I can explain it only one way." He settles into his seat. "Osira is in a time of transition. As the Gods have pulled the veil of blindness over her physical eyes, they are unveiling the spiritual world to her. I understand her distress, but I cannot relate to it. I have no connection to the realms beyond and can only offer her guidance from my experience with the Oracles before her. Unfortunately, this is no vast knowledge. I am as blind to her new world as she is now to ours." He clears his throat.

"However, you have some knowledge of value as the mortal counterpart to a God. Being an Oracle means she can see what the Gods reveal, with spiritual eyes wide-open. Being an Instrument of the divine means you can see only what your God allows you to when your eyes are closed. In dreams. That is why the servants are called Blind Ones and the Oracles are the Unveiled."

"I have read of this, yes."

"When Osira reached out with her new sight, she saw you and... you became tethered to one another. Your tie to each other is kismetic."

"Like, fated?"

"It would appear so." He smiles mildly. "She established a bridge between you that exists only in the eternal God-land. You can cross it. That is the channeling."

"When she crossed this bridge that night... I became her." I try to make my words make sense. "I couldn't see. I felt fire and heard the Gods. I felt her wolf in my presence. It's why I wasn't frightened of him today. I knew him."

"And Osira was in you. She felt cold, if I remember correctly. She woke me in the night, telling me." He strokes his chin. "She said she felt a pain in her shoulder... and water in her lungs."

I swallow back my words. She sensed the injury King Arias gave me... and my past.

"You are both in for quite a gauntlet run, that's for sure," he sighs.

"Why me?" I ask. "Why did Osira channel me? How did she even know to look for me in the God-land?"

"On this matter, I have about as much understanding as you do. Why does it happen? How? These are all questions with answers the Gods only need to know. Maybe He called her, and she came running, only to find you. Perhaps, Osira may one day need you or the power of your God." He turns to me and folds his hands.

I turn away, afraid to break the news that we should pray Osira never needs my God's power.

"I am the servant of Mrithyn, God of Death."

At the mention of His name, the candle flames explode and sputter. Dorian and I instinctively lean into each other at the flash of white-hot light. I shield my eyes with my hands but try to find the reason for it. Dorian moves from my side and stands.

"Can it be?" He asks. His hooded figure is shrouded in a fiery glow that strains my eyes.

"What was that?" I stand beside him. Shadows move atop the tree. Dorian pushes back his veil, revealing dark brown eyes. We blink in the searing light.

"What's happening to the tree?" I ask. The light either dims or our eyes adjust, but we both gasp. I move toward the tree and can make out the shapes of tiny pale leaves and red flower buds bursting into life along the branches. I look back at him, smiling before I realize he's fallen to his knees.

"Dorian?"

He sits up, sobbing with a quivering smile on his face. "I knew you would come."

He grips my hands in his. "This temple has long been unmarked, unclaimed, and unfrequented by any of the Gods' servants for centuries. My order was sure it was a Divine's temple, belonging to a God at one time in the past. None knew who we served for generations; whose blessed name would be worshiped in this hall. Instead, it's long been the holy house of the Oracles, and we their faithful priests. But I knew one day, the servant of this temple's Hallow-Mother or Father would return and awaken it."

"The Temple of Mrithyn. I never thought to look for it," I say.

"Yes." He stands and wipes his eyes. "The Temple of Mrithyn. As you probably know, each of the Gods has what our people refer to as 'Transcendants'. Objects, scripts, even places of divine nature and origin. Not every God has a temple; some have only books or other sacred tokens. Ever heard of the Chalice of Enithura? The Lamp of Adreana? Surely, you know of the Scythe of Mrithyn. Do you possess it?" He asks.

"Apparently, there is a great deal I do not know. Especially not where His Scythe is. I never cared to," I shrug. "Those things are legends buried in the annals of history... or simply mythological."

They must be. I look at the tree. Did I really awaken it? Are Osira and I really fated, connected? I think back to Nadia and the masks. Faeries, Nymphs, and other fantasies are child's play. As I told Nadia. This also seems too fanciful, but Gods and devils do exist. Perhaps these Transcendants do too. I've read about them but never hoped or believed them to be true.

"I believe," Dorian says. He presses his lips into a thin line again and I wonder if they'll permanently deflate if he keeps it up.

I turn from his scrutiny back to the tree.

"This tree makes no sense. Mrithyn is the God of Death. Not Life. How does that explain its revival?"

"The God of Death owes no one an explanation." His tone drops but then his face softens. "You spoke His name. Many times, I have muttered the names of every God in the Pantheon amid these walls. Never once did it cause a light to burn brighter or the tree to flower. You brought life to the Temple of Death."

"That still makes no sense. I bear the Death Spirit. My... Hallow-Father or whatever you called him—is Death. As in, I'm Desolation's Daughter. I'm a Reaper, not a Sower. The tree woke up for another reason." I walk right up to it and pluck a leaf off its branches.

"Don't," Dorian snaps.

The leaf melts into blood in my hand and drips onto the stone floor. We exchange looks.

"Don't do that again."

"I don't plan on it."

"Look." He points to the roots of the tree. I follow his gaze. The soil from which the tree is growing is drying up. Unnaturally fast. The tree pales even more and the leaves shrivel.

"Get water." I flurry my hands. Before I know it, he's gone. He comes running back with a pitcher, trips over something, and water splashes over the brim. He pushes it into my hands, and I drop to my knees to douse the cracking, paling soil. It soaks it up and then dries again.

"More."

"I have no more. The well is too far. It will die," He weeps. "Why did you pluck the leaf?"

I watch the soil grow drier and drier, searching for a reason. "Give me your knife."

"What do—"

"Your knife," I snap.

Dorian unsheathes the knife from his belt, and I think of the one Silas wore on our wedding day. A blade meant for sacrifices.

I wrap my hand around the blade and quickly drag it across my palm, slashing open my left hand. Blood oozes out. I squeeze my hand, spreading the blood to my fingers and digging my nails in to make it bleed more. The pain earns a grunt from me as I do the same to my right hand until blood covers both.

I focus my magic and steal a move from Ivaia's repertoire: My magic calls to the water in my blood and draws it out. I can control it. It runs down my fingertips into the soil.

Dorian gasps behind me when the water falls to the soil. The tree drinks it in but does not dry again. Instead, the soil, too, turns to water, and the dirt dissolves as the water bubbles with magic. I stop giving my power and clasp my hands together to assuage the bleeding. I stand beside Dorian and he wraps my hands up in his robe, applying pressure to my wounds. We watch in awe as the tree grows taller from a pool of my own blood and water. The leaves turn a more passionate shade of red than before and swell until they pulsate like tiny hearts. I can hear them beating in sync with my own heart.

"Perhaps you do not yet fully understand what it means to be who you are," Dorian says as we stare. "But I have always believed this place to dwell among the Transcendants. This tree is centuries old." He laughs and then cries again, squeezing my hands even harder. I wince.

"The Coroner has come unto her own, and her own will devote themselves to her." He bows deeply at the waist, lifting my bloodied hands to his brow. "Oh, blessed Mrithyn has raised up a servant for the Children of the Sunderlands when they needed His grace most."

Now he's just rambling, I'm sure. What's so gracious about giving a bleeding land a sentinel of Death? Someone to tuck the souls into the earth and kiss them an eternal good night? Then again… I look at the tree, alive from my own blood.

He fetches bandages and binds my hand. "Come again tomorrow. I will speak with Osira when she awakens. We will await you. I fear you have still much to learn about who you are— what you must do. I will educate you in the doctrine of Mrithyn and of all the Gods. I know them by heart! I've been preparing my entire life for this moment. For you."

Not knowing what else to say, I agree to come again tomorrow. Reluctantly, I tear myself from the splendor of the white and red tree of this black temple dressed in stars. An inkling of hope alights within me that being the Coroner might amount to something beautiful, not only grim.

ᘯᘰᘯᘰᘯᘰ

Apparently, Nadia the bunny-servant has a twin. Equal in beauty but with vicious yellow eyes instead of alluring sapphires. She met me in the corridor and led me back to my room, chattering beyond my attention span.

"Did you hear me, Princess?" She asks, unfathomably annoyed. I shake my head. My thoughts are still in the temple.

"No, sorry. What was your name again?"

"Moriya. I said you have a male caller." She taps a foot.

"What?" I blink at her citron eyes.

"Gods be damned, woman." She shoves open my bedroom door. "There's a male in your bed."

I peek into the room. She's right. He's in my bed. Brown curls loose and wild around his beaming face; coal eyes inflamed with pleasure as they meet mine.

"Darius." I push past Moriya and slam the door behind me.

She calls through the door, "Queen Hero will expect you for dinner."

"Thanks." I lean against the door and stare at him for a moment. I blink. There's no way he's here. In that bed. As if the bed couldn't look any more tempting. He's half-naked.

"What are you doing here?" I whisper. I smell jasmine and vanilla. "Did you take a bath?" The idea of his hulking body in that tub, covered in bubbles, lures a laugh out of me. His golden skin shimmers with oil and every muscle of his core tightens as he sits up and stretches languidly.

"Aren't you thrilled to see me, Killer?"

"How did you find me?" I ask.

"What, you thought it'd be hard?" He smirks. "It didn't take long for me to pick up on where you'd gone. I had to wait to leave camp and follow you. The only real challenge was getting that damned rabbit to tell me where your room was." His deep timbre sends shivers up the back of my legs and to my neck.

My eyes widen and a smile breaks out of one corner of my mouth.

"Well, it's… nice to see you." I gesture to his shirtless body awkwardly. He smiles and rises from the bed slowly. He closes the distance between us in three long strides.

"I imagine you had to use your charm to get her to obey you," I say, trying to steady my voice.

Standing a whole head above me, he looks down his strong, perfect nose. His hands come to my shoulders and then to my throat.

"Charm is for pretty lads. I like to use my hands to get a beautiful girl to obey me."

I push out of his arms and stalk further into the room, keeping my back to him to hide my heated face.

"And did you? Use your hands, I mean. Do you think she's beautiful?"

"Come now, Killer. Don't be like all the other girls. Quick to get jealous and petty. She is beautiful." He laughs under his breath. "But I didn't come here for a foreign beauty."

"Why did you come here?"

"You know why, delicious girl."

I hear his footsteps coming closer again. I glance towards the washing room and see the tub is still full of steaming hot water and frothy foam. That's how my blood feels when he's near. Candles are lit on the table beside the tub too.

"Enjoying yourself, were you?"

His heat warms me from behind.

"Really, Darius. If you thought you could just show up and—"

He spins me around and catches my face in his hands. He searches my eyes and then kisses me. Lust enraptures me. I burn like a candle, heat lighting up my face like a red flame, and melting down my body into my core. His tongue slips into my mouth, striking a match and then another to add to the flames. I try to push out of his grip, but he doesn't allow me to. He wraps his arms around my waist and pulls me into him, intensifying the kiss. Everything is hard: his chest, his abs, his... everything. He lets go of me and leaves me breathless for a second.

I close my eyes.

"Penance," I speak the name as if it were a forbidden incantation.

He pushes me back, taking his warmth away from me.

"What the fuck did you just say?"

I look down at the gap between us before stepping closer and meeting his eyes.

"Liriene said that was your name. Penance, son of Darius. Isn't that why Silas calls you 'Nance? Did I hit a nerve?"

He growls, displeased with either her or me. "My name is Darius." He turns back towards the bed, raking his hand through his curls.

"Then who is Penance?"

"Also I."

"What shall I call you then?" I ask.

He flares his eyes at me again, an inferno of lust sparking into them. He moves, hungry to touch me. "Yours."

I pull away. "You know that can't be."

"Why?" He asks.

"I told you, you can't handle me, Soldier."

"I told you, you don't scare me, Killer." We look each other up and down, circling around each other like animals. Who is the predator and who is the prey

He reaches for me again.

"Why are you here?" I dodge.

"Why are you asking questions you know the answers to?" His voice rumbles. I know I'm being tedious.

"Who else knows you are here?"

"The rabbit girl."

"And my husband?" The word tastes foul. My thoughts of Silas have been warped by that word. He made my first sexual experience with a man pleasurable, but I do not love him. I do not desire him because of his claim on me. He apologized for his cruelty and I forgave him, but all thoughts of him as the beautiful man with charming, honey eyes, have been reduced to ash. Thinking of him as my husband, allocating him the role of lover... No.

"He's preoccupied. Hasn't left Liriene's side. Hasn't mentioned your leaving to anyone." He stops and cracks his neck, pocketing his hands. "No one's said a word. It's like you never fucking were."

That hurt. Not even my own husband has mentioned me. Does no one wish I'd come home? Did anyone even notice I'd left?

"I came. He didn't." He reaches for me and catches my hand this time. "What more do you need to hear?"

"How did you know where I went?" I try to put distance between us with more questions.

"Last time I saw you, you were wedding another man. The time before that we were running through the dark together. You fell into my arms. I thought you were dead. Ice cold and pale. Hours earlier you were in my arms, hot and wet. You lit me up and would have opened your sweet little body for me if he hadn't stolen you."

He latches onto me again and my resolve weakens.

"If he hadn't claimed you—called in your debt to marry him. If he hadn't touched you, I would have been the first man inside you." He reaches down between my legs and I gasp.

"If you hadn't run without even fucking looking back, you would have seen me right behind you. Ready to run too." His eyes darken. "And now I'm here. Touching you. Did you think about me when he fucked you? Were you praying to your God for me to come and take his place? Well, I'm here now."

His fingers work at my core through my clothing. I lean my head back to look into his eyes as he kindles the fire in me once again.

"And all you want to do with me is play games? Interrogate me? Piss me off and make my dick hard for no reason?"

I struggle to lean back away from him. "Darius," I moan. "I need to know that you're here for me and not for something I can't give you." I break free of his hold.

He steps back, understanding. His eyes tell me his surrender is temporary.

"Attica told me it wasn't safe for you."

Prying, old Weaver.

"What do you mean?"

"She told me not to follow you. She warned me it could cost me my life. That your world was full of death, darkness, and chaos. Said I'd follow you to ruin, and Ro'Hale was lost."

I cross my arms and rub the chill from them. Attica never told me that stuff. Cost him his life? She never mentioned danger to me, only secrets. My stomach turns at the ill-thought. "So, you're here to bring me home?"

"No. We both know you're more dangerous than most things, even here. Still, I had to come make sure you were okay. She told me you were being watched. She didn't know by who, but she could See it."

"See it?" I furrow my brow. "She's a—"

"A Seer. Yes."

"How do you know that?"

"I've always known. Since I came to the Ro'Hale clan." He stops as if that's enough of an explanation. I widen my eyes, goading him to continue.

"She was prone to staring at my brother and me. One day, I asked her whether she enjoyed the view." A corner of his mouth kicks up. "She told me she was Seeing us. She told us all about her secret gift when I was a pup. So, I've always known."

"What did she See in you?" I ask.

Darius rubs his hand on the back of his neck. "I'll tell you another time."

"She warned me before I left. She was outside my tent in the rain. It was weird." I say.

"What did she tell you?" He asks.

"That there were secrets in my veins as deep as rivers. That I must beware, basically."

He rubs his chin where a light scruff has sprouted on his chiseled jaw. "So, you're a dangerous woman. I'm a dangerous beast myself."

I pause, allowing my eyes to wander over him. He's drawn toward me like a moth to a flame, moving almost instinctively. He couldn't stop himself from following me— not this time.

"I watched you leave the wedding early." Bitterness laces his voice.

"I couldn't be there. I had to get away from it all," I barely explain. I couldn't bear to marry Silas with Darius watching

"With him," he adds.

"He's my husband, Darius." I frown at my own words.

He licks his lips, stopping his reply.

I take another step toward him. "I'm not walking away from you now."

I hate admitting to myself that I still want him like I've never wanted anything in my life. He does more than turn me on. He matches me in that fiery, dangerous way. Sex, lust, and love have always fascinated me. When my thoughts turned violent, they would usually turn sexual right after. Adrenaline is a roguish thing.

When I was alone under the trees and the cover of night, I would explore my body, the delightful ache between my legs. I never shied away from the thoughts of pleasure or of power. Struggle with my divinity and curse? Yes. Struggle with my sexual curiosity and nature? Never.

Sex with him would be the kind of violent delight I imagined when I was the only one who heard the noises my body could make. The kind I read about in those sacred few of my mother's books. Who ever saw this coming? Probably not even Attica.

I don't need the gift of Sight to see what I do to him too. He went after me behind Silas' back. To take me any way he can get me. His eyes shamelessly caress my body and his own rashly responds to me. He desires me as much as I desire him, and I love it. He craves me. He makes me aware of the raw seduction of my body, my voice, my strength. Makes me see something in myself I never did before. Silas certainly didn't.

I'm no damsel in distress, I don't need his protection and he knows it. It's a lame excuse to be near to me. As much as I burn for him, he hungers for me with an ache I gave him.

But I am forbidden fruit. Therefore, so is he.

I stop a breath away from him. Watching his mouth, I ball my hands into fists and the ring on my knuckle stings my skin. My vows matter to me, whether I wanted to make them or not. I've sworn before my God to remain faithful to my husband. To be with Darius now would be to go against one of my core beliefs. I can't just turn my back on my own standards. Not for lust.

Other people may have made the decision about who I marry for me, but I'm still in control of this. Though it hurts to hold back from something I know I want so badly if I'm being honest with myself. The hard truth is I wouldn't be betraying Silas... I'd be betraying myself, and that would hurt me more.

"I have... things to attend to here at court. I cannot leave." I look at the bed. "And you cannot stay here with me."

He smiles mischievously at that. Taunted. "Oh?"

I hold up a hand between us. He takes it quickly and bites it.

"Darius," I whisper.

"Don't worry, Killer. I arranged for a room in the village. Wouldn't want anyone thinking less of you."

"So, you lounged half-naked in my bed to avoid confusion of who you were looking for?" I bite back a laugh.

"Mmhmm," he licks my fingers. I bite my lip watching him. Everything in me wants to push him back on the bed and have my way with him. But I can't. I'm shackled to one wall and he to another. We can only meet in the middle but never touch.

Memories of Silas flash into my mind when Darius touches me. Like an innate, moral alarm. I can't help it. I must think of Silas as a life-partner now. And Darius as... something else.

"I have to find someone. Will you help me? I can't ask the Queen where this person is, I don't want her to suspect me. She's lethal."

"Mmhmm," He brushes his thumb over my lower lip.

I smile against my better senses. He's here, it's true. I can't just pull away from him. We don't work like that.

"His name is Paragon Kade, Commander of the Queen's armies. Ask around," I say.

"I didn't come here to find you another man." He raises a brow.

"Just, help me. Please."

"Say that word again," he demands.

"Please?" I ask.

"Gods, that word looks delicious on your mouth."

"I'll see you tomorrow." I hand him the marked map. "Meet me here. It's a temple. My temple."

"*Your* temple?" He gives me a big smile and plucks the map from between my fingers.

"Yes, mine." I try to bite back my smile.

"That word looks even better on your lips," he says. "Mine."

I let him kiss me goodbye, telling myself it'll be the last time. I watch his backside, enjoying his figure. But then all I see is a back to put a knife into, and it belongs to Silas. My stomach winds into knots. I look to the bathtub again, then the closet doors. A short while later, I leave for dinner.

Thankfully, Hero isn't on the table, but at the head of it. Rydel sits to her right, and next to him is an open chair for me. I think twice about sitting there and he notices. He flashes me a smile that's far from reassuring. Having no other choice, I take my seat beside him. Across from him and I sit Nadia, Moriya, and another bunny-servant with deep purple eyes who introduces herself as Faye. Triplets. Queen Hero's ladies-in-waiting.

Hero is cackling, swinging her glass of red wine and spilling drops of it onto her long black gown. Tonight, she's wearing a corpse's spine that runs between her mostly exposed breast, from neck to navel. The neck of her gown dips into a low 'V that passes her navel. Spiny extensions of the long backbone, claw at her gown, keeping the edges in place. She also wears shoulder blades like pads on her own shoulders, and from them hang long black feathers. A set of dark wings for this raptorial Queen.

Her eye makeup is dramatic; dark green and gold line her crystalline eyes. She painted her lips a purple as deep as Faye's eyes. Her platinum blond hair is bound in an intricate braid that wraps around her skull. Atop it is the Crown of Bones.

I remain in my lace blue dress, having merely pressed a light rouge to my lips to seem more put together. Giving my blood for the Heart-tree in the temple drained me. Doesn't help that I didn't eat this morning. I could use a good meal. But whether I'm rosy or pale, I look nothing close to royal, and Hero looks far from benevolent.

"Faye, darling you must give it up!" Hero chides.

"Really, sister. It's not doing anyone any good under lock and key," Moriya adds.

"And Gods know what good it can do!" Nadia moans as she catches my eye.

Rydel keeps his peace, smiling as the three of them jeer at Faye—who looks absolutely mortified.

I make a plate of roasted garden vegetables for myself and fill a bowl with potato soup. I pile slices of bread onto the dish, slathering them with butter. Perfect for dipping.

"Cousin," Hero takes a gulp of her wine. She slams the glass down and looks at me, red wine dribbling from her mouth as she slurs, "Do you not agree it is futile for a maid to refuse to lie with a man? Outside of marriage, that is."

I look at Faye, who's staring at her still-full dinner plate.

"Our sister is still a virgin!" Nadia laughs.

"Tis a shame she's such a prude," Moriya adds.

"No." Hero raises her glass once more, whirling towards the other two. "She is unrivaled for purity amid the likes of us. Bless her for not whoring herself as you two do!"

Moriya and Nadia both "Humph!" at the same time. "Not fair!" and "We do not whore!"

"By the looks of you little bunny rabbits, your cottontails are far from snow-white," Rydel says before a sip of wine.

They giggle drunkenly.

Hero smirks at him, "I hardly think they're pink either."

At that, Moriya snorts wine out of her nose, which earns a ballad of snorting laughter from the lot of them.

I will not be drinking in Rydel's company. I wonder if they are under his influence. Whatever that means. Too disturbed by the idea of him slipping in and out of my head this morning, I forget to laugh at Hero's joke. I look at Faye, who's blushing a fierce shade of crimson.

"I was a virgin when I wed," I say.

Their laughter dwindles nearly as soon as I admit it.

"Wait." Hero leans across the table, inspecting me. "Are you serious?" She chortles.

I lock eyes with Faye. "I was. It brought my family and me honor."

"Honor?" Moriya laughs. "Fuck honor, pleasure feels better."

"And lasts not even half as long," I bite back.

Faye beams at me and I fill my mouth with a spoonful of soup. Moriya flutters her eyes, toying with a tomato beneath her fork. Nadia coughs and folds her napkin in her lap. I feel their eyes on me, but I continue to eat.

"Is that your wedding ring?" Moriya asks.

I rub the breadcrumbs from between my fingers and force a smile as I say, "It is."

"Is your husband a good lover?" Nadia leans on her hand as she watches me fidget in my chair.

I swallow my food. "He is."

I think back to the one and only time we had sex. The room falls silent, their dinners growing cold as they lean in, expecting me to disclose more.

"Does he bring you to climax?" Moriya asks brashly.

I feel a blush stealing my composure. *What kind of question is that?*

"Not that you deserve the answer, but my husband is a fine lover. A sworn knight protector. As dignified as he is passionate." I try to sound impressed by the man I married against my will. I'm competitive, it's a fault of mine.

"A knight protector?" Faye pipes up.

"We know knights for their long… swords." Nadia giggles. Hero smiles at her and then glues her eyes back on me.

"Who is your Knight Lover?" Hero narrows her eyes.

Again, there is a moment of silent expectation.

His name tumbles off my tongue, dropping into my soup and ruining my appetite. "Silas. Son of Solas of Ro'Hale. And of Seraphina," I add, hoping to get a hint about her.

Moriya shoves her chair out from beneath the table, slams her hands on the table. She gives me a glare sharp as my own blade and dripping with poison.

"Silas?" Nadia asks as if she didn't hear me, her hand landing on Moriya's arm as if she must keep her from leaping over the table at me.

"Yes." I smile, pretending not to realize what they've just told me without speaking.

Moriya snorts at me, rolls her eyes, and storms out of the room. She chucks her napkin to the floor at the door. Faye bows to Hero and runs after her sister. Nadia laughs into her napkin. I look from her back to the Queen and Rydel.

Hero flashes me a toothy grin. "Lions don't lay down with rabbits, anyway." She smiles over the rim of her glass. "I'm sure Moriya knew this day would come."

Nadia explodes into a fit of laughter and tears line her sapphire eyes as she swats the Queen's arm with her napkin. "Knew it? She had the whole wedding ceremony planned."

My attention snaps back to her, and she composes herself, remembering who I am: The Wife of Silas.

"Silas and Moriya were together very long?" I ask. My blood boils and the fumes of irrational thoughts rise into my head.

"Until now. Since she was fourteen." Nadia's smile sneaks back into the corners of her mouth. "I told her she was a stupid girl."

"I'm sorry." I shake my head. "You mean he's been fucking her for years?"

"You do love that word, Coroner." She smirks.

And he was jealous of me kissing Darius? Hypocrite.

I excuse myself from the table, not bothering to give Nadia any more attention. I just sent Darius from my bed, mentally pep-talking myself out of breaking a vow that never mattered to anyone but me. A vow that is worth nothing. Now I know the truth about Silas.

"Oh," Hero says and stands too. "Cousin, I need to speak with you." She pushes these revelations aside, dropping her napkin stained with purple kisses onto Rydel's lap.

I nod and follow behind her long black wings.

"Let's kill him as I said before," the Death Spirit says.

20: Three Maidens and a Bear

I preserved myself for useless tradition. Out of obedience. Out of fear.

Silas' secret stared at me through vicious yellow eyes tonight. The truth—her. Moriya.

This is where he went when he left the clan throughout the year. To visit the bed of his secret lover.

"I need to know," he'd said.

"I have been with no man, Silas."

On our wedding night, he swore never to hurt me. He begged forgiveness for shaming me. Didn't he know I would find out about her if I came to court? He hasn't come here to prevent me from meeting her. He didn't have the decency of showing up, even if only to make an excuse or another lame apology. Darius said he's stuck to Liri's hip. Hiding. I wonder if Liriene knows about Moriya, considering how close she is to Silas.

Queen Hero leads me down the same corridor that heads to my room, past my door, and then up the winding staircase. Rounding turn after turn, climbing higher and higher, my body grows hotter and hotter with rage.

His jealousy rushed me into his bed. He needed to claim me when he saw me with Darius. I preserved my first time for *this*. What a disappointment. What an embarrassment to be married to someone who treats females this way. Not that I feel for Moriya, but seriously. For years? He didn't have the decency to at least give her the truth—that he was marrying another girl. She was planning on wedding Silas. Hoping and dreaming.

By the time we reach the seventh floor, I'm so deep in my thoughts I trip on the train of Hero's gown. I catch my step and go back to twisting the wedding ring on my finger.

"Make me yours then," I'd said before I opened my body to him and bore my vulnerable soul. Attached myself to the wrong person. It should have been Darius.

Until death, Silas will never be the right man.

"Just take it off. Stop licking your wounds," Hero says over her shoulder.

I press my hands against my legs and smooth out my dress. "I'm fine."

"And I'm female. I know what that means," she says.

We push through a huge set of doors and emerge in what I assume is Hero's bedroom. She strips her wrists of bracelets, sheds the exoskeleton, and even steps out of her dress. Naked, she pads off toward her bed and gestures for me to sit with her.

"Really, Hero. At least put on a robe." I avoid eye contact.

She laughs and takes off her crown, freeing her hair from the braid. I take the scarlet silk robe that's on the floor and toss it to her.

"Your virginity is showing again, cousin," She mocks as she wraps herself in the robe. I sit at the foot of her bed.

"It isn't such a sin to save oneself for marriage." I sigh.

My morals are in complete upheaval. I should be able to do whatever I want with Darius if Silas has been doing whatever he wanted. We've been betrothed since my infancy. He didn't let that stop him. Why should anything change just because of this damned ring? It's just a manacle at this point. I see that now.

"It is a deadly sin to betray oneself." She tilts her head at me. "You wanted to be with another. You married Silas out of duty."

I snap my eyes to her. "How did you—"

"I, too, was to wed a knight."

Oh, right. And she killed him, or so Rydel said when he mind-fucked me. My Death Spirit loved that idea, hungry for senseless bloodshed as usual.

"How did you get out of it? My mother penned a letter, giving Silas the rights to me."

"Oh, piss." She rolls her eyes. "My mother penned the same letter. I burned it and I killed the knight."

My shock is not rehearsed. I half-expected Rydel was lying.

"Because you did not want to marry him or..."

"Because he wanted to be a king consort more than he wanted to be my husband." She smiles, unabashed. "I don't share power."

I swallow back my words as her crystal-clear eyes watch my face. Those diamonds peering at me are so rough, I don't know how to reply.

"Who was the gentleman caller—the naked one in your bed? I've seen Silas here at court and that male was *not* your husband." Her eyes widen and her lips curve into a smile. She wants to know my secrets; I want to know hers. I'll play along. Besides, I need to talk this out. I miss Katrielle. She would have been the first person I'd have turned to in a time like this. Now, she's gone and I'm sitting on a deadly Queen's bed, miles from my friend's grave.

"A soldier. A friend from the Clan." I cross my legs the way she does and face her. She leans forward.

"The one you wish you'd been able to choose."

"Yes," I say, and it's a relief to say it.

I let my hair down too.

"Will you kill Ser Silas when you see him?" She asks.

"What? Like, literally kill him?" I can't suppress my giggle at the ludicrous thought. "Hero, no, I won't murder my own husband."

She sighs and rolls her shoulders back. "I mean you could—"

"No, no, no. There's enough senseless death in the Sunderlands." I tuck my hair behind my ear. "I won't lie though. I'd love to wrangle Moriya's skinny neck."

"Why?" Hero stiffens. I pause and tilt my head at her, trying to understand why she doesn't understand.

"Moriya is as hurt as you are, if not more. *She* actually loves Silas and you do not. You're possessive."

"I am no—"

"Do you think she planned for her knight in shining armor to be no better than a whoremonger? She loves him and I can attest she didn't know about you. I've been hearing her drawl on and on about him for a decade. I told her she could never have him because she is low born and he is noble. I didn't know he was engaged either. I've cared little for your family before, to be honest, and never bothered to account for you. Silas and Moriya did not matter enough to me to warrant meddling either."

My thoughts leap past her indifference and straight to the part where she disagreed with me. "You're defending her?" I ask and regret it. I don't want to piss her off.

"Yes." Her expression hardens. "Females need each other, especially when we're hurt. She is not the other woman who stole your husband, Keres. Although, you probably see her that way. You don't know her. You know Silas. Hate the man who made her into what she is to you now— his dirty little secret. She may be the secret but he's the only dirty one."

I stop and think about that.

"Whether it was Moriya, or someone else, and you... Silas is the faithless one and he would have proved himself to be so, tarnishing any woman in the cross-fire." Hero says.

I raise my brow at her.

She returns the look with a smirk and says, "I don't do self-pity, darling."

She's right. Sitting here regretting my first time, regretting Silas, resenting Moriya... it's useless. It's the least of my issues. How does she know so much about this stuff? How is she this confident? I shouldn't be wasting my time alone with her, caught up in trivial fancies like my boy-problems. I should be more concerned with *her* boy-problems.

"You and Rydel make an interesting pair," I lead with him because he is my first suspect. The one closest to her may be the one manipulating or plotting against her.

She licks her lips and closes her eyes, "Ah, yes. The little devil." She quirks an eye open at me. "In Elistria... the males have a certain way with their lovers. An ancient art they still practice. Sex is about more than bodies winding in silken sheets or creating life. It's about energy, the connection, the nature of love and desire. Sex is art. It is a lifestyle that focuses on emotional and physical fulfillment."

"Did Rydel teach you that?" I ask.

"Among many, many other things." She smiles back. "Rydel showed up here some months ago, carrying a lonely banner with a sigil I did not recognize."

I close my mouth, trying not to interrupt.

"His message was of peace. From Elistria, he traveled alone to find me. He'd heard of my mother's death and came to extend his condolences and his aid. We shared an instant connection."

I'm sure they did. He probably burrowed into her mind, using all this talk of love and next-level sex as his ruse.

"He's been at my side ever since. His love has led me to a deeper understanding of life and pleasure. Of myself."

"Through sex?" I can't hide my disbelief.

"Yes. He triggers my desire. He helps me see I have power. Sexually, he's freed me. And that liberation started a ripple effect in my life."

I don't like where this is going. What I'm hearing is that she has no boundaries.

"I know no fear. I feel no regret. I have transcended."

I have a hunch he's manipulating her mind. I try to smile but I want to growl. I'm even more worried for her now. Keeping her on the throne may be harder than I thought. If there's anyone who wants her off it, it's most likely him. Faking his love for her; his message of peace. He's using her, distorting her mind as much as her appearance is distorted. Wild eyes, running around dressed like a skeleton, killing innocents, but talking of peace and sex and love. What the fuck is going on here? A higher power is at work here, for sure.

I've gotten too lost in my reeling thoughts. She's silent, awaiting my reply.

Wiggling my eyebrows, the way I've seen Ivaia do, I add, "I have a book." And she's piqued. "I must show it to you one day. On page seventy-four, there's a picture of a position that boggles me." I force another shy smile. "The girl goes on the bottom but upside down. And the man—"

She explodes with laughter. "How odd! Have you tried it?"

I blush. "Hero!" I nudge her hand.

"Promise me you'll try it with your soldier," she purrs.

"I can never be with him." My smile dies.

"That's bullshit. Then again, you are a more traditional woman than I."

She calls for tea and someone attends us as if they'd been waiting outside her door.

I notice the servant who answers isn't one of the three bunnies. She passes me a glass filled with liquid the color of Silas' eyes and takes her seat beside me. I don't want to drink this tea. Rydel's tricks have traumatized me. I wonder if he's been using the Faery wine on her too.

"Our mothers were very traditional." She looks at me. "Or so I used to believe."

She rises from the bed and walks to a shelf beside the window. While she's scanning the shelves for the book she wants, I dump my tea in the plant pot beside her bed.

"I see it in you, Keres."

I freeze, thinking she saw me dump my tea.

"The drive to do right. To make your own choices, to lead. A trait both our mothers possessed in their own ways."

Hero is smiling, I can tell by her voice, as she bends to pluck a book from the bottom shelf. I hold my empty cup in my lap.

"It is in our blood, to feel as you do. It's who we are." She presents the book to me with a broken smile. "My mother's diary."

I don't dare touch the worn black leather.

"I happened upon it when I was searching for clues about my mother's murderer. I've read it many times, and each time I do, I feel as if I never knew her."

Funny, I've been feeling the same way about my own mother. What mysterious sisters the three daughters of Ro'Hale were. She thumbs it open, eyes the page, and points to the delicately handwritten passage:

My lover, the King of Kings.
A mighty Bear, grizzly and untamed.
I live for him, I worship.

He is the God of my idolatry.

I look at Hero and she urges me to keep reading.

Man among men,

Strength of two bears.

Hair black as ravens,

Eyes blue as a stormy sea.

Let me die in those eyes,

and he will forever mourn for me.

Until he closes them for all time,

And returns to me.

Man among men,

King of all Kings.

I live for him,

My sweet King Berlium.

"What?" I jump from the bed. "King Berlium of the Baore—leader of the Dalis army that assaults us... was her lover?"

"Yes, but before you ask, no, I am not his daughter. My father was an Elf. Prince Tamyrr of Elistria," she says.

I fall into the bed, and she tumbles down next to me, landing on her belly. "Look at this," she paws the pages.

I broke my sister's heart today. She begged me not to send her, to marry her off to the clansman. But I did, and I broke her.

What kind of sister am I? I cannot protect those dearest to me. I used her as a pawn. Giving Resayla to Kaius will erect a wall between us. She begged me and I broke her anyway. For politics. For the damned treaty. The clans need this. They need her to go to them and make them whole again. They need us both; a Queen and a Princess.

Did she love Ser Indiro and wish to marry him? He cares for her. And Ivaia's run off with her knight. It should have been her——the traitor. I betrayed Resayla's heart, broke it. Sold her to a people she owes nothing to. For my crown. I am ashamed to bear it, but I must. I pray to the Gods for forgiveness, for sacrificing a beloved sister.

"Oh." My jaw drops. "Well, shit."

My parents' marriage was arranged? What was supposed to become of Ivaia? She was supposed to marry my father?

"Ivaia betrayed Herrona?" I pick the most appropriate question.

"Yes, according to my mother. Look here."

Ivaia ruined it all! This is what I get for falling in love with a Human.

Her magic is strong, and I know her motives were true. She broke the spell to save me—— now, I must live with a hole in my soul. Unending heartbreak was the price I must pay to be free of the spell.

Would it not have been easier to let me love King Berlium? To let him marry me and bring peace between our kingdoms?

Now the people are asking me to banish her. They needed the alliance.

Humans and Elves might forever be at war from this day forward.

She sought only to free me, but in doing so damned our people to the wrath of the Baore.

I cannot marry him now, though I yearn to. That Grizzly King.

Knowing he tricked me——poisoned my mind, to make me love him.

I thought I'd die for him and I very well might have, had it not been for Ivaia.

Still, the people rage. She exposed the lie, she angered the King, she lost us the ally who will now be our enemy until the end of his days. If his days ever do end.

"What does she mean *if his days ever do end?*" I rub my neck.

"I haven't got a clue either. Sounds like she thought him immortal."

"It can't be."

Hero shrugs. "Apparently, King Berlium had a spell put on my mother to make her swear herself to him. Ivaia broke the spell, setting my mother free. She later details her marriage to my father, and how it was necessary to ally the Elven kingdoms, Ro'Hale and Elistria."

"Why didn't she marry my mother or Ivaia off to an Elistrian Prince too? Why to my father, a poor clansman of Massara?" I ask.

"To establish the treaty our kingdom now holds with your clans. You do know the history of the Ro'Hale Clan you call home, don't you?" She asks.

"Yes." I put it all together. "Their marriage solidified the alliance and birthed the clan. My mother, her knight, and others from court left the kingdom to live among our clan-kin, and members of the other clans came to live with them. The clans were given a part of the kingdom. My mother and the kingdom... was given what?"

"Allegiance." She holds her head up higher. "With our people united, we are all stronger."

"My thoughts exactly," I say. "That being said, your silence is a surprise, Hero. Since the alliance that founded the Ro'Hale clan still stands."

"Nothing can be done. My armies are against me."

"That's treason." I brush my hair back. "How can they be against their Queen?"

"Perhaps, they hate me because I am young and powerful and beautiful. I doubt it is because they miss my mother. Battle-hardened warriors do not yearn for dead monarchs. Or maybe it's because men closest to the crown are the ones who can commit treason easiest."

"Why doesn't Rydel run back to the King of Elistria and ask him to use his army, to help you get your army... to help us?" I flurry my hands, talking way too fast and I know it. Got that from Riordan.

Queen Hero chuckles. "If only politics were that simple. King Gemlin of Elistria has no interest in rising against the Dalis simply because he fears King Berlium. After his eldest son, my father, was killed in an ambush by Dalis men, he swore never to give another of his sons to the Ro'Hale princesses. I doubt he'll give his soldiers either. Also, your mother and Ivaia were both powerful mages. Elistrian princes may not be with Magic Women, to begin with."

"Sounds like King Gemlin has a problem with women in general."

"Yes." She nods.

"He should fear the Heralds of War more. Or the Imperial Council."

"Why? Neither have reprimanded King Berlium or halted his siege of the Baore and now our lands. He owes the clans nothing. He is not part of the alliance we made with them. And we owe King Gemlin a debt none can pay. The life of his firstborn," she says.

"True, except King Berlium owes him that. Herrona didn't kill your father, the Dalis did."

"Jealousy killed him. King Berlium learned of my mother's marriage sometime after, and if he couldn't have her no one could. News that the Queen was with child flooded the kingdom. He offered another peace treaty. My father set off for the Baore to sign the accord and reclaim the chance for peace that Ivaia stole from us."

I don't bother defending Iv. Not yet.

"Berlium's men ambushed my father and his men. One survived. He brought the news home about what had befallen my father." She caresses the pages. "They say my mother never wept for him. I understand why because of her diary. She loved King Berlium. I just wish I'd known my father. I hear he was gallant."

"I wish I knew more about my mother," I say.

Hero's composure cracks.

"I found the documented prophecy about her." She turns to the back of the book and hands me the three separate letters that were tucked into a pocket-page.

"Ivaia's and Queen Herrona's are also there. Take them all. They're boring to me. My mother's prediction was 'Stillness in her blood, Chaos in her wake.' I assume that means no magic in her, but as her diary tells there has been great chaos in the kingdoms and between Baore, since her."

I glance out the window and see night has fallen. "It's a dark hour," I say. "Did I keep you up too late?" I stand up.

"No," she says.

"I have one more question."

She turns her eyes from the book to me.

"The Child Oracle, Osira." I straighten my back. "I wish to take responsibility for her safety. My father educated me at a young age about the actions your mother took to preserve the well-being and dignity of the Hallowed Children. I wish to see that order upheld."

"That's not a question, and Osira has a Priest. Dorian." She narrows her eyes at me.

"That temple is the unmarked Temple of Mrithyn. I feel it is my duty to preside over it as the Coroner."

"And how do you know this?" She asks.

"My God showed me when I visited Osira today. I will see her again tomorrow. I will do my best to aid her in interpreting her dreams and visions. As a Blind One, I may be of some help to her. It helps you to let me help her. Will you?"

Hero stands up, a wild look glazing over her eyes. The scent of Osira's answers on the wind puts her into a frenzy. She needs closure. I need insight.

"Very well, cousin. I grant you charge of her."

I bow to her and thank her for her time. She allows me to leave. As I close her door, I see her approach a vanity table and pick up the ornate hand mirror. She speaks to it in a language like the one Osira spoke.

21: Desolation's Daughter

My bed still smells like him, like ginger. I sit cross-legged, next to the imprint his body made in the sheets. Ink stains my hands as I fill page after page of an empty journal I found in the nightstand. Like a little ant, frozen in amber, I sit stuck at the bottom of a long list of names and issues. As the Coroner, how many times have I sat with a list of names before me? Never once did I spare pensive hours, racking my brain for solutions because the names on all those lists were of the dead. Most of the people on this list are not dead. They are very much alive. Even those who have passed are still causing problems for us left behind. Problems I need to solve.

Osira's Veiling is unorthodox.

Osira speaks the language of the Gods.

Dorian knows the doctrine of Mrithyn and wants to teach me.

The Temple of Mrithyn... awoke when I entered it. The Heart Tree seems to be linked with me.

A disembodied voice told me to, *"Curse my God and die."*

My mother wore shoes.

Darius....

Silas has been fucking Moriya for years.

Herrona and Berlium were lovers because of a spell she was under.

Ivaia broke the spell to free her sister.

Ivaia started the civil war between Humans and Elves.

Herrona gave my mother to my dad against her will.

Indiro cared "deeply" for my mother.

Rydel is an ambassador from Elistria.

Rydel is close to Hero. Too close. His power to seep into minds may be what's influencing Hero.

I stop writing and touch the soft feather of the quill to my nose as I think. I put the hand-written prophecies on the bed with everything else: my wedding ring, Katrielle's prayer beads, which I'd forgotten buried in my rucksack, all the letters, and my crimson shawl.

I open the prophecy that's garnished with my mother's name:

Princess Resayla of Ro'Hale

Mother of nations, bringer of light.
Power will drop from both her palms into two pools.
One pool like blood, the other like starlight.

The second is decorated with my aunt's.

Princess Ivaia of Ro'Hale

Power that begins and ends inside her
but continues on through her.

I already know Queen Herrona's prophecy because of Hero. My father told me he wished he could have presented me to an Oracle as a baby. I wonder why he nor my mother ever did. I take a moment to indulge in the idea of Osira giving me a prophecy about myself. I'd like some answers about my own fate, more than I care about Herrona's alleged murder or the powers that be. Though, I'd never admit that to anyone.

I feel my heart beating in my chest and it reminds me of the temple;

the throbbing red leaves of the white tree. My purpose as Mrithyn's little monster might not be so terrible after all, if my power birthed something so beautiful.

Power will drop into two pools? I reread my mother's prophecy and deduce that the two pools might be Liriene and me. I represent blood because I'm the Coroner. And Liriene is like starlight... because of her gray eyes? I rub my temples. Tangled. I feel tangled in a web of secrets and revelations. The funny thing about secrets is you're never sure whether you know them all.

Darius saunters into my thoughts, stalked by Silas. I tell them both to leave. I think of my father. Of home. I've only been gone a couple of days, but I can feel it. I've never left home before. Never been away from Ivaia and Riordan or Indiro and Liriene. Picking up Katrielle's prayer beads, I rub my finger over the stone bead. The Past. She got that from the river.

I remember her laughing at a book we read. Every other line her giggles interrupted my quiet reading. Was it merely days ago she died? Not years? I examine the ant frozen in time. The present. I wonder how Liriene is coping with her loss.

The white bead is Mrithyn. Orange for Elymas. Oran, yellow, and Adreana, dark blue. Gold is Katrielle and Red is me. The glass one is the future. I dangle the beads in front of my nose, "Be strong," I tell myself her words. I gingerly slip the beads back into the pouch. *"Wherever you are, whatever you do, be like an ant. Be strong, no matter whether anyone notices. Mountains move one pebble at a time,"* I recall, looking at the list again. One pebble at a time. I close my eyes.

Arias is in my mind, asking me to go to court. I see each pair of golden eyes. I hear the hypnotic voice in my head: *"The spirit of one may be greater than an army. And although alone she would not win, every fire starts with a single spark."* He stood up for me. *"While you slept, she claimed the lives of your oppressors. She claimed vengeance, and in silence, she carried out her duty to your dead."*

I hear my people as if they are in the room with me.

"You said she nearly got them killed, what of Thaniel?"

"Tell us, does a God bleed?"

"She is to blame for Hishmal's destruction!"

"If we hand her over to the Dalis, whose blood is on her hands, they will stop hunting the innocent!"

Kaius is suddenly in here too, giving me away to Silas. *"I give you my treasure, my youngest daughter. Do well to honor the gifts you receive this day. Swear to love and serve each other until Mrithyn takes one or the other."*

Silas is kneeling before my bed, growling, *"I was wrong. I was jealous. I needed to make you mine the minute I saw him touching you... Are you still afraid?"*

"I came and he didn't." Darius cuts Silas off in my head.

I open my eyes. I scan the room. Grains of sand cascade into the bottom half of an enchanted hourglass that turns over on its own every hour. Memories crowd the room; the past pushes in from the walls. I can't stop remembering. Even the room is feeling overly familiar. I feel as though I've slept in this bed all my life. I shake my head and cover my eyes with my hand.

One of the closet doors opens. Startled by the sound, I lean forward on the bed as it creaks out of place. The fragrance of the dying bouquet within leaks out into the bedroom.

I'm ambushed by the memory of being shaken out of bed by the news that one of the nine dying soldiers was choking. I jump from the bed.

I didn't wash my face, I didn't dress. I ran.

I run into the darkened closet and the door clicks closed behind me on its own.

The decrepit hut before Ivaia's loft. I'm there again. *That hungry door, swinging and creaking on its hinges. The pitch blackness throws its hands over my eyes, and the door slams shut behind me.*

Pulses of energy reach for me. Enveloping me in the smell of floral decay. Death and life. Beauty and entropy.

A thrumming begins in my stomach and my bowels turn to water as the strange sensation ravages my nerves.

Wards.

I do not shy away from the energy or the rising panic it creates in me.

The candle on one table sparks. I look at my hand and see it poised as if I just snapped my fingers. The candlelight gleams off the mirrored surface of —

The shoes.

I run to the couch and take the shoes off the table. The cold mirrored glass lights up my senses when I touch it. Like a finger touching a spindle. I place the shoes near my feet and battle with putting them on.

How many times have I done this?

Never.

No, too many times to count.

What's wrong with me?

I push one foot in and then the other. They fit perfectly, molded to my feet. I sigh with relief. I gasp with horror. Duality takes a hold of me as I tear into two selves. Me... and someone else.

I'm walking now, tall in these glass slippers. Compelled by something other than my own will. The Other and I stride down the aisles, running our hand over the garments fondly. I pluck a green dress off the rack and hold it against our body. I remember this dress. But it's not my memory.

My mind wars with whoever has taken over my body as we walk

through rows of clothes, remembering a life I never lived—but she did. The mirror on the wall stops me. The woman within; her shining green eyes. Green as envy. They look like my own, but the wide smile and the graceful stance differ. I am now taller, I'm far more beautiful, I'm blond. I'm not me at all.

"Mother?" My voice is not my own.

I twirl in place, feeling my body laugh. Giddy with pleasure at my own, yet not my own, beauty. I'm trying on jewelry.

"It was a gift," I say to the vision of a servant that appears before me.

"From who, my lady?" She's piqued and raises a brow at my jewels. The shape of her eyes, the slant of her nose, the frame of her face...

"I cannot tell you, Attica." I laugh again with the jingling voice I heard only as a child.

The doors open and the ghost of a beautiful woman with long black hair and crystal blue eyes glides in. "Resayla." Her voice is sharp like she's in unending pain.

"Yes, Herrona." I stop twirling, I hold my hand to my neck to hide the necklace.

"You're still not packed." Herrona's ghost frowns. She stabs a look at Attica, who bows her head.

"I got distracted." I flourish the skirt of my gowns. "I don't want to uproot my life. I don't want to pack." I spit the last word onto the floor between us. I catch the mixed tones of my own voice and my mother's when I speak again. "It's not fair. I want to keep my room here in the castle. I want to know I can come home." I stomp a mirrored foot. Light glints off it at the movement, glaring in Herrona's bright blue, dream-hewn eyes.

"You will always have a place here." Herrona's eyes brim with tears. "But you must stop dallying. The chariot will be here at dawn." She turns to go. "Leave the shoes, they will offend your new husband."

"I will never love him. You ruined all chances of me being with the one I love." I scream at her disappearing back, gripping my stomach. Something flutters there. I stop and revel in the feeling, rubbing my hand gingerly over my navel.

"That wasn't me, dear sister." Herrona regains our attention. "Ask Ivaia what she's done before you judge me for what I must do."

In a pain-stricken voice, Herrona's ghost says over her shoulder, "Attica, leave her to pack. You encourage her insolence by gawking."

Herrona's apparition disappears as the servant scurries out of the room after her.

The candle blinks out. The room is dark. I'm me again. I feel it. I snap my fingers and the flame returns to the wick. In the mirror, I see myself in a lace blue dress and enchanted shoes.

"I walked through her memory." I shiver. My green eyes are pale compared to hers. My long white hair looks dead; my skin looks sickly. I look so little like my gorgeous mother and nothing like Hero's breathtaking mother.

Do you know what men see before you take their life?" The memory of Ivaia in the cave steals my mind's stage. I kick off the shoes, trying to rid myself of the urge to remember and remember and remember.

"An executioner with the abysmal darkness of death in her eyes, and blue fire glowing under her skin as divine power charges through her veins. A cloud of white hair floating around a jagged face."

I hear my mother's angelic voice. I taste her words still on my tongue. *It's not fair.*

"A voice comes out of somewhere deep inside you; out of the realm of the Gods. Your voice sucks the air out of lungs, your throat swallows up life like a chasm into the pit of the earth."

I attempt to twirl in the mirror like my mother did. Tears stream down my face as I watch my death-touched bones move. She was so graceful. Would she be proud of what I've become because of her sacrifice? Is this what she wanted? I twirl until I can't see myself in the mirror.

"When you move in on your prey, time slows. Your hands reach for life. Your arrows bite at their souls."

I spin until I'm so dizzy I fall.

"You tear these humans from the world with a smile on your face."

I look again into the mirror and if I close my eyes, I can still see my mother's smile. I doubt mine ever looks as comforting.

PART 3

THE FATE OF THE SUNDERLANDS

My fingers brushed away her long black hair,
turning each strand white as the full moon.
My hands wandered along her body,
giving her my strength and power.

The Fire of Elymas courses through her veins,
He staked His claim on her before I could.
She need not know, She needs only Me.

I covered her mouth, eyes, and ears,
gifting her with the senses to behold My world as it is.
I placed a seed of darkness on her tongue, a mite of My power.
She swallowed it.
Wiped a streak of blood from her mouth with the back of her hand.
It took root in her soul,
Making her Mine.

When she awoke in the realm of my Beloved,
I filled her mind with a solemnity so that she did not grieve any loss.

—Mrithyn

22: DISCIPLE OF DEATH

You told him to meet you tomorrow, ass.

I keep myself awake for most of the night, debating whether I should go find Darius. Trying to think about anything but the closet and my mother's shoes. The fluttering I felt in my womb. Or was it my mother's womb? Ugh. I don't even want to contemplate it or the feeling of being torn into two people and walking through someone else's memories. Strange magic. Naturally, my thoughts turned toward home instead— to Darius. Now, I can't get him out of my head.

It's the middle of the night.

Reason and desire fill my head like thunder and lightning. Go get him. Go to sleep. Moriya's yellow eyes are lighting up dark corners of my head. Memories of sex with Silas churn in my stomach. And painful lust burns between my legs for Darius. I'm stuck between thoughts of the two men in my life that I'm attached to, and the ghosts and secrets latching themselves onto me. I entertain the lovers.

Silas has been unfaithful to his promise. Why shouldn't I?

Versus…

"We're not married yet, Silas." What I told him when he caught me kissing Darius in the River Liri. He wasn't married to me when he bedded Moriya. Maybe he loved her.

"As good as mine," he'd called me. Did we already belong to each other

when he was loving her—giving her false hope? When I was crossing lines with Darius.

I kick the blankets off and pace the room. Ignoring the door, ignoring my cloak. Urging myself not to get dressed and leave. Demanding I get back in bed and behave. Who even is Darius to me? A week ago, he was no one. Then he was in my face. Now, he's in my head. Now, I want him inside my body. "What the fuck?"

I run my hands through my hair. It's tangled from tossing and turning. I light a candle; the sharp smell of the burning wick scrunches up my nose. The fragrance of the melting wax pours into my head. The only sounds are of my shuffling feet as I walk around the room.

Silas is the person I've been jealous over for years. I thought my sister had him tied up too tightly around her finger, and he was mine, so I wanted him. Then I learned of her affections for Katrielle and my jealousy over Silas broke down into absolute disinterest. Darius attracted me in a moment of rage. What does that say about us? Can't be good. But I want him. He stoppered my anger but unleashed a whole new type of frustration in me. He's here. He came after me. Silas didn't. Silas probably wants to keep as much distance between himself and both his women. The three of us in the same place would have exposed his lie.

"Fucking sod," I kick a pillow I'd knocked off the bed.

I told myself I'd be betraying myself by breaking my vow. My standards. What about being loyal to myself and what I want in life? Hero called self-betrayal a great sin. Am I betraying myself if I go against my values and break a vow? Or am I betraying myself by not going after what I want and submitting to a meaningless tradition? Which is the worse offense? I've never imagined myself to be the disloyal type. If I loved Silas... if I chose him of my own accord, I would feel differently. I think. But I didn't choose him. I know I don't love him. I don't love anyone. Not even myself.

Not a day goes by where I don't wish I could be someone else. Power of Death aside, what kind of person am I becoming? Who is this girl everyone else made me to be? I feel like the only things I have control over are where I go and who I fuck. What I am, my power, my purpose? Up to the Gods. Who do I belong to? Again, up to the Gods and my family.

I don't know this woman. I don't honor her. She's a mess and she's hard. But will breaking a standard of mine move me toward restoring my relationship with myself or damage it? Gray is not the color of my comfort zone.

I've lived in this morally clouded realm for so long, I've grown accustomed to not being able to see myself clearly. Everything's so blurry. I've been crawling, pawing at darkness like a feral beast, looking for answers all my life.

Mrithyn, will You ever show me what this is all worth? What is this power really for? This curse? Why did You spare me? All I'm doing with my second chance is fucking up, it seems. Did You really make me into this divine creature, just to hand my reins over to every other mortal in my life? My jealous knight is the worst among them.

Is Silas worth being loyal to? Does his worthiness determine what's right and wrong for me to do? Darius could be my someone. I wonder what he's doing right now. Can he take away this misery?

I can easily wield a weapon and take lives. That's power from Mrithyn. What about my personal power… over my life? I want to write my own story, but no one will let me hold the pen. Guess I'll have to write it in my own blood if I can't get my hands on any ink. Is there anything else out there in the world for me, other than what's been given to me? How much further do I have to go to get it?

More than half of me wants to bang on every inn door until I find Darius. He'll open it for me. I can smell his skin already. I can taste his lips if I let myself go into those lovely parts of my mind he's taken over. He's in there somewhere, lying on a bed of wishes, half-naked. Besting me with his strength. Submitting me to his touch. Grazing my body with kisses and fury and bruising my self-control.

Self-control. I laugh at the thought. The Death Spirit laughs too. Self-control is something I've been lacking for quite some time. That's one thing I know. I'm compulsive. It's a fault of mine. A different beast roams hungrily under my skin tonight. This isn't fair.

The last piece of me clinging to logic throws itself on the bed and lets out a gravelly sigh. I'd have to look for him. I'd have to wander alone in the dark like a pathetic wanton and search for him. I'd have to follow him like he followed me here. Like a tamed mare.

No. I sit up and resolve to walk across the room and blow the candle out. They will not make me as low as Silas. Fuck fair. I will not break my vows and throw away my honor.

"Fuck honor, pleasure feels better," Moriya's voice screeches in my head.

"And lasts half as long," my unfortunately correct retort whimpers in reply. I let out a growl and push myself from the bed. I won't let my mind rehash every conversation, everything that's gone wrong. Anxiety and frustration will not steal my sleep. I blow out the candle.

Morning splashes the sky with gold. Cotton clouds dab at the gilded spill, absorbing some of the warming light. I turn over in the luxurious bed and groan at the thought of leaving. I wish I had curtains heavy as night's shade on those windows.

"Gods be damned," I mutter as I wrestle with the blankets.

I strip out of my nightclothes and consider putting on something… else. I don't want to. Someone washed and folded my own traveling clothes. I stare at the neat pile of my former self and resolve to revisit the Temple of Mrithyn as I am. I turn my back on my mother's closet and pour myself into my tanned leather pants and white peasant top I brought from home. I gather my weapons, the hand-written prophecies from Hero, and my prayer beads from Katrielle. All things I want to show to Osira and Dorian.

Yesterday, Dorian insisted that belonging to the Divine is beautiful. The Tree, the temple itself, the Transcendants. He believes. I find it hard not to believe... but still. He insists on praising me. He wants to numb Osira to her loss— to Unveil her. A child.

I was once a child who was chosen by a God. I know how damaging it is. Let him take one look at me, my weapons, my armor, my crimson cloak. He will see what Mrithyn has turned me into. A killer. Will he try to tell me how beautiful it is, then?

I can't help but compare him to Ivaia. She looked at me as a spectacle. I don't want him doing that to Osira. I must show him the dark side of the Divine, so he knows how serious a charge it is to protect and listen to Osira. The way no one did for me when I was in her position.

My white hair is loose. I line my eyes with black kohl and dab a deep, dark red rouge onto my lips. My eyes look healed around the edges and the green of them is an explosion of contrast to my still-pale face. I need sunshine. I look out the window and realize it's midday already. They are expecting me. Darius will meet me there. I wrap myself up in my crimson shawl and leave.

Hero, Rydel, and Nadia are in the corridor. All three of them are arm in arm, taking up the entire width of the hall. Hero's laughing as Rydel whispers in her ear and Nadia watches them with what seems like heavy desire. I wonder if they all lay together too.

"Good morrow, cousin," I call ahead to them. They turn in perfect sync, but their expressions are all very different. Rydel's is a charming opalescent smile. Hero's is a cocked eyebrow and a delighted grin. Nadia's is a low-lidded gaze and puckered lips.

"Good morrow," Hero opens a link of arms to allow me in. "Will you join us?"

"Not today. I've things to attend to at the temple."

Hero drops all signs of pleasure and folds her arms across her chest. A plain black gown, not a bone in sight.

She rubs a chill from her arms, "I hope you get some answers. For Osira's sake."

I nod. "Going to the Pleasure Gardens?"

"No, to the graveyard. There's an execution." Hero straightens up and lifts her chin.

"You've found a worthy suspect?"

"I've uncovered another lie. And someone must pay. If no one confesses, more will die. That's the rule. If you didn't have Osira to attend to, I'd hand you the axe."

"Did anyone see your mother die?" I dare myself to ask.

Rydel moves to speak but Hero speaks first, "Yes. I did."

"What did you see?"

Nadia and Rydel are both attentive to Hero. Intrigued to a degree that makes me wonder if Hero has ever talked about this.

"I called for my mother at a late hour and she did not answer. When she did not come as she always did, I went to her bedroom. It was empty. Much colder than the rest of the palace. A window was smashed open and there were rocks and glass on the floor. I ran to the window and saw her standing in the garden below. A hooded figure bent on one knee before her. I heard his deep voice begging her to take the apple he held out to her. She argued that she could not, would not. He stood and grabbed her by her throat, demanding she obey. I called out to her.

The man released her but did not turn my way. She kept her eyes on him, but I heard her cry, 'Not in front of my daughter.' Still, he pressed the apple to her mouth, and she bit it. As soon as she did her body slumped to the ground and he ran. I called for guards and went out to the garden, but the hooded man was gone. The apple was gone too. And she was dead on the grass."

"A poisonous apple?" I ask.

She shrugs. "Or magic. It could have been anyone. He knew I was watching, and he didn't care. I froze. I was useless. He was very tall and much bigger than her. I could never have fought him. I've trained in combat for sport, but in a real fight against a male three times my size, I'd be no match. It happened so fast, all I could do was watch and scream."

I don't have a reply because I too was helpless when my mother was killed. I still think Rydel might be influencing her, but this is all Hero. Truth. So, she will kill again today in her mother's name. Haven't I taken lives in the names of those who were killed?

"Sometimes I kill men who fit the part. Other times I kill those who simply disagree with me. Either way, I'll feed my vengeance with their bones until I find who fed her the apple." She holds her arms up in triumph, "I will drink the blood. I will wear their bodies upon mine and they will fear me. Obey. It's all that matters. The throne of mirrors, and the mirror. Sweet, sweet calming shards of glass. Windows. Broken windows..." She murmurs, running shaking fingers through her hair. Her eyes glaze over with madness.

Rydel is at Hero's side again. "The mirror," He snaps at Nadia. She runs to fetch it.

"What is with you and the mirror, Hero?" I draw nearer to her. She isn't there, she's locked in her mother's casket, in her mind. Asleep with her eyes open and speaking in the common tongue but not making any sense.

"It was her mother's mirror. Herrona gave it to her. After her mother's death, she began to have fits of madness. Panic, rage, sorrow.

At the time I came, we'd learned that the only thing that could comfort her were her mother's belongings. The mirror specifically," Rydel says.

Nadia reappears and holds the mirror in front of Hero. Its glass is black and holds a blurry, dark reflection. More ornamental than useful, but nothing is odd about it beside her obsession. She takes it with greedy hands and caresses it, staring into it. Rydel ushers her towards the throne room. Last night she seemed so normal. Until I spied her talking to the mirror after she'd thought I'd left.

"May I see it?"

"No," Hero barks at me with such viciousness, I flinch.

"She won't let anyone hold it, save to give it to her," Nadia says. "She killed a servant who held it for too long."

"Go, Keres. Don't worry, we will care for her." Rydel turns his back to me as he and Nadia escort Hero off. Knowing how Herrona died may help me draw answers out of Osira's visions and dreams.

🔲🔲🔲🔲🔲

A storm threatens the afternoon and trees bow in submission to the violent winds. I wrap myself tighter in my shawl and hasten through the village streets. The temple calls my eyes to it from blocks away and my heartbeat quickens. The bitter chill in the air hitches a ride in my bones.

The doors grate against the floor as I slip inside, earning a rumbling growl from Cesarus. The warmth of the innumerable candles melts into me and the lights brighten as I advance toward the altar. The blood-blossoming tree seems fuller and taller. The tiny heart-like leaves are glowing as they pulse.

"Keres," Osira says from some dark corner.

"How'd you know it was me?" I ask, taking off my shawl. Most of her hair is gone. I doubt the rest will last until tomorrow.

"Your God comes with you like winter comes with a chill." She steps into the candlelight. Her long veil sweeps the mist off the floor at her feet as she nears me. Cesarus prowls behind her.

"Do you know His name?" I ask.

"Dorian told me who you serve. Mrithyn, God of Death." When she says his name, nothing happens. No burst of light. No changes with the tree. I look at it and smile, taking a step closer to it.

"He told me it is beautiful."

I look back to her, unsure how she knows I glanced at it.

"White bark and red flowers pulsing like tiny hearts. I can see it."

"You can?"

"Yes. After you awakened the temple, the tree appeared in my darkness. I can see only the tree. I can feel its hearts beating, especially when you're near it."

I walk right up to the tree and rest my hand on it.

Osira gasps. "I see you!"

Tears line my eyes as I smile and wave at her.

"I see you Keres!" She jumps up and down, waving back with both hands. More hair falls from her scalp with the movement.

"White hair. Green eyes. Your red cloak and scythe. What's that in your pocket?"

"Prayer beads."

"No, the letters."

"Prophecies given to my family by Oracles before you."

Her expression sours. "I do not want to see prophecies even when I can see the physical world."

I take my hand away from the tree.

"I can't see you anymore."

"I'm sorry."

"It's alright. No one can stay hugging a tree all day, just for me. It's the worst part about this." She gestures to her eyes. "I remember seeing everything. Colors and shades. Light and dark." She smiles. "The broken heart will never forget it was once whole."

I frown at that. No child should have to grow up this young. I needed someone when I was a kid. Not Ivaia… but someone who still recognized me as a child and not just some Instrument or weapon.

"Osira, I think I can help you. Where is Dorian?"

She tilts her head and frowns, "Went out to get food. Should be back soon. Go on."

"As the Coroner, I am a Blind One," I begin.

"Yes?"

"I was even younger than you when Mrithyn chose me. Ever since then, I've been having dreams. He tells me things. I know how hard being chosen can be. I can help you sift through the visions and dreams. Interpret them."

"Will you only be able to help me learn Mrithyn's voice?" She asks.

"I will try to help you any way I can. You channeled me, and Dorian says that means it binds us to each other by fate." I touch where the scratches have healed around my eyes. "You asked me to come help you when you channeled me, so here I am. I've spoken with Queen Hero about you. I won't allow her to harm you."

"You promise Hero won't harm me? My hair is nearly all fallen, and still, I do not understand the voices or the tongue of the Gods. I can't—" She shudders, choking back a sob. She hangs her head and catches it in her hands. I rub circles over her back.

"I'm here to help you."

She straightens up and steadies her breathing as she wipes her eyes. "I dreamt a bird of prey circled me in the sky, looping closer to my head as I walked through a desert. It came close enough that I looked up and it plucked out one of my eyes. I ran, holding my eye. I did not bleed. I ran for seven days and seven nights. Then I woke. What does it mean?"

I take a seat in a pew, leading her by the hand to sit with me.

"When did you have this dream?" I ask.

"Guess."

I take a moment to think through all the dream symbols I've encountered in my own unwaking life.

"The bird signifies the Pantheon of Gods. A bird of prey circles its food... It plucked out one eye and left the other. You did not bleed—This was your first vision."

"Yes." Osira smiles.

"Of the Gods choosing you. This was your loss of sight and gain of Vision. I don't think the seven days and seven nights have anything to do with the length of your Unveiling—"

"Today is day nine since then. I'm glad you did not fall for that. You think it means something else?"

"The seven days and nights of running signifies seven years of constant change, but progressive change. Seven years still to come. This bodes well for you, Osi."

She nods but her smile fades and she shifts in her seat. "The night it happened I was in my father's house. It was dark, but I awoke from this dream and knew the darkness that met me wasn't natural. We kept candles burning, and the starlight danced through the roof of our hut right above my cot. I knew I was blind, and I screamed, waking my family. I wept as I told my father I could not see. I begged him for help. He told me to wait a while in silence, while he ran and fetched a priest from the temple. When he returned, my father pulled me up from the floor and held me in his arms. It took me a moment to realize he was holding a knife to my throat."

"What?"

"I heard another man's voice begging him not to hurt me because I was precious to the Gods and the people. I recognized my father's voice near my ear as he demanded payment for me, or else he'd kill me.

Dorian paid and I've been here ever since."

"And your father?"

"Queen Hero granted him an estate, lands, and a title, for giving his 'precious' daughter to serve Gods and mortals."

"What?" I slam my hands on the pew. "Osi, I'm so sorry. That's insane, that's...monstrous."

"Men seldom aren't monstrous." Dorian's voice carries in from behind us. "This boy was loitering on the Temple steps. He claims to know you, Keres."

I stand. "Yes."

Darius winks at me and approaches with Dorian, who is still veiled. Butterflies gnaw at my stomach. The tree draws Darius' eye and he lets out a whistle. "What a beauty."

I smile at him and notice his great sword sheathed on his back. "Come, we are discussing Osi's dreams."

Dorian flinches when he hears my nickname for her. I need her to feel like she's still a normal girl. I'll keep calling her that even if he presses his lips into so thin a line they disappear.

"I've been dreaming of an oasis," Osira says. Darius and Dorian stand before us.

"Springing out of the oasis is a single tree. Oranges grow from it, so big and heavy with juice they pull its branches lower. I stoop to wash my face with the water. Whenever I touch the surface of the water, it ripples into waves that form at the edges of the pool and travel toward the center where they beat against the tree. The tree shatters at their touch and disintegrates into the water. The surface quiets but oranges bob on the ripples to me. I pluck one out and eat it. It turns to dust in my mouth." Osira rubs her arms and whimpers.

She's still as stone beside me like all her energy's been swallowed up into the depths of her body.

"Osi." I catch her as she slumps down in the pew. Darius and Dorian reach out. We all share her weight as we carry her to the altar. As we lay her down, she groans and hisses, forming words in the Divine tongue with a raspy voice that sounds nothing like hers.

"Osira." I keep my hands on her shoulders.

"Let her—"

"No," I snap at Dorian.

I tear myself away from her and run back to the tree. I reach out and touch the bark and she sits upright and stares at me.

"Keres." She points at me. "There you are."

"I'm right here," I say to Osira. "I'm coming in to talk," I say to Whoever else is seeing me through her.

I close my eyes and focus on the feeling of the tree. Her ragged breaths fade into whispers again and the beating of the blood-blossoms grows louder in my ears. There must be a way for me to channel her if she can channel me. My thoughts run deeper and deeper into the shadows of my mind as I search for a way, a door, to the other side she's living on. I hone in on the sound of the pulsing, on my own heartbeat.

I hear Cesarus growling and feel his timbre in my chest. Darker and deeper, I meditate until I feel the thin tether pulling my mind to hers. A door appears and I knock to the rhythm of the beating hearts. It opens and I cross over into the Other realm.

"Keres!" Osira screams and wraps her arms around me. All around us is abysmal darkness just like the first time she channeled me. But this time there is no fire. Beneath our feet is a stone bridge.

"I'm here." I push her behind me and scan the eternal shadows, looking over the edge of the bridge. "Whoever wants this girl must come through me!"

"Keres." She tugs on my shirt. "Do not anger Them."

"I do not fear the Gods." I throw my fist at the nothingness. "What more can They take from me when They already own my soul?" My pulse is bounding, and my hands sweat as adrenaline tightens up my voice and makes it airier. "Talk to *me*."

"Osira is Our child as much as you are," A disembodied voice storms all my senses and tinkles against my skin like rain drops.

"Mrithyn," I lose my breath and fall to my knees.

Osira bows beside me.

"Yes," He replies. I know His voice from my own dreams. This feeling is all too familiar.

"Their fear?" Osira asks.

She pauses a moment, listening and nodding. "Yes, I will."

"Who are you talking to Osira? I can't hear them."

"I will drink the bones," she cries.

"Osi, who is it? What are they saying?" I turn on my knees, bringing her face into my hands. Her eyes are normal. Big beautiful brown eyes like Katrielle's were. Not scaled with blindness. Not here. She looks straight into mine, but her expression is wild.

"I must drink the bones," she says.

"What do you hear? What kind of voice?"

"A bright voice. Melodic and humbling." She shivers. "I must drink the bones of what the people fear most. She commands it."

"How do you drink the bones?" I reach for her shoulders, but my hands disappear. I retract and try to clasp my hands together, but they're gone.

"What's happening to me?" I gasp and watch as darkness eats up my arms.

"Go, Keres," Mrithyn's voice drips into my ear. "If you want to help Osira, you must kill the beast and bring its bones to her."

"I must drink the bones," Osira mutters to herself. "Their fear. Drink it."

Osira fades from my Vision and I sense a presence looming over my shoulder. One final glance into her eyes and I see a reflection in them of a cloaked figure behind me with heavy black wings.

I open my eyes. I'm back in the temple. Osira still writhes on the altar and my hand disconnects from the tree. Darius stands at my back as if he was prepared to catch me from falling.

"She won't wake up." Dorian searches Osria's face. "Her visions never persist this long. You were gone for almost an hour."

"Something is holding her inside."

"What did you see?" He whips his head around to me.

"I heard Mrithyn. Osira heard another—maybe all of them. I don't know, I only heard Mrithyn."

"What did Osira say? Who is holding her in the Other realm?" Dorian asks. "Was it Mrithyn?"

"Not Mrithyn. A Goddess. She said she has to drink the bones of what the people fear most."

"How do you drink bones?" Darius asks.

"I don't know. Mrithyn told me that if I want to help her, I must kill the beast and bring its bones to her. She said she needed to drink them. What beast did he mean?"

"He didn't tell you? Why are the Gods always so fucking vague?" Darius shakes his head.

Dorian's jaw drops. "Wait here." He leaves Osira's side and Cesarus walks up to sniff at her as she twitches on the altar. She's still muttering in the Divine tongue. He returns with a thick, dusty volume and opens it on the floor. He turns the weathered pages, scouring the scrawl for...

"What is this book?" I ask.

"It is the Tome of Transcendants." He licks his finger and turns the page. "I've read about Oracles in the past. Some many, many years ago, there was an Oracle who required a strange feeding to interpret visions and convey prophecies. Ah." He points to a paragraph. "Here. The Oracle, Delphina, once requested 'the sorrow of the trees for chewing.' None knew how to acquire this for some time, until by the bravery and intuition of Ser Percival..." He hums, skimming over the text. "She required willow-tree leaves and bark that she would chew at the time of her visions. This seemed to aid in interpreting Enithura's voice and prophecies. The Goddess of Life commanded her to eat and she ate, therefore, she knew..." He scans the rest of the page before looking up. "Drink bones of what the people fear most."

"The beast," I add.

"Queen Hero?" Darius asks.

Both Dorian and I look at him and then at each other.

"I hope not." I think back to all the courtiers dressed as beasts of prey. Queen Hero, the lone huntress.

"Queen Hero may be a madwoman, but her cruelty does not rigorously reach beyond her palace walls. She is neglectful of the realm and province. She plays with her pets at court. The people do not fear her in their homes where she does not see them, and they do not see her. They only grumble." He stands and strokes his chin. "No, they fear something else."

"The Dalis?" Darius asks.

"The Grizzly King Berlium," I add.

He turns but doesn't meet my eye as he rubs a callused hand over his face. The gesture makes me think of the masks the courtiers wear to the Pleasure Gardens.

"Monsters," I say. "People always fear monsters, whether they are Men or beast."

"Monsters." Dorian looks up at me. "Monsters!" He claps his hands. "There is a monster—a true beast."

"I don't know how that's good news," Darius says and stuffs his hands in his pockets.

"Come with me." Dorian runs from the temple. I cast a worried glance back at Osira and see she's stilled. She is now pointing to the ceiling and talking to no one in this world.

Darius and I follow Dorian down the aisle, through the heavy doors, and out to the temple steps. Dorian lifts his robe just past his ankles as he skips down the stairs and into the crowded road.

"Hello, Good afternoon." He tries to attract the attention of passersby.

"Good morrow, Father." A stout, hefty Elf inclines his head toward Dorian as he passes.

"Wait!" Dorian reaches for his shoulder. "Trethermor. Have you any news of Trethermor?"

Where have I heard that name before?

The stout Elf stops and rubs his prickly chin, perusing his memory. "Trethermor? Ah, the glade." He snaps his fingers. "Do you need a decoction? I highly recommend Mormont—"

"No, no. I do not need Mormont's brews, I need to know about Trethermor."

My mind snaps back to the Pleasure Gardens and the two masked courtiers discussing the "chamomile tea" Rydel told me was Faery Wine. They mentioned something about the glade too. And a beast.

"Trethermor is lost. The beast in the parts has torn it up properly. Pity to see. And the Apostates are nowhere to be found. Gone missin' which ain't like them. Haven't had the gall to turn my feet toward the glade for nigh on a week since the last full moon. But hey, don't you go gettin' no ideas, Father." He holds up a handkerchief and dabs at the beads of sweat that have broken out across his brow. "It's dangerous is all I mean. You best not be going into them parts alone is all I wanted to tell ye'."   .

"Yes, yes. Thank you, child." Dorian waves him away. "May the Gods go with you."

"And also with ye'!"

Dorian rejoins Darius and me on the steps. "Trethermor is about seven miles east of here. It's a large glade in the woods that mingle with the kingdom's domain. Past the seven orchards. They say a beast has changed the face of the land there. You look like a soldier." Dorian looks Darius up and down, ignoring my hunting leathers and weapons. "Slay the beast and bring back its bones."

"And the Apostates?" I ask.

"If they're still alive, they're most likely not cohabiting with the monster. Forget them."

"And if they're dead, Dorian?" I ask.

"Then perform the rites, Coroner."

23: TWO ARROWS

My hands have been itching for the bowstring. Thank the Gods I came to the temple dressed ready to prove what being the Coroner means: being a weapon. I'll prove it in Trethermor Glade with Darius. It's a small blessing to be alone with him. My hands have been itching for him as well.

"The seven orchards. Each a mile across in every direction." Darius extends his hand to my right. "We are going East."

"How do you know how large they are?" I ask.

"I've been reading this map of the kingdom since I last saw you." He unfolds it and passes it to me. "This is where we will meet with Paragon Kade. Tonight."

I look up at him. The sunlight breaks through the clouds and glances off his greatsword. A storm brews in his eyes and in the sky.

"Together," I say.

He nods.

"So, you've met Paragon Kade? Did he tell you anything?"

"He refused to speak with me unless it was by appointment and in this place. I scouted it out after I met him. It's a brothel." At my raised eyebrow, he throws up his hands. "I left right away."

I roll my eyes. "Sets the right tone, doesn't it? Is it not disrespectful to bring me, an heiress of the Mirrored Throne of Ro'Hale, into such a place?"

"He's the commander and I thought you hated being called a princess."

I smirk. "I do. How did he seem?"

"Austere. Definitely someone we don't want to piss off. What exactly do you plan on saying to him?"

"Don't know. Guess we can figure that out when we're done here."

He nods again and looks at my weapons. "And how do you suggest we approach a monster we know nothing about?"

"I suggest we approach quietly and gather as much information as we can about it first. Track where it lives, what it eats, how it moves. Just like any other beast."

"Well, I've never hunted animals. I'm a soldier." He shrugs.

My eyes bounce back to his. "How have you never hunted before? I mean, I know we don't eat them so not everyone hunts, but where do you get hide or pelts for your clothing and armor?"

"I inherited my armor from my father. Never had another piece crafted. Probably should. They fit fine, but they're wearing."

I look at his leather breastplate, gauntlets, and greaves.

"Fine quality, despite the wear. You must tell me more about your father some time." I give him the side-eye. He knows I still want to know about his real name, Penance.

"Will you use your bow or scythe?" He switches the topic.

I hold up the bow.

"Good. I don't like the scythe," he says.

"Why not?" I cover the blade with my free hand.

"It's not as sexy as you are."

I laugh. "And a bow is?"

"A bow has curves." He leans in and whispers in my ear. "It takes a skillful hand."

Alarms go off under my skin, up and down my arms and legs. I walk ahead, avoiding his nip at my ear.

"True. But a scythe takes strength too."

He stalks me, watching my stride with hungry eyes.

"Do you have any idea how strong you have to be to swipe a man's head clean off his shoulders?" I ask.

"Do you have any idea how strongly you've made me feel about you?" I don't hear his footsteps anymore.

I stop dead in my tracks.

"Darius," I say, not bothering to look back at him. "Can we just focus on the mission?"

This can't be how the conversation goes. Not like this, not here, not now.

"If that's what you want, Princess."

He picks up the pace and gets ahead of me. I catch up and grab his arm.

"Don't call me that."

"How about I call you, Mrs. Prycell? Do you take on your husband's family name or do you keep your own because of your royal heritage?"

I feel my blood starting to boil. "My name is Keres. You don't get to call me by anything other than Keres." I stomp my foot and yank his arm, so he stops. "My identity is not my royalty, family traditions, or marriage. Not my power. Not my God. Not anyone's sick claim on me. I'm no one's princess. I'm Keres."

He tilts his head and watches me fume.

"Okay, Killer." He pulls free of my grip. I set my jaw and glare at him. That will have to be enough. It's more honest than 'princess.'

We make headway through the orchards quickly with very few words between us, and we reach the edge of the glade as the sun sets. The apple trees look as if they've been set on fire, with dramatic orange and red leaves that have started to decorate the long, wild grass. The air smells of sugar. Sweet and heady like lilacs or honey or wine. Oddly enough, not like apples. I remember the apple pies Lysandra would bake. Katrielle and I would dig our fingers into them and eat them with our hands. Absolute slobs.

He takes a deep breath through his nose and looks around. "Smell that? What a horrible stench."

"The aroma is fragrant to me, sugar-sweet... and the air thicker here." I wipe a finger across my forearm and feel the moist sheen building on my skin.

He covers his mouth and nose with his hand. "Rotting corpses. That's the aroma I was leaning toward."

I scan the territory. I don't sense anything.

Trees have been uprooted and drained of life. They're withered; their roots matted and jutting out of the soil. They lean back with their arms up as if in surrender to whatever the creature's done to them. Their leaves all fell with the change of season. But there are no piles of rich auburn flakes around. They're gone. Only the skeletons of the trees remain.

There's a dilapidated house; its wood and stone are blackened and eroded. Its thatched roof is collapsed and frays over the stone walls. Broken stairs cling to the walls, reaching for the front door. Toppled wooden chairs litter the front yard. It's past redemption.

"The Apostates?" Darius asks.

The soil itself is dusty and lacks moisture. A gray haze has settled on the glade, turning the sunshine ashen. The beast has sapped all color and signs of life from Trethermor. I imagine it was once an enchanting place.

A faint gnawing or digging sound reaches my ears. The ground is vibrating, churning with movement deep below our bare feet.

"Do you feel that?"

"Yes."

The thrumming beneath the earth grows louder and more frantic with every step I take into the wasteland. As I walk further into the glade, the smell of honeyed wine mingles with a noxious odor that seeps into the edges of my senses. My head starts to hurt, and I feel the need to cough. "Oh, is that what you smelled?" I cover my nose too.

"Keres." Darius coughs into his elbow.

He just called me Keres. I find him bent over, leaning on his knees, and hyperventilating. The odorous fog hangs on his shoulders, blurring him from my view.

"The air!" I shout, starting to feel dizzy. My breathing is still easy even though I'm farther in than him. I run back and pick him up by the shoulders. His lips are blue. Katrielle suffocating as her lungs filled with blood flashes into my head.

"Move!" I push him back toward the orchards. He coughs violently and stumbles backward as I push him.

"I can't carry you, Darius. You have to get out of here."

He opens his mouth to speak but coughs up blood instead.

I rip my shawl from my shoulders and throw it over his head.

"I've got you—follow me." I grab his arm and run, half-dragging him as he struggles for breath. His lack of air is weakening him. I don't know how I'm still breathing if he's dying.

We break through the mist and launch straight into the orchards. He keels over on his hands and knees and hacks up phlegm and blood. I rub his back, kneeling next to him. The fresh air is a stark difference to the haze enveloping the glade.

"Just breathe," I whisper as my hands tremble on his back, keeping him upright.

He wipes a drop of blood from his mouth. His coughing subsides and I offer him water from my calfskin canteen. He sips, swishes the water, and spits out the last of the blood in his mouth.

"Well, this will be harder than I thought," he says.

"I still hear it." I turn and squint my eyes at the fog, listening for that unrest beneath the ruined soil. It's moving toward us.

I leave Darius on the ground and run back into the hazy glade. "Stay here."

"Hear what? Keres, don't."

The sound is closer to the surface now. And angrier. It can only be the monster. It's underground. I can feel it. I can hear hearts beating. There are either seven monsters or it has seven hearts. I feel every pulse. I hear its joints clicking and bending as it crawls beneath me. Planting my feet in the dirt, I dig my toes into the ashy soil and close my eyes. I can hear its every crackling breath. Its many legs drum into the earth, digging, moving pounds of the earth with every step. I feel the ground crumbling open for it. I hear it boring tunnels in zig-zag patterns.

I stomp my foot. It stops. Whatever this thing is, it needs to die. If this thing reached the villages or moved on to my clans.... Gooseflesh breaks out over my arms and every hair on my body rises.

I stomp my foot twice. As if I'm knocking on its door. *Come out to play.* Stomp. Stomp. Stomp. It's listening too. What curious little snack has wandered into its lair?

Me. Death incarnate.

I crouch down to listen. It scurries through the dirt; heart rates quickening. It's wild with curiosity at my taunt. I start stomping around in circles as I nock an arrow to my bow and ready myself for it to come breaking through the ground.

I dance my monster-summoning dance, pounding my feet into the earth. "Here, beasty, beasty!"

I've never hunted a monster that wasn't Human before. I'm sweating with anticipation. It heightens all my predator senses. It's coming to make me its prey. The Death Spirit isn't roiling within me, begging for control. It's quiet and that perturbs me. Does it fear the beast?

I wouldn't want to hand over the reins in a fight like this. I wouldn't want to miss out; numb to the wonder and terror of risking my life in a battle unlike any other I've faced.

A tree to my right shivers and creaks. Dried roots snap and the earth regurgitates something black and long.

One spindly leg like a spider's that ends in a heavy, sharp knob, shoots out from between the tree roots. The tree falls back and the ground collapses as three more legs reach out and dart into the ground. The creature pries itself from its burrow and launches out.

I take a step back and draw my bow. My arrow follows the trail of its long, undulating body, and up its poised, curved tail that hangs over its own head from behind. It splits into two sharp pincers that arc out toward me, snapping at me.

It spears its tail at me, and I dive to my left, tumbling in the sooty soil. As I plummet into the soil, the dirt poofs into a thick cloud of black dust, coating me in a second skin of dirt.

I shift onto my knees and shoot an arrow straight for one of its innumerable yellow eyes. It moves with surprising speed and dodges. It's smarter than it looks. Raising itself to its full height on its stilt-like legs, it screeches with a bubbling, clicking voice.

Its underside is one long slit; a mouth, with thousands of dagger-like teeth. A seam torn wide open. It could swallow me whole.

I shoot an arrow into its belly and it screeches.... But it doesn't die.

Its mottled, hairy body quivers, and every fiber of hair oozes a slick reddish slime that rains down on the soil. The earth sizzles where it lands.

It drops back down onto its front spidery legs, hiding its hungry underbelly.

I dance backward, tripping and nearly landing on my bow. I've never tried to kill something... and failed! I ready another arrow.

"You're one ugly, Gods-forsaken fucker aren't you?"

Panic grips my chest. Mrithyn's power has never been futile against any of my opponents. The Death Spirit is completely silent, and I'm starting to feel like my God has forsaken me.

It can't be. Mrithyn will never leave me. He promised.

The monster's jaw extends into another set of arced pincers, which it snaps at me, showing off rows and rows of jagged teeth in its sputtering mouth. As if it needed more.

I consider using magic, but every move the beast makes sends shivers running up the tree trunks and my bones, alike. My hands shake and I want to say it's from the adrenaline, but it's not. For the first time ever, I might be out of my depth.

The beast lurches towards me. I jump back and don't stop. I keep moving to the edge of the haze. I'd hate to see this thing ruin the orchard, but I don't know if I can fight it alone and Darius can't fight it here. I shoot my next arrow and strike its skull. It bounces off.

Bounces right off its head!

"Oh, come on." I skip reaching for another arrow and take off running for the orchard. I make a mental note. Only its belly seems vulnerable. It won't show me its mouths unless it's sure it can eat me— I jump over a patch of rotten ground.

The damned thing spits acid at me.

"Fuck you too!" I shout over my shoulder. My voice has never sounded so brittle before.

It's following me. I run all the way back to the orchard, hoping to lure it there.

Darius is at the ready, his blade bouncing a ray of sun which glimmers in my eye. He keeps a steady gaze at the monster that follows. I run up to him shouting, "Arrows bounce off its top! Weak underneath, lots of teeth! It spits. Don't touch it."

"Use magic!" He shouts and runs straight for it as I skid to a halt where he'd been standing.

Ugh. Fine.

I whirl around just as the monster comes barreling into the serene orchard, charging down the row of apple trees. With every step of its twelve legs, the green grass melts and the soil turns black. It shakes its body like a wet wolf as the fresh air hits it, and its bristles stand up against the chilly air. Toxic goo flies off its body as it shudders.

The trees that catch the acid rain wither like fragile little roses. Their branches snap, the apples tumble to the ground, rotting and melting with the soil. The monster screeches again.

It pauses, appraising Darius as he roars and lunges for it.

It swings its head, deflecting his sword with its pincers and nearly disarming him as it knocks Darius back. He stumbles but regains his footing.

I bring my hands to my chest and allow that overly familiar warmth to boil inside and spill out of my pores. Fire sparks into the palms of my hands and I throw bursts of fire at it. When my fireballs make contact, it flinches and clicks back in a nasty tone. The monster lashes out its legs one at a time, taking jabs at Darius.

Darius returns the gesture with his blade, dancing around at a still-dangerous distance and letting his sword reach out for him. I continue throwing and kicking fireballs at it, trying to follow their mad dance down the orchard aisles. I'm getting drained quickly.

Trees topple over, roots snapping. Darius swats away an attack, slicing open the creature's leg. It rasps and hisses, shuffling back from him. He roars when he lunges, and the hoarseness of his voice tells me how raw his throat is from the bout of coughing. I notice the air getting visibly thicker. It's corrupting the environment. The air will soon be too dangerous for Darius to breathe.

"Darius, move!"

Fire erupts in the palms of my hands and runs up my arms to my shoulders, coating my skin in blue flames. I raise my hands from my sides and gather the flames to my chest before extending my arms and propelling the fire in a burst of light toward the monster. Blue and white flames shoot from my palms and scorch everything in their path. I hear the monster cry out and know I've hit my mark.

Fire magic has always come easiest to me, naturally as thinking the flames into existence. I don't prefer to use magic, but in this situation, it came in handy.

I recharge, bringing my hands back to my chest. The monster rears up again, exposing its belly as three long tongues loll out of the seam of teeth. Darius rolls back into its path and thrusts his blade into its stomach. I hear one less heartbeat and it screeches in pain and fury.

"Now!"

The monster darts its tail at him, and he jumps away, crashing to the ground and losing his blade from the impact.

I run closer and allow the flames to move with the wind up my arms. Again, I throw all my magic fire at the beast and watch the outline of its massive form; following its movements as it tries to escape. Darius catches my eye in my periphery. He's shielding his eyes, watching the monster burn with a laugh playing at his mouth.

The only thing I didn't see coming was the monster boiling. Its skin melts the way the earth did. Yellow eyes flicker open and closed, orbs dimming in its wide, burly head. Its screeches are silenced, and every poisonous hair and inch of skin has been charred. The stench of its reeking burnt body and boiled toxin fill the air with smoke. Darius breathes heavily as we approach the sizzling carcass.

"Stay back." I hold my hand out across his chest.

He bends down and picks up his sword, pushing past me without breaking eye contact.

"I need to find the nearest pint of stale ale as soon as possible," he says, coughing into his elbow before pounding his fist against his chest.

"I need to find the nearest blank page and well of ink as soon as possible." I poke at it with a fallen branch.

"Want to write me a love poem?"

"Fuck poetry. I want to write about monsters," I say. "Glorious ugly bastard. I want to write down everything. This was the first time in my life that I shot an arrow and my target didn't die. Two arrows. Hit and nothing. My first real combat challenge." I stand and start laughing, watching it sizzle. "I don't know how or why my Death Spirit was ineffective against this monster—maybe this just proves my point that I am a monster. Even playing field. Can you even believe this thing lived in our world?" I laugh at it.

"It's a wonder we've seen nothing like it living in the woods."

"I wonder why it's here. According to the books I've read, monsters live on the other side of the mountains. In Illyn."

"According to my books," he says in a mocking, scholarly tone, "The creature can be found in its natural habitat—"

I smack his arm and his laugh breaks down into a cough.

"I'd love to know why your lungs gave out and mine didn't." I look back at it.

"Maybe you should keep reading monster books and find out."

I look at him and smile. I plan to read *all* the monster books now. The Sun breaks through the clouds just as a rainstorm starts. We stand there, panting. Him from the chokehold of the noxious air. Me, from the adrenaline of bringing down something so marvelous. The rain sizzles on the monster's corpse.

I glance around the orchard.

"No one got hurt. That's good." Something on the ground catches my eye. "Look."

The grass is back. The fog in the air lifts, and the trees return to normal.

"What on Enithura's good green earth just happened?" Darius looks around too.

We make eye contact before running back to the monster's burrow. The air is clear, the soil is plush and moist. The trees are intact, save the one the monster burrowed under, and autumn leaves wisp around the roots where they've fallen.

"Who's in there?" I turn and see Darius readying his blade as he approaches the house. Only, it has transformed into a beautiful cabin. There are wind chimes adorning it, and the steps climb to a brown door. The wicker rocking chairs out front are back in order. Candles burn inside.

"We are harmless," a woman's voice lilts through the open window. The door squeaks open and four Elves in intricately draped robes that barely cover their bodies step out into the revived glade.

"Who are you? What's going on here?" Darius orders them to stand in a line by gesturing with his sword.

"That's an awful long sword you've got there, handsome," The dainty one with a piqued nose and giant blue eyes pipes up. Her wavy blond hair is woven into a bun with decorative sticks jutting out of it.

"And he's not afraid to use it." I draw my scythe. She gives me a daring smile.

"My name is Famon," the only male states. He's bald and his long ears stretch high above his long, oval head. His eyes are a deep shade of auburn brown that glow red when the sun hits them. "These are my companions." He gestures to the three females beside him before folding his hands in front of his bare chest. His leather vest covers only his collar bone, shoulders, and sides. A big cut-out leaves his chest and chiseled abs on display.

"Emisandre," the blond one says as she steps forward and runs her fingers along Darius' sword. He lowers it and she leans on his shoulder. She twirls her finger through a curl and plucks out a hair.

"Ouch!" He grabs her hand. She holds up the strand and giggles. "I want to make you something."

"Careful, little witch." I spin my scythe and bare my teeth at her.

"We are the Alchemists of Trethermor Glade."

"Alchemists. Others call you the Apostates. Why?" I ask.

"Because we have abandoned our duties to the palace. After Queen Herrona died, we left."

I look from face to face.

"This is Iantharys." He gestures to the female on his left. "And this is Diomora," he takes the hand of the female on his right.

"We would like to each give you a token of our thanks," Diomora says.

"For what?" I ask, keeping Emisandre in my peripheral vision as I lock eyes with Iantharys. She's stunning. The most beautiful of the four. Her hair is ash brown, pin-straight, and reaches to her waist. A thick braid sits on either of her shoulders. Her eyes are as close a shade of green to my own, but her skin is fairer than mine. Freckles dance around on her cheeks, across her chest, and down her arms, following the loose strap of her dress. I love freckles. I was always jealous of Katrielle's.

"For slaying the Gnorrer," Diomora says. She's also lovely and her features are bolder. Her eyes are like gold, her skin is like the earth, and her short black hair makes a halo of innumerable tight curls around her head. Her body is lean and slender, but her cheeks are full and so are her lips. Darius seems to find her most appealing.

"That's what it's called?" He smiles at her sheepishly. Emisandre follows his gaze to her companion, Diomora, and smirks at me.

"What was it?" I ask. "The Gnorrer, I mean."

"Few know enough about the creature. We know its birthplace is Illyn, the Mother earth of Monsters. It prefers wooded lands well irrigated by lakes and rivers. Its legs make effective tools for burrowing and tunneling. It uproots trees, preferring to steal the water from their roots as it gnaws its way through the soil. Its saliva and secretions are toxic, and both emulsify natural matter as it digs, while also absorbing nutrients from the territory it occupies."

"Is that why everything was rotten?"

"Nothing rotted away." Famon gestures to the wholly unravaged glade.

"We saw it."

"Its toxin pollutes the air. The atmosphere above the underground burrow turns sour for the mind. It causes many people to hallucinate. As you can see, the only damage done to the glade and the orchard where you slew it was from the physical barrage of its gnashing teeth and powerful legs."

"Is it a magical monster?"

"It may be. That remains a mystery."

"But it is dead?" Diomora asks.

"Burnt to a crisp."

"Good!" Famon sneers.

"Everybody thought you were dead or gone," Darius says.

"We were terrified. The Gnorrer didn't bother us when we remained inside. Whenever we opened the door, it resurfaced. Thank the Gods you came when you did, we have just run out of water."

"We came for its bones," I say. "I'm glad we could help you in the process."

"Now, let us help you." Iantharys steps forward. She approaches me, smiling as she presses a smooth stone into my hands. "It is called Krovos by our people. It is the bloodstone."

"Bloodstone?" I ask, flashing her a reassuring smile. Of course, I get the bloodstone.

"A gift from the Hallow-Mother of all, Enithura. It represents all life, rebirth of the spirit, and physical health. It will channel nurturing, healing energy and shroud you with the All-Mother's protection to ward off any evil that would threaten your growth. I've carried it all my life. Now, you will."

"Wow," I say and turn it over in my hand. The dark green-gray stone fits right in my palm and has blood-red and orange accents that swirl through it. "Thank you, Iantharys. I will treasure it always. You don't know how meaningful this is to me."

She beams, every freckle in her face lighting up like the stars of a constellation. She bows to me.

"Horro root." Diomora reaches into the pouch Famon is holding open and pulls out a small jar filled with what looks like pine needles. She approaches Darius.

"Do you smoke?" She asks, her voice thickened by an accent.

"Occasionally." Darius rubs the back of his neck. Diomora smiles and soft lines ripple at the edges of her eyes. I watch her glide his way until they're inches apart. She's almost as tall as him. "Put this in your pipe before a battle, warrior. It will heighten awareness of your surroundings and enhance your agility."

"That's fantastic." Darius holds the little jar up in his massive hand and smiles. Sunlight bounces off the cloudy glass and glimmers across his coal eyes, lighting them on fire as he smiles back at her.

"Oh," Emisandre gasps and her smile falls off her face. She looks from me to Darius. "She will give you words."

Darius and I exchange glances.

"You will be her tongue." She approaches Darius without the same flirtatious swagger. Her steps are heavy and fast.

"What do you See, Emisandre?" Famon steps forward.

"A master of snakes will try to silence you." She walks around Darius in a circle and the clouds eat up the Sun. A chill runs down my spine.

"You will need a stronger voice than your oppressors." She rounds to face him. "You will need this." She removes one of the accessory sticks from her hair and wraps the strand she plucked from Darius' head around it before handing it to him. It looks like nothing more than a red wooden stick, but the strand of hair starts to burn. A gold line etches into the stick where the hair was.

Darius looks at us both before taking it from her.

As it leaves her hand it grows. Darius steps back, holding it away from himself as it lengthens into a rod.

"Emisandre, are you sure you want to give—"

"He will need it." Her peculiar voice silences Famon's.

Darius is now holding a scarlet ornate staff bearing an etched golden snake which winds around it.

"Pophis will show them who you are," she says.

"Pophis," he repeats. "Thank you, Emi, but what do I do with it?"

She laughs. "You will know." She bows her head and I count the many more magical sticks she's got sticking out of her hair. Six. All different colors. As she raises her head once more, she gives him a sensuous smile.

"Your woman will not like this." She snatches his face in her hands and kisses him.

I tighten my hand on my scythe and move for them, but before I can make her stop, she's already back at Famon's side.

"How dare—"

"My apologies." Emisandre tilts her head at me and raises a sheer yellow hood above her bun. The sticks in her hair poke against the fabric like a row of tiny horns. "I had to strengthen his tongue."

"I'm sure you did—"

"You will give him words." Her full attention snaps back to me.

I close my mouth.

"Words are weapons. He needed a stronger tongue. That is also my gift. He accepted it; it does not matter if you do."

I glare at Darius. He rubs a hand over his mouth.

"Whatever. Let's go." I turn to leave.

"Coroner," Famon's voice is soft as a sparrow.

"How did you know who I am?" I look over my shoulder.

He steps forward and thunder breaks open the sky. The rain comes heavier, drenching us and streaking through the layer of dirt on my skin.

"The same way I know we will meet again." He holds out a tiny, dark purple vial filled with a darker liquid. "Until then, take this."

I turn and take it gingerly between two fingers. "What's inside?"

"My gift is Scorn. A potion brewed from rose thorns, lamb's blood, and pearl powder. Suspended in water, blessed under the seventh full moon, housed in a vial of amethyst."

I hold it up at eye level and tilt it so the contents swirl.

"One drop to calm the masses. A swallow to stay one's hand."

"Thank you." I look into his auburn eyes. "Can I ask you one question?"

"One." He smiles.

"Why couldn't I kill the Gnorrer in one shot? I've been the Coroner for thirteen years. My arrows never fail because of Mrithyn's power."

He folds his hands behind his back and straightens his spine. "Gods, and what you're referring to as monsters, are cut from the same cloth, so to speak. Monsters—beings both malignant and benign, sentient and insentient, were the First Children of Aureum. The Monster and Spirit Dominions reign above Elf and Man—"

"That's fairly heretical," Darius says. "Do you not believe the Aurelisian Doctrine's teaching, that the higher Dominions, born to rule the lower, are those created in the image of the Gods, Elf and Man?"

"Have you yourself looked upon the image of a God? How does any mortal know what the image of a God is, and therefore, who has been made by it?"

"Don't the Oracles know? Or Blind Ones—the servants?" Darius turns to me.

"I have never seen Mrithyn, nor have I read of any other servant seeing a God. I've only heard His voice, and from my experience with Osira, she only hears Them too. In the Divine Tongue."

"So, you see? What may seem heresy against your personal interpretation of the Doctrine, may be canonical to my own interpretation. As the Doctrine states in the At'lara, verse fifteen, 'The Dominions were created by order, and by order shall they abide. So that Elf, Man, Monster, and Spirit, and all between, may live in perfect unity with their Creators. The First Children and then the Second Sons," Famon says.

"Haf'naar, verse seventy-three, 'Humble thyselves, putting your spirits of pride to the test and natural order. That one Dominion may rule the other.' Verse seventy-four, 'Even among the Pantheon there is such a tree. A tree with roots in both Life and Death," Darius says. "A tree of natural order. Nature has asserted itself, giving preference to the Second Sons. Man and Elf rule the world, quite literally, from civilizations that advance. Monsters do not. That sounds like the natural order to me. Would you really prefer to believe the uncivilized First Children were meant to rule the Second Sons? A Gnorrer has dominion over an Elf? Makes no sense."

"Careful, boy. You're starting to sound like the Dalis, who believe the Elves are savages and beneath them in the same regard. The divine order of nature is not comprehensible by finite minds. I do not dare to make assumptions of the Gods' will based on the trivial accomplishments of Man." Famon gives him a toothy grin.

"It's perfectly comprehensible by anyone with half a mind—"

"I'm not here to argue religious views." I put my hands up. "I don't care who read what, where, or who lives by whose word. I want to know why I couldn't kill the damned creature with my natural weapons— whatever it is."

"You are the Child of Mrithyn, akin to Him and the First Children," Diomora says.

"So, you're saying I'm a monster?" I ask.

"You use that word very carelessly. I do not know if you understand it." Emisandre smiles.

I glare at her.

"Are the First Children and Gods equal?" Darius crosses his arms.

"The Deities and Dominions are not equal. However, the First Children are closer to their nature than the comparatively domesticated Second Sons."

"Did you read that in the Aurelisan Doctrine, as well? Because I never did." Darius looks unimpressed and unconvinced.

Famon smiles at him, the way I imagine a wildcat would at a bird. "You named the Tree of Order. Stemming from the roots of Life and Death is the Pantheon of Gods which comprise Aureum. Branching from them are the First Children, and then the Second Sons. A fruit of this tree.

"Uh-huh," I goad, silencing Darius.

"Because you are the Child of Mrithyn, you have been reborn in His nature, but closer to the God-roots of all," Diomora says.

I pinch my eyebrows together.

"A First Daughter," Famon nods.

"The Gnorrer and all other Monsters or Spirits are your brethren. Harder for your power to overtake. They have their own powers which the Second do not possess."

"The Second Sons… meaning Man and Elf? So are the Elves even my kin?"

"What divine servant is kin to any mortal?" Emisandre laughs. "You take part in power they will never know. You speak in a tongue they cannot hear, and you possess the Death Spirit. Clearly, you do not know what you are but know this…. You are no longer of the same blood as the Second Sons. You are in between."

Her words ignite tingling sparks under my skin, and I feel the flush of my foreign blood from my cheeks to my toes. I push away the idea. Just because she's saying it doesn't make it true.

"Thank you Famon." I switch the subject and turn, "I will spread the news of your survival, and speak of your kindness to the Queen—"

"No," Iantharys says.

"We prefer to remain out of her eye for a while," Famon expounds.

I look at each of them. "As you wish."

"Thank you for your gifts," Darius says and waves at them, winking at Emisandre before following me back to the orchard.

"We need to collect some bones." I walk ahead of him.

"What do you think she will do with them?" He takes a few long strides to catch up with me. "How do you think anyone can drink bones?" He nudges me with his elbow.

"Don't know. Don't care. All I care about is sawing off enough legs to take back to Osi."

"Okay?" He nudges me again.

I glare at him.

"What?" He steps in front of me so we're toe to toe. "What's throwing Keres into another one of her explosive moods?"

My jaw drops, but I pick it up and lock it shut.

"Come on, Keres. You're this big bad killer, right? An *in-betweener?*" He steps closer and locks a hand around my throat.

"Give a girl a weapon and she'll slash you to bits. Give a girl a choice to say how she really feels and she's the one in pieces."

I stare up at him.

"Let's go. Give me what you've got bubbling up inside that white-haired head of yours. What things do you want to do to me now? You're jealous she kissed me? Or are you just reeling from the fact that you're not an Elf anymore?"

"I am an Elf. I will always be an Elf."

"Good. So, what's bothering you?"

I hold my breath and his grip on my throat gets tighter.

"You're possessive of me. Emisandre kissed me and I let her. I didn't even flinch." His thumb digs into my pulse. I lift a hand to his, trying to wriggle a finger under his palm and alleviate the pressure.

"Still got nothing to say?" He uses his other hand to yank back my hair.

I drop my bow and scythe and dig my nails into the back of his neck, doing the same to him, winding his curls around my fingers.

"Keres, you want me. You know you do." That doesn't work, so he says, "I can still taste her mouth and feel her."

"Stop." I push a breath out through my nose.

"Or what? You going to kill me? Is that how you deal with your problems? You kill or you run, right?"

"Stop talking," I shout back. "You don't know anything about me."

"Oh, but I do." He pulls my head back and brings his face right up to mine. His eyes search mine wildly, darting back and forth in his skull as they try to pinpoint a hint of submission in mine. "Tell me, Keres."

"Tell you what, Darius?" I growl.

"Tell me what I should do. Should I go back there, march up to that cabin, and call Emisandre out? Take her out for a walk into the woods and have my way with her? I know she wanted me the same way I know you want me. I can smell the desire pouring off you. It smelled just as sweet and promising on her."

"If that's what you want I—"

"Or," He speaks over me, "Do you want me to lay you down and fuck you, right here, right now." One of his hands lowers to caress my collar bone and then scales my clothing, dropping down to my hips and wrapping around to grab my ass.

"Do you want me, or should I want someone else? Tell me right now." He bends closer and bites my neck.

My eyes flutter closed.

"In case you didn't notice, I walked into this kingdom for you. I ran headfirst at a monster for you. I'm betraying my brother in arms, your husband, to be here with you. So, do you want me to fuck you the way your body is aching for me to, or do you want me to walk away? Tell me you want me. Tell me I can be yours."

"Darius," I breathe into his shoulder and he begins raining kisses all over my neck, behind my ear, my hairline, my collarbone. His breath is so warm it's melting me. Shivers arrest my body, climbing up my spine and down my legs. Adrenaline rediscovers my nerves.

"What is it that *you* want? My body, or me?" I ask with greater confidence than expected.

He pulls back. "Only you would avoid answering my questions by asking your own." His mouth crooks into a sly smile.

"I'm trying to understand what *this* is. What are we doing, Darius?

If I say I want you, then what?"

"Then I give you everything, no holds barred." His voice deepens and warms, but his grip tightens a bit more. "I can make you one promise, Keres." He places his hand over his heart. "I won't ever be the guy who takes from you. The only thing I wish I could take from you is your pain, but I know I don't have the power to truly do that."

His eyes burn into mine and everything fades around us. "All I can do is give you what you ask for. If you ask for me, I can give you myself. That's all I have to offer, and this won't be an equal exchange, I know. Because if you give me the privilege of holding a place in your heart, it would be worth far more than my attempts to satisfy you."

He pushes my hair back behind my ear and replaces his hand on my neck.

"Every day since that night we met in the forest, I've been waiting for the moment I could tell you that you're the most inspiring person I've ever met. You've endured trial after trial with a tenacity I respect and a cleverness I admire. Most of all, with a fire I see as a match to my own."

Holy shit.

"I'm not your noble knight. Knowing you, your naked soul, would be the only honor to my name. Penance."

My eyes widen but he silences me with a kiss on my forehead. "That's what I want. That's what this is. But if you don't admit your desire for me, to yourself and to me, I'll leave right now."

My heart is pounding against my ribs, hungry for his. Bucking against all restraints.

"Just say it." He crushes his body to mine. I can feel the solid length of him through our clothing. He releases his hold on my neck and—

Silas.

I'm married.

I'm...

"Yes." It comes out so softly, I'm almost unsure I even said it.

"What was that?" His hands wander all over my body, finding their way to my pants and undoing my belt.

"Yes, Darius." My voice breaks and I hold his face back. "I choose you. I want to give myself to you. And I want you." I grab his face in my hands. "You say this won't be an equal exchange, but that isn't true because you've already helped me claim something worth far more than all the pleasure in the world."

He leans his forehead against mine.

"Freedom."

Our mouths crash together, hungry and ready to feast.

24: CONTROL

"Darius, take off your clothes," I command.

His brows shoot up with delight and a smile quickens on his delicious mouth. The breeze is warm and sticky from the rain, and my skin flushes with heat as the dirt is washed away. I can taste him already. I can feel him. My body is ready for him, my sex is already soaking through the panties I'm wearing.

Slowly, he lifts his shirt above his head. Revealing his golden, glorious body. Rain slicks his skin as I circle him, appraising every inch. He's a delicacy and I'm starving. Since my first time with Silas, I've been feeling hollow. Yearning for a man's touch. For Darius' touch.

This isn't me letting loose. This is me taking control, taking my reins back from unworthy hands. I want him in a way I've never wanted anyone before. I can't keep betraying my truth. If the choice comes down to me breaking an empty promise or being honest with myself… brutal honesty is the right one.

I lick my lips, thinking of all the delectable things we will do to each other under the rent-open sky. Darkness is falling on us and stars are winking into view. The rain is as persistent as our desire and thunder echoes in the hollow spaces of my body.

His eyes constrict with lust as he watches me rake my gaze over him. I allow my fingers to trace his chiseled abs as I face him. His eyes are filled with smoke and fire. The entire luxurious length of his cock presses against his trousers and I lean into him. It pokes into my stomach and my skin pebbles from a feverish chill. I undo the button and set the beast within free. He growls, grabbing me by a fistful of hair, pulling me into his kiss that still tastes metallic from the blood he coughed up.

Our mouths crash greedily into each other and I allow him to turn my willpower to ash. He pulls my head back and exposes my neck. His warm breath fans against my pulse, which quickens as he presses gentle kisses against it. A shiver erupts over my skin, leaving me covered in goosebumps.

He undoes his greaves and kicks his pants off his ankles before telling me, "Your turn, Killer. But let me do it."

He turns me around and I feel his hardness pushing against my ass. I arch my back, flaring my hips against him as he pushes my white top further off my shoulders. He bites my neck, kissing his way down my shoulders as his fingers undress me. He pulls my shirt free of being tucked into my pants and lifts it over my head. I hug my chest to shield my breasts from the cold rain.

"Let me see," he whispers.

I drop my arms down at my sides as I face him again. My nipples stand up at attention and my breasts are heavy with desire, begging him to touch them. He reaches a hand toward me and I freeze, anticipating the feel of his calloused skin against my sensitive nipples. He pinches my breast, massages them as he stares. My mouth waters.

He pushes my pants down to my ankles and I kick my feet free. I want him to touch me everywhere. I don't care about the nearby house of the Apostates or the huts in the orchard. My skin craves his warmth, those rough hands.

"Touch me."

He obeys, taking me in an embrace. My bare breasts graze against his chest, setting my core on fire. His hands wander up and down my back, cupping my ass before giving it a rough slap. The sound echoes but is then gobbled by the open air, and his next touch soothes my stinging flesh.

"Mmm," he moans, "I've wanted to do that for a while now." He laughs under his breath, his whisper sending shivers through me. My legs are weak from his timbre, and his hoarse voice sounds even sexier.

He spins me around and walks me toward the nearest tree.

"Hold on," he says as he pushes my back to bend me over.

I bend and lean on the tree, holding onto its rough trunk with my hands. He grips my ass firmly in both his hands and shakes it so my body jiggles. He spanks my ass again, letting out low murmurs of approval. He grabs my hair in his fist and pulls me back to nibble on my ear as his cock caresses my entryway.

"I know you feel how wet I am for you, Darius." I shift my weight on my feet, relishing the feel of him behind me and the rain-soaked grass beneath my feet.

"You're soaked," he whispers against my ear.

"Fuck me, *please*." I use his favorite word.

"Lay down," he orders.

I listen, thrilled by the commanding tone of his voice. I turn to face him before lying down in the grass. I want him to dominate me. I lay on my back and open my legs to him. My bared flesh splayed before him. His eyes drink in the dripping wetness of my naked sex. His stare is feral, hungry to feed on me. I lower my hands, desperate for warmth between my thighs as the rain splatters off the tree leaves, splashing on my stomach and legs.

He growls in disapproval. "No."

He lowers himself to me, catches my hands, and pins them above my head. "I will give you your pleasure."

His body exudes so much heat it melts into my skin as he shields me from the rain and sends waves of fiery lust to my core. I tilt my hips upward and graze myself against his long, silken shaft as it hangs between us. He's heavily endowed and I cannot help but stare. His sinewy body is teaming with raw, sexual power. A hulking mass of muscle laden with desire. The rain soaks his curls and runs down his face, a drop trailing over his lower lip.

He bites my lip so hard he draws blood. He pulls back and licks the crimson droplet off my lips before lowering toward my hips. He releases my hands and I place them over my stomach, fidgeting with anticipation as he positions his mouth above the apex of my thighs. His hot breath fans against the sensitive flesh, igniting me. Raindrops spritz my nipples and face as the grass tickles the back of my legs and my neck.

He caresses my thighs with tender kisses before gripping them with his rough hands. We lock eyes as he plants a kiss on my most sensitive flesh. I gasp at the abrupt touch. As soon as it's there, it's gone. All warmth gone with it. I want to fight him for it, demand he brings his mouth back to me. But his eyes silence me. Again, he buries his face in my groin, kissing and licking my inner thighs and teasing my center with heavy breaths.

He licks me up the middle and my core contracts. I pinch my eyes shut. The sight of his coal eyes staring up at me from between my legs is too much.

"Look at me," he says.

I pick up my head and force myself to watch as he slowly but surely begins his ministrations with his mouth. He looks as if he's feeding on me, drinking in my arousal. His eyes flutter as he licks and sucks on my clitoris. I gasp, my lungs desperate for air. My hands wander to my breast, pinching my nipples as he grazes me with his tongue. He inserts a finger inside me and I clench around him.

"You're so fucking tight, Killer." He groans and he adjusts my body's position to give him more access. "It's like you're still brand new. Your body has been waiting for me, hasn't it?"

"Please, Darius, I need you inside me."

"You'll get me, one finger at a time."

I groan; a storm brewing inside me with every pulse of his fingers. He slips another finger inside, giving me a moment to adjust. I grind myself into his hand, forcing his fingers deeper inside but he pulls them back.

I'm tempestuous. His touch does things to me Silas' never did. He starts fires under my skin. I've never even known what to want from a man until now. I want all of him.

"Darius, I don't want your fucking fingers. I want your cock."

He slaps my thighs, punishing my rashness. But he wants to please me, he wants to give me what I want. It becomes unclear who is in control here. He sits back on his knees and licks his fingers, giving me a chance to sit up. I point at the ground beside me, silently demanding he lay down.

I push him down into the long grass and crawl over him. I begin to slowly grind my hips against the length of his rock-hard cock. I've only ever been with one man before him and I didn't know what to do. But I've never been shy. All I know now is I want to move on him and feel every inch.

He grips my hips and breasts, biting his lips as he watches me writhe. I'm off him in seconds and between his legs. I want to taste him and kiss him the way he did to me. Silas did that to me too, but not like Darius.

I kneel before him as he sits up on his elbows, I grip his member with both my hands before lowering my mouth onto him. He groans with pleasure but yanks me off by my hair again.

"What do you want to do to me, Killer?" He asks.

"I want to kiss you here. I want to please you the way you've pleased me."

"Have you ever done this for your husband?"

The 'H' word sends a bolt of fire through me, but it excites me even more that I'm defying Silas and everyone else who has sought to control me.

I shake my head.

"Good," he says and pushes my head down abruptly.

His cock breaks through my kiss and plunges into my mouth. For a second, I'm unsure how to move with him blocking my airway, but I close my eyes and try. I take him in deeper and experiment with ways to move and lick and suck on him.

It's tricky and my jaw is beginning to hurt, but I taste him. His salty and heady flavor fills my mouth. I get used to the pressure he creates on my throat and relax a little, making it easier. I swirl my tongue around the head of his cock and lick him up the sides of his shaft. I use my imagination and desperately try to conjure up memories of the pages from that damned book of sex and Hero's scandalous stories.

I use my hands and mouth together to cover the entire length of his shaft. Letting him touch the back of my throat, allowing myself to choke shamelessly on him. I've never been afraid of a challenge and this is a fun one. He pushes me down a little harder, forcing me to take in the entirety of him. I can't. I can get most in though. Tears fill my eyes from the pressure.

His cock pulses in my mouth and I know I've got the heart of him between my teeth. I allow my teeth to gently graze his sensitive flesh as I pull back, leaving only the tip of him entombed in my mouth. His abs contract and his breath catches. I guess I'm doing a good job.

He moans, pushing into my mouth again and again, desperate for more. I allow him to thrust into my mouth, fucking me between my lips.

He drops his head back, knotting his hands in his curls. His coal eyes are closed, his face lined with what seems like determination not to finish in my mouth. This feels like magic. Like art. Making him weak for me.

"Up," he grits out, jolting me to my core. I shift over his body and he pulls me back onto him. He lets me take control as he finally readies his cock for me. I position myself above him and slowly lower down.

My heart is beating wildly against my ribs. My breath is ragged, my lungs desperate. Sweat beads on my brow as I try to relax, slowly allowing my body to open and adjust for him.

Darius sheaths himself inside me. I sink down until I feel he's as deep as my body will allow him to go. Everything seems right from on top of him. I move and he moves inside me, and everything fits perfectly. As the rain washes over us, I use my legs to lift myself up and lower back down. Shifting my weight to allow my hips to control the depth and rate at which I fuck him. My rhythm is a little offbeat at first, but I move until I find a way that works for me. His cock brushes against a sensitive spot inside me, startling me.

"Right there?" He reads my expression and bites back his smile.

"Yes." I rock my hips again, trying to bring him to that spot inside me. I'm so wet that every movement sounds like a kiss. He pulses his cock into me, matching my movements so we're grinding against each other and he keeps hitting that fucking spot.

My body goes rigid and bucks against him as he continues stroking me from the inside. I feel my muscles locking and unlocking as my pleasure is growing into a wave. Cresting and pushing me over the edge. I buckle from the power of my orgasm, but he holds me still above him and thrusts up into me harder and faster. Drowning me in pleasure, keeping me afloat.

"Fuck," I moan.

He flips me over onto my back and effortlessly reconnects our bodies. He enters me, allowing the length of his cock to fill me up, slowly, inch by inch. He grips my thighs and pulls my legs to rest atop his shoulders. Again, he's moving inside me. My core clenches, taking in more of him and holding him captive as I claw at his back. He fills my tight body, pulling out and pushing in repeatedly

"You begged me for this." His eyes light up with wicked pleasure as he slows his pace and steers his movements toward that spot again.

I lock on to his gaze as he watches me respond to his cock splitting me open from my center. I'm brimming with ecstasy. It overruns me; his power destroys and rebuilds me. His power is relentless. His passion is endless, and his heat knows no bounds. I buck against him and scream as he fucks me raw. We fight each other. Fire against fire. Desire against overwhelming desire.

"Admit it, Keres."

"Yes—" I can barely breathe. Between moans I confess, "You. Not him. I needed this cock to fuck me. Fuck me harder!" I drop my head back and let him take me.

I scrunch the wet grass in my fists behind my head and hold on for dear life as he makes me moan with a voice I never knew I had.

Every inch of him within me reaches a depth Silas never could. He's giving me everything and holding back nothing. He breaks me with bliss and cuts me open with every touch. He lowers his mouth to mine and I claim him hungrily.

Every kiss steals my breath. Gentle in moments, he gives. Rough and smooth, devoted and reckless. I take and take and take from him until he's given me all he can, and all that's left to take is his willpower to be mine and only mine.

In the last ragged breaths, I thrash against him, but he pushes himself out of my body and explodes with pleasure, unleashing all over me. With a moan of satisfaction, he collapses onto me.

I want nothing more than to lay there in the wet, scrumptious warmth of him. To rub myself against him with greed for more. More. I want more and more of him. I don't know if I'll ever stop.

Stop? No. Not yet.

I allow him to rest but I cannot let this be over yet. I've waited too long; I've held out for a marriage I never wanted. No more holding back. No more obeying the rules or living by a vow I wish I could take back.

The world melts from awareness. It's not raining. We aren't on the ground beneath the faltering foliage of the orchard in autumn. We're in paradise. Where no one can find us or drive us apart.

His eyes are closed, his breathing is steady.

"What should I call you?" He asks again.

"Yours."

I creep down, placing myself between his legs. I take his cock in my mouth, and his eyes spring open.

"Keres," he gasps.

Once again, I use my mouth to bring him to the brink of needing me. He doesn't protest. He can't resist me. I'm everything he wanted me to be, and he's everything I need. My inner little monster tries to convince me I can't keep him. We can't stay here. I'll have to give it all back when I'm done and put a ring back on my finger. But I'm not done. More. Again.

Sheer animalistic desire takes over me as I make him ready to fuck me. It doesn't take much. He's wanted me since he first saw power within me—a match to his own rage and passion. Whose lust is more powerful? It seems we are equal.

This time he has me on my knees, bent over and facing away from him. He spreads my legs open, pushing my back down until my face is buried in my hands on the ground. He splays my flesh, making way for his huge cock. And he enters me from behind, angling to hit new places inside me. The pleasure is almost too intense. He holds onto my hips as he rides my body.

I push back against him, throwing every ounce of power he pushes into me back into him. He spanks me, and his fingernails bite into me as he thrusts into me harder and harder. I throw my hips back into his, needy for more.

I wish I could see him, but he's got me by my hair now. Yanking my head back, arching my back. My core throbs with need as he pounds into me. He's driving his cock so deep inside of me, hard as fucking iron. Dominating me completely. My breasts bounce with every hit. I lick my lips, biting back a growl.

"Do you like the way I fuck you?"

"Yes—oh, Gods, yes."

"You want more, don't you? Deeper and harder." He quickens his pace, intensifying each movement inside me. My body bounces off his, the sound of our skin slapping together echoing out into the night and imprinting in my mind. Drowned out only by his guttural growls of pleasure and my high-pitched moans.

"You love that I spread you apart and shove my cock deep inside you." He taunts me. "You know I was supposed to be the only one inside you. Not Silas." His words shouldn't arouse me more, but they do. I grind myself against him, near to orgasming. "Yes."

He reaches a hand underneath me and rubs my apex as he fucks me, making me lose my mind. His other hand clutches one breast. My harsh intake of breath excites him. My sounds fuel his fire. He pulls out and rams back into me, "Say my fucking name again."

"Darius," I gasp. "Please, don't stop."

He is tearing me apart from the inside out. He's claiming me with sex and I know we're dabbling in some dark, dangerous magic. He doesn't stop, he keeps driving himself into me. Giving like he said he would. His fingers massage my clit as he finds that perfect point inside me and burns into me.

Stars explode in my eyes. Heat surges through me, mingled with pleasure. My body sucks him deeper in as he climaxes too. He tears himself from me before he can fill me with his come.

He crashes onto the ground next to me, a lazy arm wrapped around my shuddering body. As my heartbeat settles down, I turn onto my side and look at him. He lays there with his eyes closed and curls a mess; naked and breathing heavily and perfect. We'll stay like this for a little while longer. If the Gods are kind for once.

The rainstorm ends. But a new truth strikes me like lightning: I don't know how we will go on living like this.

25: To Drink Bones

"We are supposed to meet Paragon Kade in an hour." Darius juggles the long leg-bones of the Gnorrer with Pophis, the staff from Emisandre.

"So, we go there first," I say.

"I don't think we'll be welcome in a brothel, towing a monster skeleton."

"We don't have time to return to the temple first if we want to meet with him tonight. Let's just go," I say.

"And leave Osira in a trance or whatever that was?" he asks.

I chew on my lip, weighing the options. Go help the girl I just promised my allegiance to or detour and seek the answers I agreed to find for the Gryphon King?

"This is my only chance to see Paragon Kade. He's one reason I came here. Osira can hold out a little longer. We'll make it as quick of a visit as possible." Guilt gnaws at my gut.

"Alright, we should wrap these in your shawl then. Make carrying them easier."

"Good idea." I go to remove my cloak and catch him watching. I smile at him, teasingly swaying my body as I take it off. He smiles back.

"I've always wanted to know what you had going on under there," he says.

"And now you do."

He winks at me.

We pick our way back through the orchards, passing glances and the bundle of bones between us. Taking turns trying to fill the silence. If my feet could move as fast as my thoughts, I'd have made it to the other side of the seven-mile stretch in seven minutes. He seems preoccupied with his thoughts as well.

"Do you hate me now?" He asks, startling me.

"Why would I hate you?" I ask.

"I've watched other people make you do things you didn't want to do. I see you resent them. Now, I feel like I've corrupted you somehow, even though you assured me of your choice. I feel I've led you into sin. I'm worried you'll resent me too." He says.

"I could never hate you, Darius. I was already corrupted. I thought you knew that," I add. "I chose you, Darius. For the first time in my life, I decided who I am and what I want. It would have been a sin not to set myself free."

He beams at me. "Good, then it's settled." He slings the make-shift sack over his shoulder and takes my hand.

"What is?" I ask.

"From here on, I go where you go."

He says it like it's so simple. "You're only saying that because I'm going to a brothel," I say.

He laughs under his breath. I glance at him out of the corner of my eye.

"I'm serious. We go together." He squeezes my hand and gives me a boyish smile.

"Together," I nod and smile back at him quickly before turning my attention to the far side of the orchard. Together until we go back home and can never be alone together again.

🔲🔲🔲🔲🔲

Women are loud when they're drunk and half-naked. Swaying in her customer's lap, a whore sings in a language I don't recognize. One that makes her sound like she's holding a lot of spit in her throat. He laughs as she serenades him and his comrades. They're boisterous, clanking their tankards together as she raises her own. On the final note, they all drown her lyrics in alcohol, belch, and cheer.

"That's him." Darius draws my attention from the revelry to a lone soldier seated in the back of the brothel. A girl with her hair done up in a disheveled bun of wild golden curls slinks around the round wooden table. She leans forward to pour more ale from her pitcher into his glass, and the sleeves of her top fall off her shoulders. One of her breasts peeks out at him, and he smiles at her before noticing us approaching.

"You again," he greets Darius before taking a swig of ale. It dribbles down his beard.

"Paragon Kade?" I ask in disbelief.

"The one and only, lass."

Darius and I cross glances. Paragon Kade's armor is scattered about his corner of the common room. I can't believe it's just lying around. The earnings from one stolen piece of it would feed a family. Its quality boasts his station: a gold-plated steel cuirass lies on the table next to the bones of his meal. The chest piece is connected to the backplate by leathers with solid gold buckles. He's still wearing his chainmail hauberk, gambeson, leather bottoms, and greaves. His gold-plated helmet sits beneath his left foot. And his sword—

"Is that a Cedenic blade?" Darius plops into the vacant chair at the table, dropping the shawl full of bones on the floor. He's ogling at the unsheathed great sword Kade had stabbed into the floorboards.

"Aye, it is." He belches as he looks at the blood-colored blade with contempt.

Darius' jaw drops. "There are only fifteen Cedenic blades in the world. Where did you get one?"

"From the same man who crafted the other fourteen."

"You've met the Rift Crafter?" Darius looks like he could faint.

"Didn't I just say I did?"

"Paragon Kade—" I try to interrupt. Darius grabs my arm.

"Fifteen Cedenic blades in the world. The rare metal doesn't rust, conducts spiritual energy, and resists magic."

"I see." I smile at him and look back at the repulsive man this exquisite sword belongs to.

"Do you know who I am, Ser?" I ask.

He looks at me from white-haired head to bare toe. "You're the dead Princess's daughter."

"How did you know that?"

"I know Resayla's eyes in any skull."

"My name is Keres—"

"I know yer damn name, lass. Not that I care to. The whole soddin' kingdom's been talking about the hound of Mrithyn keelin' at the Queen's side."

Darius' hand catches mine before it fists.

"Do you know why I've come here?"

"To bother me?" He lifts his drink back to his mouth. Then rakes a nasty look over my body. "Or to sit on my lap?"

I slam my free hand over his tankard, pushing it back down to the table. A little ale spills on him and he's only upset by the mess because he didn't make it.

"I want an honest answer."

His brown eyes shutter in his head as he searches my face.

"Why won't the Ro'Hale army march against the Dalis to save the Sunderlands?"

"The Sunderlands are beyond savin'." He stands to his full height.

Darius stands too and the brothel grows a little quieter.

"You don't know that."

"Doesn't matter what I know. Matters what the Queen says. She's the one givin' the orders."

"Liar," I snarl.

Darius puts his hand on my shoulder.

"She said the armies are against her," I accuse. "Why?"

"Everyone is against her. You'd be smart not to get yerself outnumbered."

"Maybe we can settle this diplomatically, over another drink, perhaps?" Darius asks in a softer voice before I can reply. He stuffs his hands into his pockets, and I know what that means.

"I've got nothin' to settle." Kade sits back down and finishes his drink. "I've played my part in this kingdom's fate. I risked my life for the crown."

I pull up a chair from the neighboring table and spin it so I can sit facing the back of it. I lean my arms on the back of the chair and stare at him.

"This isn't storytime, Keres. Go back to yer wet-nurse for that." Paragon Kade disregards me and retrieves his tankard of ale.

I'm not leaving without answers.

Kade relents. "Oh, bloody hell. When Queen Herrona's husband was murdered, I was there. I was part of the King's Guard. King Berlium played the crown with a false promise for an alliance. King Tamyrr left to seal the ruse of a treaty with the Baore. On the road to Dale, they ambushed us. I was the lone survivor."

I remember Queen Hero mentioning there being a single survivor to me in her room.

"How did you get away?" I ask.

"I don't quite know me'self." He waves at a wench, beckoning for more ale. "The fight was vicious. A blurred fray. Bear gilded breastplates, blaring horns, men gruntin' and shittin' themselves. I cut down the assassin that was closest to the King, but I was too late. He was fatally wounded. I fended off the Dalis cunts as I dragged his body back through the Gods' Woods. Refused to leave my King there, for his bones to be picked clean by thieves and vultures. That's how I survived."

"The Gods' Woods?" I ask.

"The area of the Sunderlands Forest that lies between the Baore and the clan Massara," Darius says, "Some say it's haunted."

I don't know how I've never heard of the Gods' Woods. I've never even seen it on a map.

"How did you make it through towing a dead body?" Darius asks.

He nudges his head toward the Cedenic blade sticking out of the wood floor. "Vanya."

"You named your blade?" Darius lifts a brow at the drunken warrior.

"I named my bow." I shrug.

"Vanya conducts spiritual energy—you said it yerself. And there were spirits, but they weren't any Gods. Wraiths. Nasty fucks; cloaked spirits that screech at yer and strike with talons like a Gryphon's. Almost tore my soul from my body. They wanted the dead King, but I wouldn't let them have him. Vanya conducted their ilk back at them, some shit I don't quite understand, but I could hurt 'em. *That* I could wrap my head around. I picked him up on my back after that. Walked 'till I laid him down at the dead Queen's feet."

Interesting. Another creature I'd like to read up on. If Cedenic blades affect Wraiths, I'd like to get my hands on one. It'll be good for my new monster-hunting hobby.

I sigh and stand from my chair. "Riveting tale. Although, not an answer to the question I asked."

"I answered yer damn question. I risked all for Gods and Crown.

I'm done with it. The army's done with it. The Killer Queen is a lunatic and everyone knows it."

"You're a coward," I say.

"And you're an ignorant bitch," Kade snaps.

"Watch your fucking mouth." Darius stands, slamming his hands on the table.

"Let's go, Darius. We won't get what our people need from a useless, drunken, whoremonger."

Turning away from Paragon Kade, I hear Darius' seat scratch against the wood. The Gnorrer's bones rattle as he slings the shawl-sack over his shoulder, and his footsteps follow me out of the brothel.

🔳🔳🔳🔳🔳

"There you are." Dorian leaps to his feet. Osira's still on the altar, entranced by the Gods.

"Did you get the bones?"

Darius drops them at his feet. "We defeated the Gnorrer and freed the Apostates of Trethermor.

Osira's voice breaks into a scream. She sits up as we approach the altar. She continues screaming in another tongue as she points at Darius.

"How does she see me?" He asks, stopping in his tracks.

"She senses you," I say.

"Darius, don't move," Dorian says.

Osi recoils from him, and Cesarus lurches between Darius and the altar, warning him not to take another step.

"Easy, wolfy," Darius raises his hands in surrender to Cesarus, and shows that he'll stay right where he is. Cesarus sits and Darius lets out a sigh of relief.

I take the bones and follow Dorian down a hall and into the abbey scullery. He's got a pot of boiling water already waiting on the fire.

"The bones," He waves his hands toward the pot.

321

One by one, I watch them sink into the bubbling water. He splashes what smells like vinegar in after them.

"Now what?" I ask.

"We wait."

And we do. For hours. Dorian scrapes foam and fat off the top of the water as time passes. He adds in chopped vegetables, I guess to make it more palatable.

"I've been thinking," I say.

"As have I," Dorian smiles.

"The Gnorrer had claimed the glade. The Alchemists, Famon in particular, inferred that the reason my Death Spirit's power was weakened against the beast is that I have been reborn. Remade into one of the First Sons, therefore, equal to monsters and spirits in power."

He stops stirring the broth. His smile vanishes and his lips pinch together as he looks at me. He no longer wears the veil and his eyes are piercing.

"Famon quoted Aurelisian doctrine. Darius was surprisingly well-versed, and they debated some points. I said I wasn't interested... but I am. I want to understand my divine nature. I believe it's the first step in disciplining myself to control the Death Spirit. I blame only myself for my weakness, but even my mentor, a powerful mage, has been unable to help me control my power. The truth is, I fear being corrupted by my curse and bloodlust. Liriene, my sister, also says I will lose myself to this divine nature. I need to understand. Can you help me?"

"A significant change of heart, Coroner." His eyes lower to his hands and he watches the broth swirl as he stirs it. "A few days ago, you doubted the Transcendants, your ability to revive the Tree. You called my beliefs myth."

"I apologize for my ignorance about these things." I stop and swallow, my throat uncomfortably tight. "I used to believe faith was weakness. In the Glade, when my first arrow failed, I feared that Mrithyn had forsaken me. It was a moment of weakness, cowardice. When Mrithyn made me His, He promised He would never leave me. In that moment of fear and doubt, I remembered His vow, and my faith became a strength. I ran." I laugh. "I may be cocky at times, but I'm no fool. I needed Darius to help me win. In that moment, I ran also from my doubt. I was moved by my faith: The Gods gave me a comrade, someone who would fight alongside me. I knew that was the answer. I was not alone."

"All who seek peace shall be anchored. All who request mercy shall be forgiven. All who magnify the Gods shall be uplifted. All who trust shall never have cause for fear. Barathessian twenty-two, verse sixteen," Dorian says and adds more spices to the broth.

"That's beautiful," I say.

"You want to understand your nature, to better control your power. This will come with study, but you can start with this passage. A depiction of the relationship the Gods intend for us to have with Them. An open communion. You can study doctrine, title your beliefs, live by a system or commands, and never truly grasp the simplicity of faith. When we believe the Gods' promises to us, that is faith. Religion is a matter of lifestyle. Faith is a matter of living."

We spend the rest of the wait in silence, and I try to commit the passage to memory. The whole night passes and the Sun rises again. Finally, he strains the bones from the broth, and pours the broth into a wooden bowl.

We bring it to Osira. Darius is sitting on the stone floor, legs-crossed, drifting in and out of consciousness. Cesarus is sitting vigilantly between him and Osira, who's still groaning on the altar.

"How long can she stay like this?"

"Hopefully, she won't have to stay this way much longer. Osira, drink." He holds the steaming broth to her lips, and she drinks.

I nudge Darius with my foot, and he snaps awake, standing up. We watch until she has swallowed the last drop. Dorian steps back and Cesarus moves to stand beside him as we all wait for something to happen.

"Keres," she says and sits up, but she doesn't turn in my direction. She stays fixated on Darius.

"What's wrong?" I look between her and him.

He holds up his hands again. "Should I leave?"

"Yes. Run," Osira says as she tries to climb down from the altar but falls to the floor.

"Osira, what's wrong?" Dorian's at her side first.

Darius walks back towards the door with a nervous look on his face. We exchange glances. I signal him to go. "I'll follow."

Osira collapses into Dorian's arms, and Cesarus nudges her with his muzzle. She reverts to writhing and weeping, praying in the divine tongue.

She finally comes back to us again, sputtering and coughing against sobs.

"What did you see?" Dorian presses.

"Keres," she says.

I kneel before her, "What was it, Osi?"

"As your ancestors before you have come before the Oracles and received a prophecy, so will you kneel before me. I have word of your destiny."

My stomach explodes into what feels like swarms of ants running around inside my torso. My palms sweat and I battle intense nausea.

With a vast, startling voice that is all her own, Osira speaks with confidence and with understanding. "One lost soul to guide all others. Marked on a map written in the stars. One life to another tethers one death and all our wars."

Dorian stands from her side and looks at me. I look from one to the other.

"That is your destiny, Keres." Osira smiles and holds out a hand for Dorian to help her stand. "I understand it all now. I can hear them each in their unique calls. I spoke with them all and they sang to me. Drinking the bones—it helped me. I can interpret for them and prophecy." She is talking more to Dorian now than to me.

"Who killed Queen Herrona?" Against my better judgment, it's the first thing I blurt out. "Did they tell you?"

They both turn towards me. Dorian looks to Osira, and she scratches her scalp where the last bit of hair falls.

"You must leave this place, Keres," she says.

"I need answers. King Arias of the Gryphons sent me here to spy on the court. I can't leave until I have—"

"Your people are in danger and you will not find help here. You must go to them—but the boy..."

I wait.

"Penance will die for you if you let him. You cannot let him. He's the one whose death I sensed before. I feel it in his presence."

"I won't let him."

"You must stay away from him or he will die for you. Remember, God is coming."

"Which God, Osira?" Dorian asks.

"All of them." She touches her hand to her brow, her fingers trembling against the veil. "Don't let him love you, Keres. He will die. You must forget him, you must—"

"I get it." My voice cracks. *How can I forget Darius?*

I look into her scaled eyes and see a foreign clarity within. She stands to her full stature now. "Leave tonight. You must reach your people by morning. They will need you. Go."

"There's still so much for me to learn. I want to be a disciple of this temple. I need to know these things." I look to Dorian and back to Osira. "I want to be here with you Osi—"

"You do not belong here. Not now."

"I have to help Hero too. Who killed Herrona?"

Dorian holds up a hand to me. "We will meet again, child. We will study the doctrine of Mrithyn another time. If she says there is a danger, listen to her. It seems her Veiling is complete. Trust her. You will always be welcomed here." He gestures to the tree. "This place will always be open to you. And you said you sought more than her visions, that you sought to help her—"

"It wasn't just about the answers, but I cannot return to Hero without one. Please just tell me who it was," I beg.

Osira takes in a long breath.

"Do not tarry, do not return to the palace. Leave Darius or he will die. Take my answer to those who sent you. Not to the Queen. Promise me these things, Keres."

I think of Hero and Rydel. I never got to speak with Seraphina; my mother's things are in her closet waiting for me to claim them.

"I promise. Will you tell me who killed Herrona? Was it King Berlium? Was it Ivaia? Who was it?" My fingernails are digging into the palms of my hands.

"It was Queen Hero."

26: THE LION'S DEN

The doors of the temple spit me out into the balmy afternoon. I'm lightheaded and sweaty, my heart races along a new track of thoughts. *Is it true?*

I wrap myself in my cloak, trying to shut out the forces of power in this world that are bombarding my life—my world—with relentless, malicious force. I step over the threshold, over another demarcation line in my life, and feel lost. Darius is leaning on the wall next to the door. I run down the steps, yank him by the arm and pull him down the steps with me.

"Slow down," he says.

"Can't. We have to go."

My bare feet skid in the gravelly dirt of the road. A small cloud of dust takes its first and final breath at my feet. My muscles are shaking, and my blood is roaring in my ears. I feel a bead of sweat roll down my neck as I turn to him. Dread snakes its way through my gut and coils up.

He will die.

"Darius, go home."

"What happened? What's wrong?" He grabs me by the shoulders, ignoring my dismissal. His eyes are burning holes into me, and everything inside threatens to pour out through them.

My life is like a bow. I choose an arrow and my target. I know exactly what I want. Holding my bow, I'm steady. I know what I'm doing when I draw the string back. Taking control of my life's direction, I aim. Tension strengthens me and I'm so sure I'll hit my mark. I make choices, I give parts of myself up, but I'm always aiming my path toward destruction somehow. The bowstring slips from my fingers and I can no longer control where that arrow is going. It soars, spirals wildly, and eventually plummets.

My arrows are my choices. Targets, hopes and motives. Too often I resent who I am, and what my life has become. I resent the stress and strain of making heavy choices and holding steady.

I've been trying to stay strong and be who I am. I've been trying to let the arrows fly, let go of what I can't control—praying to my God that I don't miss my mark. But no matter what I do, I can't outrun Death. I can't protect or defend *anyone*.

"So, it's true," a shrieking voice interrupts my thoughts.

A woman with sandy brown hair and honey-golden eyes crosses the dirt road in a few purposeful strides. She marches right up to Darius and me. Out of the shade of a neighboring hovel behind her, Moriya slinks into view. She glares at me.

"Moriya told me you are a whore, Keres." The woman jabs a long bony finger at me and raises a brow so high her forehead creases deeply on one side of her face. Her lips flare as she says, "*Resayla's* daughter. I've trapped my son into wedlock with a slut."

"Seraphina?" I push away from Darius.

"You will address me as Lady Prycell, Keres. Don't assume because your mother tricked me into sealing my only son's fate with yours that you may call me by my name." Her voice comes out so low, her words so quick and sure. "You were a black-haired baby girl the first time I saw you. If Moriya hadn't told me who you were, I'd never have believed you were that same child."

"Lady Prycell, call me by my name once more and I'll send you with my mother." I step forward to meet her. "You will call me Coroner. That's who I am."

"Who you are is my son's *wife*. A woman I assumed would be raised in virtue and honor. You've turned your feet away from home. And here you are, bedding another in his absence." She puckers her lips with distaste.

"You heard this from your son's mistress..."

"Moriya was not his mistress. He wasn't married to you when—"

"He was promised to me. That bind goes two ways." I point my finger toward those livid yellow eyes. "Moriya's just jealous."

"Jealous, yes. Rightfully so. She loves my son and it's clear you do not. She told me you're a dishonorable woman. For the sake of your mother, I didn't believe her. Until now." She knots her hands together. "It's clear you will never love my son. Better she acts on her convictions and in his best interest. It makes her more worthy to be my daughter than your claim does."

"Till my body is cold in the earth, Silas is mine and I am his." My voice breaks.

"I do not recognize your vows. I don't accept them."

"I vowed before the Gods and my people. Hate to break it to you, but your opinion doesn't matter."

"*Your* people are not my people or my son's people. I will have this marriage annulled."

"You can't—you have no authority," I say.

Osira told me I can't be with Darius. If my marriage to Silas is no longer in the way of being with Darius, I won't trust myself to avoid him. And he'll die.

"I will speak with the Queen," Moriya chimes in.

"I share blood with the Queen. If you think your words will sway her over mine, you're out of your mind, Moriya."

"Come, Moriya, we will speak to the Queen directly." Seraphina gathers up her skirts and Moriya follows. They can't do this.

"Hey!" I walk after them, but they ignore me. "You won't accomplish anything by doing this!"

"Then you have nothing to worry about," Seraphina calls over her shoulder.

Suddenly, my muscles are shivering with anger. How close is Moriya to Hero? Will Hero nullify my marriage based on Moriya's words? After what Osira told me, I can't predict her. What if she's just a liar? What if she really listens to them?

Darius' hand touches my shoulder and I freeze. "Is this not a sign from the Gods?" His face is blank with shock.

Darius. Here I am, defending my unwanted marriage. In front of him.

"Keres, don't you see? This is the answer. If Queen Hero annuls your marriage... you'll be free. We can be together."

"Darius—"

"This is what you want, isn't it? To be rid of Silas." He catches my hands in his. "Don't run after them. Don't try to stop them. Let them try and if they succeed, run with me this time. Last time, you ran and didn't look back. I told you I was right behind you. I'm still here, Keres. Come with me. We can hide out in the inn. They won't know."

"We can't just hide."

"You've already given me so much." He touches my body shamelessly. "Why take it all back now? To give yourself to Silas—he doesn't even love you. He didn't come after you. I did."

"Darius we can't."

"We *can*. We can go anywhere." He smiles and tears rise to his eyes. "We don't even have to go back to Ro'Hale. We can go away from all

330

this pain and find our happiness. Together." He grabs my face, "You know it's me. I'm the one you wanted. Not the one who took from you, but the one you gave yourself to."

My heartbeat is pounding so hard against my ribs, I fear it'll break through my chest. I can hear his too, matching mine. Tears brim in my eyes.

"You must have known from the minute you caught me in your bed, that I followed you here against all warning because I wanted you, Keres."

"Not like this, Darius." I glance around at the people passing us by on the road, eying us like they might run and tell the Queen too.

"But it's true." He laughs, "You're the first girl to ever see me as I am. To feel what I feel inside." He places my hand over his heart. "The pain, the anger, the passion, the power of what you do to me. Our hearts are broken but the pieces fit together."

That earns a sob from me. "No, Darius."

"Why?" He pulls back. "Why are you fighting me on this? Tell me the truth. Tell me what I see in your eyes. I'm not fucking blind, and I'm no fool. You're already mine, you just won't admit it to yourself. You don't belong to him no matter how loudly you swore it in front of the Gods. This—" His hands snake around my waist and latch on. "This." He kisses me, biting my lip. "Mine."

I stutter and gasp back my tears. One of his callused hands flies to my throat and the other wipes a tear from my cheek. "Don't lie to yourself or to me. I told you before not to play games with me. When I laid you down in that orchard and made your body weak for me, you told me you were mine. You told me not to give myself to anyone else. Don't take back what you fucking said, Keres."

His eyes study my face and I close mine, allowing the tears to be pressed out.

Shaking me gently he says, "Please, be honest with me. Right now, Keres. Right fucking now, tell me the truth."

"I can't."

"*Tell me.*" His grip tightens on my throat.

"Darius." I swallow hard and recollect the shreds of my voice. "I have to go. You have to go. Osira said you would die—"

"I am not afraid to die. I'm not scared of Death Herself either." He smiles and a tear escapes his eye. "I am afraid to live without you. And we have this one chance."

"It's not our chance." I try to push out of his hands, but he holds me tighter. "We will never get the chance we deserve! And I will never take a chance on losing you—"

"Then don't lose me—"

"Your *life*, Darius," my voice comes out in broken sobs. "I have seen so much death. I have caused it. I've hunted, killed, and lost too many people. My mother. Katrielle. Your brother. I've failed them all. The Gods have shown Osira I will cause your death, and I can't allow that to happen, Darius. I can't lose you, too. I am the worst part of you and you don't see it, but I'm seeing it now for the first time. You should have listened to what people told you about me. That I'm dangerous, wicked. Isn't that what you told me?" I feel tension in my neck.

"If I'm free from Silas, I'm free to hurt you. I don't trust myself to stay away from you if I'm unbound from him. It's too risky. This time, this monster needs to stay in this cage."

He tears himself away from me, running his hands through his hair. I count his heavy breaths. His shoulders rise and fall. I hear his lungs moving in his chest; his throat tightening. He lets out a sigh and lifts his hands to me. Open and waiting. Those ember eyes ignite with passion. Our tempers burn to the same degree as our desire.

"What am I supposed to do then, huh?" His voice thins. "Where am

I supposed to go if I can't follow you? I've lost everyone I ever cared about. Now you want me to give up the one person I have left? I'm not leaving, Keres. I will not turn my back on you. Are you telling me you will stay here? Or are we really supposed to go back to camp and go on living like you're not the best thing that's happened to me since Hayes died? You're delusional if you think that will work."

"I don't know where I'm going to go or what will happen to me. All I know is you have to be somewhere safe." I flurry my hands, "You have to go…"

"Where?" He asks again. My mind reels with the idea of him being gone from my life.

Osira said I must return to my people. He can't come with me, but he's right. How could we ever pretend? I want to go back to the orchard. I want to go back in time, before my wedding, before the nine, before——

"King Arias." I step up to him and take his hands. "Go to the Moldorn, Darius."

"What? No bloody, fucking way."

"Please!"

He stops and his fiery eyes settle on me.

"Please, go. Take a message for me." I remember Emisandre. *You will give him words.* I reach into his pocket for Pophis which had turned back into a small stick. I put it in his hand, and it transforms again into a staff. He watches it and realization dawns on his perfect face.

"Somehow, Emisandre saw this would happen. Something Other is at work here. Can't you see it? I am giving you these words straight from the Oracle's mouth." He looks back at me and I look around to make sure no one is listening. "The one who killed Queen Herrona was her daughter, Queen Hero."

"Is that true?" His brows shoot up.

"If it is, then it is also true that I will cause your death."

He runs his hand down his face and clamps his delicious mouth shut. He throws Pophis to the ground and wraps me in his thickly muscled arms. Lifting me into his embrace, he kisses me passionately, desperately. I'm shattered. My resolve, broken.

Please, don't let time move, I pray to some distant God as I revel in the taste of my sin. *Let us stay here like this.*

But no comfort comes. My blood is chilled. Where there should be an unquenchable inferno of lust and emotion erupting within me, there is a chasm yawning open and I must fill it with ice to stop a flood of pain from springing up. I will be the death of him.

"Darius, you have to go. King Arias awaits the message. Tell him about the court, about Paragon Kade, about Osira." I look into his eyes, trying to bury all my feelings under a mound of snow within me.

I fail.

"I'll go. For you. I'll do anything for you... except for one thing." He stays toe to toe with me and touches my face so tenderly it breaks me. "I will never forget you or stop looking for you. No matter how many times you tell me this bullshit prophecy about my death. I'll never stop needing to find you. I will find you again. We will be together, and life will be different. We will conquer anything that stands in our way, stand by each other's side, and keep fighting for each other. This is my promise to you, Keres. I'll make good on it one day."

I throw my arms around his neck and hold on for dear life. The only reason I let go is because of Death.

🔲🔲🔲🔲🔲

I should have listened to Osira.

Upon entering the throne room, my stomach turns to water. Hero looks almost naked in a mesh and skeletal bodysuit. Her face is smeared with blood, and her platinum hair is knotted and stiff with it. She's dragging an axe behind her across the marble floor. Sparks fly from beneath the blade as it grates against it. A headless corpse is slumped over on the floor behind her, leaking blood onto the floor of the crowd. Still wearing their animal skins, the courtiers cling to each other and whisper prayers to the Pantheon. Armored guards line the edges of the room, towering over everyone in suits of gold armor like Paragon Kade's.

"As you know!" Hero continues her sermon, "All those who defy me shall pay the same price as he." She lifts the axe with one hand toward the body. Looking up briefly into the menagerie of courtiers, she sees me.

Osira claims Hero killed her own mother. Then why does she continue to do this? Is it a facade to distract from the truth? Is this merciless, murderous queen her true face? Is her mask the face of a vengeful believer? She smiles at the obvious confusion on my face.

Rydel croons, "My Queen, your Coroner has arrived."

"I see her, thank you, my devil." She flashes me a toothy grin and beckons me over with a red hand.

I pass through the wide-eyed crowd, closing the distance between us with slow steps and heavy regret. Her smile does not fade, her lurid eyes do not dim. She's radiating bloodthirst. I see, for the first time, the face of the feared Queen who wears a crown fashioned of her own people's bones. Not a girl grieving the death of her mother. For the first time, I look at the face of a ruler who is enthralled by violent tyranny. And for once, I do not know her at all. Should I really be trying to keep her on the throne? Is she any better than our Human enemies?

"Come, cousin, show our people their Goddess." She hisses and twirls her axe at the crowd. I walk to meet her at the foot of the Mirrored Throne.

"I wield my weapon like an oil lamp. It will burn endlessly, lighting my way to the truth, or it will consume you all!" Spit flies from her mouth.

The smell of blood is a heavy stench in the air. It's an unrivaled assault on the senses; the kind that makes you see red when you're not even looking.

"Here is our Coroner. Our Goddess of Death." She holds out the axe, offering it to me. "The White Reaper." She snorts back her laughter. She moves like she's drunk, and I know it's on blood, not wine.

Her offer wakes up the monster inside me. My palms itch for the axe. Though there is no wind here, I feel a familiar chill creeping along my bones. I swallow back a growing knot in my throat. The smell of blood is so heady and creates an ache in my chest that makes me want to drown in it. My peripheral vision darkens. I shake myself, trying to focus through the frenzy that's creeping up my spine and into my head.

This is my curse. This is my true nature. A dangerous, wicked monster that revels in the sights and smells of bloodshed. Death.

Thoughts of Darius barrage my mind. I would have been his downfall. I'm not worthy of love like his. I have been reborn as one of the First Children of the Gods, kinswoman to monsters. Dizzy and heartbroken, I want to give into what my Death Spirit is hungry for.

I reach for the axe. I just want it all to end, to float away into oblivion.

"Her arrows do not fail; her blades do not miss. She cannot be equaled in battle." Queen Hero's words are like an incantation, summoning the beast inside of me.

I close my eyes and wrap my fingers around the cold, steel shaft of the axe. It soothes my clammy palms. I tighten my grip and a bead of sweat rolls down my forehead. As she releases her hold on the weapon, my hand sinks with the full weight of it. It's sticky with blood.

"She is the Hallow-World's Hound!"

"A soldier."

Queen Hero's chanting voice fades into the background and Ivaia's fills the void.

"An instrument of the divine." Ivaia waved the long lighting stick drawing with its smoke. *"A Mage."* She blew out the flame. *"A three-headed hound."*

Anger shook my voice in that cave. My desperation echoed against its walls.

"This life comes with a curse. You marvel at the monster the Gods have made me into, what the curse does to me. A three-headed hound, as you said. Still only a dog bid to do Their will!"

A smile breaks my mouth open, and I open my eyes to see Queen Hero watching me. I hand her back the axe and take control of myself. A frown ruins her face.

"Oh, Divine Executioner." She tosses it to my feet, ignoring my rejection of it. "Who here shall we have next? I'd like a pair of gloves." She rubs one hand over the other, pointing at each knuckle.

I catch sight of Rydel. His countenance has fallen, eyes jumping from his beloved Queen to me.

"Coroner?" Queen Hero demands my attention again. "Are you not our Avenger?"

"She is no more than a common whore."

There she is. Seraphina glides forward. "The Coroner is guilty of adultery."

Queen Hero twists her neck to watch Seraphina approach. She curtsies, lowering her eyes to the blood and marble floor. Straightening her spine, she clasps her hands before her chest.

"She is as unfit to carry out Divine Justice for you, my Queen, as she is unfit to be married to my son. Her sin is of a nature which brooks no apology. I humbly beg you annul her marriage to my son, Silas. Your Majesty, please heed my testimony. I am a mother concerned for her only child. Keres is a depraved woman. A witch!"

Queen Hero doesn't even look at me. The entire court is dead silent. Licking her lips, Hero picks the axe back up and rests it on her shoulder. Finally, she looks at me. She examines the blood under her fingernails before tilting her head at Seraphina.

"You dare accuse my own cousin—the blood of my blood?"

Poising myself beside Hero, I flash Lady Prycell a feral grin and beckon her to come a little closer. Seraphina's face creases and she lowers her eyes back to the pool of blood between her and us. I can't believe she tried. *Now*, when the Queen is ravenous for blood and gristle. Moriya shuffles forward with her sister Faye at her side.

"We are not accusing without evidence." She lifts her hand in supplication to her Queen.

"Oh, I see." Queen Hero grins at her. "My little rabbit wants her lion. What evidence do you have?"

"I saw her lover in her bed-chamber—I told you of this the day he came."

"I was there," Faye says. "When Moriya told you."

"Enough." Hero twirls on her toes, swinging her axe. She spins and points it at me. Spins and points it at them. Spiraling among us in a circle of decision.

"Kneel, Lady Prycell."

Seraphina trembles as she kneels, hands knotted in her scarlet gown.

"Lean forward."

"Your Majesty, I beg of you." She bows her head forward and Queen Hero readies her axe. "Send for my husband. Let me see him, I beg of you. I never meant to upset your Highness. I only wish to—"

The axe slips clear through her neck and clangs on the marble floor. Another burst of blood paints the white floors red. Moriya and Faye scream, along with many of the courtiers. I turn away and steady my breathing. My husband's mother's body thuds against the floor, and her head rolls to my feet.

All sounds dull in my ears from the shock until Queen Hero points a bloody hand at Moriya and says, "You were sleeping with my cousin's husband—"

"Before he married her!" Moriya interrupts, taking several steps back.

"Cadathan," Hero says and snaps her fingers with her free hand. An armored guard steps forward. "Restrain my servant. She's spoken out of turn."

Moriya yelps as Cadathan's hand lands on her shoulder. "Please, don't hurt me!"

"Please—my Queen, let her go," Faye says and drops to her knees. Blood seeps into her sky-blue gown. I scan the crowd quickly for the third bunny but don't see Nadia anywhere.

Rydel paces behind us. Queen Hero approaches Moriya and levels the blade of her axe at her throat. I don't like the girl, but I don't want another person to die. Not over pettiness.

I thought Queen Hero liked Moriya. She defended her the other night when I spoke badly of her. She's lost it. I don't know whether I should speak up or remain silent. Moriya hums to herself, whimpering as Hero touches the blade to her neck. I can hear Moriya's heart fluttering in her chest. I can hear Rydel's and Faye's. Every heart in this court is beating like the leaves of the tree in the temple, pulsing fast and hard. Drumming a battle hymn. Except for Queen Hero's. Her pupils dilate, her gestures slow. Her heart is steady and dull. I can hear the blood coursing through her veins as she considers spilling Moriya's.

"You've slandered my cousin before the court. You have no evidence of your claims, nothing I could stake my cousin's marriage on. Aside from that, her husband is not here, and should the marriage truly be in question, it would be his testimony that matters. Not his mother's or his former lover's. Garnish it all with a little disrespect for your Queen, and it's safe to say you're asking for an execution." She raises the axe to strike.

"Stop or I'll tell everyone about the women!" Faye screams.

Queen Hero tosses her head back, her blood-curdled hair sticking to her face and neck. Laughter bubbles up in her throat.

"I'll tell them all. They'll overthrow you." Faye charges at Queen Hero, but another guard catches her and holds her back.

"Tell them," Queen Hero barks. "Better yet, I'll show them myself. Rydel."

"My Queen," He says, stepping forward and bowing.

"Summon Andraste."

I step back as Rydel passes me and is escorted out of the courtroom by three of the Queen's guards. Faye crumples to the floor beside her sister. Moriya's yellow eyes brim with tears at the sight of Faye on her knees. She mouths something to her sister, and they reach for each other. Moriya grabs onto Faye with both hands as the guards attempt to separate them.

"No," Faye says.

"Seize Faye." Queen Hero flutters her fingers at Cadathan.

"No—you can't have her," Moriya growls. Cadathan lifts Faye up from under her arms.

"Please," Moriya flings herself onto the floor, prostrating herself before Queen Hero. Lying in the blood. "Spare Faye. She doesn't know what she's doing. Have we not served you faithfully for years, my Queen? Please, do not punish her rashness. Punish me instead."

"It's okay, Mor." Faye says as the guard puts her in chains. She doesn't resist.

"It will be okay." She gives in as Moriya continues pleading with the Queen.

I turn away, not able to watch as they drag her away. My mind is filled with only one name: Liriene. Her face replaces Faye's and it feels like every nerve in my body is aflame. Millions of tiny matchsticks under my skin. Tears drown out my vision and I wipe my eyes, also trying to wipe away the vision of my sister in shackles.

Moriya kicks and screams, trying to fight for her sister as another guard grabs her by the hair. "Not my sister," she roars. "*Please.*"

I watch through my tears as Cadanthan pushes Faye through the crowd and out of the courtroom.

"Fuck you," Moriya spits at Hero. "Damn you—if you hurt her—"

"Jorah," Queen Hero says. "Make her quiet." The one called Jorah kicks Moriya in the stomach, knocking her onto her hands and knees. Doubled over, she curls into a ball. Her wheezing turns into sobbing.

Rydel returns with someone following him. Her black and gray shaggy robes cover her from head to toe. As they approach, I glimpse her face beneath the hood. Her skin is dull and dark gray. On Rydel's heels, she approaches the Queen and keeps her black eyes on the floor. Her nose crinkles and her mouth tightens as she walks through the blood. Queen Hero circles around her and tears the hood of her robe back, revealing silky straight black hair that reaches her waist. A strange shadow hangs around her neck like a torq, something easily recognizable as supernatural.

"Sing for Moriya, Andraste," Queen Hero leans in close to her ear, and continues stripping away the woman's robes. She's naked beneath, but she does not cover herself. Instead, she allows Hero to strip her. She holds her hands at her side and opens her mouth. Two sharp fangs jut out from her top row of teeth and her tongue lolls out of her mouth, split like a snake's. The black of her irises takes over her eyes; like ink pouring into milk, until there are no whites.

Her voice sounds far away at first, a high-pitched whistle tone that swells and deepens until it fills the room and collides with everyone in it. In the wake of her song, the palace quakes and people stumble over.

The chandeliers shiver and chime. Relentlessly, without taking a breath, her song endures. All we can do is try to keep our balance.

The robe slips down her frame to her feet and she steps out of it, raising her hands and her voice to a near-deafening pitch.

Moriya screams as she touches her ears and finds blood on her hands. I cover my ears, but the sound breaks through. A headache splits my skull and my teeth chatter.

I finally notice her swollen belly as she steps forward. Her bare feet trek through the blood. She rolls her neck back and trills her voice, orchestrating a hymn of destruction. People fall to their knees as she passes by, her shadowy torq draping over her shoulders and trailing down her body. Moriya convulses. The strange woman's vibrato rings in my bones and raises every hair on my body. Her voice dissipates into a distant whistling tone once more, and the song ends. Moriya does not stir.

Queen Hero's applause earns a pointed smile from the woman. There's only one explanation for what she is. People cower as she turns and walks back to Hero's side. Her hands lovingly careen over the edges of her abdomen. I wipe a drop of blood from my ear lobe and stare at her. Queen Hero places her hand on the woman's pregnant belly.

"Andraste is a Lamentar and fugitive of Illyn," Queen Hero says. The crowd roils, waving their fists and shouting obscenities at the foreigner.

"She was a slave in her homeland, raped and impregnated by her former master," Hero raises her voice.

The crowd's rage simmers down but some mutter still.

"A monster!"

"She fled Illyn, crossed the Rift, and stumbled into our land. Alone, exhausted, famished, and with child. Dying. Our men found her collapsed in the woods. They brought her here, to me. I had her fed, clothed, and gave her shelter here in the palace. Hid her."

"You knowingly welcomed Aureum's enemy into our land?" A courtier shouts.

Queen Hero shakes her head and laughs. She draws back and throws the axe. It somersaults through the air and lodges in his rib cage. Blood spurts from his chest and gurgles in his throat, silencing his scream.

I flinch but not from fear—from the overwhelming rush of pleasurable adrenaline.

He flies backward and hits the ground, sliding into the crowd. People dash out of his body's way, shrieking and sobbing. Hero obviously has some combat skills I didn't see before.

"There are others like her under my care. The women Faye mentioned, who were enslaved, sold, abused, and broken. Who have found their way into our lands and into my care." Hero opens her arms to the courtiers. "Judge me as a traitor. Accuse me of conspiring with our natural enemy."

Nobody dares speak.

"Or praise me as Savior of the damned."

"What about your own people?" My voice comes out stronger than I expected. "The damned of the Sunderlands."

Queen Hero searches the crowd for the person who dared question her, not immediately realizing it was me.

I lift my hands. "You have been very generous in your mercy to these refugees. I am sure they would praise you as you deserve. But what about your people in the clans?"

"I have spoken with you about the army's disobedience," she says.

"And I have spoken with your advisor, Rydel. With Paragon Kade himself, who denies rebellion. He accuses you of ordering the Legion of Ro'Hale to abandon the clans."

"What do you accuse me of, Coroner?" Queen Hero stalks closer to me. "What else have you heard? What lies fly like fiery arrows?" She stops and points her finger toward the palace doors. "What has your beloved child Oracle told you?"

I look around at the sea of eyes trained on me. Reminding me of my kinsmen in the clans.

"Sweet Queen," Rydel intervenes. "I do not think your cousin is accusing you."

"Are you siding with her?" Hero snaps at her lover.

"As the ambassador of Elistria, my duty is to be objective." He smiles at her. "I am not here to take sides, but to ensure that peace is kept."

"There will be no peace for the Sunderlands. This land is lost to us," She says. "War and havoc will purge this land with a fiery storm."

"The only thing this land needs to be purged of is the plague of humans, their control, and oppression." I ball my hands into fists. Several courtiers cheer in agreement.

"Our war is with the Baore. Not with each other. Look around, Queen Hero."

Her eyes dart from me to Rydel to the courtiers.

"The longer you reign with terror and bloodshed, the farther you will drive your people from you until they have no choice but to rise against you," I say.

"They fear me because they are guilty," she says. "My mother's blood is on their hands!"

She crosses the distance between us, getting in my face. "You told me you believed me."

She crumples, leaning forward, and puts her hands on her knees. "Please, Keres. Someone must believe me." She stands again and knots her fingers in her hair.

I lock my mouth shut.

"Say you have an answer for me. You've been to see the Oracle. Tell me her revelations." She runs back to the body where her axe is and rips it out of him.

"You went to see Osira. I gave you charge of her. You told me to let you help her, to get answers. I want my answer *now*."

"Hero—" my hand goes to the scythe at my hip.

"I have waited long enough. I get my answer from the Gods today or the girl dies."

The room is spinning. My head is feeling fuzzy. My hand tightens on the scythe hilt.

"Do you know the truth?" Rydel's voice slips into my mind.

"Osira gave an answer."

"Will the truth get you killed?" He asks.

"It's looking that way."

"If you lie, the girl dies."

"Yes," I say.

"Then you must choose."

Lie and get Osira killed, or tell the truth, and accuse the Queen of killing her own mother before the court? Accuse the Queen, earn her wrath, and endanger my own life. Or worse— stir her people against her. They will usurp her if they learn the truth. If I allow that or if I kill her myself, I'll have failed my duty to protect her. I'd be making the Mirrored Throne vulnerable to our enemy, King Berlium. Breaking this kingdom wide open.

Or do I sacrifice Osira? Tell the Queen she doesn't have an answer. Let her take her frustration out on the child. To keep us safe from the Baore. To save my own life and make my escape.

Is my life even worth it?

I think of what Ivaia must have felt when faced with the choice to sacrifice her sister to King Berlium: to maintain the alliance or to break the spell, free her sister, and cost our kingdom everything. She got herself exiled and was disowned by the very family she was fighting to save. She chose her sister's life over her own, and over the fate of our entire Province. She must have known what her fate would be.

But if I know Ivaia, I know exactly how she made such an impossible decision: by faith. Since I've known her, Ivaia's unwavering belief in Elymas and her God-given power has driven everything she's ever done. Adept and tenacious in her magical practice, Ivaia revealed a curse on the Queen of Ro'hale. A curse so binding and dangerous, she felt compelled to break it no matter the cost. She sensed darkness in the Grizzly King's hold on her sister. She stayed true to herself despite the consequences and severed the tie between the Baore and the Sunderlands without a second thought. For the love of her sister, for the sake of our people, for faith in herself. Now, a hero in exile.

I stare down the Huntress in this court of beasts and draw strength from the lessons I've learned under Ivaia. Resenting my power isn't helping anyone. Passing blame—it's cowardly. Is my life worth saving at the expense of an innocent girl? If I save myself at her expense then, no, I don't deserve to live. But I don't have to die and neither does Osira. Not for a liar.

"My friend Osi said the Gods are coming to the Sunderlands." I draw my scythe. "But One's already here with me."

Queen Hero has a power that holds her spine straight when she walks and clears her throat when she speaks. Confidence that turns heads and mercilessness that sends them rolling across the floor. A perversion of Mrithyn's power that I despise seeing in one of my own kin.

But I possess a power too. One I've long resented. No more. The Death Spirit in me grins and I bare all its teeth at Hero. It's time I had a little faith.

Queen Hero grips her axe, wringing it as if it were Osira's neck.

I turn toward the crowd of courtiers, "My name is Keres Nyxara Aurelian, right hand to the God of Death. An heir to the Mirrored

Throne, I came by blood right to this court. On behalf of King Arias and the Heralds of the Moldorn..."

At that, Hero goes rigid and the people whisper.

"To question the actions of mortals and measure the influence of meddling Gods." I hold up my scythe. "For years, while you've slept behind the palace walls in peace, the clans have suffered at the hands of the Dalis. In the darkness, I sowed Death's vengeance and reaped the souls of our enemies. I stood as a bulwark against their waves of assault and tempered their power over our lands. I know I've done well, for you have not felt the losses the clans have."

The court is silent, watching my every move. Hero fidgets with her axe.

"Within the palace, you are sheltered, you remain ignorant of the blight on our land. I slew the beast of Trethermor Glade, a Gnorrer that crossed the rift into our land from Illyn. I brought its bones to the Oracle and helped her interpret the Gods' revelations so you would be blind no longer."

"Well?" Hero raises her axe toward me.

I hold up a quieting hand and lower my voice. "They have revealed the late Queen Herrona's killer in a vision."

Rydel backs away from Queen Hero and folds his hands behind his back, watching me. In my mind, I apologize to King Arias for failing my mission. I pray to every God in the Pantheon that the Mirrored Throne is protected from the Baore's grasp in Hero's downfall. I'd rather see it in Rydel's hands than King Berlium's.

Queen Hero murdered her own mother and would go to the lengths of killing Osira to protect her lie. Whether Osira never got an answer from the Gods or learned the truth, Hero would have killed her. She was toying with me, making me believe her. No more. The Sunderlands deserves better, and I won't let Hero make Osira her scapegoat.

"I am merely an Instrument of the divine, and the Gods accuse Queen Herrona's murderer through me now." I point my scythe at the Huntress Queen. "Queen Hero slew her own mother."

The uproar is deafening. The courtiers close in on Hero, but her guards draw their blades and kill anyone in their path as they run to her. I step back, searching for a way through the crowd. Queen Hero snarls and runs toward me, slamming into a noble instead. Andraste raises her voice, bellowing in defense of her rescuer. I look for Rydel but can't find him. Stumbling backward and ducking down out of Hero's sight, I reach for the bottle of Scorn in my pocket.

A buxom rabbit girl with long red hair grabs my hand. "Keres, this way!"

She pulls me through the crowd and down a passageway. I shove Scorn back into my pocket.

I don't allow myself to stop or turn around. Tuning out my kingdom's cry for help, I turn a cold shoulder to the emptiness of my cousin's soul. I run. Hopefully, after my escape, I'll be able to channel Osira and warn her. My skin pebbles, the hairs on the back of my neck rise, and a sense of impending doom overrides my thoughts.

Hurrying in silence with Nadia, I pay no attention to the grandeur of the palace or the screams of its exotic, misfitting residents.

We burst through the white door into the deserted pleasure gardens and sprint down the rows of banquet tables. At the other end of the gardens, there's an ivy-covered gate. She stops here and pulls my rucksack from behind a bush. Shoving it into my arms, she opens it briefly.

"Your mother's necklace." She says.

"How did you know—"

"Run east, ford the river, and go home. Don't look back. Don't stop until you're there. I'll get to Osira."

"Nadia—" I grab her shoulders. "Why are you helping me?"

She brushes me off and catches my face in her satin-soft hands. She kisses me full on the mouth. My body locks in shock.

"Goodbye, Keres." She smiles and her blue eyes deepen a shade. She opens the creaky gate and pushes me through, locking it behind me.

Go home. Your people are in danger and you will not find help here. You must go to them.

"I walk through a strange land, cast under the shadow of the wings of Death..." I toss my rucksack over my shoulder and point myself east. "Ancestors, guide my steps. Gods, go with me, and I will fear no evil."

27: THE ACCURSED

The Ro'Hale Kingdom claws at my back and nips at my ankles as I try to leave. I have no choice but to move forward despite so many secrets that are yet to unravel their truth. I'm leaving the Ro'Hale Kingdom with more questions than I came with.

Why did Hero kill her mother? What will happen to Osira? Will Elistria seize the Mirrored Throne through Rydel? What God holds sway over the kingdom? How long will Aureum be safe with Illyn fugitives leaking into our strongholds?

I have no choice but to do as I'm told and return home. As usual. I'm a frozen ant. I grip my prayer beads in sweaty palms.

What I did back there took a spark of courage, but now that fire is dwindling back into fear. It's like I caused an explosion at court and turned my back to the flames. I know my decision to protect Osira and flee will have consequences. I'm also trusting the Gods are on my side.

"Move on, Keres." The Death Spirt hisses. But the burning question in the forefront of my mind is, how will the people of the Sunderlands get the help they need? I stirred the people and they will rise against Hero, but they won't rise for the clans. They just want to survive; want to end her bloody tyranny. I just want to survive myself.

I can't stand alone forever. Which means I've got a witch to visit.

🈁🈁🈁🈁🈁

The decrepit hut and its wards attempt to repel me, but I approach despite them. More than the magic, my pride halts me at the creaking door.

I hear a wolf howling somewhere in the distance.

"Oh, Gods." A bit jumpier than usual, I stop short, making eye contact with another wolf.

Its shaggy, gray fur and beady eyes regard me. Its teeth bare. It looks me up and down, and then just howls back in reply to its distant kin. I walk away slowly. It doesn't seem to care about me though. It just lets me slip by. I pick up my pace, never letting my attention wander again.

I push through the unhinged, broken door, and walk forward through the darkness I know so well, melting into it. I'm one step closer to reuniting with Silas, and one step farther from Darius.

Old feelings ambush me. All over again, I want to be someone else so badly it might kill me. I feel myself backsliding into bitterness. My curse is still lingering above me like a blade.

Gods know I'm trying. They've heard me begging all my second life. No help comes. Now, I'm running from enemies surrounding me, not just from the enemy within. If anyone else could see the things I've done... if anyone else could feel the things I'm feeling... they'd end it here. Cross the threshold to eternal darkness.

I think of Liriene, my beloved, exasperating sister. So pure in her intentions. She had her own secrets too—a secret love. Nothing dark or twisted about that. She floats through this world, benign, like a feather. And I am... me.

The mirage spell melts away, and I'm left staring at the loft nestled in the trees and the beacon of warm, glowing lights behind the windows. Every star of my favorite constellation is missing from the deepening evening sky.

Ivaia and Riordan aren't expecting me. No one waits for me at the foot of the steps to lead me by the hand up the spiral staircase into the trees. But I'll go anyway, and I'll make things right. I don't want to go backward. It's time to outgrow this angst.

The stairs creak under my feet and I cling to the banister for dear life. Peeking into the windows as I ascend, I glimpse them. A feeble knock on the door awards me with nothing. I sigh and knock again with more conviction. I hear the locks sliding out of place. All three of them. The knob turns. The door pushes me backward.

A pair of diamond eyes blink at me, and then the other set of diamonds in a curl-framed face appears.

Her eyes fill with tears before mine do. The three of us melt into each other, a huddle racked by blubbering apologies. Whoever is petting my shoulder and whose hair I'm crying into—it doesn't matter. I pull back and scan both their faces. This is my favorite constellation: these two sets of starlit eyes.

"Ivaia, I—"

All at once, they're both talking. "Hush, girl. I know. We're glad you came home. How are you? Would you like some tea?"

I follow them into the loft and am welcomed by the aromas of smoldering firewood, flowering plants, and freshly brewed herbal tea. The air outside is crisp, the trees mostly bare. Inside the loft, a fire is going strong and heat soothes my pebbled skin. I'm crossing over yet another threshold on my way home.

Why then do I feel as if I'm going farther from it?

Riordan pushes his favorite teacup into my cold hands; white bone china with hand-painted red wolves. My finger wanders over the rim, marking the chip in the edge. From heavy use, no doubt. The tea smells like jasmine flowers and honey. I inhale the steam and venture a sip before returning my attention to them. I drink and wash Darius' name out of my mouth.

Traditionally, we take our usual places on the body-sized pillows and fur throws. Each of us cradles a cup of tea for comfort. I'm swallowed up by the plush forest green pillow, and my toes dig into the fur at my feet. Riordan takes his spot between two long-leafed plants, reclining with his feet near the firepit. Ivaia sits on the ground beside him, leaning back into him. He wraps an arm around her, and she rubs her hand over it.

"I went to court," I start.

They nod. I assume he told her.

"As King Arias asked to meet with Queen Hero. To investigate the army. The Oracle said I'd need to be back with the clan by tonight. Said they needed me. But I had to see you first."

They both smile.

"At first I felt Hero was not as mad as everyone claimed. I saw things in her I've seen in myself. I related to her chaos because we both lost our mothers." I cling to the cup of tea, looking at the crumbled tea leaves within. "I justified her actions." I look back into their eyes. "She's executing her own subjects—wearing their bones." I shiver. "Publicly punishing those who disagree with her, by death. She dresses her courtiers like animals, and she is the huntress of truth. I arrived, and she was wearing a crown of bones on her head, dressed as a bird of prey. In a blood frenzy." I shake my head. "I accepted her because I saw myself in her. Ruthless power, unbridled grief. Pain, loss of control. Nothing good, I now realize." I frown. "But Osira's Unveiling finished. I met her in the temple of Mrithyn." I look to Ivaia.

Her expression alters, but she doesn't interrupt me.

"The Oracle revealed that Herrona *was* killed." I hesitate, still reeling from the truth myself. "And Hero is the one who killed her."

Ivaia flinches.

Riordan's free hand is at her back, rubbing soothing circles over the thin mesh gown.

"I'm sorry, Iv. To bear such terrible news."

"I don't believe it," Ivaia says flat out.

"Can we doubt an Oracle?" I ask.

She looks up at the ivy crawling along the ceiling. We both know the answer's not there.

"I don't believe it," Ivaia whispers.

She's always spoken ill of Hero. Believed she was mad. I thought she was just misunderstood. Which, even if it were true, is just as bad. A misunderstood girl is a dangerous thing. But Ivaia doesn't suspect the insane heiress on the throne? Not even with Osira's testimony?

I believe Osira. I've been in the Other realm with her. I stood beside her on our channeling bridge and heard Mrithyn. I know He's with her, and He never lies to me.

"I sensed the influence of a God at court. It's the only explanation. At times, Hero's mind was sound. Then she'd snap. She craved her mother's mirror and spoke in the Divine tongue—I believe she's a servant, like me."

"The servant of Ahriman?" Riordan asks.

"Isn't it possible that she is?" I ask.

"No one knows who the servant of Chaos is, if there even is one," Ivaia says.

"If there is, I suspect it might be her. She's hosting Illyntar fugitives under her protection. Cavorting with our enemy. She turned her back on her people. Murdered her own mother. Gods know if she's the right hand of War, but if she is... that makes her my natural enemy."

"I don't think there is enough proof she is a Servant," Ivaia says. "Does she exhibit any power?"

"None. Unless her power is manipulation. She seemed to have some combat skills that she made seem underwhelming early on. Things got bloody in the throne room." I think for a moment. "There was her lover, Rydel. An ambassador of Elistria. He showed... something."

"What?"

"At first, I thought he'd drugged me. Used a potion or something in my tea. But the second time it happened he used nothing. Except what I now see is his power."

"What did he do?" Riordan asks.

"I heard him in my mind. Talking with me in my thoughts. He slipped in and out of my head like a dream."

"Perhaps he is the servant. Elistria has no great love for Ro'Hale after King Tamyrr's death," Ivaia says.

"I met with the lone survivor of the ambush on King Tamyrr, too. Paragon Kade, captain of the forces," I add.

"And? Will the army aid the clans?" Riordan asks.

"He says Queen Hero won't allow them to. She claims they won't obey."

"One of them is lying," Ivaia says.

"I instructed Darius to deliver that information to King Arias. He might send help—"

"Darius?" Ivaia tightens her mouth. Riordan raises his brows.

"Yes," I breathe.

"The young man who accompanied you here the night the Oracle channeled you?" She asks.

"Yes." Thoughts of him swarm me, heating my body. My mouth goes dry and I lick my lips, fidgeting in my seat. I take another sip of tea. I already miss him. "He's headed to the Moldorn."

I look to Riordan for relief, but he laughs, "You slept with him."

I close my eyes and rub a hand over my face.

"By the Gods, girl." Ivaia picks up her tea. Before taking a sip, she adds, "I hope you at least read page seventy-nine," and smiles into the steaming cup.

I toss a pillow at her. That damned, holy sex book.

"Doesn't matter what happened between us. He's gone. Carrying my message to the Gryphon King. Hopefully, they will intervene with Hero and our people will get the help they need." Hope sparks within me.

"*If* he makes it to the Moldorn with that message. Our Queen has abandoned us. He's our only hope now," Ivaia says, the light in her eyes dimming.

I shoot a silent prayer, quick as an arrow, heavenward. For his safety. For our deliverance. I'm predisposed to despair, and I often give in to sinking feelings and wallow in my misery. Darius... trekking south to relay a message that may stem the tide of bloodshed and turn the war. With that in mind, I can keep hope. I have faith in him. I remember his promise to me: *We will conquer anything that stands in our way, stand by each other's side, and keep fighting for each other. He'll be our saving grace, and then he'll come back to me.*

"I don't understand," Riordan stands. "No matter what Hero did or didn't do, her kingdom is in shambles and the Baore is on her doorstep. If she wanted the throne enough to kill her own mother over it, she'd defend it. Does she not care that her enemy is approaching with an army?"

"King Berlium doesn't cross her mind. She's too busy orchestrating a never-ending trial for her mother's killer. To protect herself. She cares only for herself." I shrug. "I don't get it either."

"Which only makes me wonder if she's allied herself with the Baore." Riordan crosses his arms. "It would explain why she doesn't fear them. Preparing for their affront would be the most self-preserving thing she could do."

He's right. Why didn't I think of that? I'm so unschooled in this. My whole life, my only politics have been Elves versus Men. I never considered that she would ally herself with our enemy.

"Would the Baore be willing to ally themselves with our kingdom, after the failed attempts at exactly that?" I ask. I remember Ivaia's role in the war between the Sunderlands and the Baore. She looks at me, reading my face. She knows I know.

"You saved her," I say. "You sacrificed everything for Herrona."

"And look what it got me." She says.

"Freedom," I say.

I'd give anything to be truly free, beyond what I felt with Darius. The deeper I wade into the darkness of my homeland and of my bloodline, the more I feel embedded in it. I envy Ivaia for her bravery.

"Did you ever look back when you ran?" I ask.

They lock eyes and smile. "Never."

"And run we did," Riordan beams. "All over the world. Accomplished things you'd never imagine. Suffered defeats, too."

"Why is it that the three daughters of Ro'Hale seem to have lived the most interesting lives? I heard my mother had many adventures as well, before marrying my father."

I think back to my night in her closet, wearing her shoes. I skip that, though I'm dying to know who my mother loved. Was it Indiro? Bringing up the fact that Ivaia was meant to marry my father is too uncomfortable.

"We did, we wild three." Ivaia smiles faintly.

"Perhaps it's time we tell Keres of our greatest accomplishment?" Rio looks lovingly at her.

Her brows pinch together, and she folds her hands. Looking at me, warmth returns to her diamond eyes and she smiles, every line in her face settling. "Where to begin?"

Riordan offers to start. "Aureum's seven provinces are each shared by two ruling kingdoms—a team of kings and queens to better their land for the people. There must never be one ruler in a province. Always two sets."

"As we know, the Baore Province has one ruler. King Berlium," Ivaia adds.

"Prince Berlium killed his father and took his throne in Dale. In Dulin, the Baore's second kingdom, his father's brother sat on the Dulin throne. His uncle."

"Oh!" I recall some hazy details from my dad's lectures. "The Brother Bears. Leto and Myromer!"

"Yes, Berlium killed his own father, Myromer. Took the throne; and then killed his uncle, King Leto of Dulin. Took his throne, too."

"Took both thrones, uncontested?"

"Oh, he faced many competitors. His own brothers and cousins. But he spared his youngest brother, Oraclio. Exiled him."

"But every kingdom in any province answers to the Council of Perl in the Cenlands. King Arias said that the council would deal with him, but they haven't. How can we trust the council's supervision? How have they allowed him to stay seated on two thrones?" I ask.

Ivaia picks up there. "The council has its shortcomings. Aureum is a vast land, and they are its ever-watchful guardians. But they cannot succeed alone. The Heralds of War are theirs. The council also chooses two Mages every decade to act as ambassadors on their behalf. One for the northern provinces and one for the southern provinces. Magisters. Their purpose is to observe political affairs, hold the kingdoms accountable and report back to the council. Agents with power."

"Why have we never seen a Magister?"

"Because one is beside the King of the Baore, and the other... was me. Before me, it was your mother."

"No," My jaw drops. "You and Mother were Magisters?"

"Yes," she says and frowns.

"How?"

"Twenty-three years ago, Herrona gifted us each with a knight." Her hand goes instinctively to Riordan's thigh. "She blessed me with this lug." She squeezes a smile out of him.

"And your mother got Indiro. Thus, we continued the tradition of our ancestors." Her eyes glaze with memory. Resurfacing, she continues, "Your mother and Indiro traveled to the northern province east of the Baore; the Ressid Province. There, they got involved with the Guild of Shadows and its very powerful leader, a man named Emeric."

"Guild of Shadows?" I repeat.

"Yes. Another story for another time. All you need to know now is that your mother's actions there earned her the nomination to become a Magistress. She accepted it."

"Then all hell broke loose." Riordan chimes in.

"I broke a spell—"

"The spell Berlium cast on Herrona," I say, excited to know about it.

"Well, Hadriel's spell."

"Who?" I ask.

"Berlium's advisor is a powerful Mage named Hadriel. He's the one who cast the spell on Herrona, for Berlium."

"Oh," I say.

"He was the second Magister. Still is, to this day."

"So that's why Berlium got away with killing his family and taking both thrones? That's why everyone fears him. Because he has the other Magister in his pocket?"

"Basically," Riordan says.

"About twenty-two years ago, I broke Hadriel's spell, which as you now know, ended a would-be alliance between our kingdom and the

Baoreans," Ivaia says.

"And then everyone got pissy with you." I smile.

Ivaia doesn't smile. "The people wanted me executed. Called me *Accursed* for my power. If I had to do it all over, I'd choose the same every time: My sister over my people."

I nod.

"In my sister's mercy, Herrona refused to kill me. Marrying me off was adequate. The alliance that binds our kingdom to the clans of the Sunderlands was founded on a marriage."

"I know." I lower my eyes and sip my tea. "It's weird to think about."

"I wouldn't allow Iv to marry anyone that wasn't myself," Riordan says. They look at each other with an immeasurable, unstoppable love.

"We'd sworn ourselves to each other." They each hold out a hand bearing matching tattoos.

"So, you ran away." My heart melts.

"And it sealed your mother's fate." Ivaia takes a sip of tea. "My desertion nearly cost us a second alliance between the kingdom and the clans. The Dalis sent spies into our Province, and some tried to convince the clans to surrender. To join a coalition with the Baore. The clans refused, but they knew they didn't have a choice. The Boare would take them by force. The Sunderlands was about to implode. They forced your mother to marry Kaius. To take my place and solidify the alliance. It cost her the role she'd worked for. She stepped down from being Magistress to support her people here."

"When she came back, we left the Sunderlands."

"And went where?"

"To the Cenlands. We devoted our attention to making connections in Perl and established the Imperium of Magic: A school for training mages." They lock hands.

"What?" I put the tea down for good now.

"Establishing the institution earned me the nomination that my sister gave up. I took it. It ended when your mother died. I returned to the Sunderlands to take you in."

"Wow." I don't know what else to say. "That *is* a lot of great accomplishments."

"And still not our greatest," Riordan smiles.

"We left the Cenlands and all we'd worked for behind. But we also left behind our son."

My body freezes. Guilt clamors through my being. They have a son? They left a child behind to come care for me?

"We couldn't have any children of our own, so we adopted." Ivaia's eyes brim with tears, "A baby boy. His name is Monroe."

"Well, he isn't a baby anymore." Riordan wipes a tear from her cheek. "He's a little older than Liriene."

My stomach does a somersault. "What?" I ask again.

"A woman named Saber traveled to Aureum from Illyn, in the west. She was a slave whose master impregnated her and sought to kill her for the pregnancy."

Sounds familiar. Seriously, what is going on in Illyn with these masters impregnating their slaves?

Why do they even have *slaves?*

"She fled his estate and eventually across our border after childbirth. She came into the Sunderlands with only the clothes on her back and the baby. We met her in our travels, and she gave us the baby because she resented him. We took him as our own."

"Queen Hero is harboring women like Saber. Illyn refugees. Their children," I say,

They exchange a glance.

"Where is this Monroe now?" I ask, stunned.

"In the Cenlands at the Imperium," Ivaia says.

"Why didn't you take me to the Imperium? Why didn't you bring Monroe to live here?"

"Monroe is our child, but he is also a powerful mage. He's better off with the Ministry."

"Better protected, too. I made enemies as Magister," Ivaia says thoughtfully.

"I can't believe I never even thought… that you might have children of your own."

"We tell no one of Monroe to protect him," Riordan assures me.

"The daughters of Ro'Hale have many enemies," I ponder. It raises another question. Who would want to kill Queen Herrona?

"Hero told me a story about Herrona's death. Said she saw it happen and detailed the whole thing to me."

Ivaia perks up, fidgeting with the hem of her gown.

"She said a man killed her with a poisoned apple."

Ivaia's face turns gray.

The sound of a moaning horn interrupts us. We all jump up, spilling tea, and Ivaia drops her cup. It shatters on the floor.

The horn is bleating frantically.

"The clan!" I gasp.

We disperse like ants from an anthill that's just been doused with water.

We all know what that horn means:

War.

28: The Assunderance of Children

I never knew fear until I saw him. For a moment, I thought he was Mrithyn in the flesh.

I forgot to breathe.

Move, dammit.

I will myself to take a step but can't. My ears fill with the sound of my blood rushing to my head. Somewhere beyond this pulsing sound, Ivaia's muted voice is screaming at me to move. My peripheral vision is blurred. I'm still not breathing.

"Move!" A sharp voice cracks through my stupor.

A body slams into mine pushing me out of the way of the charging mare. We narrowly escape the hooves of the massive black stallion with red eyes. The greatsword wielded by its rider clips his shoulder as it sails toward us in a wide, low arc. I'm on the ground. The last bit of air has been knocked from my lungs.

Breathe.

My chest is heaving, caving in.

"Breathe," his voice cuts into me again.

I take in a sharp breath. Wafting smoke makes me cough and I gasp for air. I try to lift myself up.

His hands are on me; his powerful arms are lifting me up from the ground. His hands steady me as I get my footing. There's no time to thank him. He saved my life from the Death-like sentinel on the Night Mare.

People are screaming. Somewhere to my left there's an explosion.

"We have to go, Keres."

I look up and am met by honey eyes. An angry gash crosses his brow. I lift my hand to his face, to his blood. *Silas saved my life.*

He grabs my forearm and leads me around the back of a tent. I look around for Ivaia and Riordan but don't see them. I don't see anyone else I know. I only see hundreds of Humans—the Army of Dalis Soldiers.

"My bow." I dropped it. I've never dropped my bow before.

"No time, use the blade," Silas orders.

My hand goes to my hip where the short-hilted scythe is bound to my belt. Its cold iron feels like an electric shock to my palm. The curved black and silver blade smiles at me, moonlight winks off it. I smell blood.

We evade attackers, trying to get wherever Silas is leading. There are so many of them, I don't know how we manage to stay out of sight. *Am I in shock?*

"In here," Silas ushers me into a tent.

"Keres!" My sister steps out of hiding. With her comes Attica, the Weaver.

"Oh, child—you're safe."

"We are *not* safe. When did they get here? What's going on?" I ask, stupefied.

"They attacked at nightfall," Attica says.

"Where is father?" I ask.

"He's out there fighting." Liriene frowns.

I turn to Silas. "Then we go, too."

He nods and draws his sword.

"What? You can't go out there," Liriene squeaks at us.

Nearby footfalls rattle the tent.

"It's not much safer in here, Liri. We should move out. Now."

Her and Attica look at each other.

"Alright," they agree.

Silas takes the lead. Attica and Liriene crouch behind him, and I bring up the rear.

"Where's Thaniel?" I ask.

"Where's Ivaia?" Silas asks.

I weigh the two. "We find Ivaia first."

"Where is Indiro?" Attica asks.

She stops, Liriene stops behind her, and I'm forced to stop, too.

"We must find Indiro," Attica insists.

"When was the last you saw him?" I ask.

"He went with Kaius," Silas says, beckoning us to move into cover. "When the attack first happened, he and Kaius went to the front lines."

"No, no." Attica's hands fly to her wrinkled head. She takes Liriene by the hand. "He's supposed to be here. Not you," she sneers at Silas.

"Attica—"

I'm interrupted by a man's scream.

I evade his sword, sinking low, and swing back my scythe. The blade hooks around his throat and nearly tears his head off.

I'm already covered in blood.

"We have to move," I shout.

"To the gates," Attica screeches. "We must find Indiro."

"She's right, the battle began at the gates. They broke through—"

Another attacker charges us, this time aiming for Silas.

We're faster. Silas quickens his steps and flurries his sword. I lunge and hook my scythe around the man's arm, severing it from his body. He falls over as I dance around him. He drops his ghastly weapon—a wooden club with blades jutting out of it. Chains and manacles jingle when he hits the ground. I stoop and take inventory of his body.

"Chains. Are they taking captives?"

"Young women your age and hers," he tilts his head at Liriene. "That's why I hid her."

"That's why we need Indiro," Attica urges. The hairs on the back of my neck rise. *Has she Seen something of this battle?*

Pushing around the edges of the camp, we round the walls, killing Dalis stragglers as we go. Lightning and fire erupt out of the center of a fray and strike a tree. I assume that's Ivaia. I mentally mark her position and listen for her voice. I don't hear her, but I sense her magic coming in waves of power as it sweeps over the battlefield.

I start to pick faces out of the warring crowds. Lucius' father is fighting two men. A bent-boned elder is dead on the ground. We step over bodies, hurrying toward the gates where the fight is still the thickest. Our people don't have the numbers or weapons these Humans do. But we're using the walls and the forest we know so well. They can attack our land, but they don't know it like we do.

Many of us are fighting, winning little battles here and there. It all blurs past us. As we go, Silas and I jump into skirmishes and defend helpless kinsman. Dead older women and young children are scattered around the campgrounds.

We were unprepared for an attack like this. Even Indiro's efforts would not be enough in preparing our pacifistic people for outright war. We don't stand a chance without reinforcements. Osira said my people needed me. I came too late. I went back to the palace—wasted time on Moriya and Seraphina. I could have been here when the gates were broken down.

Osira was right. My belief that she was right about Hero solidifies, too.

The gates are in view; badly splintered and nearly unhinged. More and more Dalis soldiers file through, pushing against a wall of shields marked with White Stallions. My people are fighting like the hope's been sucked out of their bones. Brittle and breaking quickly.

The sounds of steel shattering wooden shields and clanging against iron ones ring in the air in pulses and echoes.

Screams. Curses. Barked commands.

"Hold!" I hear a familiar voice. *I know that temper anywhere.*

"Where is he? I hear him. It's Indiro." I try to see above the crowd.

I duck the next breath, and a sword whirls above my head.

"Liri— Attica!" *If I go down, they do too.*

I kill the assailant. Blood erupts from his sliced throat, spraying my face. I spit out the taste and wipe my eyes, spinning to look for Liriene.

She's on the ground.

Her knees are pressed into the dirt, hands busy—trying to stop the blood gurgling in a soldier's throat. Blood and dirt streak her sweaty face.

Attica's pulling at her, trying to get her to leave the soldier. I kill a Human who lunges for them, and in the momentum of the killing blow, I tumble to the ground beside Liri.

"No." I gasp as I right myself. My voice disappears from the strain of shock. "No—"

Tears blur my eyes.

Liri's fingers are trembling, inefficiently plugging the wound to his throat. He sputters, choking on his blood. Weakening by the second, but that's not the worst of it.

His armor is shattered, cracked open like a walnut. His innards have spilled out through the massive gash splitting him from navel to sternum.

"Girls, I'm sorry but we have to go," Attica's screaming.

"Keres," Silas shouts. "Liri—leave him, there's nothing we can do." He grunts as he crosses swords with an attacker.

"He's still alive!" Liri screams.

I'm forced to stand, to avert my eyes—I bury my father in my heart and am the first to leave his body's side.

"Liriene," I say and pull her up from under her arms with a newfound strength rooted in anger.

"No—Papa!" She sobs.

His choking stops, the blood seeps from his throat as his chest stills. She's rocking on the ground next to him.

Tears threaten to compromise my vision. *He's dead.* I send a quick and ragged prayer after his soul.

"Liri, I have to get you to safety." I groan as I pull her weight up.

She kicks and swings her fists at me, fury and tears blinding her. She screams his name. Every word is a prayer for his revival.

My voice is weak with shock. With pain. "Liriene, he's gone now."

"Hold!" That voice comes again.

"It's Indiro." Silas points his sword.

Liriene still fights me but I get her to her feet. I've got her under my arm, and we are exposed in a clearing amid fighting soldiers.

"Fetch Indiro," Attica orders Silas.

"I'll move her." I nod at him.

We split up. He dives into the fight, hurtling for that wall of shields near the gates. As he goes, I watch him pick up a shield off a dead body. Then he's gone.

I drag Liriene away from our father's body without sparing him another glance. I can't bear it. If I look, I will get us killed. Maneuvering through our enemies and comrades requires my attention, my energy.

Liriene is mumbling incoherently and her eyes glaze over. When we make it closer to our walls, she pushes out of my hold and sways, staring at the starlit sky.

"The Sun." She spins in place.

"Liri, stand not amazed," Attica calls.

She wanders toward two Humans who have their back to her. She's staring up at the sky.

"It's so bright." She cries. "My eyes—what's happening?"

I look up at the moon and stars and am baffled by what she's saying. There is no Sun. I feel Attica leave my side, and chase her toward Liriene. She reaches my bewildered sister first and takes her by the shoulders.

"What do you see?" Attica shouts in Liriene's blank face.

Horror spans across her eyes as she stares into the sky. Her eyes are wild; an ocular shiver like she's reading an invisible book.

"The black wolf hunts the white hart."

Where have I heard that before?

"What's happening to her, Attica?" I snarl.

"She's Seeing," she answers me.

I look into Liriene's eyes, trying to keep the outskirts of my attention on the battle happening around us.

"You mean—"

She cups Liriene's face in her bony, callused hands. "What do you see, Liriene?"

"God." She points to the sky, "The Sun God. The world." She twirls. Her elation turns to sadness, and Liriene weeps. "A black wolf." She points into the battle and tears pour from her gray bulging eyes.

"The black wolf hunts the white hart."

Something startles her, and she turns as if someone tapped her on the shoulder.

"*You.*" She says to no one. Her body relaxes, her expression is peaceful.

"Liriene." I grab her by the shoulder. The smell of blood is luring something dark out of me. I grip her, trying to grip my own sanity as well. She ignores me and continues staring into nothing. I get in front of her, trying to make eye contact, but she looks around me and then back at the sky.

"What's your name?" She asks nobody.

Attica's watching her, as stunned as I am.

"Who's there, Liri?"

She scowls.

"Don't talk to—"

"Thane," Liriene says.

"Who?" I ask Attica. She shrugs.

"He's coming." Liriene smiles. Finally, she looks back at me. "For you."

My reserve shatters. I grab Liriene and shake her roughly. "Liriene, stop."

She continues smiling but is still crying. "He is." She grabs my shoulders too. "I will—" She says.

"Ah!" Attica's voice breaks.

I push Liriene aside in time to stop the soldier from stabbing her through the back, narrowly avoiding his blade myself. Attica's behind him on the ground, blood spurting from her chest.

"Agh!" I throw every morsel of my power into my swing. My scythe lobs his head off and I kick his body to the ground.

Liriene turns and looks at Attica's body. "She tried."

I whirl back to her. Grabbing her by the wrist I pull her further along the wall.

Ivaia where are you? I need you.

"*You need me, not Ivaia.*" The Death Spirit clamors into my thoughts.

"This way, Liri." I lead her onward. We leave Attica dying on the ground. She struggles to speak as we go. "Eyes... open—"

I can't risk a moment of mourning; I can't stop to comfort her in death. I'm not *that* Coroner today.

Today, I am Mrithyn's Hound.

That familiar, otherworldly beast claws at my rib cage, beating against it with every heartbeat, begging to be unleashed.

"Come out to play," I invite the Death Spirit to the surface of my mind.

I see Cesarus in my head, guarding Osira. That's me, next to Liriene—*I am the beast.*

I scan the battlefield for a familiar face. I smell blood and excrement wafting on the biting wind. It's intoxicating. I welcome the tangy flavor of the blood on my lips, and a feverish hunger for souls gnaws at my belly. I prowl into the thick of the war.

My sister is a lamb and I am her lion.

No one can have her. No one can touch her.

I cut down soldier after soldier, baring my fangs and cleaving their souls from the bodies. They scream when they see me, and I know they see eternity in my eyes. I hunt them shamelessly. Digging the fingernail of my blade under the skin and spilling their lifeblood onto my bare feet.

The phantom breeze caresses my face, kissing the part of me that is so like it.

"Go, Keres," Mrithyn's voice hisses.

So bitter. So brutal and unforgiving. My mind swims with the smell of blood thickening the air. Mrithyn is here; His power takes hold of me.

I am His blade. I am His right hand. His might reaches for souls through my very fingers.

Silas and Indiro are nowhere to be found. They break the barricade of shields our soldiers had made. Most of our warriors lie dead at the front. Humans pour into the campgrounds, cutting down everything in sight.

A bolt of lightning shoots into the sky. "There you are." I follow that beacon.

One hand is locked with Liriene's, the other on my scythe. I pull her behind me. She's walking too slow, still staring at the sky.

"He's so beautiful."

"Thane?" I ask, making conversation to steady my nerves as I usher her through the middle of the battlefield, toward sounds of volcanic eruptions and lightning strikes.

"Oran."

"You see Oran?" I try to keep her mind occupied before she loses it.

"Yes, I am His family." Liriene giggles deliriously.

A soldier jumps at us. I yank Liriene behind me and deflect his knives with my scythe blade. He stumbles back but lurches for us again. I push Liriene aside and catch his wrist with a speed that startles him. Coming alongside him, I break his arm with unnatural strength. His scream delights me.

As he falls to his knees, I catch him by his hair. I pull his head back to expose his neck.

"You should have worn better armor," I say and drag my blade across his throat.

I reach out and Liriene slips her hand into mine.

We move on.

"Liri, try to focus."

"I see all." She lists dangerously to one side.

"*Liriene.*" I tug on her hand and she stumbles after me. I can't fight pulling her around like this, but I won't leave her. For a moment, I bristle, realizing I'm endangered, vulnerable. Only as strong as my weakest link, which is her right now.

But I have faith. Mrithyn is with me even now. Maybe her God is too.

"You see that tree?" I point to a tree engulfed in blue flames.

She looks.

"Ivaia is there. We have to go. She will help us."

"She won't," Liriene says, a frown crossing her face.

"Yes!" I pull her again.

We walk through the waves of blood, and I clear a path with my scythe. We forge into the heart of the campgrounds. *What if Ivaia isn't there? What if it's a Human mage?*

I kick doubt from my mind.

Keep going. If the Gods march tonight into the realm of mortals, I'm marching too.

My vision heightens. The color of fire against the night sky dances in my eyes. I see more Humans than Elves now.

And they see me.

The real me, the executioner with the abysmal darkness of death in her eyes.

Fire glows beneath my skin and divine power charges through my veins.

Finally, we break through the crowd into the center of a fray. The horseman of death has a clear path to Ivaia. She's glowing; blue, fiery light glows beneath her skin. Her wild hair flutters in a violent wind as she calls storms. The horseman counters her magic. I now realize he wields a staff in one hand and a great sword in the other.

I stop short, watching their magic in a cataclysmic confrontation.

Soldiers howl and roar at them, cheering on the Death Rider.

She raises her hands above her head, calling forth all manner of magic. Her voice is multi-tonal and her words are not of the common tongue. Spells.

She hisses a hex and fumes rise from the ground, Putrid yellow steam swirls around the horseman's field of protective magic, which I now notice originates from an intricate glyph on the ground. The steam coils and undulates against his barrier and the friction sparks blue lightning. His shield sizzles and splinters. He throws up his hands and enhances the shield. It vibrates, shrinking and expanding, pulsing with heightened energy. With a mind-numbing burst, it evaporates smoke that threatened to disable it. Startlingly fast, he places another glyph, another shield goes up between them.

Her lightning bolt refracts off a protective field of magic and ricochets back into her. She isn't fast enough. She falls.

"Ivaia," I scream. I struggle with the decision to leave Liriene and go help Iv.

I can't lose another mother figure. Compelled by this desperation, I let go of Liri's hand but I'm too late.

It happens so fast, but I feel time crawling like an ant on my skin.

Someone in the wild crowd throws a lance.

A body crosses in front of Ivaia, shielding her from the blow.

Two sets of golden-haired heads fall to the ground.

I try to scream but nothing comes out.

My voice fails.

My body locks into place.

My mind warps.

My world shatters

The beast within me howls.

The Night Mare paws the earth and stands up on its hind legs, victorious. The horseman cackles, not at all deterred by the fact that someone else made the winning strike.

I run toward their bodies.

"Rio!" I find a scratch of my voice. "Iv!" I stumble through the crowds. I listen for their heartbeats, but my own is so loud. I push my senses farther, like the tendril of a vine, reaching along the ground toward them.

One steady heartbeat meets me at their bodies. Only one.

Tears blur my eyes.

"No!" I cut a Human down out of my way.

Both their bodies move.

Ivaia's underneath Riordan, his full weight resting on her. He's not moving. But she is.

I choke on a sob, still pushing through the crowd. My muscles tremble wildly, making me weaker. I stumble over my faulty legs.

Ivaia pushes Riordan's body up. The spear has impaled him through the chest. Drawing closer, I hear his faint heartbeat now, too. He's still alive but coughing blood onto her face. He won't last much longer. I must get there.

I push myself onto my toes, struggling to see as I forge through bands of armored soldiers. Ivaia's face goes white. His blood splatters it. He's choking. Blood oozes from his wound and pulses from his mouth.

Her fists are locked around the lance that connects them: It went through him into her.

She roars as she pushes his impaled body off hers, and the spear exits her body.

"No!" I scream. She was hit too—I can't lose them both.

Her magic, like gold and silver rays of light, lifts Rio into the air, pulls the spear from his body, and lays him on the ground. His sacrifice earned the silence of the crowd, and nobody moves as she shifts to lean over his body. Blood sputters out of her mouth as her lips tremble. Her voice breaks through her mouth, "Rio."

Her bloody hands shake, lingering over his wound. I can sense his soul departing. As if she can feel it too, she digs her fingers into his tunic, knotting it in her fists. Trying to tether him to this world.

Ivaia looks into her beloved knight's diamond eyes as they dim forever. I hear his faint, final heartbeat. She clenches her hands into fists, lifting them to her face, and I remember the tattoo on her palm. Her heart rate quickens but it's thready.

She struggles to stand. Wiping the tears from her eyes with the palms of her hands, smearing her face with his blood. Like war paint.

A soldier steps in front of me, and I can't see her now. I cut his throat and push him aside.

I look and see the horseman, his black eyes trained on her failing body. Her shoulders hunch forward but she raises her arms at her side with characteristic grace and stares him down. Her crystal blue eyes are shrouded in crimson blood.

She shoves a fist into the massive puncture wound in her abdomen. It's not good enough.

With her free hand, she calls fire into her palm. Blue fire billows into the air, a torch against the night. A beacon of her resolution. With a final battle cry, she drops to her knees and punches her flaming fist into the ground. Magic violet flames explode, blasting back the soldiers around them, and consume Ivaia and Riordan's bodies.

My eyes widen to take in the height of the fire's reach. A tower of tumultuous flames rises into the night sky and burns into my memory.

A soldier turns on me when I try to shove him. He grabs me by the hair.

"Look." He taps his comrade on the shoulder with his gigantic free hand.

"Let her go," Liriene's voice bleats behind me.

"Grab that one too—they're both of the right age."

I hear her scream as someone grabs her behind me.

"No—" I kick at his legs. He grips my throat.

I steal a look back to Ivaia and Riordan. The fire dies, no longer fueled by her magic. Their bodies are entangled with one another in a final embrace. Charred and crumbling to ash.

My blood boils, my magic erupts within me. An inferno ravages my bones, breaks through the surface of my skin, and scorches the soldier's hands.

He drops me. I swing my scythe at his legs, removing them from his body. He falls to the ground. I grab his face in my hand and push my pain and magic into him. His face combusts, his head explodes.

I push myself up with a roar and see the Horseman's smile at the scene left in Ivaia's wake.

A scream—a voice from the realm of Gods, rends the air like thunder.

All attention is on me in the next second.

The horseman looks through the crowd straight to me.

The earth moans and quakes.

Soldiers fall into the chasm yawning open in the ground at my will.

I'll bury them.

For the first time in my life, I hear myself: The divine tongue, the voice that sucks air from lungs. I curse them. I curse them, my Death Spirit imbuing me with an understanding of the strange words.

"Your souls belong to Mrithyn. Your blood belongs to me."

I aim my scythe at the nearest soldier. He yelps as the ground beneath him gives way.

I watch him fall.

The Horseman's black eyes narrow on me.

"I claim your life in the name of Death."

"Die." Magic pulses from somewhere deep inside me.

The energetic power blasts from me like an icy wind, freezing everything in my path.

Except him.

My power stops at his feet.

The shield of magic surrounds him still, unbroken.

Savage power seizes my bones. But it's not my power.

My blood curdles in my veins, I go completely stiff.

He's controlling my body. My magic is no match. I can't force him out, I can't repel his power.

"Got you." A thought that doesn't belong to me sails into my head like an arrow.

"Stop," my mind reels against him. I'm choking now too.

"Stop fighting." I hear in my head.

"Never!"

"Have it your way."

The world goes black.

29. The Maws of Men

Regaining consciousness feels like pounding on the surface of a frozen lake from beneath it in its frigid blackened waters.

The ice thuds against my pounding fists, stinging my flesh.

Then it cracks.

Each crack splinters.

Until the ice shatters.

I lay here now, lost in my new reality.

Where am I?

I push up on my elbows. Every inch of my body hurts.

"You're up," Liriene says in a hoarse voice from behind me.

I roll over to face her. It's dark and I can barely make out her form in the shadows. The smell of wet earth and stagnant air confuses me.

"Are we in a cave?" I make no movement.

"Yes."

I rise into a crouching position. Her hands grope in the darkness. We lock onto each other's forearms.

Her skin is cold. I finally realize I'm shivering. We huddle together for warmth.

Hours pass before our sleepless eyes in a stretching and recoiling shadow. Silent hours. My mind runs through the battlefield into the clearing where I watched Ivaia and Riordan die. The Night Mare's whinnying and snorting chase me into the recesses of my thoughts. Silas' body slams into the dark place of my mind and leads me into the tent where I found my sister and Attica hiding from terror. I wander behind the visions, watching them replay.

Ivaia and Riordan's love goes up in flames. I chase down the horseman. I slam into his wall of magic. My mind beats its fists on the shield between him and me.

His pitch-black eyes watch me through the crowds of thoughts.

"Memories will destroy you," Liriene whispers. She sighs. Whether I open or close my eyes, darkness shrouds us. A perfect backdrop for the memories to play against. I can't ignore them here.

"Do you remember having visions?"

She stills beside me. Her bones shudder and I know it's not from the chilly, dank air.

The voice that escapes her next is ethereal—it glows in this dark, but her words are deeper than the shadow. "Violence. Terror. Chaos. These events come from the twisted side of my wildest dreams. What am I becoming?"

I turn toward her and feel for her shoulders. They're fallen forward and her head is bowed. I lift her chin and push her back upright. "Liriene," I breathe. "You are not becoming anything. I won't let the Gods—"

"How can you stop Him? I saw Him." She begins to cry. "He sees me even here beneath the earth. He is showing me ruination. War. Death."

I dig my fingernails into her shoulders, trying to steady her, trying to prevent what's taking hold of her.

"He has revealed to me my own demise."

"No." I grit my teeth. "No, the Gods cannot have you too. You are not going to die." I shake her. "Ignore Him. Block out His voice, close your eyes."

"I can't." She wraps her hands around my forearms and bows her head against my chest. I take her in my arms.

"Everyone thinks Oran is a child-like God. That He is giddy and bright." She picks her head up.

"It's not true. He's terrible. He sees all, knows all. These visions are blinding." Her whispers are frantic. "He is not a *Sun* God. He is Revelation, and He shows me such darkness. Adreana does not hide Him from us—she hides us from His Truth."

Her words chill me. Could this God really have chosen her? Is she truly a Seer?

"What does He want? Why claim you now?"

"I don't know."

I shake her again. "The darkness was meant for me. Not you, Liriene."

Her shaking stops, her shoulders roll back under my fingertips, and she places her hands on my face. I can feel her breath when she says, "We all have both light and darkness within."

Approaching footsteps bring us to our feet. We cling to each other. Firelight blazes through the shadows, casting them back into the depths of the cave as the torchbearer nears us. Heavy, armored footsteps ring out as what sounds like a multitude approaches. The light burns my eyes and Liriene shields her face as they come into view. First, I see torches wrapped in fire, then the hands carrying it.

Faces.

Men's faces.

Broad-bodied soldiers dressed in silver and black armor march in unison down the long corridor of the cave. When their light reaches us they stop, drawing their blades.

I hear screams and cries of fear coming from somewhere deeper within the cave, and guess those in the darker depths must see the light coming. Liriene and I step closer together until our hips are touching. She pushes me behind her, earning a glare from me.

"State your names." One deep timbre shakes the cavern walls.

Liriene squeezes my hand, halting me from replying.

The leader steps forward, sword drawn and aimed in our direction. We push back into the wall instinctively.

"From what clan do you hail?" He questions us again. His eyes are sanguine, burning red in his long, lean face. His ash brown hair is tied neatly into a short braid. His skin is fair as a lily.

"Hishmal or Ro'Hale?" Another soldier asks behind him. Less appetizing to the eye, this one has grayed skin and giant black eyes with no whites in them.

There are survivors of Hishmal here? As well as our own people? Liriene and I exchange a wary glance.

"Ro'Hale," she replies. Her voice is stronger now, clear. All traces of despair are gone. I stare up at her placid face and mercury eyes. Her scarlet hair is a furious shade of red in the firelight. I sense newly awakened power undulating in her veins.

"Names." The leader demands.

Her eyes are orbs of divine warning, and the soldier visibly recoils when she speaks again, "You first."

Her very presence is terrifying.

He laughs at her before his posture settles. "I am Lord Varic," he says. "Master of Tecar."

"Tecar?" I ask.

Liriene's eyes widen with realization. She squeezes my hand once more. She knows where we are. I look to her for an explanation but she locks her eyes on Varic.

"Shepherd of the Lost," she snarls at him.

"Ah, so, you have heard of me?"

"No, I have *Seen* you. I have Seen your death!" Her fiery hair floats about her face, but there is no wind. She grows in stature, her voice tears through the cave like a thunderclap.

"We are no little lambs, Shepherd—We are wolves. And we will never be slaves of the Baore—you will let my people go," she says.

All humor deserts Varic's expression. His jaw tightens and his brows set with determination.

I grin at my sister and straighten my back beside her. I wonder how dangerous we seem to these Men. The contrast of our appearances must be startling. Snow white hair and flaming red. Claws and fangs to match. Sisters, one marked by death, the other by fire.

"Witches." One spits on the ground. I come abreast with Liriene and glare at the one who spewed the insult.

"Try again," I dare.

"I recognize her." One points in my direction. "She was in the clearing when Magister Hadriel slew the Witch."

"She's a Mage."

"Daughters of Despair."

Magister Hadriel. I recognize the name from my conversation with Ivaia. He's the one who magicked Herrona into loving Berlium.

"Then it seems we have who we were looking for." The leader turns and walks away. "Take her and kill the other."

"No! I go nowhere without my sister." I lock arms with Liriene.

"We want the Instrument of the Divine only." The leader turns back to me. "But I'm sure the King will find that very interesting."

"We are both servants to the Gods," I say.

"Which of you serves the God of Death?"

Liriene and I both hold our tongues.

"No answer?"

"She has white hair! She must be the White Reaper."

"But she has hair the color of blood. I sense greater power in her." The soldier with all-black eyes flourishes a staff. A mage or a monster?

"Take her then." He points to Liriene.

"Touch her and I'll kill you." I sink into a ready stance, hands opened as magic charges and sparks at my fingertips. I'll fight them for her. I'll die on their blades for her.

Liriene mimics my stance and bares her teeth—*fangs*. Her hands uncurl and the length of her nails have grown into small talons. I almost forget to look formidable in my surprise.

I tear my eyes from her and meet those of the guards. Their armor displays the insignia of the Grizzly King. We are in the Baore. We are in King Berlium's slave den.

"And what makes you think you can?" The black-eyed one hisses.

This fight will be too dangerous. I don't know what power Liriene has—I don't know what she is. And I can't trust this cave to prove an even playing field. I hate being caged-in.

"I demand your King grant us both audience," I growl.

Liriene shoots me a glare sharp as knives.

"You are in no position to be making demands," Varic sneers, his red eyes inflaming.

Liriene whispers to me. "Do not—"

"We are the daughters of Resayla Aurelian. Daughter of Adon, King of Ro'Hale."

Liriene bites back her words, hiding her fangs once more.

Does she even know she has them?

Varic looks back to one of his men, who nods.

"Bind them both."

Liriene's eyes urge me not to struggle or fight back as they lock manacles around our wrists and chain our ankles. They shuffle us out of the cave. The smell of fresh air seeps into the cave as we approach the gaping exit and the daylight beyond.

Night has passed and we are in a new day—a new world.

In this world there is no one I know but my sister, and I don't even fully understand what she is. I watch her as she walks ahead, shoulders shoved by the angry, yet tentative, hands of Human guards. They fear her. I sense it in their blood. The telltale stench of prey. I wonder if she senses it too. I wonder if she knows what she is. I don't.

Does their fear excite her—does she, too, revel in blood?

What have the Gods created?

They lead us through corrals meant to keep people in.

Elves.

My people.

Molten rage surges through me as I take in the sights. I can see the palace northward and the Sunderlands Forest to the south; a long stretch of mighty trees with impenetrable shadow beyond their boughs. A magic-brimmed woodland filled with horrors and wonders. Home.

The trees have lost their leaves—bared for the bone-chilling winter to come. No clans to light their fires within. Except for Massara, if it still stands. One thought pushes a weight of despair from my shoulders. Darius is beyond the Baore's reach. Heading to the Gryphon King among the Heralds of War, to safety. He may not be able to save us—we are beyond saving, in Man's domain. At least Osira's prediction saved him. I'm sure if he had followed me home, he would have died.

I stare from this side of the tall fence that hums with energy. Magic wards—not to keep others out but to keep us in. I look to the palace— its fine stone walls that reach heavenward. Flying buttresses and towers. I wonder if Berlium thinks himself a God to reach so high with his castle. To erect pillars and build walls, to build a staircase into heaven as if he belongs there. Dulin is a mighty fortress, sewn into the rim of the mountain range that wraps around the backside of the Province. Dale is

East, a twin in glory.

There are Elves everywhere. Armored Human guards whip them and drive them to labor. They're building walls and monuments. I keep my eye on my sister and the guards harassing her but can't help getting distracted by the massive statues of bears and stone houses. The most exquisite temple made similarly to the Temple of Mrithyn. Not a cathedral and spire, but a black stone house, sparkling like the night sky. Pillars spanned by arches surround the square-shaped house of worship.

A guard shoves me from behind and I lose my footing. I sprawl out on the gravelly ground, and my bound hands do little to break the fall. My teeth are singing in my head as two guards hoist me up.

"He said *unharmed!*" One snaps.

I shake the pain from my head and try to move closer to Liriene. She walks peacefully, but her steps are heavy. As if she were bearing a tree on her back. I try to get near enough to whisper to her, but she ignores me as if lost in her own mind.

The guards nudge us, keeping us from slowing or getting too close to each other. I follow her gaze to a large, elevated stone table in the center of the yard. Elves keep a healthy distance from it as they tow rocks and pickaxes. No one dares approach it, even the guards. It's as if a magical repelling shield of energy surrounds the stone platform and those who near it bounce away in quickened steps.

The guards shout orders to comrades on the other side of the pen, and the gates swing open. The magic buzzing in the fence zings louder and louder as a path is cleared for us through the gates. We file out, following the silver helmets with wings on either side. Those outside the yard eye us with suspicion. They stare at Liriene, barely noticing me.

She's a phoenix, aflame amid men. The shade of her hair is wilder, more vivid. Her eyes are melted stars, gray as ash revived by fire. Red smolders around the rims of her gray irises. Her skin is radiant, glowing with an aureate sheen. Her body is light and heavy at once—her sleek frame moves with grace, but her presence is intrusive. The sunlight filling the sky seems to focus on her, gilding her in gold.

The men stare, their eyes alight with a mix of desire and fear. I simply watch, forgotten in her shadow. I can't help but watch her either. She is a rising Sun and I, the paling moon.

The Palace swallows us whole.

The Ro'Hale Kingdom is diminished by the majesty of the Kingdom of Dale. King Berlium and his forefathers have outdone the World of Aureum. Theirs is a realm of such grit and steel, power and fortitude, it's no wonder they're a threat to all. Seeing where the Human terrorists come from—the stone cloud from which they rain... I can only imagine the man behind the army.

The guards lead us through a pair of heavy stone doors that grate against the stone floor, sparks flying from beneath them as they open. We enter the throne room. A mausoleum dressed in scarlet robes. Drapes the colors of wine and blood fall heavily from the rafters, tapered to the walls' curves and corners. The insignia of the bear sits on each, roaring proudly in silver thread. The room is longer than it is wide and ends in a wall of latticed windows. The daffodil-yellow light of morning saturates the room.

The gray stone is cold beneath my feet as we're ushered closer and closer to the throne. I smell nothing natural in here. The heavy fabric is no doubt laden with dust. Not a plant or animal present. Just a man.

He is the storm-bringer. The man upon the throne locks eyes with Liriene and then with me. His stare is unnerving because it is dark, cold, and stunning. Black hair and stormy-ocean blue eyes. A wide, strong jaw and prominent cheekbones. His thick brows set close to those brooding, almond-shaped eyes, and his full mouth curves into a smile at our approach.

His fingers play at his sensuous lips, and he bows his head toward us, letting a wisp of raven hair fall out of place across his brow. He stands, boasting an immense stature. Tall, broad-shouldered, and thickly muscled. As he prowls toward us, a tempestuous ocean roils in his eyes.

His hand caresses the dark scruff at his jaw until he crosses his arms over his rich, burgundy tunic. Black trousers dress his long, strong legs, ending under the cuff of black leather boots. A belt dotted with rubies hangs from his hips and bears a rapier with a black and silver hilt.

Still silent, he approaches Liriene. She doesn't move or breathe as his hand reaches her face. The touch is gentle, appreciative of her beauty. She meets the watery depths of his stare with an ashen glare. His fingers linger at her jaw before wandering to her crimson tresses. He wraps a lock around his finger—and then he smells her. Teeth bared, eyes closed, hand wrapped around her slender throat.

I move toward them, but a guard stops me.

He moves her face this way and that, sniffing at her carotids. His tongue flicks out and grazes her porcelain skin, but she doesn't flinch. When he releases her, she doesn't shrink back. She doesn't push him away. She stares into his eyes, a brilliant heat blossoming on her cheeks.

I watch them, the beast rattling my chest bones like cell bars.

And then his attention is on me. As if he heard the Death Spirit growling, he whips his head toward me. His composure cracks, an odd emotion sailing across his eyes. He looks to me, then back to Liriene, who watches his every movement.

In three long steps, he's at my throat. His hands nest in my hair. He pulls my head back and breathes against my pulse. I don't know what he's trying to discover, but I assume he finds it. King Berlium releases me and his eyes widen, the tide of what seems like joy swelling within them

King Berlium's hands tangle in my hair again and pull my face to his.

I barely have time to react—he crushes my body against his, sending shockwaves of fear into my core, and claims my mouth with his own.

The kiss is possessive, passionate, and unreserved. As if he's kissed me a thousand times in his life.

He sighs against my breath with something akin to relief. His hands move against my body, wandering over my curves and edges as he deepens the kiss.

Powerless, I can't pull away, I can't push him back. His body is hard against my own as he assaults me with shameless lust.

Gods know why, but my body reacts without hesitation, without a need for explanation. The only need I have is for him, his body.

In the back of my throat, I taste magic. It's burning my throat like strong liquor, but his mouth is sweet.

"Enough," Liriene speaks.

My body revolts, shoving him off and he's taken aback.

His wild eyes swirl with a lust that washes away in a wave of rage.

"Who are you?" He's in Liriene's face in a flash of movement.

My mind and body are reeling from the effects of his seduction—magic or not, he is powerful. His desire reached through him into me and made me believe it belonged there. His lust is brutal, his affection is lethal. I push my hair back off my face, racking my brain for confidence and understanding of what just happened to me. Only a name comes to mind: *Herrona.*

I don't hear her respond, but she must have because he roars at her.

Liriene stands before him, a girl smiling at the gnashing teeth of a black wolf.

Elegant and beguiling as a deer stilled in the forest.

Listening, watching the stillness for a glimmering hint of its predator's next move.

Her skin is white as death, robbed of her former blush.

Her hair is the color of fall.

A white hart in an autumnal wood.

The black wolf hunts the white hart. I see her prediction playing out before my eyes.

"Get away from her!" I scream.

He whirls on me, teeth bared. "Which of you possesses the Death Spirit of Mrithyn?"

I bare my teeth right back. That's what he wants? My inner monster? Well, I'll give him the beast and all her fury. I'll show him exactly who I am; the power coursing through my veins. If he touches my sister, I'll be the Goddess everyone fears. The one they whisper about in the dark.

"Tell me," he bellows. I slide my eyes over to Liri. Her expression is brittle. My rage collides with doubt. If I tell him I'm the one he's looking for, what will he do with her?

"What do you want?" I ask.

"If you're the Coroner, you know what I want." His voice rumbles in his throat.

He wants the power to stem or swell the tide of bloodshed. Power to determine the fate of the Sunderlands... to take over yet another province. He craves the power of Death, to rule the living.

Is this power enough to save me if it is enough to damn me?

Am I going to make it out of here alive, and will Liriene too, if she's of no use to him?

"If you tell me... If you surrender," he addresses us both, "If you lay yourself at my feet, as a knight promises his sword in fealty, and offer yourself as the divine weapon that you are; I will spare the people of the Sunderlands."

Liri and I exchange wide-eyed glances.

"If you deny that either of you is the White Reaper, I will kill you both." He laughs. "If you bind yourself to me, you will gain freedom.

You will gain the world." He steps toward Liriene.

"Bow to me. Bend your will to mine."

"And forsake our people? Liriene asks.

"If we surrender the power you seek, you will use it to destroy our people. And if we deny it, you will slay us," I say.

"Your spirit for their lives, or your blood and their demise," he growls back.

When I was a child, I died. The God of Death granted me a second chance at life on one condition: that I kill for him. That I let the Death Spirit consume me. Possess me wholly. A second chance that culminates in this moment.

Do I succumb to the King of the Baore, and sacrifice myself to spare my kin?

Or do I defy him and accept Death? Escape it all to oblivion?

Free from this curse, this power, this life stalked by Death. Free from the body that houses horror. From the Monster. I look into the oceanic eyes of King Berlium, and I see another monster in there too.

No.

In his eyes, I see my reflection and I realize Liriene was right. We all have light and dark in us.

Darius saw something in me—something more than wickedness or danger. The longer I stare into those eyes, I see something in myself I never saw before. I see the truth of what I am... my purpose. I feel it blooming into life within me, like the swelling and beating heart-leaves of that blessed tree in the Temple of Mrithyn. My heartbeat strengthens, pounding its familiar battle hymn.

The King is asking for my demon to come out and play. He's tempting me. Testing a God's power. He's begging me to dwell in his darkness. To give in to his own power and lay myself under the heavy hand he's holding over my people in their stead.

He thinks his brute force is stronger than my beast?

His lust for power dares to rival my thirst for blood?

He believes his demon is meaner, and his bones are colder than mine?

I laugh in his face. I've made my choice.

We all have our inner monsters, but mine is the hungriest of all.

EPILOGUE

SILAS

"I lost her."

He tells me to be patient. He promises we will find them. We watched her fall, and then her sister. Neither of us could have moved faster or more desperately. The battle was over; the Humans won.

I killed whoever stood in between us, but I wasn't enough.

I suddenly felt the way she must have on those hunts in the dead of night. One person facing down an army, trying to do right by the ones she loved. I felt Death and Chaos on that battlefield. I ignored the reaching hands of my fallen soldiers, begging me to kneel beside them in their dying moments. She was the only one I saw, and hers was the only scream I heard.

"I can't sit here while he goes—"

"Emeric's men are the best chance at Keres' survival."

I cross my arms in front of my chest and sink back under my hood, tightening my jaw to avoid saying something I'll regret. This is so fucked. What if he gets to her too late? We've already wasted so much time. I'm counting the days, and every sunset drives me deeper into the darkness within. I'm losing it.

Today is day thirty-five since they took her.

I thrum my fingers on my crossbow and dig the heels of my boots into the dirt. Indiro lights up his smoking pipe.

"It will take him at least a fortnight to travel to Dale. He's wasting time."

I watch him as I clean my crossbow. His mouth curves into a sinister smile, and his blue-green eyes appraise me from beneath his hood. A man dressed in shadows, too preoccupied with a tapestry of the night sky, to go rescue my wife.

His brother-in-arms watches me, his mismatched eyes glowing hungrily at me. Their power is strange and ancient. Their presence sets my teeth on edge. Humans shouldn't have this affect me, but they do. I'm not a fool, and I'll admit when I'm beyond my bounds. I just don't see what Indiro sees—how can he trust them?

"Thane is doing this his way. We can't question it." Indiro's heavy hand claps on my shoulder and forces me to look at him. "He told us to wait here," he sneers. "And we *will* wait here."

"I cannot wait. How do you expect me to sit idly by? I don't trust these Humans, I'm not you. If they get their hands on her, who's to say they're no less threat to her than the Grizzly King? They're his kind. Not our kind. She will never be safe in the hands of a Human, king or shadow."

Emeric laughs, a dull sound. And he continues to laugh as he lights up his smoking pipe too. His men turn towards me, circling around me.

"You use the word Human too loosely, boy." Their leader glares at me from beneath his hood.

"We are not his kind and he is not ours. The Stone King and my kind… we are not cut from the same cloth, the way a bear is not a dragon. No one else is what we are."

"And what are you?" I stand to my full height. Every muscle in my body goes rigid and the hairs on my arms stand. Emeric coughs as he laughs, and smoke plumes from his mouth, filling the dimly lit hall with haze. Indiro is no longer at my side but melded into the crowd of Shadows that surround me.

"You need to understand only one thing." Their leader steps forward. "We *are* the only chance Keres and Liriene have of surviving."

🔲🔲🔲🔲🔲

DARIUS

"She cast me away."

Vagabond in a strange land, wandering farther from my lover's arms.

Her words echo in my mind with every step.

"I can't."

I sensed the truth behind her eyes. I tasted it on her skin. She could love me; turn my world on its axis with her love. If she could be honest with herself and if she stopped giving in to the will of the Gods. She could be with me.

Still, she sent me here. Away from her—cast off.

And I obeyed because I cannot resist her. Her wish is my command. No matter the cost, no matter the pain.

I delivered her message to the King of Gryphons and in return, they have harbored me. Bid me to remain in the camp's hospitality of Lydany. These people are a strange coalition of Elves and Humans; allies. All standing vigilant watch against the borders of Aureum's Republic and its neighbor, Illyn.

There is movement in the West. Shadows stir and the bitter winds whisper predictions of strife. Ruination.

They told me when my homeland fell. They tell stories of the battle around their fires.

The Sunderance of Children.

They say the King took her and her sister. They say Ivaia of Legend was slain on the battlefield by none other than the feared Magister Hadriel.

First Hishmal was wiped off the map, and now my clan Ro'Hale.

Massara clings to the fabric of existence by a thread. I pray daily for my kin, but I cannot go back. King Arias has forbidden me to leave and to hunt for my lost lover on bare feet across a cursed land. I will fulfill my promise to Keres.

The King of Gryphons bids me stay with *her*. The fearsome General Vyra, leader of the people of Lydany.

"I'll make a warrior out of you," she says and laughs, her brown eyes delighted by the threat that is also a promise—a dare.

Epona, a native warrior of the Moldorn and the General's right hand, watches my every move with distrust.

King Arias has warned me that the Sunderlands has fallen into ruin, and the Moldorn is the only safe place for me. That if I wish to live, to see Keres again, I must remain.

I pray my mother has fled Massara, that she finds refuge. I curse the Human scum that have taken everything from us. I wish to fight for *my* people. My hands ache for my blade, and my skin crawls knowing that bastard, sick-fuck King has my woman.

They talk of Queen Hero. Saying she was crazy before, but now her mind has snapped and she's never coming back. Her mind has been shattered, and she talks only of dark magic—a man within the hand mirror they cannot part her from. She says he will kill her if she looks away from the glass. They allow none near her, and she doesn't sleep or eat.

They say she pleads with the mirror, asking repeatedly why he will not let her be. She then answers herself in strange words and a voice unlike her own, "He must pay. He must pay."

All this talk of destruction. An ending of a time.

I cannot listen. Fuck this news, fuck these Humans.

I want to go, to fight for my homeland. To hold her in my arms again.

THE SUNDERLANDS

Vyra urges me to fight alongside her and her men, but I refuse. This is not my battle. My fight lies with the Humans of the Baore. Not the refuse of Illyn. Although, theirs is a danger none can ignore.

I push aside this battle and fight only with my desires and regret. I'm barely coping with my losses.

My thoughts lie only with her. When I am alone on my cot, in this borrowed tent among strangers, I close my eyes and I see hers. I hear those soft noises she makes. I remember the way it feels to be inside her. I allow my mind to relive the time I had with her, stopping and rewinding before she can tell me to leave.

When I wake up, I'm here. She's gone, and I feel lost.

A stranger. Once a soldier, once a lover. Now a man with nowhere to belong.

On the horizon, they say they see war, but I see nothing except her.

Now the fun begins. This series continues in...

World of Aureum Series, Book Two

KINGS OF SHADOW AND STONE

ANASTASIA KING

ACKNOWLEDGEMENTS

Thank you to my sisters, my forever beta readers, for listening to me drawl about this novel for over a decade. Thank you for reading it enthusiastically and cheering me on always.

Thank you to my parents for what you taught me about reading and writing. Thank you to all my friends, online & offline, for supporting me throughout my self-publishing journey.

Thank you to the professionals and the Beta Readers who collaborated with me throughout this novel's production. You made the journey that much sweeter.

Made in United States
North Haven, CT
06 February 2022